from *The Man from Tibet*

The doors to the Tibetan Room were locked, both doors. Frantic pounding brought no response. The quick-thinking brain of Jed Merriweather took instant command of the situation. He and Vincent had just come in from the lake, their clothes dripping wet.

They were heavy doors, the archaeologist explained in quick, terse phrases. It would take time to batter one open. Wasted time in which a human life might be saved. There was another alternative.

They raced up the stairs, Westborough, forgetful of the miraculous recovery his ankle was displaying, with them. A straggling group of panting, frightened people: Vincent, Jed, Alma, Janice, Chang, the lama, Wilkins, the other servants. Everyone in the house, in fact, except its master.

Vincent had brought a rope from the boathouse; Jed was knotting it about the balustrade with the swift, deft touch of one accustomed to the intricacies of packsaddles. "It may be, probably is, only a faint," he flung out hopefully. "Janice, go to the phone and call Doctor Walters. If Walters gets here soon enough we may be able to save him."

Westborough noticed the sudden tenseness of her body, the equally sudden relaxation of its taut muscles, and then she was gone with the swiftness of a paper borne by a gusty wind. The historian's gaze traveled downward to the beams above the Tibetan Room. They were spaced fairly close together; one could walk across them without difficulty and drop (about a six-foot drop, he estimated) to the floor. But there were no signs that anyone had done this. Quite the contrary. The layer of dust on the top surfaces of the beams had been at no place disturbed.

The Man from Tibet

A Theocritus Lucius Westborough mystery

by

Clyde B. Clason

with an afterword
on the author by
TOM & ENID SCHANTZ

The Rue Morgue Press
Boulder, Colorado
1998

The Man from Tibet
was first published
by the Doubleday, Doran Crime Club
in 1938.

New material in this edition
© 1998 The Rue Morgue Press

PRINTED IN THE UNITED STATES OF AMERICA

Contents

The Man from Tibet

LAKE MICHIGAN

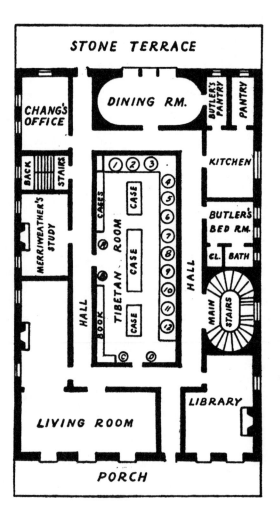

SHERIDAN RD.

Plan of First Floor of Meriweather Residence

Lake Michigan to the east; Sheridan Road to the west. The center glass case in the Tibetan Room contains musical instruments; that to the west is devoted to demon masks; that to the east holds charm boxes, turquoise earrings, turquoise and coral necklaces, rosaries, prayer wheels and the two Tibetan *ka-tas*.

A. Yellow King
B. Red King
C. White King
D. Green King

1. Pal-den Lha-mo
2. Dorje Pa-mo
3. Drol-ma
4. Padma Sambhava

5. Tsong-ka-pa
6. Maitreya
7. Amitabha
8. Sakyammuni Buddha

9. Chen-re-zi
10. Jam-pe-Yang
11. Chana Dorje
12. Yama

PART ONE: The Man from Chyod
(Monday, July 19)

ADAM MERRIWEATHER added half-a-dozen drops from a vial to a goblet half filled with water and swallowed the faintly tinged liquid. It was in addition to the regular dose prescribed by the doctor who was taking Pressinger's place, that young fellow Walters, but he knew his heart would need it. Unusual visitors were always upsetting, and this one, to judge from last night's telephone conversation, was going to be a very unusual visitor indeed. Merriweather was not sure that he felt equal to the interview. His heart pained him; yes, that same dull pain that was now with him almost constantly. He reflected on his way downstairs that no one in the house (with the possible exception of Janice) had any idea of the suffering he was forced to undergo.

Reaching the first floor, he walked with a pontifical tread to the entrance of his study. The stranger was already there and was making himself at home very much at home. He had seated himself in one of Merriweather's eighteenth-century curule chairs and was drumming his fingers carelessly on the satin-smooth finish of Merriweather's prized eighteenth-century Italian table. Merriweather drew back slightly in surprise. The voice which he had heard last night over the telephone had certainly not conveyed the impression that its owner was an Oriental.

Yet this fellow with his sleek black hair, prominent cheekbones and light brown skin looked like a Jap if there ever was one. The stranger rose to his feet.

"Mr. Merriweather?"

Merriweather (who didn't like Japs) nodded swiftly and evaded the outstretched hand. "I'm Jack Reffner," the Jap said.

Reffner! Good heavens, he was the right man after all! And he had brought it with him, for Merriweather now noticed that an oblong package wrapped in brown paper was lying at one end of the Italian table. Merriweather, however, considered it beneath his dignity to apologize.

"You're Reffner? I took you for a Japanese."

9

Reffner's smile revealed a double row of dazzlingly white teeth, which made him look more of a citizen of Nippon than ever.

"My mother was Japanese," he answered. "I can remember her dimly. One of those exquisite little doll women."

"Oh!" Merriweather was conscious that the exclamation alone sounded rather weak. "Your father was not Japanese, then?"

"No. An American of full-blooded Anglo-Saxon descent. I was born in the United States and brought up by him."

"Very interesting, I am sure," Merriweather observed. "Please be seated, Mr. Reffner. Last night you mentioned you had an original Tibetan manuscript to show to me. I presume you have it with you?"

Reffner nodded toward the oblong package on the table. "There. Shall I unwrap it for you?" Removing the brown paper, he exposed a covering of heavy yellow Chinese silk. "There are three layers of this," he explained. " 'Clothing.' Tibetans call it. To them a book stands for everything which distinguishes man from the lower animals. They consider it's almost indecent to leave one of their sacred books uncovered."

"Yes, yes, I know," Merriweather said impatiently.

Reffner peeled off the last of the silken covers, revealing the heavy boards between which the unbound pages of the manuscript were strapped. The topmost board was decorated by two faded gilt figures which were drawn in a stiff, conventionalized style that was something midway between Hindu and Chinese arts. Both gilt figures were seated cross-legged in the usual Buddha fashion. One of them was, in fact, the historic Buddha, or Sakya-t'ubpa, as he was known to Tibetans. The other figure wore an impressive miter topped by a long feather and was depicted as being seated among the petals of a luxuriant lotus.

"Padma Sambhava," Merriweather observed, using the Sanskrit name. "The Precious-Teacher-Born-from-the-Lotus!"

"Right!" There was nothing of the Japanese in Reffner's clipped, terse speech. "He's supposed to be the author of this."

"So you explained to me last night. A copy of one of the little-known writings of Padma Sambhava."

"Who said anything about 'copy'? Didn't I tell you that this was his original manuscript?"

"What!" Merriweather ejaculated. "Why, that's unbelievable!"

Reffner nodded carelessly, saying, "I had it on good authority."

"Are you aware of the age in which Padma Sambhava lived?"

"Eighth century, wasn't it?"

"Yes, the eighth century. Do you mean to tell me that this manuscript dates from the eighth century?"

Reffner shrugged his shoulders. "Well, why not? Tibetans could make paper and ink then. And they knew how to write."

"Yes, yes, I know, but--"

"The dry cold of Tibet preserves manuscripts indefinitely, I've heard. Other writings have been found that are known to date that far back. Why not this?"

It did look old, Merriweather acknowledged to himself as he scrutinized the opening page. The paper was soiled and yellow; the letters had faded to a dingy gray. Merriweather turned over several of the unbound leaves. The pages measured about ten inches wide by four inches deep, and each bore six or seven long lines of extremely cursive script. Merriweather wasn't able to read a word of it.

Each line was a jumble of complicated Tibetan characters. The words were run together without spacing---one of the practices which make the Tibetan language such a difficult one to translate. Occasional vertical lines, both single and double, marked the ends of clauses and of sentences. Merriweather was sure of that much, anyhow.

Well, it might be authentic. But these things could be faked, had been faked before. Chang would be able to tell about that, though. Chang or Jed. No, Chang could do it without Jed. Damn Jed anyhow!

Replacing the leaves he had turned over, Merriweather made a pretense of deciphering the opening line of the manuscript.

"Very interesting," he observed. "May I ask, Mr. Reffner, what this work purports to be? Or do you know that?"

"In a general way. I had parts of it translated by a friend of mine in Darjeeling. Not too much of it; I had to be careful. It was the very devil to smuggle it out of India. It's a book of Tibetan magic. Old magic that's long been forgotten."

Merriweather's pale blue eyes glistened. Merriweather's pudgy white finger traversed the soiled paper with the feather touch of a caress. "What kind of magic?"

"Spells. Incantations. Things they call *tantras*. I don't know much about it, except that this old fellow Padma was supposed to be the tops of them all when it came to wizardry. They won't talk too loudly about him even now in Tibet, I've heard. His magic was strong stuff—far too hot for the average lama to handle."

"I am aware of that fact." Merriweather stared suspiciously at his visitor. "What I do not understand is how a manuscript of the nature you claim this to be came into your possession, Reffner."

Reffner cleared his throat, perhaps a trifle nervously. "It is odd, isn't it?"

"Very."

"Well, let me tell you a few more things about it first. The tradition is that when Padma disappeared from Tibet he left behind him a number of writings. They were supposed to disappear from human sight until they were needed again by the Buddhist religion. But whenever an emergency arose---some real danger to Buddhism—a lama who had acquired a lot of merit from his past lives would be destined to find one of these documents. That's how this one was found a hundred or so years ago. It's been kept hidden ever since at a lamasery—a *gompa* on Lake Manasarowar in the southwestern quarter of Tibet."

"How are you acquainted with all these facts?"

"I had them direct from the head abbot—the *kanpo* himself."

"Then you must have been in Tibet," Merriweather speculated.

"Yes, of course I was in Tibet."

"It is difficult to believe. Tibet is a closed country closed to all foreigners, even to the Chinese."

"Foreigners sneak in occasionally. Some of them have even managed to get to Lhasa. Lhasa wasn't my goal, but I did get across the frontier and a good way inside the country."

"Yes ?" Merriweather laughed inwardly, wondering how far the fellow would dare go with his preposterous story. "And this manuscript?"

"It belonged to the high lama I told you about. Tsongpun Bonbo."

"You stole it from him?"

"No."

"No ?"

"No, I did not."

"He gave it to you, then?"

"In a way."

Merriweather coughed, a cough that was meant to convey a warning. "You expect me to believe that a high lama gave to you, a foreigner, a work of such a sacred nature as this? Do you know the extreme reverence in which Tibetans hold their religious books?"

"Maybe better than you know it," Reffner answered impudently. "I've been to Tibet. Have you?"

Merriweather again coughed warningly. "Reffner, I have a brother who has crossed the Tibetan frontier. Perhaps you have heard of Doctor Jedediah Merriweather?"

"Jed Merriweather, the archaeologist? He's almost as well known as Roy Chapman Andrews. Funny I didn't connect the name. So you're his brother!"

"I am. And he is going to be here within a very short time. To be exact, on the day after tomorrow. I received an airmail letter from him this morning. So if this article you are offering for sale was—shall we say 'manufactured'—outside of Tibet, it will be just as well for you to admit the truth of the matter now."

"See here," Reffner pleaded conciliatingly. "You've got me all wrong! In a way I don't blame you, because it is a crazy yarn. But it's true, and the least you can do is to listen to it, isn't it?"

"Very well." Merriweather pushed a pearl button on the surface of the desk to play his trump card. "I will listen while Chang takes down your conversation in shorthand. If your story is true, as you say, you won't mind that."

"No, I don't mind it. Who's Chang, by the way?"

"My Tibetan secretary."

"*Tibetan?*"

Merriweather smiled, enjoying the other's discomfiture. "Yes, Tibetan. If you have visited that country you must know how to speak the language. Chang will enjoy conversing with you. Poor fellow, he obtains so little practice in it nowadays."

Chang entered silently without knocking. That trick had frequently annoyed Adam Merriweather, but it didn't today. Reffner, caught off his guard, started visibly as Chang opened the door. Fellow had probably never seen a genuine Tibetan before.

"This is Mr. Reffner, Chang. He has brought us this manuscript to examine."

"Very happy," Chang murmured and extended his hand. He was dressed immaculately in a freshly pressed Palm Beach suit; for a Tibetan Chang had developed a surprising fussiness about clothes. And he was grinning as he usually grinned—that silly oriental grin which might mean everything or nothing.

"He tells me that it dates from the eighth century," Merriweather added. "It's supposed to have been written by Padma Sambhava---Guru Padma, as I've heard you call him. Mr. Reffner found it in Tibet."

Chang's grin didn't alter one iota, but he got the point all right. Chang was quick mentally. Now that he understood English so well it was never necessary to explain things a second time to him. Chang said something to Reffner in Tibetan. Watch the fellow be shown up now for the impostor he was! He and his fake manuscript!

But Reffner was talking right back at Chang and in a language which Merriweather couldn't follow. Tibetan? It must be Tibetan. Chang knew no other languages than that and English. And as Reffner continued talking Chang's manner toward him altered. Not perceptibly, but if you knew Chang well you could tell that it had altered. Chang was always polite to everyone, but he was just a shade politer now. More polite to this fellow Reffner than he had any business being. Treated him almost as if he were Jed. Then Chang began to examine the manuscript.

"This is very old writing," he pronounced. "Like old writings found by Sir Aurel Stein. Old paper, old writing. Tenth, ninth, maybe even eighth century."

"My God!" Merriweather breathed. "Chang, are you sure?"

"Old alphabet," said Chang, "slightly different from present one. Many Bonpo names—Buddhism not yet universally triumphant. Use of *shad* different from that of today. Old writing! Maybe it is by Guru Padma. Who can say?"

Merriweather gasped breathlessly. If Chang were right this was a find indeed. Greater by far than anything else in the famous Merriweather collection of Tibetan manuscripts. An almost priceless find. And Chang wasn't wrong very often. Jed had trained him too well.

"What is it about, Chang?"

"Very hard to read," Chang replied after due deliberation. "Not like modern language. It seem to be a work of Tantrik Buddhism. Magic for my superstitious fellow countrymen."

"Magic!" Merriweather cried delightedly. His eyes were gleaming. "Reffner, if you can prove you have the title to this I'll pay you—well, what do you think it's worth ?"

"Ten thousand dollars," Reffner replied promptly.

"Humph! You're asking a high price."

"For a rare object, the only thing of its kind in the world."

"I'll buy it at ten thousand—if you have the right to sell it. Get your notebook, Chang, and take down what Mr. Reffner tells us. He says that he can explain how this article came to be in his possession."

Reffner smiled—the smile of one who has the game well in hand. "I didn't steal it, and it wasn't given to me. It came to me in a way that you might almost call an act of God."

"Act of God!" Merriweather echoed.

II

Chang's notebook was already in his pocket. He was an efficient secretary. Not that he had ever showed any gratitude for the money Merriweather had spent on his education.

"I'm an electrical engineer by profession," Reffner began. To Merriweather's horror he had tilted back the curule chair so that it was resting on two slender, fluted legs. "That's how I got the chance to go to Chyod."

"Chyerd?" Merriweather repeated.

"C-h-y-o-d. Two dots over the o. That's the nearest you can come to expressing the sound phonetically. It's a sliver of a kingdom along the

Himalayas, sandwiched in between Nepal and Sikkim." Merriweather started to open the expensively bound atlas which he kept on the table for reference. "You won't find it on many maps," Reffner put in quickly. "There's a prevailing misconception that it's a part of Nepal. Most of that country's still a sealed book to us, you know. As a matter of fact Chyod does pay tribute to the maharajah's government, but for all of that it is practically autonomous. The people are Bhotias—Tibetans—and one hundred per cent Lamaists. They have as much love for the Gurkhas of Nepal, who are orthodox Hindus, as an Ulsterman has for an Irish Free Stater."

"Very interesting, I am sure," Merriweather murmured. "You say that you have actually visited this almost unknown territory?"

"Oh yes, I spent several months there. Chyod is under a hereditary ruler they call the *penlop*, who is a fellow with modern ideas. The greatest ambition of his life is to keep up with the maharajah of Nepal. Since the maharajah has a power plant in the Kathmandu Valley, the penlop couldn't be happy until he had one too. The company I worked for sold him the equipment, and for some reason or another I was the one they picked to go over there and install it for him."

He paused, waiting for Chang's pencil to come to a halt. "I'll skip over most of the details. The stuff was shipped by rail from Calcutta to Darjeeling, and after that it was up to me to get it over the border. All I had to do was to move the heavy equipment forty miles by coolie power, dig a ditch, lay down a pipe line, cut timber for flumes and bridges, build a dam at the waterfall in the jungle, erect a powerhouse, get the turbines installed, teach natives how to run them so the plant would keep working after I'd left the country, and finally build a five-mile transmission line from the powerhouse to Reta-puri, 'the town of hungry devils,' as the penlop's capital city is known. You can believe that I'd been let in on a job that was no picnic.

"The worst of it was that there wasn't another white man in Chyod to help me—only a crowd of grinning, jabbering Bhotias, who didn't like work any too well and had no more idea than a pack of monkeys what I was trying to accomplish. Only one man in Chyod knew any English, and he knew precious little of it. My first job was to learn how to speak the native language, which resembles pure Tibetan about as much as a dialect such as Cornish resembles pure English. The written language of Chyod is Tibetan, but I never did find the time to learn to read or write it. What I was after was an oral vocabulary large enough to make my coolies understand what I wanted of them, and when I'd acquired that we began to make progress."

Refiner brought his chair down on its full four legs, to

Merriweather's considerable relief. "Well, we did get the penlop's hydro station finished, but that's not the story that interests you. Up beyond the Himalayas was Tibet, and Tibet fascinated me as it has a good many other people during the last hundred years or so. I made up my mind, as soon as things had settled down to a comfortable routine, that I wouldn't leave Chyod without a try at slipping over the frontier.

"Every once in a while I had to ride over to Darjeeling to order the things I needed, and it was in Darjeeling that I struck up an acquaintance with an Englishman named Hilary Swithins, who taught English to the Sikkimese kids during the day and worked nights at compiling a Tibetan dictionary. An Oxford graduate and a white man if there ever was one. Tibet was his specialty, and it soon became mine too. Swithins wanted to get up there more than he wanted anything else in his life, but he didn't have a ghost of a chance of making it from Sikkim, since the passes along that frontier are now guarded so tightly that a mouse can hardly sneak across. The Chyod frontier, however, isn't watched nearly so closely. Chyod is as closed to foreigners as Tibet, and its inhabitants are of the Tibetan race and religion. I got to wondering if I couldn't make it from Chyod.

"Swithins and I used to have some long arguments. He was dubious about my chances, but the more I studied the situation, the more it seemed to me that I would be able to get away with it. The frontier was my first trump, but my face was also a priceless asset. I didn't look like a *pyi-ling*, as the Tibetans call the British. I didn't have 'white' eyes nor 'gray' hair. Tibetans call all light hair 'gray' and all blue or gray eyes 'white,' and they think that every pyi-ling is invariably possessed of these features. So the face I inherited from my Japanese mother was my second trump.

"Trump number three was that I was learning enough Bhotian to be able to pass anywhere in Tibet as a native of Chyod. Even Swithins admitted that I held three high cards, but he was as stubborn as only an Englishman can be. The final outcome of our arguments was that we fixed up a little bet---one thousand rupees, he said, that I wouldn't be able to get far enough over the frontier to take pictures of one of the big lamaseries. I had learned that there was one of these just three days march from the top of the last Himalayan pass. It was known as Dawa Gompa, the 'House of the Moon in the Solitude,' and it accommodated about a thousand monks, which was large enough to satisfy Swithins. He agreed to pay me the thousand rupees if I was able to show him some films of Dawa Gompa.

"At my headquarters in Chyod I began to keep an open house for all the Tibetan traders who came down from the uplands. It cost me several bales of brick tea and countless hours wasted in apparently interminable harangues, but at last I began to get a clear picture of the road to the boundary and beyond. Also, piece by piece, I acquired a complete Tibetan dress: cloth boots laced with red woolen garters and a red robe with long sleeves and a high collar which reached clear to my knees. A Tibetan ties a sash about the middle of his robe, and it makes a pocket above the waist in which he keeps his eating bowl, purse, knife, spoon and various other odds and ends. Chang is the only Tibetan I've ever met who doesn't look like a woman seven months pregnant."

Merriweather's secretary continued to write as though he had not heard the last remark. "Both Chang and myself are thoroughly familiar with the appearance of a Tibetan costume," Merriweather observed coldly.

"Then I'll try not to bother you with unnecessary details. The penlop, even though I was now on fairly intimate terms with him, couldn't be expected to advance my plan since he was honor bound to Lhasa not to allow any of the pyi-ling to enter the sacred land of the lamas through his kingdom. So I had to fool the penlop—as well as his ministers, his army and all of his citizens. It wasn't going to be any too easy.

"I waited until the last insulator had been placed on the last pole of the transmission line and then struck at the psychological moment. When the penlop had pressed the button and seen his palace windows gleaming with his beautiful new electric lights he was so pleased he could hardly talk. It wasn't enough to pay me in gold as he had promised. Was there anything else he could do to show his gratitude?

" 'Yes,' I answered, and explained that I had a sickness from remaining for so long in the lowlands. My heart ached to visit the Himalayas, the abode of eternal snow, where I could be cured of my illness. Might I have his permission to travel there before I left his realm forever?

"The penlop fell for it and gave me a pass that permitted me to travel anywhere in his kingdom unmolested. He didn't even ask me to promise not to enter Tibet; I don't believe the idea that I was planning such an attempt ever crossed his mind. It was May when I started, and the *datura* trees were flowering---hundreds of white, bell-shaped blossoms well over a foot long on every tree. It was magnificent, as you can imagine. Orchids were so common that I stopped looking at them, and rhododendrons followed me all the way up the slope of the Himalayas. Rhododendrons of every possible color—pink, white, cream, yellow, violet and even a deep blood red.

"I had decided to make the journey on foot, but I bought a mule to carry my outfit. One of those sturdy little Tibetan mules that can climb over rocks like a cat. I called her Jenny when there were no Tibetans or Chyodians near to hear me; she was a good beast but greedy. When Jenny was loaded she looked authentic. She had the usual kind of wooden pack saddle (they use it interchangeably for horses, mules or yaks) with a skin bag fastened on each side of it. Everything I brought had to go in one of those rawhide bags, but I didn't bring much. Brick tea, yak butter, parched barley flour, a little mutton—I had spent several weeks training my stomach to keep down Tibetan grub. I had a few pots and pans for cooking, a blanket and an old sheepskin for bedding, and of course my Tibetan costume. As soon as I was away from Reta-puri and well hidden in the jungle I took it out and put it on. Then Jenny and I continued our way.

"Two days walking brought us out of the tree ferns and into a country of oaks and silver firs. It was remarkable how completely the vegetation altered in character as we climbed upward. Finally we were above all timber and right in the heart of the rock country. Huge boulders were everywhere around us—dainty little calling cards that had been left behind by the last glacier. Some were as round as marbles and twenty feet or so in diameter. I had to scramble my way over them, and the going got tougher and tougher. My path, like most Tibetan roads, had to be taken on faith a good share of the time. Tibetans will call any craggy course a highway if enough people travel it to wear away some of the grass. Several times I nearly lost the way, but I kept zigzagging up the rocky slopes northward toward the Rongbo La—a saddle-shaped gap between peaks that looked from below like a mouth full of hungry teeth. You don't know what mountains can be till you try climbing the Himalayas. We think the Rockies or the Sierras are something, but there isn't a peak in this country (outside of Alaska) as high as fifteen thousand feet. The Himalayas have seventy peaks above twenty-four thousand feet and, I understand, around eleven hundred over twenty thousand feet. That's the kind of range you have to cross to get into Tibet.

"I thought I was in good physical condition before I started. I'm pretty wiry and can stand lots of exertion, but the Himalayas got me. Got my wind, that is. I couldn't do more than thirty or forty yards without stopping, so it was slow going. Lord, how I used to envy Jenny! That crazy mule didn't seem to mind the climb at all, and rocks bothered her about as little as they'd bother a mountain goat. She was an optimist, that animal! Every time I'd halt she'd lower her head to graze, and if she did happen to find a few blades of coarse grass sticking out of the snow patches she'd munch away as happy as if you'd put her in the finest pasture.

"So we climbed and we climbed. It was a queer sensation to spend day after day traveling through that country of ice and snow and naked rock. I seemed to be out of this world altogether and in an incredible region between earth and heaven where time stood still. I had almost lost count of the days when we reached the top of the Rongbo La.

"I don't know how high that pass is. It's never been surveyed. Maybe it never will be. My guess is that it's between seventeen and eighteen thousand feet, and nearer eighteen than seventeen. A heap of stones decorated with yak horns and skulls marked the top, and there were also long poles decked with wind-torn cloth streamers bearing Tibetan prayers. I caught just a glimpse of this, staggered forward and fell flat on my face. I was all in and no mistake.

"I spent the night at the top of the pass. Something no Tibetan would dream of doing, but I was suffering so horribly from the effects of the rarefied air that I couldn't have moved another step. Tibetans have a name for that sickness which may be translated as 'pass poison.' It feels like a combination of giddiness and nausea, together with the type of headache that splits your skull open. The worst case of seasickness you can imagine is nothing at all to it.

"I managed to crawl over to Jenny and hobble her feet so she wouldn't be able to stray too far. Then I huddled into a cavity between two boulders to shiver miserably under my sheepskin. It was as cold as interstellar space, a fiendish cold that whipped through my clothing and into my very vitals, but in spite of everything I did get an hour or two of sleep. That helped some. When I woke I had recovered enough to be able to stagger onto my feet.

"It was about three o'clock in the morning and black as ink. 'Come on, old girl,' I whispered to Jenny, who gave a cheerful snort as she heard me approach. 'Let's go down where we can find some breakfast.' So I strapped on her saddlebags, and we started downhill on the Tibetan side of the range.

"I hadn't counted on encountering the frontier station so soon. We had only traveled a short distance when it loomed out of the early morning darkness, a bulky round tower that nearly scared me to death. I would have been willing to make a wide detour to avoid it, but I couldn't. There was a sheer rock wall on either side, so I had to pass right by the very door of the watchtower. 'Jenny,' I whispered, 'not a sound, or we're sunk.' And I'll swear that mule understood me. We crept by the tower like two ghosts.

"Believe it or not, but there wasn't a sentry on duty. You see, I'd spent the night on the pass, which no Tibetan would do, and hence arrived at an hour when the garrison didn't expect any traveler could be coming, and so were all happily sleeping within. It couldn't have worked out more beautifully, but I can't take any credit for planning it. I couldn't have gone on from the top of the pass that night—not if I was to be hung for staying there.

"I began to feel better with that watchtower behind us. We continued to go down and down until presently we came to trees again: scrubby little junipers, whose pungent twigs are burned by the Tibetans as incense. Then the sun burst out in a great flood of gold to give me my first view of Tibet.

"After the magnificent scenery I had encountered on the way up there didn't seem to be very much on the plateau to get excited about. Nothing but flat, treeless plains, with tier after tier of barren mountains in the background. Everything yellow or brown or gray. A bleak land, arid and windswept and desolate as one of the eight cold hells of the Buddhist.

"I stopped beside a stream to make a fire with my Tibetan flint and tinder (it's a trick to learn how to use them) and boil my breakfast tea. The plateau didn't seem like it would be hard going after the Himalayas, but I soon learned better. Punctually at eleven o'clock the wind came up, the terrible Tibetan wind that whistles like a howling dervish and brings with it a cloud of gritty dust. It blew into my eyes and my nostrils and my mouth and left me with a sore throat that lasted all the time I was in Tibet. But that was nothing at all compared to what I felt when I met my first party of Tibetans.

"They clustered around me---men in shaggy fur tams and long gowns, like my own, which they wore over their left shoulders to leave their greasy right shoulders bare. (When the sun is out Tibet can get nearly as hot as it can get cold.) All of them seemed to be asking questions at once; it was amazing how curious they were.

"It wasn't that I was in any way suspected, but no Tibetan will leave a stranger without putting him through a lengthy catechism. I had expected something of the kind and had the answers ready. I was a native of Chyod, I told them. That was plain from my speech, one said bluntly, but where was I going in the land of Bhod?

"Spinning my prayer wheel and intoning the sacred formula written on the roll of paper inside it, I answered that I was bound on a pilgrimage to the lamasery of Dawa Gompa. They twirled their own prayer wheels piously as I talked; nearly every Tibetan carries one of these gadgets. Finally they left me, with their heartiest good wishes, and I continued my march across the desolate plains.

"I met several other parties of Tibetans with equally happy results and was feeling quite pleased with myself by the time I reached Dawa

Gompa. I never will forget my first glimpse of that lamasery. It's magnificently situated on the crest of a hill and looks like something out of Hollywood—whitewashed walls, golden roofs shimmering in the brilliant Tibetan sunlight. Spellbound, I stared for fully five minutes before I remembered that if I didn't get pictures I couldn't prove to Swithins that I had actually seen this architectural wonder.

"From where I was standing the gompa was rather far away, but, as I could see the robed figures of lamas moving about the buildings, I didn't dare to move closer for my photographic operations. I reached in the pocket above my waist and withdrew my Leica cautiously from the fold of my voluminous gown. Holding it level with my eyes, I took several quick shots of the gompa.

"If you have ever used a Leica you know how hard it is to keep watch on what may be going on around you. The first inkling I had that anything was wrong was the noise of stones rattling down from the path above me. I turned my head and was horrified to see a detachment of soldiers.

"Needless to say, I whipped the Leica back inside my robe in nothing flat, but they had already seen me. There were eight or ten of them—uniformed like British soldiers with khaki caps, tunics, trousers and puttees. The commander sported a Sam Browne belt with an automatic pistol, but the long turquoise earring which hung from his left ear didn't fit the modern military picture.

"Two of the rank and file held me while the gentleman of the earring reached inside my robe. He had seen me trying to hide something there, all right. His hand closed upon my Leica, and he stared at in a puzzled manner. Ordinary cameras are known, at least by hearsay, in most of Tibet, but it was evident that none of the soldiers had ever seen a camera that looked like this one. However, they knew very well that it was a foreign article that had no business being in Tibet; it was plain that I was one of the pyi-ling.

"I had to admit that I was; lying would only have made matters worse. But I refused to divulge the nature of my Leica, remembering that many Tibetans are said to hold the belief that a camera is able to steal the soul from the object photographed. Very well, my friend of the earring told me, I would have to go before the governor of the district, the *dzong-pon*. They were perfectly polite and seemed not at all unfriendly, but I didn't like the situation any too well for all of that. Floggings are a frequent punishment in Tibet, and a Tibetan flogging, in which they lash your inner thighs with rawhide thongs (with every two lashes counting as one stroke), is no laughing matter.

"The dzong-pon lived three or four miles away in a stone castle on a hill overlooking the surrounding plains. Yes, 'castle' is the word. With its rounded towers, its battlements and its massive walls it might have come straight from the period of William the Conqueror, had it not been for a certain delicacy of line, a beauty of proportion which no Norman builder could have achieved.

"As we entered the courtyard the rays of the afternoon sun glinted upon a row of giant, barrel-shaped prayer wheels. They were being turned by wrinkled crones whose withered lips never ceased their mumbling of the sacred formula that was written over and over, millions of times, upon the great paper rolls within the huge cylinder. I was allowed only a glimpse of the activities of the courtyard, however, before I was forced to climb a steeply pitched wooden ladder. The ladder, although placed on the exterior of the building, was the only staircase to the upper story where the dzong-pon maintained his living quarters and business office. After a brief delay we were admitted to his presence.

"Dressed in a magnificent sky-blue kimono of stiff Chinese silk, he sat cross-legged upon a cushion as we entered. The room was sparsely furnished: a few chests along the walls, a few dragon-carved tables of the folding Tibetan type, but not a single chair. Bright-colored silk paintings ornamented the walls, and a niche held a small *cho-ten*, a gilt model of one of those fantastic bulb-shaped monuments so commonly seen throughout Tibet.

"I was not allowed to stand but was compelled to be seated upon a small mattress placed directly on the floor, as a rigid etiquette forbade that my head should be higher than that of the dzong-pon during our audience. He received me graciously, ordering tea to be served. Using as much as I could remember of the special ceremonial language that is required for addressing high Tibetan officials, I told him my story. He listened without comment until I had finished.

"I waited with growing nervousness for him to speak Slowly, very slowly, the dzong-pon lowered his delicate porcelain teacup and with the third finger of his right hand flicked a drop or two of liquid upwards as a sign to his servants that he did not wish the cup refilled. His face remained inscrutable while he told me that I had committed a serious offense in entering Tibet. It was not only an offense against his government, but also against the government of the pyi-ling.

"I bowed my head to express my deference and said that I could only trust to his justice and mercy. He replied —greatly to my relief— that both justice and mercy would be shown to me, but I must leave Tibet at once. The *ru-pon*, the captain who had arrested me, would escort me to the frontier.

"That was getting out of the situation so nicely that I ventured to ask for the return of my Leica. But upon that point the dzong-pon was firm. He was no petty provincial officer, but a sophisticated aristocrat from Lhasa, who had learned enough of foreign customs to recognize a camera when he saw one. He called it by a word that meant 'devil box' and insisted that it must be destroyed at once.

"While I watched helplessly the ru-pon shattered it to pieces against the stone flooring. My beautiful little Leica! Back in America it had cost me over two hundred dollars, and I didn't value it much more than I did my right eye. And added to its loss was the loss of the thousand rupees which I now had to pay Swithins, since the terms of our bet had been distinctly that I should return with pictures of Dawa Gompa. However, I could do nothing. I had no choice but to leave the dzong in the escort of the ru-pon's detachment.

"They accompanied me back to the round watchtower and as far as the top of the Rongbo La. Standing by the stone cairns and fluttering prayer flags, they waved their good-bye while I scrambled down on the other side of the frontier at as fast a pace as Jenny could go. Since I had already spent one night on a Himalayan pass I wasn't any too anxious to repeat the experience."

"And the manuscript?" Merriweather inquired. "The manuscript which you claim to have procured in Tibet?"

"I'm coming to that," Reffner answered. "Just before sundown that day I reached a good camping spot. Several soot-blackened stones, which had been heaped together by the last traveler, provided a place on which to set my cooking pot. There were juniper branches for fuel, and a tiny rivulet coursing down the rocks supplied enough water for a mess of tea. 'Mess' is the right word for Tibetan tea, I think. You take a hard brick that makes you think of a plug of chewing tobacco, break off a chunk of the compressed leaves and twigs, and boil them with soda until you get a thick black liquid. After straining out the tea leaves you add salt and yak butter (if the butter is rancid it makes no difference), churn them all up together and throw a double handful of tsamba, or barley flour, into your eating bowl. The best table etiquette is to mold the flour into balls with your fingers and use them to sop up the tea. I was just in the middle of preparing a meal of this kind when I happened to look down the path and saw a traveler climbing up from below.

"He was on foot, as I was, and he led a mule which might have been first cousin to my own Jenny. He wore a lama's plum-colored robe that reached to his ankles and was tied around the waist with a yellow sash. Also he wore a peaked yellow bonnet with great long earflaps, which told me that he was a member of the Ge-lug-pa or 'Yellow Hat' sect, the established religion of Tibet, which you might almost term the Church of England of that country. As he reached my camping place I bent low and touched the bottom of his robe with my forehead. Tibetans invariably show the greatest deference to the religious order, and it amused me to keep on playing the part of a Tibetan. 'You have undergone hardship,' I said, giving him the conventional greeting between travelers who meet on the road. He answered in the usual manner: 'No, it is you who have had the hard time.'

" 'Will your holiness honor me by partaking of my poor repast ?'

"He thanked me and brought out his wooden lama's bowl. Squatting to face the embers of the fire, we drank our tea while the sun sank below the horizon, tingeing blood red the crests of the peaks towering far above our heads. He informed me that his name was Tsongpun Bonbo; the *ts*, the way he pronounced it, sounded like the sputtering of firecrackers. In return I gave him my own name—the Tibetan name I had assumed for this journey—and told him that my home was in Lhasa. That was taking a risk, but the lama did not appear to notice the peculiarities of my Chyod accent. His own home, he said to me, was a gompa on Lake Manasarowar, or Tso Maphang, as he called it. Unworthy as he was, the lama continued, he had the honor to be the kanpo of that gompa.

"I scented something wrong in that statement. The head abbots of these Tibetan monasteries are important persons. They are believed to be reincarnations of past abbots, and many of them are worshiped as living gods. They live like princes and travel, if they travel at all, with a formidable retinue—a yellow silk umbrella to be carried over his holiness's head, and that sort of thing. Yet Tsongpun Bonbo, who traveled on foot without a servant and with only a single mule, claimed to be one of these mighty prelates. None of my business, of course, but curiosity wouldn't let it rest there. As deftly as I could word it I inquired why he was now so far from his lamasery. He took no offense but replied that he was returning from a pilgrimage to a spot even more holy than Tso Maphang, which is considered to be one of the most sacred spots of the Orient. He had been to Budh Gaya."

"Budh Gaya!" Adam Merriweather echoed.

"Yes, holy ground indeed! Centuries ago, when Babylon was falling to the troops of Cyrus, an Indian prince squatted there to meditate beneath the branches of a fig tree. And because of what took place in that one man's mind the history of half the world has been altered. Is it any wonder that Buddhists consider that small village in northeastern India to be the most hallowed spot in the entire world? But to get back to the lama. He told me the reason for his pilgrimage. To this day I don't know how he happened to tell that story to a stranger, even though one, as he thought, of his own race and religion. Maybe it was because we were alone in the overpowering vastness of the Himalayas, two human atoms clinging together for companionship while the stars popped into the sky by the millions, by the billions. Under such circumstances even a Yellow Hat lama might—"

"May I ask nature of story he told?" Chang interrupted. Although his brow had knit into a barely perceptible frown he gave no other sign to indicate that the conversation had taken a turn distasteful to him.

"I'm coming to it now." Reffner's manner showed plainly that he had no intention of allowing himself to be hurried. "That was back in 1934. What was the year 1934 called in the Tibetan calendar?"

"Wood-dog year."

"That's it! Fire-dog, earth-dog, iron-dog, water-dog, wood-dog. Every twelfth year is a year of the dog. Is that right ?"

"You are correct," Chang answered, bowing politely.

"Well, every dog-year the head lama of Tsongpun's gompa is compelled to make a pilgrimage to Budh Gaya. He must be humble as the Buddha was: go unattended and, if possible, go all the way on foot. Tsongpun confessed with shame that he had not felt able to remain away from his gompa in order to make the whole journey as the great master would have wished, and so he had taken the train from Darjeeling to Gaya and back. However, he must have walked over five hundred miles to reach Darjeeling from Manasarowar and now he was walking an equal distance from Darjeeling back again. One thousand miles on foot, crossing and recrossing the highest mountain range on earth! I tell you that religion really means something to those people!"

Chang frowned again—the slight frown which only Merriweather could detect. "Please may I ask object of journey ?"

Reffner pointed to the manuscript. "About a hundred years ago the kanpo of Tsongpun's lamasery—Tsongpun is supposed to be a reincarnation of him—discovered this sacred manuscript in the secret place where Padma Sambhava had concealed it. With the book Padma had also left instructions concerning its use. The magic properties of the work, the instructions said, were dormant from long disuse, and to restore their original virtue the kanpo must carry the manuscript with him to Budh Gaya in order to spend a night in meditation at the site of the famous bodhi tree. This act, however, was good for only twelve years. Every year of the dog the pilgrimage must be repeated by the kanpo and by his successors."

Well, it was possible, Merriweather admitted to himself. Almost anything might be possible in Tibet, Jed had once observed. Merri-weather gave to the storyteller a look of cold disapproval.

"So you did steal it from him?"

"No." Reffner said, his dark skin revealing an indignant flush. "I've already told you I didn't."

"There's no other way in which it could have come into your pos-session."

"Yes, one. We stacked our saddlebags side by side; we each had two—yak-skin bags of the type common throughout Tibet—same size, same shape. We broke camp in the early morning before sunrise. I strapped two bags to Jenny's saddle that I could have sworn were my own, called out the usual 'Go slowly' to the lama, and took the trail down. That evening when I made my next camp I found this manuscript. I had taken one of the lama's saddlebags and left him with one of mine."

"Did you make an attempt to return it?"

"No. How could I? Tsongpun Bonbo was in Tibet by that time, and the Tibetan frontier was closed to me. I might have left the manuscript with the penlop of Chyod, trusting that he would see it returned to Tsongpun, but the penlop wasn't supposed to know where I'd been, and although I wasn't particularly afraid of him he still held my pay in trust. If I told him what I'd been up to he might take the opportunity to confiscate the sum due me; you never can foretell the tricks of an orien-tal potentate. Besides, I figured that the Tibetans owed me something for smashing my Leica and making me lose my bet to Swithins. I was sorry for the lama, but the manuscript seemed to even the account."

"Have you offered the work to other collectors?"

"No. No one has seen it but Swithins, who translated parts of it for me in Darjeeling. Swithins advised me, if I wanted to keep it, to get it out of India in a hurry before the lama had time to start an inquiry. He said that the officials of the Indian government are very sensitive to complaints from influential Tibetans. And from India I went to China, where I had the good luck to stumble onto another electrical engineer-ing job. After that I cruised around the Orient, spending my money foolishly but keeping out of British territory. I didn't land back in the United States until two weeks ago, and I landed here practically broke or I wouldn't be selling this now. Now that you know the truth, is it worth ten thousand dollars to you?"

"Ten thousand dollars," Merriweather began ponderously, "was the price I agreed to pay only if I was satisfied that your claim to the work was valid. I am not so satisfied. Legally, as well as morally, you have no title to it."

"It isn't likely that a Tibetan lama will be over here to sue you for it in an American court," Refiner vouchsafed.

"That is not the point," Merriweather opined. Jed would be here on Wednesday, he was thinking. Would it be best to wait for Jed's opinion?

No, he decided swiftly, the manuscript was genuine. Chang had said so, and Chang could tell as well as Jed. He would buy it now in order to have it when Jed came. Jed, for all his explorations, had never found an object of anywhere near the value; he would turn green with envy when he saw it. Yes, Jed would turn green with envy, Merriweather mused, chuckling. Then, too, he would be itching to translate it, but one could make excuses to keep him from handling it. Keep him on pins and needles for a few days, perhaps even as long as a week.... Adam Merriweather chuckled again and reached in the desk drawer for his checkbook.

"Good!" Reffner ejaculated. "I thought you'd see things my way." Merriweather's pen paused after dating the check.

"Not altogether. Since you do not have legal title to this work it is obvious that I cannot pay you the full price for it. However, I am not the sort to take advantage of you. I will give you five thousand dollars."

"Can't you make it seventy-five hundred?"

"Five thousand is my only offer. Do you choose to take it or not?"

"There are other collectors who will pay more."

"I do not believe that you will find them in the United States. Perhaps you will find a few such collectors in England, but by your own admission it is dangerous to try to hawk this in British territory, since there is an excellent chance that it will be confiscated and returned to Tibet. I constitute your only market for this work, my friend. Do you accept my offer?"

"Payment to be made in full?"

"Payment to be made in full immediately."

Reffner shrugged his shoulders.

"I'll take the five thousand."

Merriweather made out the check, and Chang carried it to his office to run it through the Protectograph. He brought it back for Merriweather's signature. Affixing his name with its usual flourish, Merriweather gave the slip of paper to Reffner. The latter folded it into his wallet rather wryly.

"You've done a nice stroke of business," he observed.

And so he had, Merriweather exulted when he was left alone in the study. Five thousand dollars! A nice stroke of business indeed. Half of what the fellow had asked, and he hadn't asked anywhere near the amount which Merriweather would have been willing to pay. He chuckled gleefully. "I constitute your only market for this work, my friend." That sentence had been a really masterly touch.

Chang returned to bring the evening paper; Merriweather unfolded it upon his desk. The same tiresome headlines! War in Spain—Seventeen Rebel Planes Shot Down. Well, who cares? War in the Orient—Japs Now Threaten to Occupy Peiping. Russia ought to step in to stop them. Let the Japs and the Bolsheviks kill each other off, and what a good thing it would be for the rest of the world. Supreme Court Battle—there were some new developments which looked interesting. . . . Oh, my God, what was this?

It was an inconspicuous paragraph, tucked away in the lower half of the front page, but Adam Merriweather read every word of it three times before the paper slipped through his fingers to drop unheeded to the floor. He jabbed furiously at the pearl button on his desk. Where the devil was Chang? What was keeping him?

Rising to his feet, Merriweather strode across the room. "Chang!" he bellowed down the hallway. "Chang! Come here at once."

But Chang returned no answer. Chang was no longer in the house.

PART TWO: The Man from Carthage
(Tuesday, July 20)

PEERING FROM BEHIND gold-rimmed bifocals, the eyes of Theocritus Lucius Westborough surveyed the proof sheets with the look of a doting parent toward a newly born offspring. Nearly seventy years of age, Westborough was a small man with a triangular face, broad and wide at the forehead, slanting downward to a small, narrow chin. His pencil paused to note a correction; within only a few weeks the work, *Heliogabalus: Rome's Most Degenerate Emperor,* would be entrusted to the mercies of critics and reviewers.

The title was the selection of Westborough's publisher. The historian himself secretly considered it to be a trifle sensational but, since he relied implicitly on his publisher's judgment in such matters, had not ventured to proffer an alternative suggestion.

He marked another correction; the name of Rome's Most Degenerate Emperor had been again misspelled. The compositor appeared to have had a penchant for replacing the second *a* in the name with an *o;* Westborough had already made this same correction a great many times, and he was scarcely a quarter of a way through the bulky pile of galley proofs.

There were other corrections, too—far too many of them. His introduction had been so awkwardly constructed that it had been necessary to rewrite virtually every word of it. What perverse fate is it, he wondered, that afflicts an author with a sublime blindness to his mistakes until the galley proofs are actually laid in his hands? And at that very moment miraculously permits him to see with the blinding light of truth all of his miserable follies?

Westborough's pointed chin rested upon the palm of his small-fingered hand as he lost himself in contemplation of his account of the battle of Antioch. His treatment now appeared to be rather sketchy. Could he be quite sure that the memorable occasion was covered as fully as it deserved?

The unbridled strains of Swing floated to his ears from a radio on the opposite side of the hotel court. He rose to shut the french door to the balcony, murmuring to himself as he did so:

" 'Sometimes a thousand twanging instruments will hum about mine ears; and sometimes voices . . .'"

But such twanging instruments, such voices could prove very disconcerting to one whose thoughts must be centered upon the reasons which had induced the Emperor Macrinus to desert in shameful fashion his victorious army. Even closing the door did not hush them a great deal. And, as if these noises of the ether were not enough, Westborough's telephone chose that instant to commence a noisy jangling.

Sighing in vexation, the little man picked up the instrument. "Yes, this is he speaking. Oh, Lieutenant Mack! It is certainly a great pleasure to hear your voice again, John."

The voice which was such a pleasure to hear said gruffly: "Listen, Westborough! Doing anything special right now?"

Westborough directed a rather rueful glance toward the stack of unfinished galley proofs. "Nothing of grave importance."

"Good! Grab a taxi and come over to the Pilgrim Deluxe Hotel on Eron Street. Room 414."

"The Pilgrim Deluxe Hotel on Eron Street? Yes, I shall come at once. May I ask---"

"Murder !" Mack grunted tersely.

"Murder! Dear me! May I know---"

But Mack was no longer at the other end of the wire to answer questions. Westborough opened the engraved hunting case of the thick gold watch which he had carried for fifty years. Eight-thirty in the morning did not seem a likely hour for murder, but perhaps the crime had been committed earlier. The Pilgrim Deluxe Hotel on Eron Street? No, he could place neither the hostelry nor its address. But he had promised Lieutenant Mack that he would come at once.

As he reached the door he glanced back regretfully at his galley proofs. It did seem a shame to leave them now. But he supposed that the battle of Antioch could wait a little longer for his analysis. It had already waited nearly eighteen centuries.

A canary-colored taxi was waiting conveniently before his hotel. Westborough gave the driver the address and settled back against the leather seat. The cab turned south among the ancient brownstone fronts of Rush Street. A most interesting quarter of the city. The newer parts of Chicago, no matter to what hoary age they attained, would never possess one tenth the character of narrow Rush Street, Westborough reflected. The cab turned westward on Eron Street.

The street was shabby and dingy and grew more shabby and even more dingy with each block they traveled. After traversing a quarter of a mile the driver halted the cab before a grimy brick building, black with the encrusted dirt of forty years or more. A number of people had already congregated in a little knot upon the sidewalk.

Paying his driver, Westborough attempted without any degree of marked success to make his way to the main entrance. The crowd was babbling excitedly; it was clear that in some way a hint had leaked out that an event out of the ordinary had occurred inside the grimy build-ing. A bulky policeman brusquely ordered them all to "move along." Reluctantly the crowd began to disperse, permitting Westborough to approach the entrance. "Yes, you too," specified the officer. "There ain't nothing here to see, so get going."

"But I wish to go inside," Westborough protested.

"Oh, you do, do you? There ain't nobody going inside while I'm on duty."

"Dear me," Westborough lamented. "I fear that Lieutenant Mack will be vexed if he fails to see me."

The officer, turning his gaze downward, saw a shrimp of a man with scraggly white hair, a scrawny neck, gold-rimmed spectacles, a broad forehead and a dinky little chin. All of these details were committed to memory in one quick glance.

"What's your name?"

"Westborough. Theocritus Lucius Westborough, to be exact."

The officer nodded. "You can go in."

Westborough stepped through a revolving door. The Pilgrim De-luxe Hotel had evidently been a fine establishment in its day, he con-cluded as he noted the tiled floor and the marble fountain of its lobby. But time had taken its revenges; sly and malicious ones they were. The basin of the fountain was dry and desolate; the marble youth with the uplifted urn had a chipped nose and stood badly in need of a liberal application of the liquid he falsely purported to purvey. And the lobby, despite its enormous crystal chandelier, was appallingly illuminated. To eyes which had been adjusted to brilliant July sunlight it seemed like the interior of a cave.

The desk was deserted, but Westborough could see a second uni-formed officer lounging by the elevator shaft. The little man crossed the floor.

"What the hell do you want?" the officer inquired. His tone was not rude; it was merely the tone of one who seeks information. Westbor-ough supplied it.

"I believe that Lieutenant Mack wishes to see me."

"Your name would be . . . ?"

"Westborough."

"It's all right, then." He opened a door of wrought-iron grillwork to the elevator shaft. "Get in the car, and I'll run you up there."

No hotel clerk? And now no elevator pilot? It appeared that the Police Department had completely ousted the staff of the Pilgrim Deluxe. Only a grave emergency, Westborough realized, could warrant such an intrusion.

"May I ask what unfortunate event has transpired within these precincts ?" he inquired as the elevator wheezed asthmatically upward.

"Guest here has been bumped off. Some damned Jap! No great loss, if you ask me. Them little squirts are going to start a war with us someday."

"The Japanese," Westborough said gently, "are a much maligned race. Do you know why Lieutenant Mack wishes to see me?"

The officer stopped the car and flung the door open. "You'll have to ask him that question. Down that corridor and turn left to 414."

Westborough was stopped in the corridor by a third policeman, a plainclothes man attached to the Homicide Squad whom he knew slightly. Smiling, he extended his hand.

"Mr. Carnavan, I believe."

The detective grinned. "Right the first time. Do you know that Johnny Mack wants to see you?"

"I do not know why."

"Trick writing," Carnavan said laconically.

"Trick writing?"

"We found some on---" He terminated the sentence abruptly. "I'd better let Johnny Mack do the talking on that. He thinks that you'll be able to translate it for him."

"Lieutenant Mack honors me far too much. This writing is not by chance Japanese? If so, I fear that---"

"Mack doesn't think it's Jap writing," Carnavan cut in. " 'S funny he doesn't, because the fellow who was killed looks like a Jap if there ever was one."

"Dear me," Westborough murmured as he resumed his walk down the corridor. The door of room 414 was open, and he could see some of his old acquaintances within. Jimmy Seizer, that spectacled youth from the Identification Bureau, and the short, globular Dr. Hildreth from the coroner's office. Only Lieutenant Mack appeared to be absent.

Dr. Hildreth was bent over something on the floor, and Westborough's own glance traveled automatically downward.

The man who was lying on that worn, faded carpeting might have been a Japanese. His relatively large head, straight black hair, oblique eye sockets, and the sparse, almost nonexistent eyelashes were certainly all characteristics of that race. But the face was livid, blackened; the brown fingers clenched in a futile desperation; a bloody tongue protruded from between blood-flecked lips, and the small eyes were fixed wide in a frozen stare.

Shuddering, Westborough averted his head. He had never known that the impassive Japanese features were capable of expressing such stark, such unbelievable terror.

II

Lieutenant Mack popped out like a big-nosed jack-in-the-box from the interior of a closet. He grinned his recognition and shook the historian's hand in a hearty grip.

"Glad you're here. Want you to look at—" He noted that the rotund Dr. Hildreth had closed his instrument case and was straightening up from the floor. "Through already, Doc?"

"Guess so—for the time being. Not hard to tell what happened to this fellow."

"Strangled ?"

"Certainly. Do you see the ecchymosis in a circular line around the neck? That's where the ligature was applied."

"What the hell is an ecchymosis?" Mack wanted to know.

"How can I tell you?" the doctor snapped. "Call it the pouring out of blood into the skin tissues. Eight words to express one simple medical term, and I still haven't given you the precise shade of meaning!"

"Call it a mark," Mack suggested amiably. "That's only one word. What sort of thing was used to strangle him ?"

"Almost anything except a rope or a cord. The depression is a wide, comparatively shallow one, which suggests the use of something softer and more yielding than a rope."

"A silk scarf?" Mack asked.

"Yes, a scarf. It wouldn't have to be a silk one necessarily. A big handkerchief. A necktie. Or even a window curtain. All of these could effect the necessary constriction of the windpipe." He began to write in a notebook. "What's the unlucky Jap's name?"

"He's down on the hotel register as Jack Reffner.""

"Reffner?" The doctor paused in his writing. "Nothing Jap about that."

"No," Mack agreed.

"Home address?"

"Chicago."

"Just Chicago?"

"That's all that's on the register."

The doctor jerked his pencil abruptly away. "You mean to tell me you haven't been through his papers yet?"

"What papers ?"

"Those in his billfold, of course."

"What billfold?"

"Didn't he have one?"

"He did not," Mack growled disgustedly. "If he'd had one he wouldn't have had any bills to put in it. He wouldn't have had even two coppers to rub together. He was cleaned out as slick as a whistle."

"Well, there's the motive for you."

"Yeh," Mack grunted. "Some sneak thief?"

"Sure, why not? Jap comes in and finds the thief in his room, and the thief strangles him. Looks to me like you have a clear case."

"Yeh? No one's going to let himself be strangled without putting up a fight. That'd turn the room topsy-turvy, but everything's in good order. Think a sneak thief would stop to straighten up the furniture? And besides, do you see anything here that could be used for strangling ?"

Dr. Hildreth's eyes wandered around the hotel bedroom, which contained, as Westborough had already inventoried, a brass bedstead with a faded blanket under a cheap cotton spread, a rickety rocker, a straight chair of ancient vintage, a marble lavatory of old-fashioned square design, a golden-oak bureau, a battered suitcase, an unshaded lamp bulb which dangled from a cord in the middle of the ceiling, a cracked window shade and a pair of exceedingly grimy window curtains. The doctor's attention focused upon the latter.

"No," Mack objected. "They're lousy with dirt; probably haven't been washed for weeks. This fellow's neck is fairly clean."

Dr. Hildreth nodded agreement. "What's in there?" he asked, pointing to the suitcase.

"Nothing. His stuff's either in the bureau drawers or hanging in the closet."

"What sort of stuff?"

"Nothing to get excited about. Shirts, underwear, socks, shaving things, toothpaste, toothbrush and an extra suit."

"Any neckties?"

"Three besides the one he has on. A red one with black stripes, a green one with black polka dots and one with a plaid pattern that's badly frayed."

"He might have been strangled with one of those."

"He might," Mack said dubiously. The doctor inspected the exterior of the suitcase.

"Have you seen these labels ?"

"Calcutta, Tokyo, Shanghai and Hong Kong," Mack returned promptly. "Doesn't help much. There isn't a hotel represented that's any closer than China, and they're having a war over there now."

The doctor returned the notebook to his pocket. "Thuggee rears ugly head in Chicago hotel. There's an angle for your reporter friends, Johnny."

"You give it to 'em," Mack directed wearily. "What time would you say he was killed, Doc?"

"H'm, several hours ago, anyway. Rigor's pretty well advanced. My guess is sometime between nine and eleven last night. That make sense to you?"

"I guess so."

"Well, send our oriental-looking friend down to the morgue when you can spare him. So long, fellows."

"So long!" Mack echoed. He turned to the spectacled Seizer, who was spraying red "dragon's blood" powder over the window sill with an insufflator. "Try the doorknob. Both sides of it. Murderer had to get in and out, didn't he? And the light switch. The lamp wasn't burning when we came in this morning, and it's a cinch our friend on the floor didn't get up to turn it out."

"You telling me how to run my business ?" Seizer grumbled. Nevertheless, he raised the insufflator toward the brass fixture at the end of the dangling lamp cord. "How about giving Donovan and me a break by getting out of here for a while?"

"Good idea," Mack grunted. He turned to Westborough. "Come on across the hall with me. I've got the night clerk waiting there until I can finish talking with him. Want to sit in on it?"

The night clerk, an elderly individual in a worn alpaca coat, had the gray face of one whom life has unkindly buffeted for nearly half a century. His pale eyes were reddened and watery. "Extremely nearsighted," Westborough said, noting the thick lenses of his nose glasses.

"Back again, Dawson," Mack greeted as he entered the room. "Didn't mean to keep you waiting so long. This is Mr. Westborough, who's worked with me on a couple of cases. Now let's go on where we left off. This guy's name was Jack Reffner (at least he put that name down on the register). And you said he's been here only two days."

"Scarcely more than one," Dawson corrected. "He arrived here on Sunday night."

"Did you see him enter the hotel last night?"

"Yes."

"Remember what time it was?"

"Not exactly. I have the impression that it was fairly early."

"What do you mean by fairly early?"

"Eight or nine o'clock."

"As late as ten?"

"It might have been that late."

"Did anyone ask to see him last night?"

"No one."

"Has he had visitors since he's been here?"

"Not that I know of. I got the impression that he was a stranger in the city."

"What gave you that idea?"

"I'm not sure. Maybe it was because of the rather lonesome expression he had when he asked if there'd been any mail for him."

"Was there any?"

"No, his box was empty."

"Nevertheless," Westborough inserted quickly, "Mr. Reffner's address must have been known to at least one person, or he would not have expected to receive letters."

"Good point," Mack grunted. "Did he ever get any phone calls ?"

"Not while I was on duty."

"Lewis, the manager, takes over your desk during the day, doesn't he?"

"Yes, we each work twelve-hour shifts."

"I've already talked to him. See here, did anyone go upstairs last night who wasn't registered here?"

"Decidedly not."

"How many guests have you?"

"Twenty-five rooms are at present occupied."

"Twenty-five rooms! Not quite half full. How do you expect to keep in business that way?"

For just one instant Westborough was permitted to see the fear in the clerk's gray face. "That question, I believe, has also troubled Mr. Lewis."

Mack dismissed the subject abruptly. "Well, it's none of my business. Let me take another squint at your register, Dawson. I want to see if I can find some of my old playmates signed up among your guests."

"You left the register at the desk downstairs," Dawson informed him.

"So I did," Mack owned, picking up the telephone receiver. "Clancy? Bring me up the hotel register. And get it here right away."

"You still use the old-fashioned registration book," he remarked to Dawson while they were waiting. "Why don't you go modern and put in a card-index system?"

"In this hotel?" The night clerk shrugged. Mack laughed.

"Well, I don't think I'll have to look very far back in the book. My guess is that your guests don't remain here long."

"They don't," Dawson admitted.

Clancy, the uniformed officer who had brought Westborough upstairs in the elevator, entered with the registration book tucked under his arm. Taking it from him, Mack opened the pages.

"No, there don't seem to be any names I recognize. Wonder who came in yesterday? Here's one fellow who printed his name instead of writing it. Not many people do that. And the name is a funny one. Hamilcar Barca, of Carthage, Mo."

"Hamilcar Barca!" Westborough ejaculated. "Dear me, how surprising!"

"Why? Do you know him?"

"Hamilcar Barca was a noted general of a Carthage several thousand years older than the city of that name in Missouri. He was the father of Hannibal."

"Hannibal? Oh, sure. He's the fellow that took the elephants over the Alps and raised hell with those Romans you write about. Hamilcar Barca, of Carthage, Mo. It does sound kind of phony when you stop to think about it. What kind of fellow is he, Dawson?"

"An elderly man with a gray beard. I wasn't on duty when he registered, but Mr. Lewis described him to me."

"You haven't seen him, then?"

"Just once. He walked across the lobby last night, and I was able to recognize him from Mr. Lewis' description."

"Was he going out or coming in?"

"Going out."

"What time was it?"

"Some time before midnight."

"Before or after Reffner had returned?"

"I'm sorry, but I didn't pay enough attention to the incident to remember."

"Are you sure that you saw him only once?" Mack insinuated.

"Yes."

"Only *once?*" the detective persisted.

"Yes, that's all " Dawson broke off abruptly. "Oh, I see what you mean. No, I don't seem to remember him coming back here. But of course he must have come back."

"What makes you think so?" Mack asked quizzically.

"Why—why his luggage, for one thing. He didn't take any of it away with him. And he paid in advance for his room."

"Room on the fourth floor, too," Mack added. "Four bits against a Hershey bar we won't find him in there now."

He strode into the corridor, Westborough and the night clerk following. "This room," Dawson indicated. Mack rapped on the door but received no answer. His hand closed upon the doorknob; it turned beneath his hand, and the door swung open.

The room was empty.

III

The key was in the inside of the door. "Warded locks!" Mack exclaimed, directing a contemptuous glance toward it. "Skeleton key would open any room in this hotel. Don't touch it—there may be prints on the key tag. Let's see what else is in here."

There was a suitcase, which was as old and battered as the one in Reffner's room, but void of labels. It was locked. Inserting the large blade of his pocket knife, Mack quickly forced the flimsy catch open. The receptacle was found to contain a dozen shirts all size fourteen and of a nationally advertised make—and nothing else.

"What the hell!" Mack shouted. "Did the guy sleep mother naked? Didn't he ever change his underwear? Or his socks?"

All of the bureau drawers were empty, but they found a few toilet articles on the shelf beside the imitation marble washbasin. A toothbrush. A Gillette razor in a plush-lined case. A half-empty tube of shaving cream. An untouched tube of toothpaste. A bottle of shaving lotion, three quarters full. A shaving brush. A black hard-rubber comb. A jar of cold cream.

"Don't touch anything," Mack warned Dawson. "Might be prints here." He inspected the articles. "Can't trace these things. All nationally advertised brands—he might've bought 'em in any drugstore. Humph! Friend Barca hasn't used his toothbrush or his toothpaste. But the shaving brush is damp; it must've been wet no later than last night. And both the shaving cream and the shaving lotion have been used. See anything funny there?"

"Yes," Westborough concurred.

"For a bearded man," Mack ruminated, "Friend Barca was mighty particular about shaving." His glance fell downward. "What's this stuff on the floor?" He stooped to his knees to inspect the nearest of several white smudges. "Powder of some sort." Placing his nose close to the floor, he sniffed. "Perfumed! Gardenia or my smeller is playing tricks! A woman's face powder."

"A woman!" Westborough ejaculated. He stared reflectively at the floor. "I know very little concerning the subject of feminine cosmetics."

Mack grinned, rising to his feet. "You and me both."

"However, I have the distinct impression that face powder of a flesh-colored hue is commonly preferred to white."

"No telling what a woman may take in her head to use," Mack opined. "They shellac their fingernails—some even paint their toenails—so why shouldn't a few of 'em use white powder?" He started toward the door. "I'm going to borrow a brush from Jimmy Seizer. Don't walk around here much—you might step on one of those smudges."

He was back in a few seconds with a fine camel's-hair brush and an envelope. He printed upon the envelope: "Reffner Case, Exhibit B. Specimen of powder found in room of Hamilcar Barca."

"Exhibit B?" Westborough inquired.

"Yeh, that's right."

"May I ask the nature of Exhibit A?"

"Wait till I get this job off my mind, and I'll tell you." Stooping once more to the floor, he deftly brushed as many of the powder grains as he could into the envelope. "There isn't much here, but it may be enough. I'm taking it down to headquarters. With any luck a laboratory analysis will tell us what brand it is. And that gives me a whale of a big idea. How many women are staying here, Dawson?"

The night clerk counted on his fingers. "Not over ten," he said.

"Good!" Mack picked up the room telephone. "Put me through to headquarters, Clancy. I want to talk to the chief of detectives." The connection was made promptly. "Mack, Chief. I need help. . . . No, I want one of your female operatives. . . . Sure, the Carlin kid'd be swell. She's a smart little number. . . . What I want her to do is to call on all the women staying here at the Pilgrim Deluxe and get samples of the face powder each one uses. She can pretend she's canvassing for a face-powder firm and say she wants to take the sample back to the company's laboratories to find out if the woman is using the right shade for her complexion. Some such line of blah as that; there never was a woman yet who wouldn't fall for it. . . . Thanks, Chief. Don't think it's such a bad idea myself. . . . What's that? . . . Now don't get excited, things are moving all right. . . . Sure, I know what the newspapers are saying about you. Can I help it? . . . Sure, we're going to get results."

Replacing the receiver, he took a handkerchief from his pocket to wipe his perspiring face. "Whew! Well, that's over! Let's have a look at the wastebasket."

"There is a newspaper in it," Westborough informed him, "and below that what appears to be a crumpled towel. I did not look too closely, as I did not wish to disturb the status quo."

"The towel might be one of ours," Dawson added. "There seems to be one missing from the rack."

Mack removed the newspaper, which was folded as neatly as when it had been delivered, but with the sports section placed outermost. His fingers closed upon the towel. "It's wrapped around something," he said. "Something he was trying to hide."

Unfolding the towel, they found a braid of grayish substance and a small bottle with contents half gone.

"Crepe hair and spirit gum!" Mack ejaculated. "There's where Barca's gray beard came from. It was this shade, wasn't it, Dawson?"

"As I remember it, yes," the night clerk confirmed.

"He had his fake beard on when he left here last night," Mack mused, "but there's nothing to stop him from getting rid of it later. This stuff must've been extra makeup that he didn't want to bother to cart out with him."

Westborough had taken the liberty of unfolding the newspaper. It was yesterday afternoon's edition, but he could not seem to find the front page. He went through it carefully and saw that the front page was indeed missing. It had been torn away. Torn very neatly, too, as though with a straight edge. He looked about the room to see if it had been placed elsewhere, but he could not find it.

"What are you looking for?" Mack demanded.

"The front page of this newspaper. I am rather curious concerning the reason for removing it."

Mack rustled through the newspaper pages. "Say, it is gone, isn't it? Maybe he used it to wrap up something he carried out of the hotel."

"He was carrying no package when I saw him last night," Dawson informed them.

"Well, maybe there was something there that especially interested him. Can you remember what was in last night's paper, Westborough?"

"Unfortunately I seldom read more than one newspaper a day, and that is usually the morning one."

"There was a big story about the Supreme Court fight," Dawson contributed. "That's the only news I can recall."

"Suppose you can find a copy of this paper somewhere around the hotel?"

"I think so."

"Dig it up for us, then. And you might tell your boss, Lewis, that I want to talk to him again. Tell him to come up to the same room where we talked to you—I forget the number of it."

Dawson left to perform these errands, and Mack and Westborough returned to room 414. Mack was carrying the hotel register tucked under his arm. Selzer looked up aggrievedly as they entered the room. He was dusting powdered chalk on the rug to bring out a shoe print for photographing.

"You fellows back already? Thought you were going to give us a chance to get some work done."

"I'll give you plenty of chance for that," Mack told him. "In fact I've got a new job for you and Donovan when you get through here. Go to room 424 and go through it with a fine-tooth comb."

"Whose room is that?" Seizer questioned.

"Unless I miss my guess badly, the fellow who did this job stayed there for a while last night. He's gone now."

Seizer whistled. "Leave anything behind him?"

"A few toilet articles. They've been handled, and you ought to find some good prints there. And go over the big tag attached to the room key. No matter how careful he was, he probably wouldn't think about handling that with gloves on."

Selzer nodded. "Okay, we'll take care of it."

Mack left the two men to their work and strolled across the corridor to the room where the hotel manager was already waiting for them. Lewis, with his round, red face and protruding stomach, might have been the traditional "Mine Host" of an English inn if it were not for his hands. They were, Westborough discovered, flabby to the touch and unpleasantly clammy.

The hotel manager noted the book tucked under Mack's arm. "Is that my register you've got there?"

Mack nodded. "Brought it in to show you because we're after some dope on one of your ex-guests."

"Ex-guests?"

Mack opened the register. "That fellow! Hamilcar Barca, of Carthage, Mo."

"Oh, him."

"Didn't it strike you as being funny when he printed his name instead of writing it?"

"I didn't pay any attention."

"See anything funny about his name?"

"Italian, isn't it? Odd name, all right, but I've been in the hotel business long enough to know that it's the odd names that are the real ones. It's the plain Smiths and Browns and Joneses that you've got to watch out for."

"Know who the original Hamilcar Barca was?"

"Never heard of him."

Mack winked surreptitiously at Westborough. "Ever hear of Hannibal?" he asked.

"Sure. It's a good-sized town in Missouri."

Mack made no attempt to suppress his guffaw. "That's not all. You don't seem to be up on ancient history. Better study it a little, or you'll find Julius Caesar and Mark Anthony coming in to put their names on the register. What time did this fellow Barca sign in yesterday?"

"In the afternoon. Sometime between three and four o'clock."

"Describe him for me."

"Let me see. He was wearing a white linen summer suit and a Panama hat. An old man with a gray beard."

"What sort of beard?" Mack asked, writing in a notebook.

"Just a beard."

"Long or short?"

"A full beard."

"What color were his eyes?"

"I couldn't see them. He was wearing dark green glasses."

"Big ones?"

"Yes. They seemed to cover up a good share of his face."

"Was his skin light or dark?"

"I didn't notice."

"How tall was he?"

"Not so tall and not so short."

"What color was his hair?"

"He kept his hat on."

"You could see the hair at his temples."

"Oh yes. Well, it was gray like his beard."

Mack produced the braid of crepe hair from his pocket. "Like this?"

Lewis inspected it carefully. "That's the shade, all right."

"That clinches it!" Mack exclaimed. "Lewis, that beard was a phony. This is part of the false hair that he used to make it. Unless I'm badly out of line Barca is the fellow we want for this job. Now is there anything you can tell us that will help find him?"

Lewis fell into a silence, his flabby hands folded across his lap, his eyes staring vacantly into space. Finally he spoke. "He had a rather deep voice, but that's all I can remember. The light isn't so good down there by the desk, and as he'd paid me for his room in advance I didn't pay much attention to him. Maybe Fred Clifford can help you."

"Who's Clifford?"

"Our day bellboy."

"What about the night one?"

"We haven't any. Business hasn't been so good lately, and—"

"Yes, I know," Mack interrupted impatiently. "Send Clifford up here."

"Of all the dumbbells!" he exploded after Lewis had left the room. "He had the best chance in the world to get a good look at Barca, and what can he tell us? Gray beard! Green glasses ! That's all we know, and he's probably shed both of them by this time."

"The bellboy may be more helpful," Westborough suggested consolingly. "Youth is usually observant."

Fred Clifford swaggered into the room with the air of one who owned the place. He was a lanky youth of eighteen with straggly tow hair and an insolent slouch.

"Lewis said you bulls wanted to talk to me."

"Sit down," Mack invited, overlooking the youth's rudeness.

"Well, you can't mix me up on any murder rap, see? I quit this dump at seven last night. Got an alibi for it, too. I picked up my twist and took her out to a chop suey joint. The twist'll tell you that—"

"Who's trying to mix you up in it?" Mack growled. "All we want from you is some dope about a fellow who came here yesterday. The one in 424."

"Four twenty-four? That old mutt with the whiskers?"

"That's the fellow! What do you know about him?"

"Well, I took his grip, ran him up in the elevator to this room, and opened up the room for him. And he tipped me four bits—biggest tip I ever got in this joint."

"Who carried the key to the room?"

"Me. I opened the door for him."

"Did you place the key in the inside of the door, too?',

"Sure. That's where I always put it."

Mack groaned his disappointment. "Probably hasn't been touched since. When we get through here, Clifford, go to 414 and tell those fellows in there I sent you in to be fingerprinted."

"Fingerprinted!" Clifford ejaculated.

Mack nodded. "You heard me."

"You can't do that," Clifford objected in an angry tone. "I'm no crook. You got no right to take my prints and put me in the rogues' gallery."

"You're not going in the rogues' gallery," Mack said, displaying a patience which he would not have shown to an older man. "There are probably some prints on the tag attached to the room key. Maybe they are your prints and maybe they aren't. If they're your prints it doesn't mean a thing to us, but we gotta know. And how can we know unless you let us fingerprint you?"

"Zat the only reason you want my prints?" Clifford asked, his voice expressing considerable relief. Mack nodded. "All right, I'll do it then. Want me to go there now?"

"Not yet. Few more things I want to ask you. Tell me what this fellow in 424 looked like."

"An old guy with whiskers. That's all I know about him."

"You ought to be able to do better than that, Clifford. You look like a smart kid who keeps his eyes open. Did the whiskers run all the way round his chin?"

"Uh-huh. Full beard."

"Any mustache?"

"Nope."

"What color was the beard? White?"

"No, gray."

"Get a good look at it?"

"Not enough light in this joint to get a good squint at anything. Lewis is sure scared he'll waste a little candle power."

"Did it look like a phony to you?"

"The beaver? It might've been. I didn't get close enough to tell."

Mack produced the crepe hair. "Know what this is?"

"Sure, fake hair. It was that color. Where'd you find it?"

Mack ignored the question. "What color were his eyes?" he asked.

"He had on big green glasses. I couldn't see his eyes."

"What about his skin? Pale or dark?"

"Pretty tanned."

"How'd he talk?"

"Deep voice that rumbled up from his belly. He didn't say much to me."

"How tall was he?"

"Shorter 'n me."

"How'd he walk?"

"Walk? Oh, kinda stooped over. Like an old guy usually walks."

"Notice his hands?"

"Nope."

"Or his ears?"

"Jeez, no! Ears is all alike, ain't they?"

"Not on your life! If you want to be able to recognize a guy again, always notice his ears. They're the one thing about his face he'll never be able to change. What about his nose?"

"Jeez, I didn't notice it."

"Sure you did. You just don't remember. Was it pug?"

"No-o."

"Hooked?"

"Naw. It weren't no beak."

"Then it was straight?"

"I guess so."

"A large nose?"

" 'Bout medium."

"What about his feet?"

"Didn't see 'em."

"What'd he have on?"

"White summer suit. Panama. White shoes."

"Thought you didn't look at his feet."

"Jeez, you're right! I must-a seen 'em."

"Well, were they large or small?"

"Don't remember. 'Bout medium, I guess."

"Did you see his hair?"

"Nope. He kept his hat on."

"I mean the hair at his temples."

"Gray, I guess. Sure. It was the same as his beard."

Westborough found Mack's next question to be an astounding one. He could see no reason whatsoever for the inference.

"Think the guy could've been a Chinaman?"

"Jeez, no!" Clifford exclaimed.

"Or a Jap ?" Mack added. "They look something alike."

Clifford shook his head. "He didn't look like either of 'em."

"Sure he didn't have any Chink or Jap features? High cheekbones, for instance?"

"I didn't see anything like that."

"But you told us it was too dark to get a real good look at him," Mack persisted.

"Yeh, it was dark," Clifford admitted. "Maybe he was a Chink, but if he was he didn't look like it to me. What else do you want to know?"

"Nothing. You can go, but don't forget to stop in 414 to be finger-printed. Thanks for coming in, Clifford."

"My dear John," Westborough began when they were once more alone, "whatever induced you to embark upon such a strange line of inquiry?"

"What's so funny about it ?" Mack demanded brusquely.

"A disguised Chinese is, to say the least, a little improbable."

"Why? What are the principal things you recognize the Chinks by? The Japs too. All of them Orientals."

"The physical characteristics of the people of the Mongolian race are a subject upon which it is very difficult to generalize," Westborough opined. "There is, of course, the straight black hair."

"He kept his hat on," Mack reminded. "No one saw his hair except the bit at the temples, and that was probably as phony as his beard."

"But the oblique eyes? The conspicuous Mongolian eye fold?"

"You couldn't see 'em under the dark glasses."

"The yellowish-brown skin?"

"He was tanned, Clifford said. I've seen many a fellow down at the beach with skin about the same color as a Chinaman's."

"But the flat, stolid face? The cheekbones? The depressed nose? How are such features as these to be concealed?"

Mack shook his head. "I don't know. Do all Orientals have 'em?"

"No, not all of them. There is in northern China, for example, a tall, long-headed type which is considered by most ethnologists to be of a proto-Nordic origin."

"What does that mean?"

"That they are the descendants of people very much like ourselves."

"A Chink like that might've been able to get away with it."

"Dear, dear!" Westborough sighed. "The supposition is such an extremely unlikely one that I cannot understand why you advance it."

"Good Lord!" Mack ejaculated suddenly. "I forgot I hadn't shown it to you yet. And I asked you up here specially so you could get a look at it! Lock the door, will you? I don't want to be disturbed now."

Westborough closed and locked the door while Mack brought out an envelope from his breast pocket. "This is Exhibit A," Mack said. "You were asking about it awhile back."

The envelope contained a small and ragged triangle of white silk.

"This was clenched in the fingers of his right hand," Mack explained. "We believe that it's a piece of the cloth that was used to strangle him. Something like a white silk scarf or a big silk handkerchief. As I dope it out, Reffner tried to yank it away from his throat but only managed to tear off this little chunk. No chance for a second try, either. Strangling is an efficient way of killing. It would be all over in a few seconds."

Westborough shuddered. "But why does such a death suggest to you a Chinese agency? I confess that I fail to see the connection."

Mack placed the silk triangle on a table near the window. "Come over here to the light and look it over." Obeying this command, Westborough was able to see that a horizontal line of writing was embroidered with a black thread. There were six tiny characters, each of an intricate design that afforded the eye extreme difficulty in encompassing its outlines.

"Looks like it was written the way we write,' Mack was saying. "And the Japs put their writing in columns, don't they ?"

"Yes," Westborough concurred. "One starts at the top of the column and reads downward, then from right to left—the exact opposite of our own left-to-right procedure."

"What about the Chinese?"

"The two races use the same ideographs or picture characters, although their spoken languages are quite different. The Japanese borrowed the Chinese signs a great many centuries ago. It is true that there is a simplified form of Japanese writing known as the *kana*, which is used for books and magazines of popular circulation, I believe. Dear me! These characters are so very small!"

"Try this," Mack invited, producing a pocket magnifier.

With the aid of the glass Westborough was able to recognize the six complex characters. They were not German nor Russian nor Greek nor Arabic nor Hebrew letters. They were not Babylonian cuneiform nor Egyptian hieroglyphics. They belonged to the most perfect alphabet which man has yet invented. That alphabet which provides for the expression of virtually every speech sound and expresses it in only one manner. Sanskrit! Westborough pronounced aloud the phonetic equivalents of the characters.

"Om mani padme hum."

"What sorta language is that?" Mack demanded.

"The inscription is in Sanskrit, the grandmother of all the modern Hindu tongues. But the formula, unless I am greatly mistaken, is one that pertains almost exclusively to the Lamaism of Tibet."

"Tibet!" Mack ejaculated. "That's part of China."

"Not since 1912," Westborough corrected. "It is ruled by the head priest or pope of the state religion, the Dalai Lama." He recalled that the thirteenth Dalai Lama had died nearly four years before. "Was ruled, I should say. What the present status of government is I do not know. So little news is allowed to filter through the barriers, both natural and artificial, which enclose that enigmatic state."

"What does Om many what-you-may-call-it mean?"

"You may call it a prayer, the common Tibetan prayer designed to free the six classes of Buddhist beings from the endless cycles of births and rebirths. It means . . ."

He hesitated, wondering how he would be able to express it. "The 'jewel within the lotus' is perhaps the closest that one can come to expressing the meaning in our language. *Mani*, jewel; *padme*, lotus. *Om* stands mystically for the incarnation of the deity, and *hum* is untranslatable—very much so. It is the awesome syllable said to close the gates of rebirth in all of the many Buddhist hells."

"Whatta you mean by 'jewel within the lotus'?" Mack asked with a puzzled frown.

"Oriental symbolism. The jewel, the blessing of the Buddha's word; the lotus, the emblem of spiritual rebirth. As I have said, the entire phrase may be thought of as a prayer, one that is more commonly on the lips of Tibetans than the paternoster on the lips of devout Catholics. Laiety and lamas alike carry prayer wheels containing the mystic formula written perhaps thousands of times on rolls of paper. When they twirl their prayer wheels the sacred words revolve; each complete revolution of the phrase is expected to count in heaven—their conception of heaven—the same as a spoken prayer. And there are many types of larger prayer wheels, some of which are turned by wind power, some by water power and some even by---"

"Do Tibetans have silk scarves?" Mack interrupted.

"Yes. Ceremonial scarves known as *ka-tas*. Whenever a Tibetan wishes to--"

A knock sounded on the locked door.

"Who's there?" Mack demanded impatiently.

"Dawson."

"Well, what do you want?"

"I've found yesterday afternoon's paper."

"Well, bring it in." Opening the door, Mack snatched the newspaper from the night clerk's hand. "Thanks, Dawson. Let's see what we've got here." He read the headlines aloud. " 'Greatest aerial battle in history over Spain.' Well, that's not it. 'Jap army starts drive; first guns heard near Peiping.' That's a long ways from here—almost as far as Tibet. Tibet? What the devil! Am I going crazy or is it this paper?"

The heading which he read was a small one of two lines, pertaining to an obscure paragraph at the bottom of the missing newspaper page. It said:

TIBETAN LAMA PAYS
VISIT TO CHICAGO

IV

"He's staying at the Prescott House," Mack remarked, continuing to read. "And his name is T-s-o-n-g-p-u-n B-o-n-b-o. Nice mouthful, that! So far's I'm concerned the name is Bonbo. Bimbo the Bonbo! Lawson, before you leave I want you to do something else for me. Sit down and try taking off Barca's fake beard and dark glasses in your mind's eye. Then tell me if you get a Chinaman."

"Tibetan," Westborough ventured to correct. "The Tibetan race is ethnologically distinct from the Chinese."

"Chinaman's good enough," Mack maintained.

"I—I don't understand," the hotel clerk faltered.

"You're not supposed to," Mack snapped. Dawson sank into the chair as though he had suddenly found himself in the midst of lunatics, and Mack turned to Westborough.

"You and I are going to call on this Tibetan lama. Lama. What the hell is a lama, anyhow?"

"A priest of the Tibetan Buddhist religion. Literally, 'one to whom no one is superior.' "

"Always thought it was a long-necked goat from South America."

"Dear me, no. Undoubtedly you have confused the word with the llama, that is the domesticated guanaco of the Andes, which is allied to the camel, I believe. Surely, John, you do not profess to believe that the Lama Tsongpun Bonbo is our Hamilcar Barca?"

"What do you think?" Mack countered.

"Hamilcar Barca and Carthage should be concepts unknown to the Tibetan mind."

"They tell me," Mack answered slowly, "that a Chink or a Jap educated in this country learns to think just like the rest of us. Why not a Tibetan?"

Dawson wiped a despairing hand over his brow, a gesture which did not escape Mack's attention.

"Well, what'd you decide?" the detective demanded bluffly.

"Nothing. I didn't see him closely enough; I can't guess what he'd look like without the beard and glasses. He might have been a Chinese. But he might also have been a Turk or a Hindu or a Filipino or a plain, ordinary, everyday American, for all I can say."

"All right," Mack said. "Thanks for your help. That's all now, but later on I'll have a statement for you to sign."

"What kind of statement?"

"A record of what you've said to me—police routine." He carefully replaced the white silken triangle in its envelope. "See here, Dawson. I don't want the newspapers to know we're hunting Tibetans. If they know they'll shoot the story all over their front pages, which'll make our job six times as hard as it ought to be. I won't be inclined to kiss the guy that tips them off." He paused significantly. "Right now the only three fellows who know anything about the Tibetan angle are in this room."

"I get it," Dawson informed him, halting in the doorway. "A hotel clerk's first lesson is to hold his tongue." He added, not without a touch of bitterness, "And I have been a hotel clerk for thirty years."

Mack summoned Carnavan, the plainclothes man whom Westborough had encountered in the corridor, for a conference.

"How are the snoops taking this?"

"Not much excited," Carnavan answered. "Took plenty of pix, but I don't think the story'll be played up very big." He grinned broadly. "One of 'em told me that the case lacks glamor. He means he couldn't find a sex angle."

Mack laughed. "Let 'em go on thinking it lacks glamor. And keep quiet about our piece of white silk. I'm not ready to release that bit of news yet."

Carnavan nodded. "It won't get out."

"Here's the hotel register," Mack said, handing over the book. "I want you to interview every guest staying here."

"Every one?"

"There are only twenty-five rooms occupied. Put extra pressure on the people who live on this floor. There's a bare chance that one of them might've seen or heard something."

Carnavan nodded again. It was the nod of one who thoroughly comprehends his instructions.

"I'm leaving you in charge," Mack went on. "I've got other fish to fry this morning—outside. Two more things: Find out if anyone will admit knowing Reffner or admit knowing the fellow who stayed last night in 424. Hamilcar Barca, of Carthage, Mo., is the name he gave here, but the name's as phony as he is."

"What's the fellow look like?"

"Old looking. Average height and build. Bass voice. Straight nose, probably medium size. Wears a white linen suit, white shoes, a Panama and a pair of dark green sun glasses. Gray hair at the temples and short gray beard—but the beard's as phony as his name!"

"Hell of a description!" Carnavan observed, grinning.

"That's all the dope I could get from three people, so you'll have to do the best you can with it. Maybe you'll be able to get a better description of him. Someone may have seen him prowling around in the hall, waiting for Reffner."

"Anything else you want?"

"Not unless Selzer and Donovan find something that calls for quick action. I'll phone in around noon to check up. You're running the show, though, till you hear from me. Come, Westborough, let's try to sneak out of here. I don't want any of the newshounds to learn where we're going."

The hall, Mack noticed, as he peeked from the door, was empty. He led the way at a fast pace to the freight elevator. Mack ran the elevator to the first floor, unbarred the back entrance and walked through the alley. When they were a good two blocks away he commandeered a taxi.

"Prescott House and make it snappy."

The Prescott House will be included in any list of the big six of Chicago Loop hotels. The street-level entrance leads to a block-long tunnel lined by shops, from which tunnel branches a ramp to ascend to the capacious lobby on the second floor. Westborough was well acquainted with the hotel. James, his deceased brother, had often entertained his friends in one of its dining rooms.

Emerging from the broad stone ramp, they found the huge square lobby to be more than usually crowded. A convention of a fraternal order known as the Antelopes was in progress, and it seemed to Westborough that at least two thirds of the men who lounged by the registration counter or occupied chairs and divans were wearing giant white disks which bore in crimson letters such legends as: "My name is Chuggers. I am an Antelope from Kalamazoo."

Scarcely had he time to read the first badge of an Antelope when he felt Mack's fingers touch his arm. The detective turned quietly and walked away from the lobby and into the shelter of the ramp. Westborough followed.

"Reporters!" Mack exclaimed tersely. Standing at the top of the ramp, it was difficult for them to be seen by those in the lobby. "Sears of the *Trumpet* and Blaze of the *Bugle*. Both of 'em are watching the desk like hawks and both of 'em know me. If I go up there to ask for this Tibetan lama the fat'll be in the fire."

"Fat?" Westborough repeated. "Fire? I do not understand your sudden aversion to newspaper reporters, John. I have often heard you say that they have been helpful to you on past cases."

"It's a different situation now. There's a paper in this man's town— I'm not mentioning names—that's after the chief's scalp. If the word gets out we're hunting Tibetans they'll turn their cartoonists and smart writers loose to get the town laughing at us. And if the town laughs enough at the chief he's washed up and so am I. Get the idea ?"

"Indeed yes! Ridiculum acri fortius . . . Ridicule is often effective in cutting the Gordian knot, as Horace has so wisely observed. But how are we to get in touch with the lama without exposing ourselves?"

"Sears and Blaze don't know you. You'll have to go up to the desk and ask the clerk what room he's in."

"Returning here to report the information?"

"Yeh—no! One of 'em may get interested when you ask about the lama and follow you. You'll have to signal me the room number so I can come up later."

"Signal? In what manner?"

"Simple. After you know the room number take out your watch and pretend to be setting it to the correct time. When you walk past here on your way to the elevators hold the watch out so I can get a squint at the dial."

"The watch being set to indicate the lama's room number ?"

"That's it. Use the hour hand for the floor and the minute hand for the number on that floor."

"So that, for example, the hour of ten thirty-five would indicate that the lama was staying in room 1035?"

"You got the idea all right."

"A most ingenious code, but one slight difficulty occurs to me. I believe that this hotel has a total of twenty-five floors. And it is most probable that the lama, as a Tibetan accustomed to high altitudes, would wish to sleep at as great an elevation as possible."

"Blow your nose before you leave the desk, and that will tell me to add ten to the hour-hand number. No, that only takes up to twenty-two. If he's higher up than that you'd better stoop to tie your shoelace. Then I'll add twenty. Got it all straight now?"

"I believe so, but I am reminded of yet another difficulty. Perhaps the lama is not in his room."

"H'm, that's a problem," Mack mused. He peered searchingly into the lobby, drawing back with a grin of satisfaction. "See the little fat guy in the gray suit?"

"The gentleman reading a newspaper?"

"Pretending to read a newspaper," Mack corrected. "There's not much going on in that lobby that gets by him, you can bet your last dollar. That's Eb Vishart, the house detective. Good friend of mine. If the lama's out cross the lobby and sit next to Eb. Sears or Blaze will probably be watching you, so be careful. Tell Eb I want to see him. He has an office on the second floor, and we'll all meet up there. There probably won't be much about our friend from Tibet that Eb can't tell us."

Breathing deeply, Westborough began his walk to the desk. It was ridiculous for an elderly historian to feel such a surge of excitement, but then his last few years had been extremely thrilling ones. Four times before had circumstances forced him to enter the arena against criminals.

There had been the strange death of Elmo Swink, the tragedy of Arnold Bancroft's Wisconsin estate, the baffling problem of Hezekiah Morse's purple parrot, and finally, the most dangerous adventure of all, the death which struck twelve hundred feet below the surface of the earth in the heart of a Colorado gold mine. But none of these four imbroglios had supplied such weird complications as the present case promised. None of them had brought Westborough into contact with such an out-of-the-ordinary personage as a high Tibetan lama.

The hotel clerk rewarded his inquiry with a suspicious stare. "I'll see if he's in," he said coldly. "Your name, please?"

"It is Westborough."

"Mr. Westborough. Are you personally acquainted with the lama?"

"No, I do not enjoy that honor."

"Would you be good enough to tell me why you wish to see him? He has given positive instructions that reporters are not to be admitted."

"I am not a reporter," Westborough smiled. "I am, in my humble fashion, a scholar, or perhaps I should say a student, a student of the races of mankind. Many of the most enigmatic problems connected with that vast subject pertain to Tibet, since Tibet is one of the few corners of the world where such researches as mine cannot be carried on. The advent into this country of a Tibetan gentleman affords a priceless opportunity for consultation. If the lama will kindly grant to me a mere hour of his valuable time you may promise him that our interview will be held in strictest confidence."

The clerk nodded. "I'll tell that to the lama if he's in." He picked up his telephone and said to the hotel operator, "Connect me with 2513, please."

Westborough stooped to tighten a shoelace. Then he took his watch from his pocket and opened its engraved hunting case. With one eye upon the large electric clock above the registration desk he set the hands of his own timepiece to the hour of five-thirteen. He held the dial of the watch toward Mack, who was at the top of the ramp twenty feet or so away. The detective had keen eyesight. His slight nod showed Westborough that Mack, even at that distance, had been able to read the signal. The historian returned the watch to his vest pocket.

The clerk replaced the handset of his cradle telephone. He said blandly, "I am sorry, but the lama doesn't answer."

"Are you able to tell me when---"

"Sorry," the clerk interrupted and turned his attention to an impatient Antelope who was vociferously demanding a room with bath. Westborough began his walk across the lobby. Sears, the reporter from the *Daily Trumpet*, was staring curiously. Westborough did not deem it wise to engage too openly in conversation with Eb Vishart.

Fortunately the chair next to the house detective was not occupied. Sinking into its soft upholstery, Westborough slowly filled his pipe. It was his favorite pipe, which some years ago he had purchased in a small shop on an inconspicuous side street in Rome, and its bowl was carved to resemble a human skull. Westborough poured tobacco from his pouch, a crumb or two at a time, while the house detective perused his newspaper. Vishart did not look up from its pages, but for all of that Westborough felt that the man's gaze was now focused sharply upon his own face. John Mack, the historian concluded, had certainly been right; there would not be a great deal going on in the Prescott House lobby which Vishart would miss.

The death's-head bowl filled, Westborough restored the pouch to his pocket. He tamped the tobacco in place with his forefinger and continued the operation until he was sure that Sears was no longer watching him. He reached into all of his pockets, pretending to be fumbling for a match. Finally:

"I beg your pardon, but may I borrow a match from you?" he inquired of the house detective.

Vishart looked up from the paper. His plump face appeared, superficially, to be as guileless as that of a child, but his small gray eyes were not guileless. They bored into Westborough's very skull; there was no sin of which they were innocent, those eyes, no type of crime with which they were unfamiliar. Without speaking Vishart handed a paper packet of matches to the historian.

Lighting his pipe, Westborough took a few meditative puffs. Sears, he saw, still continued to look the other way. Westborough returned the matches. "Lieutenant Mack wishes to see you, Mr. Vishart," he said in a low voice. "He could not speak to you openly without attracting the attention of reporters."

Not a muscle in Vishart's face moved; for the moment Westborough wondered if the house detective were not hard of hearing. Then, almost without movement of his lips, Vishart asked:

"Where's Mack now?"

"Standing at the top of the ramp where it is difficult for Mr. Sears and Mr. Blaze to spy him."

Vishart's nod of acknowledgment was almost invisible.

Still without moving his lips he said, "Go up to 219 and wait for me there. Be careful. Sears has his eye on you."

Pocketing the matches, he resumed the reading of his newspaper. He might have now been miles away, so utterly unconscious did he appear of his surroundings. Westborough rose to his feet. "Dear, dear," he thought reproachfully on his way across the lobby, "how stupid I am at this kind of work. I was so very sure that Mr. Sears was no longer watching me."

Sears halted him midway to the elevator shaft. "You look like a man

I used to know in Oshkosh. Is your name Spragmore?"

"No, it is not, and I am not from Oshkosh, but from Cortland, N. Y. This is my first visit to Chicago."

"Staying here at the Prescott?"

"Yes, I have a room on the second floor. I am going there now."

"Didn't I hear you ask to see the Lama Tsongpun Bonbo? Are you a friend of his?"

"No, the lama is a total stranger to me," Westborough confessed. He must think quickly now, or the fat would be in the fire, to use Lieutenant Mack's vigorous expression. "Reading in yesterday afternoon's paper that he was stopping at my own hotel, I took the liberty of asking to see him."

"What about?" Sears asked. How much of the conversation with the clerk had been overheard? Westborough wondered. The little man leaned forward confidentially.

"Please, do not tell the hotel clerk," he implored.

"Tell him what?"

"That the reasons I gave to him for desiring to see the lama were altogether spurious ones."

"Then you're not writing a book?"

"No, not in the least." The historian knew now that Sears had overheard practically all of the conversation. "I feared that it might be impossible to see the lama if I revealed my true errand."

"What's that?"

"I have a grandson in Cortland to whom I am greatly attached. He is thirteen years of age and an ardent collector of postage stamps. I knew that he would be delighted beyond measure if I could induce the lama to give me a stamp from Tibet."

"Do Tibetans have postage stamps?" Sears inquired. His tone was that of one who has lost interest in a conversation.

"I do not know." For the first time Westborough gave the reporter an honest answer. "Do you?"

Sears grunted and strolled disgustedly away. Westborough took the elevator to the second floor. Both Vishart and Mack were waiting for him in room 219—a cubbyhole just big enough to hold a desk and two chairs.

"Saw you talking to Sears," Mack said as Westborough came through the door. "What story did you give that Paul Pry?"

"That I wished to ask the lama for a Tibetan postage stamp for my small grandson."

Mack shook with boisterous laughter. "Meet the professor, Eb. Theocritus Lucius Westborough, one of the greatest little guys in Chicago."

"You've told me about him before," Vishart acknowledged as they shook hands. "Why the sudden interest in Tibetan lamas, Johnny?"

"One lama," Mack corrected. "And is he a Tibetan?"

Vishart shrugged. "How should I know? He signed the register as the Lama Tsongpun Bonbo, Tso Map-hang, Tibet, but anyone could do that much."

"Well, what does he look like?"

"He's some sort of Chinese, all right, and he has one of the weirdest ways of twisting up our language that you've ever heard. Friendly little cuss, but down on reporters since that fool newspaper story came out yesterday and the curiosity seekers tried to hunt him up. He left orders at the desk that he wouldn't see anyone, especially another reporter, and that made it tough for us. If a guest wants privacy we have to give it to him, but it's bad business to get the newspapers down on you."

"You telling me?" Mack grunted. "If you had my job, Eb, you'd really know what it felt like to have the newspapers down on you. How long's the lama been staying here?"

"Came in Sunday afternoon."

"And the story about him was in Monday's *Bugle*. Blaze didn't waste much time."

"No, Blaze is a smart cookie. He took one squint at the lama when he registered and followed him to the twenty-fifth floor. I trailed along because I was curious about the lama myself, but the interview was the usual line of bunkum. 'How do you like America, Mr. Lama, and what do you think of American women?' I forget what the lama told him, but Blaze filled in all the stock answers. 'Your country is enormous in size, but very bewildering to a stranger. I think that American women are the most smartly gowned of any women in the world.' They stuck Blaze's bull right on the front page of his rag, and Sears was fit to be tied when he learned how he'd been scooped. He's been sitting in the lobby since eight-thirty this morning waiting for the lama to come down. The lama left the hotel at eight, and that's what we told him, but Sears is so used to dealing with liars he can't recognize the truth when you give it to him on a platter. Both he and Blaze are sure that the lama's still up in his room."

"They can wear out their fannies," Mack chuckled. "Where'd the lama go, Eb?"

"He got in a cab. I didn't bother to get the number because our responsibility toward him ends when he's outside the hotel."

"Did he go out anywhere yesterday?"

Vishart shook his head. "If he did I didn't see him, and I was in the lobby most of the day."

"And no one got up to his room yesterday afternoon or evening, you said."

"I gave you a bum steer there. One fellow did get up. He claimed to be a Tibetan."

"Another of 'em?" Mack roared. "What'd he say?"

"I heard him telling the clerk to let the lama know that he was a fellow Tibetan who could aid the lama's quest. As soon as he heard that, the lama said for him to come right up."

"Did he look like a Tibetan?"

"He looked like the lama. How the hell do I know what a Tibetan looks like?"

"What'd he mean by 'aiding the lama's quest'?"

Vishart shrugged his shoulders. "Your guess is as good as mine."

"How long was this fellow with the lama?"

"Three to four hours."

"Know what time he came?"

"Late in the afternoon. Sometime between four and five."

"Did you see him when he came in?"

Vishart nodded. "And I saw him go out, too."

"Know his name?"

"He didn't give any."

"All you know about him is that he said he was a Tibetan and that he stayed with the lama between, say, four-thirty and eight o'clock yesterday?"

"That's all."

"H'm. Can't do much with that infor---" Mack's face suddenly brightened. "Did the lama make any telephone calls?"

Vishart reached for the phone on his desk. "I'll find out for you." He spoke briefly into the instrument and hung up. "Operator says he made a call this morning," he told them. "Some Bryn Mawr number. She's got a record of it, and she's going to call information and find out who it belongs to."

"Good work!" Mack explained approvingly. Vishart's telephone bell began to jangle within a few minutes.

"It's the residence of Adam H. Merriweather," said Vishart as he replaced the instrument on its stand. "Sheridan Road address."

Mack whistled. "That Merriweather is the head of Merriweather Steel, Incorporated. Must be worth three or four millions. Why should the lama want to talk to him?"

"Adam Merriweather," Westborough informed the two detectives, "is known in other circles than those of business. He is not without renown as our country's principal collector of Tibetan art treasures."

PART THREE: The Man from Tibet
(Tuesday, July 20)

THE YELLOW KING had three eyes and a great, gaping mouth. Brass circlets six inches in diameter dangled from his long ears, and he wore a wreath of tiny skulls. He was tall—even taller than the lanky Dr. Walters, who was two inches over six feet. Above the Yellow King's dragon-embroidered silk costume his head—three or four times the size of a normal human head—loomed like an oriental nightmare.

Except for the colors of their glossy faces the Yellow King's three brothers—the Red, White and Green kings—were almost his exact duplicates in appearance. Two members of the formidable quartet flanked each of the two doors of the great room which they were now entering.

"The four guardians of the quarters," Miss Shelton explained. "Images or paintings of them appear at the entrances to every Lamaist temple because they are supposed to have the power of frightening away the enemies of Buddhism. These are the masks and costumes used to represent them in the so-called Tibetan devil dances."

Dr. Walters stared incredulously, too taken aback to vouchsafe a reply. Just the room itself was a sight worth seeing: a closed patio, in the heart of the house, thirty feet wide, seventy feet long, lighted only by the skylight above their heads. Sunlight was now flickering down from the skylight through the broad wooden beams at the second-story level. Beams painted in primitive reds and blues and yellows, from which trailed pennants bearing queer Tibetan inscriptions. But the room was ordinary in comparison with its contents.

Dr. Walters turned his attention to the array of Buddhas and Buddha-gods on the opposite side of the room from where they were standing. He saw an even dozen images, varying in height from three to six feet, which were ranged behind a low, L-shaped altar that was covered with yellow brocade and extended across nearly two complete sides of the room. Some of the figures were smiling with the placid serenity which Walters associated with images of the Buddha, but others were nightmare creatures with a multiplicity of arms or heads, scowling hideously, gnashing protruding teeth.

Scores of small objects had been placed upon the altar before the twelve gods. They included teacups with long-stemmed saucers, teapots wrapped in silk and embellished with peacock feathers, brass bowls, engraved handbells and other articles utterly unfamiliar, whose names Dr. Walters did not know, whose purpose he could not even guess.

In the center of the room there were three large glass museum cases. The middle one contained queer-looking musical instruments, which ranged in size from small conch shells to a giant brass trumpet twenty feet long. The case on Walters' left held turquoise earrings and turquoise and coral necklaces as well as a multitude of other objects he could not identify. That on his right was devoted exclusively to papier-mache masks such as those forming the heads of the Yellow King and his three brothers—masks of beasts, of gods, of demons.

"Marvelous!" Walters ejaculated, completing his inspection. Reflecting that, although he had called daily on Adam Merriweather during the past two weeks, this was his first visit to Merriweather's Tibetan Room, he added. "I'm glad your uncle had his important visitor this morning."

She nodded understandingly. Walters liked this girl, liked everything about her. Liked the slim tanned hands, one of which was now poised so lightly just between the swelling curves of her breasts. Liked the yellow linen summer dress and the air with which it was worn. Liked the small curls clustering above the lower tips of her small ears, the honey-tanned skin of her neck and throat, the warm vitality of her handclasp.

He liked her already better than any girl he knew, and he had not seen her half-a-dozen times before, scarcely spoken twice that many words to her. Until this morning, until just a few minutes ago when she had found him waiting for Merriweather. (He had already waited nearly an hour and was inclined to be in a bitingly savage frame of mind.) Until she had invited him to inspect this great hall.

"Everything you see here is authentically Tibetan," she whispered. (He knew nothing about her really except that her name was Janice Shelton. Pretty name, Janice.) "Uncle Adam has agents in both India and China. And then a lot of these things, including some of the images, were brought to him by his own brother, Doctor Jed Merriweather, the archaeologist. Have you heard Uncle Adam speak of him?"

"No," Walters whispered. He wondered if it were some quality emanating from the Tibetan gods opposite which had caused them to hush their voices. "This room must have cost a fortune."

"Don't you think that a beautiful room like this is its own justification for everything you put into it?"

"I suppose so." As a prudent afterthought Dr. Walters added, "If you can afford it."

She pointed to the checkerboard of deep, square pigeonholes which had been built along the north wall. "Those are Tibetan bookcases, and they hold genuine Tibetan books. Would you care to see one?"

"Yes, very much." Dr. Walters was not greatly interested in Tibetan books, but he was very definitely interested in his companion. "Allow me." He reached for the oblong object wrapped in silk which she was taking from a pigeonhole.

"Thank you. It is rather heavy, isn't it? But I think the glass on the top of the case is thick enough to hold it. Now we'll take off the wrapping."

Their hands touched accidentally as Walters was helping her to remove the silk covering. That touch, to Walters, was like an electric shock, like the discharge of static electricity. "I beg your pardon!" he exclaimed in his confusion.

She smiled and began to unstrap the board covers. "Tibetan books aren't bound. They are not books, as we think of them, but collections of loose pages. Tibetans have an alphabet, and they write from left to right the same as we do."

"Their writing's even worse than pharmaceutical Latin," Dr. Walters commented as he inspected the long, crowded lines.

"Anyway, they don't have to use several thousand picture-symbols like the poor Chinese. Do you know that most of these books aren't sold in the market?"

"Aren't they?"

"No. If you want a copy you have to pay to have it printed from the wood blocks which are kept in some lamasery storeroom. That makes a Tibetan book rather expensive."

"I see they have paper like ours," Walters observed, trying to think of an intelligent comment. "Here, let me put that cover back on for you."

"Thank you. Yes, the Tibetans have known how to make paper since the middle of the seventh century. Five hundred years or so before Europeans had anything but parchment! Rather a staggering thought, isn't it?"

"Paper's been one of the things I've always taken pretty much for granted," he told her. "Shall I put this away for you?"

"If you please. The end with the white tag should be out because the tag tells what book it is."

"What book is it?"

Dr. Walters enjoyed very much the free, clear note of her laughter.

"I don't read Tibetan, Doctor Walters. It's probably one of the Kan-gyur or the Ten-gyur—the Tibetan Bible and its commentary. Chang is translating them for Uncle Adam. It's a wonderful thing to do, but I don't like---"

"Don't like what?" Walters asked.

"Nothing much. Do you know Chang is a native-born Tibetan?"

Dr. Walters did not possess that information. Furthermore, he had the impression that no one was allowed to enter or leave Tibet, and he admitted to this belief. Miss Shelton shook her head.

"The rule doesn't work both ways. Tibetans can go into India or China or anywhere else they want to. Chang was trying to get out of the country when Uncle Adam's brother found him. It was just after Doctor Merriweather had his bad luck in Sinkiang."

"Sin-ja-yong?"

"The Chinese name for what we call Turkestan. Isn't all this boring you, Doctor Walters?"

"Was the caliph bored by Scheherazade?" he laughed. "By the way, I'd like to ask you a question."

"I'm not sure I'll be able to answer it. I'm no authority on the subject of Tibet."

"This is a personal question. You were talking about your uncle---"

"He isn't really my uncle," she interrupted.

"No ?" Walters exclaimed in surprise. "I thought that---"

"Father's oldest friend, but no relative. You might call him my guardian. Not that there's anything to—oh well. What were you going to ask me?"

"You were talking about the translation of these books. And you said there was something about it you didn't like."

"Yes?"

"I'd like to know what that something is."

"If you please, I'd rather not talk about it."

"I wouldn't ask you to talk about it, Miss Shelton, except that Mr. Merriweather is now my patient. Please don't think that I'm merely trying to poke my long nose into matters that are none of my business."

Her laughter rang musically throughout the room. "It isn't too long a nose, Doctor Walters. Well, if you must know, please don't tell him that I said anything about it. I don't really know anything definite. But he spends far too much time in here alone, doing—well, I can't even guess what he does." She added in a hushed voice, "I do know this much. There's only one part of Chang's translations that really interests him. The part that deals with magic."

"Magic!" Dr. Walters repeated, glancing across the altar toward a Buddhist gentleman with innumerable heads. "Magic in the twentieth century?"

"Why should the twentieth century be different from any other? And all primitive religions profess to magical powers, don't they?"

"Do they?"

"I think so. Buddhism isn't exactly primitive, but---" She broke off the sentence to whisper peremptorily: "Shhh! Someone is coming." In her normal tone of voice she resumed the conversation. "The one with the eleven heads is Chen-re-zi, the God of Mercy. Not exactly a god, but a Bodhisat, which is a being above all the gods and next in rank to the Buddhas themselves. The one seated on the throne is another Bodhi-sat: Maitreya, who is going to be the next Buddha. On Maitreya's right— oh; hello, Vin! Haven't you taken the wrong door for the beach?"

The youth who sauntered toward them was wearing only bathing trunks and a pair of crepe-soled sandals, but appeared sublimely indifferent to his clothing (or lack of it).

"Jan! I've hunted the house over for you. Good morning, Doctor Walters. You won't mind if I take Janice away from you, will you? We always have a swim together before I go down to the daily grind."

Dr., Walters answered politely, "Not in the least." But he did mind. In his opinion Vincent Merriweather was a spoiled young brat whom someone ought to teach better manners. The bathing trunks didn't suit him so well, either; he was far too much on the thinnish side. Ribs prominent, chest not well developed, arms skinny. Might be because he didn't get exercise enough, or it might be something else. Maybe he wasn't eating the right kind of things. Wouldn't hurt to prescribe a diet if he got the chance to go into the case.

"All right, Jan," the boy commanded. "I'll give you ten minutes to get your suit on."

"I'll do no such thing. Do you know it's after ten o'clock?"

"Steel can wait."

"But you can't. Be a dear, Vin, and run on."

He answered sulkily, "If you don't want to go with me, Jan, be good enough to say so. I'm going to have my swim."

Strangely enough Miss Shelton did not seem to mind the young man's appalling rudeness. In fact her eyes were wistfully following his retreating bare back.

"Poor Vin!"

Dr. Walters saw nothing in Vincent Merriweather's position for which to sympathize and said so frankly.

"Uncle Adam is forcing him to be a steel man, and how he hates it."

"A man doesn't amount to anything without a job to do," opined Dr. Walters, who had never been without work since the age of sixteen.

"Yes, but Vin considers his father's attitude unjust, and, looking at it from his viewpoint, he's right. Vin's grandfather, who was the original steel Merriweather, founded the business so well that after he died it went right on running itself, with nothing for his sons to do but spend the profits. Doctor Merriweather never was interested in money-making, and when he needed funds for one of his expeditions he didn't hesitate to sell all of his share to his brother. Uncle Adam, even if he does have the title of chairman of the board, cares very little about it either. So why should he expect Vin to make it his life's work?"

"You're fond of that young man, aren't you?" Walters inquired.

"I ought to be," she smiled. "We're to be married this fall."

Gaylord Walters seemed to feel a spray of icy water being dashed across his face. He said soberly, "I didn't know that."

"Didn't you? It's been no particular secret. A quiet home wedding on account of Uncle Adam's health. However, I'm not making a great deal of progress in showing you the collection. In this case you will see charm boxes, prayer wheels and rosaries. The lamas tell their beads—just like Roman Catholics. Do you see the turquoise earrings? Tibetans would rather have turquoise than diamonds or emeralds, Chang once told me. I can't altogether blame them, because it is a heavenly color. They love amber, too, and of course coral, as you can tell from these necklaces. There are a lot of interesting things to see on the altar. Skull caps, ritualistic dag—"

She broke off the sentence as Adam Merriweather emerged from behind the Yellow King. The collector was accompanied by his caller, a small man of dark complexion whom Walters had never seen before and at whom he stared curiously.

"Janice!" Merriweather's manner was more agitated than Walters had ever before seen it. "Allow me to present you to our distinguished visitor. He is one of the princes of the Tibetan Buddhist church, a veritable living god. The Lama Tsongpun Bonbo."

II

Just how, Dr. Walters wondered, does one acknowledge an introduction to a high Tibetan lama? Miss Shelton had already said a few words to him, but Walters had not caught them, so intently had his attention been concentrated upon this visitor from the most mysterious land in the world. Should one bow, or what? To Walters' relief the lama extended his hand in the orthodox occidental fashion. Except for his Mongolian features he did not look as one would expect a high prelate of the Tibetan religion to look. He was dressed in a conventional American business suit, and he carried a small satchel, a cheap satchel with a zipper fastener such as one may purchase at a chain drugstore for ninety-eight cents and up.

"My glad knowing you, Doc-tor," the lama acknowledged, smiling. His small hand felt surprisingly unsubstantial to Walters' touch. A wisp of a man, but probably of tougher stamina than he seemed, the doctor reflected. These Orientals often displayed amazing fortitude. The lama squinted badly; perhaps he had read too many of his sacred books under bad lighting conditions. But his voice was astonishing for so slight a person. It held some of the very deepest tones to which the doctor had ever listened.

He saw that the lama was gazing with enraptured eyes at the long row of Tibetan images.

"Tsu-stu-stu-pen-dous !" The lama beamed like a happy child as he achieved the difficult word. "*Cho-kang* like *cho-kang* ob Bhod Yul. Your *cho-kang*, Kusho Mer-ri-weat-her."

He gave an equal stress to each syllable of a word, so that his sentences were delivered in the monotone of a child reading a primer. The lama's funny deep voice, however, did not allow the child analogy to be too perfect a one.

"You like it?" Merriweather inquired.

"Ber-ry much."

"Wait until you see it at night when the floodlights are on?"

"Ploodlights ?"

The consonants *f* and *v,* as well as the digraph *th,* seemed to be impossible sounds for the lama to utter, although he did not, Walters noticed, suffer from the confusion between his *l*'s and *r*'s to which other oriental races are partial.

"Floodlights," Merriweather repeated, correcting his guest's pronunciation. "You know what electric lights are?"

The lama smiled. "Soon by me a learning is."

"Well, floodlights are big electric lights. They are hidden under the altar, and at night they shine into the faces of the Bodhisats. Beautiful effect!"

"Ber-ry nice," the lama murmured politely. He did not, Dr. Walters fancied, altogether approve of the innovation. "Kusho, your not minding my seeing now?"

"Certainly not, if Chang isn't working on it." Moving toward the pigeonholes, Merriweather reached for one of his queer Tibetan books. "No, it's still here. Evidently Chang hasn't started on it yet." He handed the book to his visitor. "Unwrap it if you want to."

The lama, to Walters' surprise, squatted cross-legged on the floor while he removed three successive layers of yellow silk. As the last covering came off he cried out several words in delighted Tibetan.

"I take it that's the right one," Merriweather observed with an amused smile. The lama glanced toward him apologetically.

"My not remembering your not knowing Bhod-Skad. Yes, Kusho, it right one—Guru Padma's own words. My taking back to Bhod Yul, helping atone por my e-bil past. Please, I now take it?"

"Not so fast," Merriweather objected. "I bought this manuscript in good faith and paid for it. It means a lot to me too. No other collector ever owned anything like it."

Hugging the manuscript tightly to his thin breast, the lama sprang to his feet. "No, Kusho! It not belonging to you. To my gompa it belong."

"In Tibet," Merriweather answered callously, "that might be true. But this is America. Since I've bought and paid for it, it's mine here."

The lama, relinquishing the manuscript, staggered back as though he had received a mortal blow. "Oh, the poor thing!" Janice Shelton cried impulsively. "How can you be so heartless? And Uncle Adam! Whatever are you wearing around your neck?"

Looking rather sheepish, Merriweather removed a long fringed scarf of heavy silk, which he folded and laid on the glass top of the nearest case. "I'd forgotten the lama's calling card."

"Calling card?"

"Yes, he laid it upon my shoulders when I first met him. It's a Tibetan custom."

The lama, greatly to Walters' surprise, suddenly thrust his satchel into the doctor's hands.

"Your not minding opening?"

Walters obligingly pulled back the zipper and, as he did so, vented a shrill whistle. Was he the victim of a hypnotic illusion or what? If the interior of the satchel was not entirely filled with currency there were at least several large bills lying on top.

"Your not minding counting?" the lama urged. Dr. Walters complied, using the top of the case for a table. Most of the bills were hundred-dollar ones, but, even so, the counting took him some little time. The lama glanced toward him inquiringly as he finished.

"Over twenty thousand dollars. Twenty thousand one hundred and fifty, to be exact."

The lama caught up the bills in handfuls and stuffed them into the satchel. When the last bill was inside he tendered the fantastic receptacle to Adam Merriweather.

"Kusho, money not to buy Guru Padma's sacred words; my giving it you. Your wishing more? My gompa habing store ob many, many gold disks; I see one be giben you. Gold not-hing; your being kind much. Your not making me go back Bhod Yul wit'out precious words ob Guru Padma?"

Merriweather's face was a study in conflicts. He said slowly, "Your offer, Lama, is a generous one, yet money means little to me in comparison with the value of such a rare masterpiece as this manuscript. However, I don't like to refuse you. Suppose you be my guest for the next few days? My brother arrives tomorrow, and I'll be able to give you an answer after I have had a talk with him."

The lama bowed with resigned calm. "Most happy. My un-wort-hy person habe new hope."

Merriweather turned to his doctor, beaming in that blandly condescending manner which Walters found so infuriating.

"Sorry you were kept waiting, Walters. Suppose today we forgo our usual examination. I feel much better this morning."

"As you wish." Dr. Walters, consulting his watch, saw that he had completely missed an important engagement. "Tomorrow at the usual hour, then? Good-by, Mr. Lama, it has been a pleasure to meet you. Good-by, Miss Shelton, and thank you for the Cook's tour of Tibet. I enjoyed it hugely."

Hurrying from the door, he narrowly averted a collision with Merriweather's butler. The butler's words to his employer caused the doctor to halt abruptly.

"Two gentlemen from the police are waiting to see you, sir."

"Police? For me?" Merriweather's face reddened as he snorted an indignant, "Outrageous!"

"From the Homicide Squad, sir. One gave his name as Lieutenant Mack."

"Oh, my Lord!" Walters ejaculated, walking back to the Tibetan Room. He felt that he had to stay there now. One could not tell what effect a visit of this nature would have on Adam Merriweather.

PART FOUR: The Man from Headquarters (Tuesday, July 20)

MERRIWEATHER'S ponderous butler returned to the hallway where Mack and Westborough were waiting.

"Mr. Merriweather will see you now, gentlemen. This way, please."

He led them down a narrow corridor and through an open door into a hall of incredible dimensions. Westborough cried out in astonishment, scarcely able to believe the evidence of his own eyes. He had heard of the Merriweather Tibetan collection, of course; he had even read a catalogic description of it. But nothing he had heard, nothing he had read, had prepared him for the sight of the thing itself.

Directly opposite the door where he was standing sat a huge gilt-copper image of the historic Sakyamuni Buddha. A beautiful piece of work in itself, but only one of the many images ranged behind the long, L-shaped platform. The others were not so commonly seen by Western eyes as the familiar Buddha, but Westborough could recognize some of them. Maitreya, Amitabha, Avalokita . . . these were particularly scintillating luminaries in the enormous Lamaist galaxy of gods and demons, Buddhas and Bodhisats. But dear, dear! He must not look any longer; he was completely neglecting the little knot of people toward whom they were walking.

There were only four of them. A gentleman in nose glasses—senatorial head atop his pudgy, pear-shaped body. A tall young man whose rugged features reminded Westborough of Gary Cooper. An unusually pretty girl. A small, dark-complexioned gentleman. . . . Westborough gasped breathlessly as he realized that this could be no other than the man whose trail they had followed from the Prescott House. The Lama Tsongpun Bonbo!

The historian stared with undisguised curiosity. One does not, after all, meet a high prelate of the Tibetan church every day of the year. The lama was a small man—not over five feet four inches. His head was shorn of all but a thin gray stubble; his beardless face was seamed with multitudes of tiny wrinkles. His lips were only a trifle thick, his cheek-

67

bones only a little prominent; his straight nose might have belonged to a person of Aryan ancestry, and his bronze skin was very little darker than the tanned complexion of the girl standing beside him. However, the lama's oblique narrow slits of eyes and his faintly marked eyebrows were plain indications of his Mongolian origin.

"I am Mr. Merriweather." The pudgy gentleman of the nose glasses moved frigidly forward. "To whom are we indebted for the pleasure of this visit?"

"My name's Mack. Lieutenant Mack of the Homicide Squad. We're investigating a murder case."

"How can that possibly concern me?" Merriweather inquired icily. Westborough wondered if that question were not an index to the man's character. First reactions were such important ones! Both the young lady and the young man were displaying an entirely normal degree of curiosity, but the lama's features had scarcely altered in expression. Doubtless the Tibetan had not understood the significance of John Mack's terse statement.

"I don't know that it does concern you," Mack answered, shrugging his shoulders. "I'm here looking for a Tibetan lama."

"Your wishing seeing me?" the lama asked with an eager smile. Mack inspected him critically.

"So you're the guy! Kinda little, you are. Need more meat on your bones. Lama, do you know a fellow called Jack Reffner?"

"Reffner!" Merriweather ejaculated. "Why, he called here only yesterday."

"He did, did he? Well, he's the fellow who was murdered last night."

"Impossible!" Merriweather exclaimed. He added as a belated afterthought, "Did you find my check?"

"What check?"

"The check for five thousand dollars which I gave to him yesterday afternoon."

"You gave Reffner five thousand dollars?"

"I did. Perhaps you found the money. Although I do not know where on such short notice he would have been able to cash a check of that size."

"We didn't find the money either," Mack said. "His pockets were as empty as the inside of a drum. Why'd you give him five grand?"

"I purchased a rare Tibetan manuscript from him." Merriweather pointed to an oblong object covered with yellow silk which was resting on one of the glass cases. "That!"

"That?" Mack did not deign to give it a second look. "You rich guys don't have much sense about your dough," he grumbled. "What time yesterday was Reffner here?"

"He came at two and stayed perhaps two hours."

"If he stayed two hours you must've done lots of talking. Can you remember what he said to you?"

"I have a typewritten transcript of our conversation."

"Say that again!" Mack directed.

"Chang, my secretary, made a shorthand record."

"Now you're talking!" the detective exclaimed. "Get it for me, will you?"

Merriweather answered coldly, "I'll ask Chang to find it," and strode with offended dignity from the room. Mack transferred his attention to the lama.

"All right, you! You haven't answered my question about knowing this fellow Reffner."

"My not habing chance, Lu-ten-ant *lags*." The lama smiled shyly. "My habing him once met—to my sor-row."

"You only met him once?"

"But once, Lu-ten-ant lags."

"When?"

"In wood-dog year." He noted Mack's puzzled glance and cried apologetically, "Sor-ree! My porgetting your not knowing our cal-en-dar. Wood-dog year, wood-hog year, pire-mouse year, now pire-ox year. Your calling it nineteen t'irty-seven."

"What kind of crazy zoo is this?" Mack demanded. "Pire-mouse? Pire-ox?"

"Perhaps the Lama Tsongpun Bonbo wishes to say fire-mouse and fire-ox," Westborough hazarded. "The lip-teeth fricative consonants *f* and *v* are not, I believe, included in the Tibetan alphabet."

"Yeh, but why the animals? Does he think he's talking about Noah's ark?"

"The years of the Tibetan calendar are not numbered as ours are, but are named, the names being formed by the combinations of twelve animals with the five elements of the Chinese: wood, fire, earth, iron and water. After a cycle of sixty combinations the years repeat themselves, I believe."

"Goofy system," Mack grumbled. He counted backward on his fingers. "Lama, was the wood-dog year in 1934 ?"

The lama nodded confirmedly.

"You haven't seen him since?"

"No, Lu-ten-ant lags."

"Where'd you meet him in 1934?"

"On way to Bhod Yul."

"Are you trying to tell me it was Christmas?"

"Bhod Yul is the Tibetan name for Tibet, I believe," Westborough proffered. He saw that the lama was nodding in a pleased manner.

Mack rubbed a hand across a bewildered forehead. "What was Reffner doing in Tibet in 1934 ?"

"My not knowing, Lu-ten-ant lags."

"Stop calling me Legs," Mack directed exasperatedly. "I'm Lieutenant Mack."

"Yes, Mack Lu-ten-ant. Lags meaning what your calling hon-or-able."

"Honorable, eh?" Mack grinned broadly. "Well, go ahead. Did you know Reffner was in Chicago?"

"No, Mack Lu-ten-ant. My not knowing only now. My not being surprise."

"Not surprised, eh? Why not?"

The lama's slight brown hands spread open in an expressive gesture. "His *karma,* my *karma,* t'ey being what your calling in—inter—inter---"

"Intertwined ?" Westborough suggested gently. The lama bowed in a grateful manner.

"Yes, Kusho. His karma, my karma being intertwined."

"What does he mean by 'karma'?" Mack wanted to know.

"It is a word difficult to define, although it may be interpreted broadly as the law of cause and effect. Perhaps the lama wishes to tell us that it was fated that his path and that of Reffner should converge again as a result of their own past actions."

The lama beamed delightedly. "Yes, Kusho, yes, yes!"

"Damnedest nonsense I ever heard!" Mack growled. "Guess I'll take a look around here."

"Excuse me," said the tall young man, crossing to Westborough, "but I think I recognize you from Barry Foster's description. We're old pals; he told me about what you did to help his wife out of a mighty bad hole. I'm Doctor Gaylord Walters—sometimes known as Gay for short."

"A friend of Mr. Foster's is indeed a friend of mine," Westborough observed as they shook hands.

"Miss Shelton, may I present Mr. Westborough?"

Mack returned from a prowl around the room in time to overhear the introduction. "Miss Shelton, do you live here?" She nodded. "What's your relationship to Mr. Merriweather ?"

"We are not relations—yet. Mr. Merriweather's son is my fiance."

"Oh, I see." Westborough could tell that Mack's attention was now centered on another matter. "There's a question I'd like to ask you, Miss Shelton. What kind of face powder do you use?"

"Face powder ? What a strange question. Baiser d'Amour."

"I don't mean the brand name. What color?"

"Rachelle."

"What's that? White?"

"White with my skin!" She laughed heartily. "Really, Lieutenant Mack!"

"Oh, all right. I just wanted to know." He turned to the young man. "I heard you telling Westborough you were Doctor Walters. Merriweather's doctor?"

"Yes, temporarily. I am acting as a substitute for a far better man. Doctor Pressinger."

"The famous heart specialist," Westborough observed. "Once I had the pleasure of conversing with that remarkable character. Is it possible that he is at last taking a vacation ?"

Walters grinned. "He was forced into it, you might say. Four of us split his practice between us, and we'll disown him if he comes back any time under four months. He's on a walking trip through the Black Forest."

"A most interesting excursion," Westborough murmured. "In my younger days I made such a trip myself. I shall never forget the experience. Indeed, I am inclined even now to envy Doctor Pres---"

Mack's eyes had spied a white object on top of one of the glass cases. From a distance it looked like a folded handkerchief.

"A silk scarf!" Lt. Mack ejaculated, shaking it out to its full length. "Same Chink laundry marks on it, too. Or are they the same, Westborough?"

"Exactly the same," the historian confirmed. He saw that the six characters of the formula had been repeated a great many times in a decorative pattern at either end of the heavy fringed scarf.

"Lama, come here," Mack ordered. "Tell me what this says."

The lama replied promptly, "Chen-re-zi's great *mantra*, what your calling prayer, Mack Lu-ten-ant. Om mani padme hum."

The six syllables, intoned in the lama's magnificent bass voice, reverberated sonorously throughout the room. Westborough, for no reason at all, thought of a service he had once attended at a great English cathedral. Mack, however, remained unimpressed.

"Is it your scarf ?" he demanded severely.

"No, Mack Lu-ten-ant. My giving it Kusho Mer-ri-weat-her."

"When?" Mack questioned quickly. The lama shrugged his shoulders in an expressive manner.

"One, two, t'ree, pour hour ago, my not knowing."

"Mr. Merriweather was wearing the scarf around his neck when he and the lama first entered this room," Dr. Walters informed them.

"Wearing a scarf in July? Doc, have you gone nuts?"

The doctor grinned, unoffended. "I'm wondering too. But he was wearing it."

"He certainly was," Miss Shelton corroborated.

"Then he's gone screwy!" Mack declared emphatically. "Wearing a scarf in July!"

"My putting it there, Mack Lu-ten-ant," the lama interposed shyly.

"You did ? Why ?"

"The presentation of a ceremonial scarf is, I believe, the universal method of conveying a greeting in Tibet," Westborough informed the detective. "Truly a delightful custom."

"Come over here," Mack directed tersely. He led the lama to a far corner of the room, away from the doctor and Miss Shelton. "Got any more such scarves up at your hotel?"

The lama nodded. "Many, many, Mack Lu-ten-ant. My bringing prom Bhod."

"Bird, Bird, Bird!" Mack repeated exasperatedly. "Here's a piece of news for you. This fellow Reffner—yes, the one you haven't seen since the year of the woodchuck—was strangled last night. Strangled with one of these silk scarves that you brought with you from Bird! Now explain that if you can."

"My not knowing how explain," the lama said simply.

II

Mack skimmed through the typewritten pages which Adam Merriweather had brought to him a few minutes ago. "Queer yarn!" he exclaimed. "Does it make sense to you, Westborough?"

The historian, who had read each page as Mack finished with it, glanced up from the sheets he was now rearranging in their proper numerical sequence.

"The details of Mr. Reffner's narrative seem to accord very well with what I have read of Tibet."

"Let me see the first page," Mack directed, selecting it from Westborough's pile as he spoke. "Yeh, here it is. Reffner admits he had a Japanese mother, but he says his father was an American, and he claims to be an American citizen himself. Did he happen to tell you where he was born, Merriweather?"

"No, he did not."

"Mention any American cities that might give us a slant on where he came from?"

"No, he did not. Practically everything he said was recorded by Chang."

"Chang? Oh, your secretary. Chinese?"

"Tibetan."

"*Tibetan*, did you say?"

"Yes. Chang is a native-born Tibetan."

"H'm!" Mack's face grew very thoughtful. "Can't be many Tibetans in this country. I'll have to talk to him before I leave here."

"If he wishes it, yes."

"He'd better wish it," Mack declared. Picking up Merriweather's scarf, he folded it into a compact bundle. "I'm taking this down to headquarters," he explained as he stored it away in his coat pocket.

"That scarf happens to be my property," Merriweather informed the detective coldly. "You have no right to remove it."

"Don't worry. You'll get it back when this thing's settled. Right now I want to talk to the lama in private. Where can we go for our powwow?"

"I have just invited the lama to become my guest," Merriweather declaimed pompously. "I do not wish him to be subjected to your insulting cross-examination."

"Insulting, eh?"

"Your whole attitude since you have entered my house has been very insulting. I will not allow my guest to be illegally molested."

Mack turned to the lama. "I'll play square with you, Mr. Bonbo. Merriweather, if I read the signs right, is about to tell me that I don't have any authority to compel you to talk with me. That's true—now. But if you won't talk I can go to the state's attorney's office for a warrant to bring you down there for questioning. Now which is it?"

"My not understanding, Mack Lu-ten-ant." The lama smiled in a confiding manner. "Your wanting talk wit' me?,'

"That's the general idea," Mack admitted.

"Most happy," the lama murmured.

Mack grinned triumphantly at Adam Merriweather. "Where can we go?" he asked. Merriweather was looking as if he could cheerfully drown all of his guests, including the lama.

"Well, I'll be running along," Dr. Walters observed, starting for the door.

"Stick around awhile, Doctor," Mack ordered. "We may want to talk to you too. Well, Merriweather ? Is there a room we can have?"

"You may have the use of my study," Merriweather yielded stiffly. He led them to a room across the hall.

"Italy of two hundred years ago!" Westborough exclaimed in delight as he glanced at the late eighteenth-century falling-front secretary,

the table with its fluted legs and mirror-polished top, the slender, delicate curule chairs. "Mr. Merriweather, may I congratulate you upon
your taste in furniture? The intarsia on your secretary is the finest I
have ever seen."

Merriweather thawed a trifle. "Thank you, Mr.---er—I do not believe I know your name?"

"Westborough," the historian supplied.

"Westborough? It sounds familiar, but I am unable to recall where
I have heard it. If you want anything, Lieutenant, press the button on
the desk, and Chang will come. Good day to you, gentlemen."

Westborough reflected, as Adam Merriweather left the room, that
the modern steel filing cabinet in a corner of the room was a ridiculous
incongruity amidst eighteenth-century Italy. He wondered why Merriweather, obviously a man of excellent taste, tolerated its presence.

Mack pointed to the curule chair nearest to the table. (They were
veritable museum pieces, those chairs!) "Lama, you sit down there.
Westborough, sit over by the desk—never saw so much fancy work on a
piece of furniture---and if you want to you can take notes. All right,
Lama! Let's begin with the time you met Reffner. The year of the
wood-hog."

"Wood-dog year, Mack Lu-ten-ant."

"Wood-dog, then. According to Reffner's yarn you two were camping together, and in the morning your saddlebags got mixed up so he
accidentally got away with your manuscript. Is that true?"

"It is not true, Mack Lu-ten-ant."

"No? What was the truth?"

"E-bil Reppner stealing Guru Padma's precious words, he leabing
blanket same shape in my saddlebag. Being un-wort-hy person in past, I
am de-lude by his trick, so losing my gompa's great treasure."

"Well, I'll be damned!" Mack ejaculated.

"But why," Westborough inquired, "did you tell Reffner of the manuscript and of your pilgrimage to Budh Gaya ?"

"My not knowing, Kusho Wes-bo-ro." The lama shook his head in a
gesture expressive of complete bafflement. "My e-bil karma! It making
me tell e-bil Reppner of Guru Padma's words. It not letting me open
bag until one night, two night, t'ree night later. He six day away when I
see gone my gompa's precious treasure."

"Go on talking," Mack ordered. "What happened then ?"

"Ne-ber such sor-row to Ge-lug-pa ob Bhod! My knowing my habing e-bil karma, or it not happening. My knowing must restore Guru
Padma's words or be reborn in lowest hell. My being de-so-late.

"E-bil Reppner—my not then knowing name---six marches away.

My habing return Chyod, see penlop, he being overwhelm wi' sor-row, he employ e-bil man, but Reppner not in Chyod. My seeing British *shap-pe* at Darjeeling. He kind man, but e-bil karma not habing worn away, Reppner not in Darjeeling when I come. My not knowing any tongue but Bhod-Skad. How I search por him t'rough land ob pyi-ling?"

"Where did you study English?" Westborough asked.

"Kusho, in Darjeeling is good school, it being taught by Kusho Swit-hins, who know Reppner. He say he tell e-bil one to leave Guru Padma's words wit' British shap-pe. E-bil one, being greatly wicked, promise but he de-lude Kusho Swit-hins as he de-lude me."

"Swithins was a pal of Reffner's," Mack observed reminiscently. "Didn't he tell Swithins what city he came from? Or where he was going?"

"No, Mack Lu-ten-ant, Kusho Swit-hins not knowing. My studying one year, two year, longer under Kusho Swit-hins. Hard it is learning your tongue, but a *ge-long* must learn by heart each year one hundred, two hundred, more pages ob sacred text. One who can do t'at can learn Eng-lish, Kusho Swit-hins say, he being right. My learning Eng-lish."

"You speak it very well," Westborough declared. The lama smiled happily but made a negative gesture.

"No, Kusho, not well. It not being like Bhod-Skad. Pire-mouse year—nineteen t'irty-six—my leabing Darjeeling."

"What were you using for money all this time?" Mack demanded.

"My gompa sending gold which British shap-pe take, gibing me rupees. He seeing I take train to great city call Cal-gut-ta. My not liking it because air ber-ry heaby, it press down on my chest. My learning not-hing ob Guru Padma's words; heaby air not letting me sleep. My seeing big riber wit' boat big as my gompa. Great is magic ob pyi-ling! My taking boat por Lun-dun.

"Ocean a-ston-ish, it being so big. Long, long time it take to reach Lun-dun, and sickness come to me, sickness like t'at we call *la-druk*, but it cannot be la-druk; where on ocean are passes? T'ey telling me it sickness ob ocean, but I know it come because ob my e-bil karma. I being glad—more I sup-per, sooner will e-bil karma wear away—but sickness leabe me. Lun-dun big city; bigger t'an Cal-gut-ta, it being ca-pi-tal ob pyi-ling. My seeing many British shap-pe; t'ey not knowing about Guru Padma's words. Perhaps, t'ey tell me, e-bil Reppner take my gompa's sacred treasure to A-mer-i-ca. I not know where is A-mer-i-ca. It big country, t'ey tell me, long, long journey away. My again taking boat.

"Ocean sickness come back; I glad my e-bil karma grow less, but it leabe. My reaching big city t'ey call Noo-Yok; it big as Lun-dun but noisy like demon city. My not liking it.

"My seeing British shap-pe. He being kind, see I talk to many people. T'ey ask many, many question about Bhod, but t'ey not know ob Guru Padma's words. T'ey tell me t'ere is ot-her big city call She-caw-go where libe Kusho Mer-ri-weat-her who collect my country's books. T'ey tell me about Pres-cott House where I get room high up so heaby air not so much bot-her me."

"When did you get this room that was so high up?" Mack demanded.

"One day ago yes-ter-day. Sun-day, you call it."

"Yeh, Sunday. Today's Tuesday. Yesterday was Monday. Why didn't you try to get in touch with Merriweather then?"

"Yes-ter-day?"

"Yeh, yesterday. What made you wait until this morning to see Mer-riweather?"

"Must spend day to reach right mind."

"What?"

"Wit-out right mind I cannot dis-co-ber Guru Padma's words, my e-bil karma being so strong. Must spend day in quiet to med-i-tate. But I am dis-turb by man call Blaze who ask many question. He ask question not about Bhod, which I know, but about A-mer-i-ea, which I not know. I see he is stupid. My not telling about Guru Padma's words because he is stupid."

"Oh, my God!" Mack choked.

"Many people asking see me because ob what Blaze write in his paper. I say no because I must med-i-tate, but each time new one come tel-e-pone ring. I am dis-turb, I cannot reach right mind. One call who speak Bhod-Skad; him I see. His name Chang."

"That's Merriweather's secretary."

"Yes, Mack Lu-ten-ant. Chang bringing welcome news; e-bil Repp-ner habe sold Guru Padma's words to Kusho Mer-ri-weat-her. I greatly joyed because I see my e-bil karma now gone."

"Did Chang tell you where you could find Reffner?"

"No, Mack Lu-ten-ant. I not care."

"Why not? Didn't you want to get after him for stealing your manu-script?"

"My knowing Reppner be punish, he habing done e-bil. Pain pur-sue wicked man as wheel pursue ox drawing carriage. So it is written in sacred book. E-bil one's e-bil karma certain to destroy him."

"Sure you didn't think you'd help his karma out a bit?" Mack in-quired. The lama drew back with the first indignation he had yet dis-played.

"Mack Lu-ten-ant, Enlightened One, great Sakya-t'ubpa, teach long ago not to kill."

"Indeed, yes," Westborough concurred. "All followers of the Buddha are forbidden to take life—even a life of the lower animals."

"Your studying Sakya-t'ubpa's doctrine, Kusho Wes-bo-ro ?"

"I know a little of its beauty, Tsongpun Lama," Westborough answered, hoping that he had achieved the correct Tibetan form of address.

"My liking teach you more, Kusho Wes-bo-ro."

"I shall be highly honored, Tsongpun Lama."

Rising, they bowed gravely to each other. "May I ask a question of you, Tsongpun Lama?" the historian inquired.

"I happy to answer, Kusho Wes-bo-ro."

"Are scarves embroidered with Chen-re-zi's great mantra commonly found in the land of Bhod, Tsongpun Lama ?"

"Yes, Kusho, such ka-tas are common."

"Thank you, Tsongpun Lama."

"You welcome, Kusho Wes-bo-ro."

Once more they rose to bow to each other. "Hey, cut the Alphonse and Gaston stuff," Mack growled. "Lama, you can answer a question for me too. Just why were you so sure Reffner was going to be murdered?"

"E-bil always create e-bil. Course ob law cannot be changed."

"That sort of talk doesn't mean much to me. Look here! The fellow was strangled with a white scarf—a scarf with your Om mani what-you-call-it on it. I don't give a damn how common such scarves are in Bird; there can't be many of 'em in Chicago. Matter of fact, the only ones I know about are the ones you have. Now you sit there and tell me you knew all along this was going to happen. What do you expect me to think?"

"My not knowing, Mack Lu-ten-ant."

Springing suddenly to his feet, Mack shook his finger directly under the lama's nose. "Who killed Jack Reffner?"

"My not knowing, Mack Lu-ten-ant," the lama repeated placidly. Beneath Mack's penetrating gaze his eyes blinked, but he did not glance away. It was the detective who finally looked down.

"All right. That's all I wanted to ask you. You can go now."

Bowing, the lama left the study. Mack jabbed viciously at the button on the eighteenth-century bureau-desk.

"Merriweather said this would bring Chang. Let's see what kind of Tibetan he is."

III

Chang, who appeared almost at once in answer to Mack's ring, waited with perfect poise in the doorway. He was taller than the lama, his face stolid and expressionless. Westborough took particular note of his nose. It was a straight one, like the lama's.

"Is Chang your first or last name?" Mack asked.

"My only name." Chang's voice, like that of Tsongpun Bonbo, was surprisingly deep in tone. "It is name Doctor Merriweather gave to me when his party find me in Chang Tang."

"Chang Tang? Where's the Chang Tang?"

"Plains of northern Tibet."

"Merriweather found you there? He doesn't look like the sort of fellow to be wandering around in that part of the world."

"Not Mr. Merriweather. Doctor Merriweather. He is brother to Mr. Merriweather."

"Doctor Merriweather, the archaeologist ?" Westborough inquired.

"Yes, Doctor Jed Merriweather."

"I've heard of him," Mack put in with a sudden flash of interest. "One of those fellows who hires a few camels and wanders over half of Asia. Some life!"

"He is a fine scholar," Westborough observed thoughtfully. "I have read his great work, *The Races of Turkestan*."

"Does he live in Chicago?" Mack inquired.

"He has home in San Francisco." Although Chang's manner was courteous Westborough sensed a reserve in him which he had not found in the friendly lama. "What is it you wish to ask me?"

"You speak English pretty well," Mack declared.

Chang bowed. "Thank you. Doctor Merriweather teach it to me during years I am with him. Later I take secretarial course before I come to work for Mr. Merriweather."

"What sort of work?"

"I translate books of Tibet."

"That ought to pay pretty well." Chang returned no answer. "Saving it up to return to Tibet?" Mack catechized. "You ought to be able to go back there and live like a king."

Chang bowed. It was not the bow of an obsequious man. "Pardon, Lieutenant, if I remind my personal affairs cannot interest you who hunt the murderer of Mr. Reffner. I am glad to answer questions bearing on that subject."

"Well, slap me down!" Mack ejaculated. His face broke suddenly into a broad grin. "All right, we'll stick to Reffner. What time did he call here yesterday afternoon?"

"At two o'clock."

"You are sure of it?"

"Yes, Lieutenant, I make note of time for Mr. Merriweather."

"How long did he stay?"

"He leave at ten minutes past four. I also make note of time."

"Now here's something we know about you, Chang." Mack's voice had grown suddenly acrid. "Yesterday afternoon, after Reffner had left this house, you went down to the Loop to see the lama. We can prove that, so don't try telling me you didn't go there."

"I do not deny that I visit the Lama Tsongpun Bonbo."

"How did you know he was in town and where he was staying?"

"I read it in evening paper which I bring to Mr. Merriweather."

"What made you go there ?"

Chang remained silent.

"Perhaps," Westborough put in gently, "I am able to conjecture the reason. You considered the lama to be the real owner of the Tibetan manuscript, did you not? You went to inform him of its whereabouts?"

Chang hesitated slightly before replying. "I am born in Tibet. Although I am loyal to Mr. Merriweather, who employ me, I do not like to see treasures of my country stolen. I tell the Lama Tsongpun Bonbo where to find his manuscript."

"Humph!" Mack grunted. "Ever strike you that there might be something funny about the lama's visit coming so soon after Reffner had sold the manuscript? Ever think that Reffner's whole yarn might be a fake?"

"Yes, I consider that possibility. I wonder if there is not plot to defraud Mr. Merriweather, to make him believe manuscript is genuine when it is only clever forgery."

"But, Mr. Chang, did you not examine the manuscript before Mr. Merriweather purchased it?"

"Yes, I examine it. I believe it to be genuine. I tell Mr. Merriweather that."

"And what did you think of this fellow Reffner?" Mack asked.

"It is strange story, but he describe Tibet accurately. Also he speak Tibetan."

"He did, did he ? Well, that ought to prove—something. What's your slant on the lama? Think he might be a fake too?"

"I consider that possibility. But it is not so."

"No?"

"As soon as I talk with him I learn that he is true Tibetan."

"Because he can talk the lingo?"

"Not that alone. There are pyi-ling—Doctor Merriweather is one of them—who can speak our language as well as my own countrymen."

"Well, what else was it?"

Chang said hesitantly, "We talk of Sacred Books. He speak of things which no one can know who has not study in large gompa."

"Have you studied in a large gompa, Mr. Chang?" Westborough questioned gently. Chang did not answer.

"Well, let's get back to Reffner," Mack suggested. "Did he leave his address with you, Chang?"

"Yes. I get it when I show him to door."

"Did you tell Merriweather where Reffner was staying ?"

"No, Lieutenant."

"Whatta you mean, you didn't? You got Reffner's address on purpose for Merriweather, didn't you?"

"If he ask me I tell him. But he not ask me."

"Sure of that?"

"It is truth."

"Maybe you wanted that address for yourself," Mack insinuated. Chang said nothing. "Or the lama? You told the lama where Reffner was staying, didn't you?"

Chang shook his head. "No, Lieutenant, I say nothing to the Lama Tsongpun Bonbo. I know he not be interested."

"Maybe you didn't know the address yourself," Mack snorted.

"Yes, I know it, Lieutenant. The Pilgrim Deluxe Hotel on Eron Street."

"That's right. And that's where he was killed. Know where that dump is, Chang?"

"I stay there myself," was Chang's surprising answer.

IV

"You stayed there last night?" Mack shouted.

Chang shook his head. "No, not last night."

"When?"

"Three years ago. On day I come to Chicago to work for Mr. Merriweather. There is no one at station to meet me because I have made stupid mistake about day I am to arrive. I decide I stay at hotel until next day."

"Why the Pilgrim Deluxe Hotel?" Mack wanted to know. "How'd you happen to pick that dump to stop at?"

"I take long walk about city, and I see it. It look like cheap hotel, and I do not have much money."

"May I ask," Westborough said gently, "why you left the employ of Doctor Merriweather for that of his brother ?"

Chang's face was an expressionless mask. "That is question you must ask of Doctor Merriweather or of Mr. Merriweather. The act was not of my choosing."

"Ever been back to the Pilgrim Deluxe Hotel since that time?" Mack demanded. Chang shook his head.

"Not even once?"

"No, Lieutenant."

"Did you tell anyone Reffner was stopping there? Anyone at all?"

"No, Lieutenant."

"Did he tell you of anyone else who knew his address?"

"No, Lieutenant, he say nothing."

"Screwy case!" Mack growled. "The lama told us a lot of stuff that I couldn't make head or tail of. That Reffner was killed because of his past Carmen, or something like that. Do you believe in that sort of junk, Chang?"

"My religion," Chang said evenly, "is personal affair that have nothing to do with murder of Mr. Reffner."

"All right, you can go."

"Talks too well," was Mack's verdict when Merriweather's secretary had left the room. "No Chinaman has a right to talk that well."

"Tibetan," Westborough corrected. "Chang is not a Chinese."

"Looks like one to me, and so does the lama. The lama talks in the sort of mixed-up way you'd expect a Chinaman to talk, but Chang doesn't. Too slick! He's holding back something, and I'll bet forty doughnuts on it. But it looks like both of them have airtight alibis for this job."

He referred to the pages of his pocket notebook. "I've got the times down here. Hamilcar Barca signs in between three and four o'clock, and he doesn't leave the hotel until after Reffner was killed—sometime between nine and eleven, according to Doc Hildreth. Well, Chang was at the Prescott House before five to ask for the lama, and he doesn't leave there until eight or so. We have Eb Vishart's word on both times. Chang's out."

"And the lama?"

"Out like a light! Remember all the thrill hunters who dropped in to see him after they'd read Blaze's piece in the afternoon paper? The clerk kept calling him each time a new one came in; he had to be in his room to answer the phone or we would have heard about it."

"True," Westborough admitted. "It seems logically impossible that either the lama or Chang could be Hamilcar Barca." He paused briefly. "But is our assumption that it was Barca who strangled Reffner justified?"

"Who else could it be?" Mack demanded brusquely.

Westborough shrugged his slight shoulders. "I do not know."

"There's only one other fellow in Chicago who might have a Tibetan scarf," Mack went on. "Merriweather. If he knew where Reffner was staying---"

"According to Chang, he did not know."

"How do we know Reffner didn't give Merriweather his address while Chang was out of the room?" Mack demanded. "Merriweather talked to Reffner a while before Chang got there. It says so in these notes Chang made."

"True," Westborough admitted. "But you cannot seriously suspect Mr. Merriweather?"

"You tell me who to suspect," Mack retorted. "This case is screwy. It's the perfect setup for an outside job—the stranger in town who's murdered and robbed at a cheap hotel. But this bit of silk narrows it down. Narrows it down too damn much! Who else in the city besides Merriweather collects Tibetan stuff ?"

"There is a very fine Tibetan collection in the Field Museum."

"Any white scarves there?"

Westborough shook his head. "Although I have had the pleasure of viewing the exhibits several times I am unable to recall seeing a single ka-ta."

"Any other Tibetan collections in Chicago?"

"I do not know of any."

"You're up on stuff like that, too."

"I am deeply interested in the history and in the customs of all races. But I must not be considered as any kind of authority on matters outside of my own narrow specialty."

"No? Bet you could talk Tibetan stuff all day with Merriweather. And you're smart, you keep your eyes open. If you stayed here you could---" He slapped his hands forcefully against his thighs. "If you stayed here . . . man, what an idea! Why don't you?"

"Stay here?" Westborough repeated in perplexity. "But I have not been asked."

"No, you haven't. We'll have to cook up some way to get Merriweather to ask you. It's the only way."

"The only way?"

"To get the truth out of this bunch. I've got a piece of white silk with some doodads embroidered on it that says Reffner's murderer came from this house. What's the answer? Stick around and find out. It's a case up your alley if there ever was one. All this Tibetan stuff!"

"But I am now in the midst of reading the proofs of my new book," the historian objected.

"That can wait, can't it?"

"I fear that it has waited far too long already," Westborough sighed.

"Send a wire to your publisher," Mack directed peremptorily. "Tell him he's got to give you an extra week on it. Just a week, that's all I ask. What's his address? I'll send the wire myself."

"It is difficult to resist you, John, but—"

"You liked the lama, I saw," Mack put in shrewdly. "He's Merriweather's house guest. If you stayed here you'd have the chance to get acquainted with him."

"The opportunity would be a rare privilege, but---"

"Think of all the junk Merriweather has in that museum of his! Bet there's nothing like it anywhere in this country. You'd have a swell time looking it over, you know you would!"

"Dear me!" Westborough murmured. "The offer is very tempting."

"Well, why don't you grab it then?"

"Dear me, I suppose that I shall have to."

"Atta boy!" Mack clapped the historian hard on the shoulder. "Just one thing left to settle. How are we going to get Merriweather to invite you?"

"Only that?" Westborough said dolefully.

"Ought to be a way to crack that nut," Mack maintained.

"But is there?"

"Sure," Mack insisted with cheerful optimism. "Here's one. You get started talking Tibetan stuff with Merriweather until he thinks you're an expert. Then you tell him you'd like to spend a few days with him going over the stuff in his museum. If he's any kind of guy at all he'll ask you to stay here."

"Impossible!" Westborough cried in horror. "I should never be able to delude Mr. Merriweather while there are two Tibetans in his home. I can neither speak nor read the Tibetan language."

"You read the Tibetan writing on the scarf," Mack said.

"Those characters are not in Tibetan but in Sanskrit —altogether a different language. Moreover (I trust you will forgive me for pointing this out, John), the fact that I came here in your company is not apt to recommend me to Mr. Merriweather as being a desirable guest."

Mack grinned. "He did pass some crack about me being insulting. Insulting when I hardly said a word to him!" He lapsed into a study. "I've got it. We'll work the old sprained-ankle gag."

"You mean that I should pretend to sprain my ankle so that Mr. Merriweather will be forced to invite me to stay here?"

"Sure, why not? I'll rush up and slap a bandage around your foot before anyone can tell whether it's swelling or not. Then you pretend you can't walk a step. If Merriweather puts you out he'll feel like a heel."

Westborough shook his head dubiously. "I do not believe, John, that you will be permitted to render first-aid treatment while there is a doctor in the house."

"Doctor?" Mack repeated. "Doctor—say, you've got something! I knew I had the right hunch when I told that sawbones to stick around. We'll get him to go in with us. Then Merriweather won't guess for a minute that our stunt isn't the real McCoy."

"Enlisting Doctor Walters' cooperation will be a feat of some difficulty."

"Oh, I don't know. I heard him telling you that he was a pal of Barry Foster's. Foster is a good friend of yours and that ought to count in your favor."

"I can scarcely believe that Doctor Walters will agree to betray a patient's confidence merely because he and I have a mutual friend," Westborough objected.

"Well, we can ask him, can't we?" Mack pushed the desk button. "If he turns us down we'll be no worse off than we were bef---- Oh, hello, Chang! You get here in a hurry, don't you? Is Doctor Walters still waiting out there ?"

The Tibetan laughed. Those who believe the stories about the sphinxlike imperturbability of the Oriental should be required to listen to hearty Tibetan laughter, Westborough reflected. "Yes, he walk back and forth in the hall. He is very angry with you, Lieutenant. He say that he is busy doctor and that you make him miss important engagements."

"Well, tell him to come on in," Mack directed brusquely. Chang bowed, a bow that was short and unceremonious. The Japanese, Westborough recalled, can be extremely insulting merely by extending a different degree of courtesy than that to which a person is entitled. He wondered if the same were not also true of Tibetans. Like the Japanese, they appeared to be an unusually sensitive race.

Dr. Walters strode indignantly into the study, clenching a stubby briar between his teeth. "About time!" he exclaimed. "Think I don't have any patients to see?"

"Thanks for sticking around, Doctor."

"Thank me for nothing!" The doctor blew a great cloud of blue smoke from his mouth, causing him to resemble, Westborough fancied, the genie who had appeared from the bottle in the Arabian Nights story. "Now what's it all about and what do you want with me?"

"We're investigating a murder, as I guess you've gathered."

The doctor grinned good-naturedly. "I'm not blind, and I've still

The Man from Tibet   85

got the full use of my ears. It was a man named Reffner."

"It was a man named Reffner," Mack repeated, stressing the past tense of the copula. "Do you know him?"

"No."

"Maybe you saw him when he called here yesterday?"

"Never saw him in my life. What's this leading to?"

"Sit down, Doc, and take a load off your feet."

Dr. Walters sank obligingly into one of the curule chairs and crossed his long legs. He had the happy faculty of making himself instantly at home. He was, Westborough decided, the type of tall young man who never becomes fat. He had broad, square shoulders, an oblong face with a heavy jaw, and a jutting nose. His mouth was large but was saved from overaggressiveness by the lines of humor which crinkled up at the corners. The teeth which clenched upon the thick stem of the doctor's pipe were excellent biting implements.

"I don't know why you want to talk to me," Walters remonstrated. "You came here to find the lama, I heard you say. Well, you've found him. I never saw him before in my life, and I don't know two words of Tibetan. Two? Hell's bells, I don't know one."

"I won't beat around the bush with you," Mack said directly. "You look like too smart a fellow. We've got good reason to think Reffner's murderer is someone in this house."

Westborough reflected that one may tell a great deal concerning the character of a man by the way he takes a startling bit of information. Dr. Walters took it calmly.

"Sounds crazy," he observed.

Mack nodded. "Yes, I know it does. But we found something---well, we won't go into that. I'll lay my cards on the table. We want your help."

"What kind of help?"

"I want to get Westborough into the house a few days—where he can keep an eye on things. We thought of having him stage a sprained ankle---"

Walters jumped indignantly to his feet. "I'll have nothing to do with it."

"No use losing your temper, Doc," Mack drawled. "If that's the way you feel about it we'll drop the idea."

"That's exactly the way I feel about it."

"All right, we're licked." Mack was silent for so long that Westborough wondered if he actually were conceding defeat—although that did not seem in the least like him. "'Didn't I hear you say awhile back that you were taking care of Merriweather for Doctor Pressinger?' he inquired.

"Yes, Mr. Merriweather is one of Doctor Pressinger's patients," Walters said in a noticeably cold manner.

"Pressinger is a heart specialist, isn't he?"

"One of the finest in the country. Why?"

"If Merriweather is one of his patients he's probably a heart case," Mack speculated. Dr. Walters said nothing. "Heart case," the detective repeated. "Fellow who needs quiet. Can't stand excitement. Has to have lots of rest. That describe him?"

"I have nothing to say regarding the case," Walters declared frigidly.

"No, of course you haven't," Mack drawled soothingly. "But you don't want Westborough in the house because strangers upset Merriweather. You're afraid his heart can't stand too much excitement. Is that it?"

"Not that alone," Walters snapped.

"But it is that," Mack insisted. "Now I'll leave it to you which is going to cause the least harm to Merriweather's heart: Westborough staying here unofficially in a quiet way or an obvious click from headquarters? Hell, you know the answer! I'll bet the very idea of having a plainclothes man in here would drive Merriweather half crazy."

"You can't put a man in here without Merriweather's consent."

"Can't I?" Mack was bluffing, of course, but his face didn't show it. "You can do lots of things on a murder case, Doctor. But if I had to go through the official channels to get a man in here it couldn't be Westborough. He's not on the force."

"Well?"

"It's up to you to say who does come. Westborough or someone else. You know Westborough. He's a quiet little guy who couldn't upset even a fellow with a bum heart. He can talk Tibetan stuff with Merriweather—they'd hit it off fine. And he'd be here unofficially; he won't be obligated to report to me at all if he doesn't want to. Which will be the least shock to your patient's heart? A man from headquarters or Westborough?"

"Westborough, of course," Dr. Walters answered. It was the first symptom of yielding he had displayed. "Certainly excitement wouldn't be good for Merriweather. But he's Pressinger's patient; I'm responsible to Pressinger. . . ." His voice trailed away, evidently unable to keep pace with his thoughts.

"If we're right about this business it may be dangerous for Merriweather," Mack said sententiously. "Damn dangerous!"

"Dangerous ? Why ?"

"Some murders go by pairs."

"You think Merriweather's life may be threatened?"

"It might be. That's why I'm going to have a man in here. You can't stop a thing till you find out what it is. I'm going to have a man here, and you can bet your last dollar on it. It's up to you to decide who that man's going to be."

"Suppose that I do play ball with you? Do you realize your sprained-ankle stunt is fundamentally unsound? Merriweather doesn't have to ask Westborough to stay here. We might ask him, but he doesn't have to. What's to stop him from calling up an ambulance to take him to the hospital?"

"We'll have to risk it."

"I'll have to risk it, you mean," the doctor snapped. "It's my professional reputation at stake, not yours. Well, suppose Merriweather does ask you to stay, Westborough? You can't go wandering around the house looking for clues when everyone knows you're supposed to be laid up with a sprained ankle."

"I believe that sprained ankles recover so that one may in two or three days time resort to hobbling with a cane."

"Then you'll be well enough to go home."

"Dear, dear, it does seem difficult."

"Calamity Jane!" Mack growled. "It took me fifteen minutes to talk him into agreeing to go into this."

"I don't blame you for hesitating. The idea's no good. Passing up the ambulance (I'd probably be able to talk Merriweather out of that) and assuming that Westborough is allowed to hobble around with his cane, it's still no good, and I'll tell you why. Merriweather's not a complete fool, and he's suspicious as a good many people with money are. He doesn't know a thing about Westborough except that he came here with you—which might mean that he's some sort of policeman. He knows that the three of us are in here talking. Now what's he going to say when we come out to stage that sprained-ankle stunt? Think he won't be able to put two and two together?"

"Good point," Mack acknowledged. "I've got to be out of here when it happens. And it has to happen later on. Say this afternoon."

"How am I to get back inside the house? How is Westborough? How are we to get here at the same time?"

"You'll get here at the same time because you'll arrange it that way. Let's make it five o'clock. If that's not okay, Doctor, say so. I don't know yet how Westborough's going to get in, but I know how you can. You can tell Merriweather you have to see him again because you're worried over his blood pressure or something. Hell! There ought to be half a million reasons you could give him."

Walters made a wry face. "I see that if you once start something like this you've got to go in it whole hog. All right, I'll be back here. Five o'clock, you said? Now for God's sake let me out. I have a few other patients to see today besides Merriweather."

"Toughest bit of selling I ever put across," Mack remarked after Walters had rushed tempestuously through the door. "These doctors! He doesn't like the idea one little bit, but he'll see us through. Now all you have to do is to think up some excuse to make to Merriweather for coming back here at five."

"All!" Westborough exclaimed in dismay. "Dear me, whatever shall I say to him?"

"That's your problem," Mack shrugged. "It better be good, and you'd better get started thinking on it because I'm having Merriweather in here right now." He pressed the pearl button. "I want to know where he spent his time yesterday from four o'clock on—at least where he says he spent it."

V

There was a smudge on the satin-smooth finish of the eighteenth-century table, Westborough noticed. Mack evidently had brushed against it during one of his frequent peregrinations about the room. Taking out his handkerchief, Westborough restored the polish. He was none too soon about it, for at that moment Adam Merriweather entered. His dignity was at least equal to that of an archbishop.

"Chang tells me that you have asked to see me."

"Mr. Merriweather, you can help us a lot." Mack had shed his hard-boiled mannerisms as a serpent its worn-out skin. "Help one, I should say, for, although Mr. Westborough is a good friend of mine, he isn't connected with the department. Would you mind answering a few questions?"

"Well, that depends," Merriweather said pompously. "What kind of questions?"

"Just official routine that I have to go through. It doesn't mean anything, but I have to go through with it. You understand, don't you?"

"I understand perfectly." Merriweather noted that Westborough was staring questioningly at the steel filing cabinet. "Useful for my papers. Fireproof and almost burglar proof. I'll admit it doesn't harmonize so well with the other furniture, but these Italian cabinets have such flimsy locks. Well, Lieutenant? I don't believe you want to chat about furniture?"

"If I did I wouldn't know what to say about it," Mack laughed. "I'm trying to find the time Reffner left your house yesterday. It's important for us to be able to trace his movements during the whole day."

Merriweather nodded sagely. "Yes, I can see that it would be. My impression was that he left here around four, but I do not remember consulting a timepiece. Did you ask Chang?"

"Yes, he said about four, too." Mack paused. "It's helpful to get things from as many different angles as we can."

"I can see that it would be. But whatever did you want with Doctor Walters? He was not here yesterday when Reffner called."

"I wanted to ask his professional advice."

"His professional advice?"

"Yes. Reffner was killed by strangling. There were a few questions about strangling that I wanted Walters' slant on."

"Reffner was strangled!" Merriweather had taken a pencil from his pocket and was nervously fiddling with it. "Is that why you're taking my scarf away?"

"Not exactly," Mack answered. It was his turn to be ill at ease.

"Scarves may be used for strangling," Merriweather persisted. "Come, Lieutenant, if I am suspected of this crime I wish you would be good enough to say so."

"You aren't suspected," Mack informed him. "Scarves can be used for strangling, but so can a hundred other things. That particular scarf interested me, that's all."

"Why should it interest you?" Merriweather demanded. "It's nothing to you that the Lama Tsongpun Bonbo presents me with a Tibetan ka-ta. And may I remind you that the scarf has a considerable monetary value? If it is in any way damaged I shall hold you personally responsible."

"You'll get it back," Mack declared. Only by the narrow slits his eyes had become was it possible for Westborough to guess the effort his friend was making to keep his temper in check. The historian decided to intervene. Relations with Adam Merriweather could not possibly be more strained than they were at that instant.

"It is a very fine ka-ta," he remarked. "One of the finest I have ever seen. These scarves, John, are made in a variety of sizes and with different grades of material. The more important the recipient, the more expensive must be the scarf which is presented to him. Hence it is easy for us to guess what the lama's opinion of Mr. Merriweather must be."

Merriweather smirked self-consciously. "Well, you've got to take the polite manners of these Orientals with a grain or two of salt. But it is a better ka-ta than any of the others in my collection."

"You have others, then?"

"Yes, two."

"Are they, like this one, embroidered with the celebrated mantra?"

Merriweather shook his head. "No, of plain white silk. I've never seen that mantra on a ka-ta before, but there's no reason why it shouldn't be there. The jewel-in-the-lotus formula is found everywhere in Tibet. 'Om mani padme hum! The dewdrop slips into the shining sea.' "

"Edwin Arnold?" Westborough inquired and was rewarded by a surprised glance from Adam Merriweather.

"You are familiar with *The Light of Asia*?"

"Yes, a most remarkable work. Particularly so when one considers that it was written by an extremely busy newspaper editor."

"Let's get back to yesterday afternoon," Mack cut in. "Merriweather, do you mind telling me what you did after Reffner left you?"

"The first thing was to read the afternoon *Bugle*."

"The *Bugle*, huh? See the story about the lama?"

"I certainly did."

"How'd that strike you?"

"It took me completely by surprise. I could scarcely think clearly, the coincidence was such an amazing one. I remember I called for Chang, but he had left the house. Without my knowledge, but I could do nothing. I am forced to put up with a great deal from Chang because he is irreplaceable. Tibetans are a proud race, and he cannot be treated as a servant."

"Where'd Chang go to?"

"I do not know. I asked him but he would not say."

"Was he gone long?"

"Gone long!" Merriweather exclaimed indignantly. "I should say he was! He did not return here until ten minutes to ten—an absence of six hours without a word of explanation. And when I asked him for one he pretended that he did not understand me and went upstairs to bed. I believe I mentioned before that I am forced to put up with a good many things from Chang."

Mack hastily jotted down some notes. "One more thing. Did you leave the house after you had finished reading the afternoon *Bugle*?"

Merriweather's shoulders stiffened in offended surprise. "I? You are inquiring concerning any movements?"

"Part of the official routine I told you about," Mack said conciliatingly. He was really handling Merriweather with a great deal of tact, Westborough reflected. "I have to ask you that question, or I'd lose my job. But it doesn't mean anything."

Merriweather unbent a trifle. "I understand. No, I did not leave the house. After finishing the paper I retired to my bedroom for a rest before dinner, since my aorta, unfortunately, is not in good condition. Alma, my sister, and I dined at our usual hour of seven-thirty. I recall that my son and Miss Shelton were absent, and we were forced to dine alone. After dinner I strolled to the terrace and remained for some time watching the moon rise over the lake and enjoying the luxury of a postprandial cigar—the only cigar that I am allowed by the medical profession."

"Was your sister with you on the terrace ?"

"No, Alma had gone to her sitting room upstairs to finish a book."

"How long did you stay there?"

"Until I heard Chang return to the house. That, as I have before stated, was at ten minutes to ten."

Westborough was only half listening to the conversation. His mind was busy with the excuse he must make for returning to Merriweather's house that afternoon. What kind of man was Merriweather mentally? He collected Tibetan manuscripts, he quoted from *The Light of Asia*. Was it possible, could it be possible that he had not bought the Padma Sambhava manuscript solely because of its historical value? Was he interested in Tibetan mysticism per se? Many people were.

The more he thought of it, the more plausible it seemed. And if so, Westborough now knew how the return visit might be effected. But he must be careful; the subject must be introduced delicately. One does not usually confess such predilections to strangers. The opening wedge? One's name, of course; there are few subjects in which a man is more interested, Merriweather's initials: A.H.M. Something might be done with that if one was astute enough to think what. A.H.M.? It should mean something, but if it did, Westborough did not know what. A.H.? Ah! Ah, indeed!

From one of the neatly arranged pigeonholes of his mind Westborough selected exactly the information he needed. He said excitedly:

"I beg your pardon, Mr. Merriweather, but I could not help considering your initials."

"My initials? What about them?"

"Your first two initials express phonetically the sound 'ah'. That is an extremely propitious circumstance, since the sound 'ah' is the syllable uttered by the primordial Adi-Buddha as he created the two crossed *dorjes* which form the foundations of the Lamaist universe."

Merriweather's eyes showed a gleam of interest; Westborough was sure of it.

"How did you know about that?" he asked.

"I recall reading it in Kustner's *Tibetan Mysticism*."

"Kustner? You have studied Kustner?"

"Yes, I am fortunate enough to own a copy of his work." He paused, knowing he must not be too obvious about it. "I ran across it quite by accident many years ago in a London bookstall and was at once intrigued by the title."

"Kustner is supposed to have gone deeper into the subject than anyone else," Merriweather informed them. "He lived for years in a lamasery."

"Yes. His material is fascinating, but unfortunately for Mr. Kustner's popularity it is presented in an extremely dull manner." Westborough paused. Merriweather was not rising to the bait at all. "By the way, Mr. Merriweather, is your own copy of Kustner the first or second edition?"

"The first," Merriweather answered. He turned upon the historian a slightly startled glance. "How did you know I owned one?"

"Any person of scholarly tastes interested in that subject would naturally acquire a copy of Kustner. He is, I believe, still considered the supreme authority."

"Doubtful," Merriweather took issue. "Kustner has been outmoded by later writers."

"I do not deny that Kustner made mistakes. Many of them were corrected in the later second edition. Do you own a copy of that also?" He tried not to display his anxiety. The whole plan hinged on Merriweather's answer.

"No." Merriweather had grown thoughtful. "I'd like to see one."

"That can be arranged very easily. My own copy is the second edition. I shall be glad to lend it to you."

"That is very kind of you."

"Not in the least. I can bring it out to you this very afternoon if you wish. I was planning upon coming out in this direction again today, as I must visit the Charles Deering Library at Northwestern University."

"But that will put you to a great deal of trouble, which I cannot allow. I'll send Chang to---"

"Not in the least," Westborough interposed hurriedly. "The trouble will be of the slightest, I assure you. Would five o'clock be a convenient hour?"

"Yes, I shall be here the entire afternoon. Are you sure, Mr. Westborough, that you will not be going out of your way ?"

"Not in the least. To tell the truth, Mr. Merriweather, I am rather looking forward to our little visit."

VI

Westborough, jolting northward in a bus, thought regretfully of his

galley proofs. He had sent the wire to his publisher as Mack had suggested, but his conscience still bothered him. Even yet it was not too
late to draw back.

No, he had already given his word to John Mack. When one has
burned one's bridge one does not dare to look backward. The bus passed
the Spanish bell towers of the Edgewater Beach Hotel. This was an adventure, Westborough reflected, one that promised to be more bizarre
than any he had yet experienced. How was it that he could not feel
more enthusiasm for what awaited him in Adam Merriweather's house?

The historian sighed and rang the bell for the bus to stop. "I wonder if I really like adventures," he mused. "No matter. They do seem to
like me."

Precisely at five o'clock the ponderous butler was showing him into
Adam Merriweather's living room.

"Right on the dot," Merriweather observed as he rose to greet his
guest.

"Punctuality is one of my few virtues," Westborough returned smilingly. He stared about him in frank pleasure. The room was extremely
well done.

Rough white plaster walls; aged tapestries from the looms of Ven-
ice. Italian furniture, all of the late Renaissance and apparently authentic. X-shaped Savonarola chairs—the camp chairs of former times—
with wrought-iron frameworks covered by purple and burgundy vel-
vets. High-backed chairs, resplendent in stamped leather and rich bro-
cades, standing as stiffly erect as the pride of their ancient owners. Massive *cassapanche*—those cushionless wooden seats that looked like uncomfortable church pews. The inevitable *cassone*. Console tables—heavens, such carving! Westborough could no longer restrain his enthusiasm.

"My dear Mr. Merriweather, never outside of Italy have I seen such
a room. You must have purchased the contents of an entire villa."

Merriweather nodded. "Exactly what I did do. May I present you to
my sister, Mrs. Gestler?"

"I am highly honored."

She was years younger than Merriweather; her heart-shaped face
bore not the slightest wrinkle. Her hair was jet black with the exception
of a single white lock; had some sudden shock occurred to turn it so
dramatically to silver? Smilingly she motioned him to be seated in one
of the X-shaped chairs. Westborough did so; he had a queer feeling as
he sat down that the iron arms on either side might suddenly constrict
about his body. Complete nonsense! Why the fancy should come to
him he did not know; he had sat in such chairs a great many times

before. But the room seemed to have grown gloomy.

He removed the book tucked under his arm and handed it to Merriweather. "Here is the work of which we were speaking today. Kustner's *Tibetan Mysticism.*"

"Thank you." Merriweather could scarcely restrain his eagerness to open it. "It is the second edition, I see. If you don't mind I shall keep it for a few days. I wish to compare it carefully with my own first edition."

"Pray keep it as long as you wish." Drawing a mental bow, Westborough fired an arrow at random. "Kustner relates some rather peculiar stories."

"Yes, I know." Merriweather thumbed hastily through the pages. "This doesn't seem to be much different from my own copy, but I'm glad to have the chance to look it over, nevertheless."

"Tibetan magic is Adam's pet hobby," Mrs. Gestler informed the historian. Merriweather turned on his sister with a look of intense malevolence. "I wish, Alma, that you'd stop speaking flippantly of matters you are incapable of understanding."

She laughed mischievously. "Ouch! After that there's nothing for me to do but order tea. You will have some with us, won't you, Mr. Westborough?"

The historian accepted gratefully. The invitation came as a godsend since Dr. Walters had not yet arrived, and it was difficult to estimate just when he would be able to get here. Crumpling out her cigarette, Mrs. Gestler rose from her chair. Westborough's eyes followed her as she walked from the room. Beneath her thin afternoon gown the muscles moved as sinuously as serpents.

As soon as they were alone Merriweather moved his chair to a confidential distance. "You have studied this subject which Kustner discusses?"

"In a small way, yes."

"Good. It is a pleasure to talk with an intelligent person. Most of the material-minded fools about us would pronounce Kustner, for instance, to be insane. Yet he was one of the greatest oriental scholars the world has known; he studied many years in a lamasery, living as an actual monk; he had every opportunity to see there the actual things he reports."

"All that is true," Westborough conceded, "but I must confess to a certain sympathy with the material-minded people you mention. Some of the incidents which Kustner cites are very difficult to—shall we say swallow?"

"They have all been verified from later sources," Merriweather contended. "Have you read Alexandra David Neel? She has had firsthand experience with them all. The *tumo*—the psychic heat that enables certain lamas to melt snowdrifts with their naked bodies. The breath-control secret that makes it possible for other *gurus* to run continuously for days and nights at a time without once halting for rest. Think of it! At the altitudes of the Tibetan plateau most Olympic champions would be winded in a few minutes of running. Yet the gurus who know this secret are able to keep up their constant pace, not for hours, but for days."

"Such feats are indeed remarkable."

"Remarkable!" Merriweather snorted. "I should say so! Mental telepathy has been developed to an exact science. Tibetans call it sending a message 'on the wind.' But all of these are nothing in comparison with the creation of *tulpas*. Do you know what they are?"

"Thought forms," Westborough replied immediately. He had that afternoon taken the precaution of refreshing his memory of these amazing topics. "Illusions which have no real existence."

"Who knows what's real and what's not? Buddhists say that everything comes from the mind; how do you know they are not right? Tulpas can look like men, can walk like them and act like them. The lamas who have learned the power of concentrating their thought can even materialize the demons that guard their religion, I've heard. These stories can't be dismissed as fairy tales; there are too many Westerners who have seen them happen. But the Tibetan priesthood guards its secrets jealously, I can tell you. Those secrets are the real reasons why Tibet remains a closed country. Someday, however, one of us will succeed in breaking down the barriers—I mean the mental barriers and not the physical ones. He who does that will have powers, such powers as---"

Adam Merriweather's voice hushed suddenly as a young man in a light gray suit entered the room.

"Hello, Dad! Seen Janice anywhere?"

"Vincent!" Merriweather exclaimed severely. "May I ask what brings you home at ten minutes past five?"

"I left the office early."

"Evidently! And arrived late as usual, I presume?"

The young man shifted uncomfortably from foot to foot. "Well, I got to thinking that Janice might like a swim with me before dinner."

"Swim!" Merriweather exploded. "Swim! Are you a young man who is laying the foundation of his business future, or are you a duck? It is difficult at times to realize that you are my son, Vincent."

"You know I don't like it there."

"We are all forced at times to perform tasks that we do not like, Vincent."

"You weren't!" the young man cried hotly. "All your life you've done only what you wanted to, and so has Uncle Jed. But it's different with me, you say. Just why should it be different?"

"We will not discuss that matter now, Vincent. We have a visitor. Mr. Westborough, my son Vincent."

Vincent acknowledged the introduction sulkily. He was taller than his father but very thin—an anemic, unhealthy thinness. His lips were curved into the pout of a spoiled child.

"And now," Westborough asked, "I have met all your family, have I not? That is, with the exception of your distinguished brother, whose great work, *The Races of Turkestan*, I so admire."

The petulance disappeared as if by magic from Vincent's face. "Oh, you'd like Uncle Jed! Everyone does. He's going to be here tomorrow."

"Within a few days at the most," Merriweather qualified. "In the last letter I received from him he said he was not quite sure of his plans."

"I hope that I shall have the honor of meeting him," Westborough murmured. But he was secretly aghast at the news. Although Adam Merriweather's house was a large one, so was his household. He already had one house guest—the Lama Tsongpun Bonbo. Now a second was expected. Could there possibly be room for a third?

Westborough did not know. Nor could he think of any way in which the subject might be tactfully broached. There appeared to be no other course open than to proceed with their plan and trust to luck. However, he did wish that Dr. Walters would make his appearance.

Footsteps sounded in the hall outside, and Westborough listened hopefully, but it was only Mrs. Gestler, followed by the butler carrying a tea tray. She supervised its placement upon a seventeenth-century stool supported by exquisitely carved cherubim.

"Will you have tea with us, Vin?"

"No thanks, Alma. I'm going to hunt up Janice."

"You will find her on the beach," Mrs. Gestler informed him.

"Thanks, I'll go out there. Well, glad I met you, Mr. Westborough."

"Young wastrel," Merriweather fumed as his son left the room. "Won't even try to learn the business and make something out of himself. Doesn't want to do anything but spend money foolishly."

Mrs. Gestler smiled enigmatically as she lifted the teapot. "My dear Adam! This, of all people, from you!"

"Well---er—hum. At least, Alma, I---"

"Cream or lemon, Mr. Westborough?"

"Lemon, please. This invitation is extremely kind of you."

Hoping to make his tea last as long as possible, Westborough sipped very slowly. From a point far down the hall he heard the sound of a bell. He listened intently. It was a doorbell, he was sure, and not a telephone.

Could it be Dr. Walters at last? No, it was only a telegram, which the butler was bringing into the room on a silver salver.

"Pardon me, but this may be urgent," Merriweather said. He tore the envelope hastily open. "No, it's only Jed."

"I hope that nothing has interfered with his plans to visit us," Mrs. Gestler exclaimed.

"No, he's on the train now—this was sent from Kearney, Nebraska, at three-sixteen this afternoon. He'll be here at eight thirty-five tomorrow morning. Wonder if that's daylight saving time or not. Just like Jed to assume we have nothing to do but memorize train schedules. Well, Vincent can look it up. He may want to meet the train."

"May want to?" Mrs. Gestler repeated, inserting a fresh cigarette into her green jade holder. "All of Clyde Beatty's lions and tigers couldn't keep that boy away from the railroad station."

Dear, dear, it would be extremely awkward if there were no more rooms available, Westborough was thinking. One could not ask—dear me, no! What could be detaining Dr. Walters? He was now at least half an hour behind his sched--- But the doorbell was ringing again. Could it really be he at last?

This time it was Dr. Walters, who was entering the living room with a physician's cool deliberation. He said with facetious sternness to Merriweather: "My conscience bothered me about letting you off this morning. You've had lots of excitement today, and excitement isn't the best thing for you."

"No," Merriweather agreed. "It certainly is not. Good of you to come back, Walters. Would you mind excusing us for a few minutes, Westborough? Walters' examination won't take long."

"Dear me, I fear that I must be going," Westborough exclaimed, returning his cup and saucer to the tea tray. "I have enjoyed my visit with you and your sister so much."

"Well, I appreciate the loan of your Kustner. Hope I can return the favor sometime. You must come out to meet Jed."

"I shall be extremely happy to do so," Westborough murmured.

He turned to thank his hostess. When he had said as few words as the dictates of manner would permit he saw that Merriweather and the doctor had already gone into the hall. Westborough followed, knowing that the spurious accident had to take place there or not at all. The hall was not too brilliantly illuminated, and there was a Persian prayer rug at its entrance which afforded excellent sliding possibilities.

Westborough stepped upon the prayer rug with a prayer—a prayer that he would be able to make it slip. He need not have worried; it slid very easily. His legs were out of control before he realized it, and gravity impelled him toward the floor a good bit harder than he had intended.

At least, however, he had succeeded in making a great deal of noise. Both Merriweather and Dr. Walters had turned and were now coming toward him with exclamations of alarm. Westborough rested both hands on the floor and made a futile attempt to hoist himself to his feet. His face twisted into what was, he hoped, a grimace of pain.

"Dear me, that was incredibly clumsy. I am very sorry, but I fear that something has happened to my ankle."

PART FIVE: The Man from San Francisco
(Wednesday, July 21)

U NDER THE multistoried ceiling of the North Western station waiting room Vincent Merriweather was one among hundreds of insignificant atoms. Atoms aloof in lonely silence. Atoms chattering like
monkeys in gregarious groups. Atoms scurrying through the station as
though the fate of the world were hanging on their arrival. Atoms walking as slowly as persons moving to impending doom. Male atoms: in
shirtsleeves, in business suits or in white flannels. Female atoms: smartly
gowned or in gingham. Juvenile atoms: well behaved (not many),
screaming and obstreperous. Hundreds of atoms! Not one knowing,
not one caring what would become of its fellows.

"A microcosm of Chicago," reflected Vincent, who was young
enough to be cynical. Strolling across the waiting room floor, he read
the legend on a blackboard above his head:

INCOMING TRAINS
Three minutes before arrival
track number will be shown below.

But the track number had not yet been posted; he was a few seconds too early. Vincent employed the time in gazing across the platform at the block-long line of track gates. So many gates! Gates for
smug commuters which swung aside each evening into suburban re-
spectability. Gates for blase salesmen to the wearisome grind of the road.
Gates for frenzied businessmen which might open on success or on
ruin. Gates for vacationers leading into enchanted gardens from which
they would be ruthlessly evicted in a fortnight. Gates for the adventurous—gates that meant new lives.

A voice above Vincent's head boomed through a megaphone: "Train
number 28, Overland Limited from San Francisco, arriving on Track
4." Vincent strolled toward the track gates. "Within three minutes—five
minutes at the most—I'll see him," he thought. "I haven't seen him in

99

over a year. Uncle Jed. But I see Dad every day. Why can't it be the other way round?"

A little knot of people had already gathered at the entrance to Track 4. Like him they were waiting for someone, waiting for the gate to open. Now the train could be heard, now it could be seen, now its hundreds of tons of weight had glided into place with a dancing ;instructor's mincing precision. The huge black mass that was the engine hissed exultation at accomplishing the arrival on schedule.

Vincent hurried down the platform. The train that had so lately hurtled the leagues across the continent had become the bulky and inert wall upon his right. People passed him: men, women, children. So many people! Where did they all come from? Redcaps staggering under the burden of half-a-dozen suitcases. Baggage carts. People. More people. And Uncle Jed at last! Black-bearded, broad-shouldered Uncle Jed, skimming through the crowd like a racing craft through surf.

Uncle Jed had seen him. Uncle Jed was wringing his hand. They were walking through the station waiting room, a redcap following with Uncle Jed's suitcase. They were pausing at the newsstand. Uncle Jed bought a paper and his face grew grave.

" 'Fighting Near Peiping; Japanese Will Land 35,000 Troops.' Vin, it looks bad. This time it isn't just another Manchuria, another Jehol. The Nanking government has been super patient, it has swallowed colossal affronts because it was playing a waiting game. The clever waiting game at which Chinese diplomats excel! But the time for that game is over; Nanking has to fight or go under. And if I know Chiang Kai-shek, Nanking will astonish the world with the fight it puts up."

"How does it affect us?" Vincent asked with an anxiety which he made no pretense of concealing. "Will it stop the expedition?"

"It will block the way in from China."

"Yes, but the western way, the one from Kashmir through Ladakh?"

"It will be open. It's the hardest, the most dangerous caravan trail on the face of the earth, but it will be open."

"What about Sinkiang?" Vincent inquired.

"There shouldn't be any fighting there. Most of Sinkiang is under Soviet influence and pays no allegiance to the Nanking government. The Tungans, of course, hold the strip of oases along the south where I plan to operate."

"The Tungans are your friends, aren't they?"

Uncle Jed nodded. "I get along pretty well with their leaders; they'll give me almost any sort of permit I ask for. And while they are a set of hard-boiled ruffians, they keep their words."

"Then what is the trouble?"

"Mostly financial. I need money—lots of it—and I haven't got it. Four men were going to back me. Two of them live in San Francisco and two in Chicago. The two in San Francisco backed out with the first rumors of trouble between China and Japan."

"Cowards!" Vincent exclaimed contemptuously.

"I wouldn't call them that, exactly. They didn't think that I'd be able to accomplish anything if I had to run into a hornets' nest, and maybe they are right. I don't think so, but that's only my personal opinion. At any rate, if the expedition is to start next spring as we planned, your father and the other Chicagoan, Salman, will have to shoulder the whole burden."

"Will they?"

"I don't know. Salman is conservative; I'll be lucky to hold the support he's promised, let alone get anything else from him. And your father—well, he's helped me three times before. It is possible that he may be a little tired of my holding out the hat."

"How much do you need?"

"At least fifty thousand."

"Is that all?"

"Is that all!" Jed mocked. "There speaks the rich man's son."

"You were a rich man's son yourself, Uncle Jed."

"Yes, but that was long ago. I not only squandered my substance but came back and slaughtered the fatted calf myself before anyone could think of ordering it killed for me. Since then I've been living on husks and trying to talk myself into believing that husks are better for the digestion. How's Janice, by the way?"

"Fine."

"You don't sound enthusiastic about her."

"Don't I ?"

"Men don't usually speak of their fiancees in monosyllables."

They walked down the staircase to Canal Street. "Janice is all right," Vincent said confidentially. "She's a nice girl, and I think a lot of her, honestly I do. But do you like to have anything---even if it's as sweet as chocolate candy—crammed down your throat?"

Jed shook his head. "I see your point, Vin."

"Why does he have to run my whole life?" Vincent demanded hotly. "Whom I should marry, where I should work, what I should do! I'm not going to put up with it much longer. I can't put up with it."

Jed laid a hand conciliatingly on his nephew's shoulder. "You take it too seriously, Vin. One of the troubles of being twenty-one. It's a great age, but one lacks a sense of proportion. Making any progress in Tibetan?"

"Some. Chang doesn't seem to think I'm doing so badly. But it's a hard language."

Jed nodded confirmatively. "One of the most difficult in the world. But you'll pick it up, all right. You have a natural gift for languages, Vin. How's the wind, by the way ?"

The question caused Vincent to wince noticeably. "Still not so good. I swim every morning and every night, but it doesn't seem to improve much. Uncle Jed, do you think I'll ever be in shape? Is there any use in my trying?"

"Of course there is." Jed laid his hand affectionately across the boy's narrow shoulders. "Is that your car by the no-parking sign? Lucky you didn't get a ticket! Would you mind driving me over to the Pure Oil Building? I want to try to catch Salman this morning."

Vincent inserted his ignition key and swung his cream-colored roadster eastward into Wacker Drive. He had a large budget of remarkable news to deliver to his uncle, and he talked without a pause all the way to the Pure Oil Building. Jed climbed down from the car.

"Thanks, Vin. Now you can drive around the block for fifteen minutes, if you have time, but you needn't wait any longer than that. If I'm able to stay over fifteen minutes with Salman things will be all right."

Vincent, however, circled the block for half an hour. He was just about to give up and drive on when he saw his uncle emerging from the swinging doors of the Pure Oil Building. Vincent honked his horn.

"You stayed longer than fifteen minutes," he said as his uncle climbed into the roadster. "Does that mean everything's all right?"

Jed's lips were smiling, but his broad shoulders drooped in a manner that Vincent had never seen before. "No, Vin, on the contrary. Everything is completely wrong."

PART SIX: From the Notebook of Theocritus Lucius Westborough (Wednesday, July 21)

I HAVE BEEN STUDYING how I may compare this prison there I live unto the world." I do not know why these lines from *Richard II* came unheralded into my mind, nor why they exercise such a peculiar fascination. *This prison where I live!*

It is, first of all, a magnificent prison. Lorenzo de' Medici himself would not complain of my bedstead, a high-post curtained affair, whose headboard and posts are loaded with a veritable garden of fruits and flowers carved in half-relief. I have Florentine monastery chairs and an ornate *sgabello*, which increases my admiration for the Spartan qualities of Venetian princes since it is probably the most uncomfortable seat devised by man. Towering above all else is an imposing wardrobe of architectural dimensions, which must have cost a small fortune to ship here. But, for all its ducal grandeur, the room has the air of a museum. I suspect that it is rarely, if ever, used for the homely purposes of a bedroom.

Even I, loving Italy as I do, turn from the Renaissance with welcome relief to my small balcony, where one may enjoy a splendid view of Lake Michigan. I should like to sit in the sunshine, on one of those very modern chairs of chrome tubes and red leather which I can see through the glass of the doorway, and watch the blue shimmer of the waters, the flash of white sails across the horizon.

But this I dare not do; by order of Dr. Waters I am today confined to my bed. Should I regain the use of my ankle too quickly, I fear that the fraud would be quickly discovered. I have had so many visitors!

Miss Shelton was the first. She came to bring my breakfast and remained to chat while I consumed my toasted muffins and coffee. Although I found her charming company, I must confess to a certain uneasiness while she remained with me. One detests the necessity for deceiving such friendly, unsuspecting persons.

Dr. Walters arrived while Miss Shelton was in the room, a circumstance which made for something of a dilemma. In her presence he did not dare to unbandage my unswollen ankle; neither did he dare refuse to look at it. And he must either unbandage it or refuse. Therefore--- well, what the outcome would have been I do not know. Fortunately Vincent Merriweather resolved the dilemma by calling to his fiancee to join him in an early morning dip.

No sooner had Miss Shelton left us than we were visited by the elder. Mr. Merriweather. Dr. Walters expressed grave concern over the state of my ankle and ordered me, in Mr. Merriweather's presence, not to leave my bed during the day. I fear that the doctor is taking a sly revenge for having been lured into this plot against his will.

Mrs. Gestler was the next to visit me. I learned from her that the summer has been a very dull one because all of her friends have been out of town. Although she would like to join them, she cannot because of Adam (I use first names merely for brevity's sake), who refuses to spend a single day apart from his Tibetan collection. Thanks to the long nose of the excellent Mrs. Grundy, Alma cannot leave Adam unless she takes Janice with her. But Janice (the pretty Miss Shelton) will not leave Vincent, and Vincent is forced by Adam to work in the steel company office, thus completing the vicious circle. I sympathized with her complicated predicament and, impelled by my avocation of snoop, directed the conversation to the subject of books.

I discovered that she is absorbed in an ultra-long novel of the Civil War period, which she has found so fascinating that the past two nights have been devoted to its perusal. I did not dare at that time to attempt to probe further. The information, although of slight value, confirms to some extent Merriweather's account of their Monday evening.

During the next two hours I entertained no more visitors except the butler, Wilkins, who came to remove my breakfast tray. Him I pumped assiduously. I began by discussing the subject of memories. Was it not true, I asked, that in his profession a good memory is one of the first essentials? He owned that such was the case. I confessed that my own memory is extremely faulty; that I could not, for instance, re-call the details of so short a time as two evenings ago. As I had hoped, he was unable to resist the temptation of displaying his superiority in this respect.

"That would be Monday evening, sir. On that evening Dr. Merriweather dined alone with Mrs. Gestler. Miss Shelton and Mr. Vincent had been invited out, I believe to a beach party. Immediately after dinner Mrs. Gestler went upstairs, and Mr. Merriweather strolled outdoors to the terrace. I did not see him again for nearly two hours."

I abridge, to some extent, Wilkins' conversation. Many superfluous details were included, showing that his memory is indeed a highly trained one. I expressed my admiration vociferously, and he left, greatly pleased, with the tray. It had been more than a trifle obvious, but I do not believe that he suspected that I had ulterior motives. I trust that he will not reveal our discussion to his employer or, most of all, to Chang. I cannot help but feel that of all those in the Merriweather household Chang alone looks at me askance. I must tread carefully where Chang is concerned. He is as alert, as watchful as a cat.

My next visitors were Vincent Merriweather and his uncle. Yes, I have met the famous Dr. Merriweather, and I have found him fully as remarkable as his accomplishments would lead one to believe. He is not tall, he is not physically imposing, but his vitality is tremendous. He is like a god—a copper-skinned, black-haired god of exploration. His personality is, in fact, almost too powerful. One seems to receive shocks from him as from an electric eel.

Despite his coarse and exuberant beard Dr. Merriweather has lost the hair of his head except for a small fringe along the back and over his temples. The tendency to alopecia appears to be a hereditary trait of the three male Merriweathers. Adam's baldness is more pronounced than that of his brother, and even Vincent's fair hair is beginning to thin over his forehead.

The question of Merriweather heredity is indeed an interesting one. Both Adam and Vincent have the same pale, almost expressionless turquoise eyes. The only difference between them is that the eyes of the father, for some unknown reason, convey the impression of emotional sterility while those of the son do not. Jed's eyes are markedly at variance. They are of a deep brown, almost black, and make one think of shafts opening into tremendous depths. But not vacant shafts.

By contrast with his dynamic uncle, Vincent Merriweather appears colorless. He is shy, obviously not sure of himself, perhaps a little spoiled. But he has an excellent mind. Our three-cornered conversation, brief as it was, touched upon a number of difficult subjects. The remarks which Vincent contributed were always pertinent ones, as I recall it. There is good material in the boy; much might be made of him if the right person would take the trouble to mold his character. The right person is, of course, his uncle, whom Vincent obviously idolizes.

Later in the day I was honored by a visit from the Lama Tsongpun Bonbo, who, having heard that "Kusho Wes-bo-ro" had been injured, wished to call to express his sympathies. He was much taken by my view of the lake and inquired if I could tell what the great body of water was named.

"Lake Michigan," I informed him. He repeated the words and added a little wistfully, "It not being blue as Tso Map-hang."

We discussed Buddhism for some little time. I listened with pleasure while he endeavored to enlighten me concerning some of its abstruse metaphysics, but may I add that I found his quaint speech sometimes difficult to follow? In the Tibetan grammar, I have read, "to be" is the only true verb. All of the other words which do the work of verbs are in reality nouns. This peculiarity of language structure may explain to some extent the lama's remarkable preference for our gerund.

I wonder how the misconception became promulgated that we of the West cannot understand Orientals? The lama's personality is no more enigmatic than that of a confiding child. He is punctiliously courteous and has, moreover, a delightful sense of humor.

Adam Merriweather, I have learned with surprise, has not promised to return the manuscript he purchased from Reffner to its rightful owner. Yesterday the lama, with engaging simplicity, offered for his precious document an entire satchel filled with currency—over twenty thousand dollars, I believe—but the offer has been neither accepted nor rejected.

Legally, of course, Merriweather has no true claim, but proof of ownership may prove troublesome to the lama. Although the notes made by Chang of Reffner's story may undoubtedly be subpoenaed as evidence, perhaps a court would not hold such notes conclusive. In that event Tsongpun Bonbo might even be forced to return to Tibet in order to secure depositions with regard to the manuscript's ownership. (The introduction of Tibetan depositions into an American court is, however, a matter beyond my powers of speculation.)

The lama, entirely ignorant of American jurisprudence, is firmly convinced that possession in this case is not merely nine tenths of the law but the law itself. Merriweather has in no way attempted to dispel this delusion. He is enjoying too much posing as my Lord Bountiful for whose favor the lama must sue if he wishes the return of his treasure. This last sentence may be unjust to Mr. Merriweather, but at the present moment I do not think so.

Of course I cannot allow the situation to continue indefinitely. Unless the lama receives satisfaction in a few days I shall have to see that he is placed in touch with a competent attorney. For the present, however, I am helpless. I dare tell the lama nothing that would imperil my own position as house guest.

Perhaps, after all, I have misjudged Mr. Merriweather. Perhaps he will eventually decide of his own accord to part with his newly acquired treasure when it has been translated for him. Chang has been working all day on such a translation. But Merriweather, when he revealed this information to me, cautioned me to say nothing of it to the lama. He feels that the lama win be extremely upset if he learns that "Guru Padma's precious words" are being turned into a tongue which the pyi-ling can peruse.

The ancient manuscript is one of amazing interest. With the aid of a book which Mr. Merriweather loaned to me from his library I have been refreshing my memory of its supposed author, Padma Sambhava, the "Precious Teacher-Born-of-the-Lotus."

He whom the lotus thus chose to honor was the exponent par excellence of Tantrik Buddhism, that cult of magic spells and mystic powers which he introduced into Tibet during the eighth century under the name of Dorje Thegpa, the "Thunderbolt Vehicle." His wizardry destroyed the shamans of the primitive Bon religion, who were hindering the spread of Buddhism throughout Tibet, and converted the demons they worshipped into defenders of the Buddha's doctrine. (It is interesting to observe that many of the more hideous figures in the Lamaist pantheon were once Bon deities.)

Having thus established Buddhism (although Buddhism of a degenerate brand, bearing little relation to the austere and intellectual beauty of Sakyamuni's doctrine), Padma Sambhava disappeared from Tibet. He did not die—a teacher of such eminence could no more die in the ordinary manner than he could be born in the conventional way—he simply disappeared, "riding a winged horse through the clouds," in the poetic language of Tibetan legends. But there is a tradition that his work in Tibet has not yet been finished.

Tibetans of the present day, I am led to understand, do not like to talk about Padma Sambhava overmuch. In their religious paintings he is usually pictured with a frowning, angry face; they look forward with dread to the time when he will be forced to return to their land.

For Padma Sambhava was no mild and gentle Buddha turning the Wheel of the Law, but a prophet of uncertain disposition, of furious rages, given to blasting out of existence those who dared attempt to thwart his will. Mere superstitions, of course. And yet Jack Reffner, he who stole the manuscript containing Padma's spells, died by a most mysterious agency. . . .

Despite Lieutenant Mack's firm conviction I cannot believe that Reffner's murderer is within this house. The possible suspects under this roof can under no stretch of the imagination be more than three. The Lama Tsongpun Bonbo is morally incapable of murder, a crime even more abhorrent to a Buddhist than to a Christian, and has, moreover, a watertight alibi. Chang, although a man of strong physique who could easily perform the act of strangling, has also an invulnerable alibi.

(N.B. Has Chang remained a Buddhist? If so, is he also a Lamaist, since the two are by no means synonymous?)

There remains, then, for consideration only Adam Merriweather. I am his guest; he has been most kind to me; I dislike to confess (even in these notes which he will never see) that I can evoke little admiration for him. But common honesty will allow me no other course.

I have observed that Merriweather is both cruel and unjust in with-holding the lama's property, that he praises Chang (who works hard for him) but little, that he bullies his son, that he is more than resentful of his distinguished brother's reputation. I have found in him neither true scholarship nor even a first-class mind. Intellectually his accom-plishments compare with those of Dr. Merriweather as a marble com-pares in size with a medicine ball.

Psychologically I wonder if it were not an unconscious desire to rival his more brilliant brother that led him to take up his strange study. In all lands throughout the ages mysticism has ever been the refuge of those who have failed in the normal life of every day. But enough of this. I have said many unkind things of Mr. Merriweather, none of which, however, point to him as the culprit for whom we search. He does not possess the ruthlessness of a killer, he had no motive for the crime, and his alibi, if not so good as those of Chang and the lama, cannot be challenged.

But just as I am forced into the inescapable conclusion that the murderer of Reffner is not among those in this household that trouble-some Tibetan scarf comes, like a toccata of Galuppi's, to unsettle me once more. I am seized with a wild fancy. I wonder if what has hap-pened so far is not but mere prologue to that which is to follow.

Heaven help all poor souls lost in the dark!

PART SEVEN: "Yun-drun! The yun-drun of Bon!"
(Thursday, July 22)

WESTBOROUGH PUSHED ASIDE the curtains of his Italian bed to glance toward his balcony. It was very early; the sun was as yet no more than a ball of fiery orange, poised at the horizon across the gray expanse of Lake Michigan. Climbing down from the uncomfortable glory of his Renaissance sleeping prison, the historian hastily donned his dressing gown and slippers.

Fortunately there was a cane in the room which he could take with him. His ankle must not show too complete a recovery. He hoped that he would meet no one during this matutinal prowl, but there was always the risk of an encounter.

He opened the door into the corridor. The house seemed to be as quiet as the night before Christmas. He crossed to the railing surrounding the interior court in which the Tibetan Room was located. From the second story one could look directly into that huge room.

Westborough gazed downward through a grating of painted beams but could see no one. He walked softly down the corridor. He passed the door of the lama's bedroom, not without trepidation. Tibetans were in the habit of rising very early, were they not? He tiptoed down the back stairs. Chang was another real danger. If he encountered Chang now, he did not know what would happen. However, he must not dwell upon these contingencies. In the wise words of Marcus Aurelius: "Forward, as occasion offers."

The noble Roman's philosophy, however, was sometimes difficult for one of a normally timid temperament to follow, Westborough reflected as his hand closed upon the doorknob of the Tibetan Room. Although he had seen no one from the second story, could he be sure that no one was within now? Was it wise to enter? He was very sure that it was extremely unwise, yet he opened the door. A row of twelve oriental images stared reprovingly at him from behind the yellow altar. But no human occupant stared with them.

Nevertheless, Westborough felt a little uncomfortable as he walked between the giant forms of the Yellow and Red kings. It seemed as if he were violating a sanctuary, the sanctuary over which those grotesque guardians kept ward. But he had now gone too far for retreat.

He had believed that Merriweather's Tibetan scarves would be in the glass case at the eastern end of the room —among the charm boxes, earrings, rosaries and prayer wheels—and the belief was well founded. He spied them immediately: two, as Merriweather had said, each neatly folded under a card with the legend, "Ka-ta, or Tibetan ceremonial scarf."

Westborough discovered by test that the sliding door to the glass case was not locked. However, he hesitated before inserting his hand. If someone in the household should catch him in this act it would look as though he were attempting a theft. Nevertheless, there was no help for it. He had to examine those scarves.

He found them both of plain white silk without embroidery, exactly as Adam Merriweather had described them. Could it be possible that the collector had been lying? That he had once owned another ka-ta similar to the one which Tsongpun Bonbo had presented to him?

And the lama. How many ka-tas did he own when he first came to the Prescott House? How many did he have now? For some reason he had not been asked these simple arithmetical questions. Westborough promised himself that the error would be rectified today. But it was entirely possible that the lama would not know. He did not seem to be so very practical.

Carefully folding the two scarves, Westborough replaced them within the case and closed the sliding door. His errand was now accomplished, but the images behind the L-shaped platform tempted him to linger. On his previous visit to this room he had been able to examine them only superficially; he wanted very much to make a closer inspection.

No, he must not stay here. He was courting discovery, it was too dangerous. But he could not dismiss them so cursorily—these important deities of the Lamaist mythology. He must at least discover the identity of the three female figures at the short eastern end of the raised platform. He could read their names from the cards placed before each image.

The first was Pal-den Lha-mo, whom Tibetans so fear that they dare not speak her name but refer to her only by the vague term, "the Goddess." Riding sidesaddle upon a long, angular mule, the Goddess had short legs, bare toes and pendulous breasts, but at this point resemblance to a woman ceased; it was virtually impossible for the human brain to conceive a more hideous creature than this dreaded fury. In one hand she carried a death's-head scepter, in the other a skull drinking bowl; on her head she wore a wreath of smaller skulls, and her saddle was a freshly flayed skin, according to tradition that of her own son, whom the amiable mother had destroyed. Westborough turned to the next image.

Dorje Pa-mo, the "Thunderbolt Sow," was, aesthetically, not much of an improvement, since she had three heads and three pairs of arms. Her right head was that of a sow, and she sat in a four-wheeled cart drawn by a herd of nine swine. The third feminine deity, Drol-ma, the green Goddess of Mercy, returned to the normal complement of arms and head. Despite her green color she was very near to Western ideas of beauty with her straight nose, cupid's-bow mouth, smiling lips and long, delicate fingers. The oblique eyes alone were peculiarly oriental.

It was now high time to go, but Westborough, turning to leave the room, found himself face to face with a gilded image of particular significance. "Padma Sambhava, dear me!" He must have at least a glance at that great wizard whose spells Jack Reffner had stolen.

Padma Sambhava frowned upon his admirer in an extremely severe manner. The mighty sorcerer was equipped with three eyes (including, of course, the conventional "Eye of Wisdom" in the center of his forehead), a Kaiser mustache, earrings which drooped to his shoulders, and a miter crowned with a long peacock feather. He was seated in the Buddha posture upon the spreading leaves of the lotus from which he had so miraculously sprung fully grown. " 'And I will restore to you the years that the lotus hath eaten,'" Westborough murmured. He fancied that Padma Sambhava's frown deepened at the atrocious pun.

Next to Padma Sambhava was another important prelate of the Lamaist church, Tsong-ka-pa, the founder of the now dominant Yellow Hat sect or Ge-lug-pa to which the Lama Tsongpun Bonbo belonged. It was this Tibetan Martin Luther who had endeavored, with some success, to free Buddhism from the Tantrik mumbo jumbo of magic and sensuality into which it had degenerated by the fourteenth century. Tsong-ka-pa's face, unlike that of the frowning Padma Sambhava, was placid and kindly. His conical miter bore a strikingly odd resemblance to the cowls which medieval monks of western Europe had worn.

The sublime features of the Coming Buddha next captured Westborough's attention. Ages hence, the historian reflected, when men shall have shrunk to mere dwarfs who marry at five and die at ten years of age, Maitreya will appear on earth to preach once more the doctrine "glorious in the beginning, glorious in the middle, and glorious in the end." Maitreya alone of the twelve images was represented as sitting in the Western fashion. His turquoise-inset copper throne was engraved with elephants, with lions and with sea monsters—motifs that were not Tibetan but had been handed down from the ancient art of India, unchanged for century after century.

Strolling rapidly by the meditating Amitabha—he whom the Orient calls the "Boundless Light"—Westborough paused before the one image in the room familiar to Western eyes: the historic Sakyamuni Buddha. The great Gautama smiled his inscrutable Buddha smile, while his left hand cuddled his beggar's bowl and the right pointed downward to call upon the earth to be his witness in his struggle against the evil Mara. On the altar, directly before the smiling Buddha, was a large brass bowl filled with stemless marigolds. They were slightly wilted, Westborough noted as he passed to the eleven-headed Chen-re-zi, the patron deity of Tibet.

In addition to the eleven heads grouped in a fantastic cone above his single neck, Chen-re-zi, the "Lord of Mercy," had also been allotted four pairs of arms. Westborough wondered idly which head was supposed to direct which arm; under any procedure the arrangement promised to be complicated. He left the Lord of Mercy for the "Lord of Wisdom," Jam-pe-Yang, whose face was that of a good-natured but not quite bright fat boy, and then moved to a large painted image of papier-mache and wood. It was the first image he had seen which was not of bronze or of gilded copper, and a card told him that it was of Chana Dorje, the "Wielder of the Thunderbolt."

The Thunderbolt God, the historian cogitated, has been one of the themes repeated over and over in the religious experiences of all races: the Greek Zeus, the Latin Jove, the Norse Thor, the Vedic Indra, to cite only a few who have been allotted the title. The Tibetan version, however, seemed to be vastly inferior to these deities. Chana Dorje was no noble Zeus, no virile Thor, no lofty Jove, but a scowling, potbellied monster who squatted like an enormous toad upon a circular base. His face was a deep indigo as became a Bodhisat of wrathful aspect; tiny skulls peeped from his hair; he had great bulging eyes, a broad nose like a pig's snout, and a gaping, snarling mouth filled with protruding gold teeth. Undoubtedly the Bodhisat heaven must boast of a celestial dentist, Westborough mused facetiously as he walked on to the last image of them all, Yama, the dreaded "Lord of Death."

Yama's image, slightly smaller than the others, was composed of a resinouslike substance painted black—the universal color of death—with bushy red eyebrows and a fringe of red whiskers. A monstrous snake crawled over his body, and in his hand he carried the sling with which he captured all who essayed the impossible feat of escaping his inevitable clutches. The Lord of Mercy, the Lord of Wisdom, the Lord of the Thunderbolt, the Lord of Death—yes, they were certainly arranged in climactic order, Westborough reflected. But (although he knew full well that he should return, while there was time, to the safety of his bedroom) he had not yet inspected the numerous small objects upon the altar.

Most of them he could identify: the eight auspicious altar symbols, the teapot-shaped holy-water vases wrapped in skirts of yellow silk, the bronze handbells so indispensable to Lamaist ceremonies, the Tantrik libation cups of human skulls, the shallow butter lamps, the three-edged ritualistic daggers ("ghost-daggers" had been the happy phrase which Rudyard Kipling had coined for them), the round bronze disks which bore the misleading label of "mirrors," and—most esoteric emblem of all—the conventionalized thunderbolt or dorje.

The dorjes—there were three of them on the altar—were shaped like small bronze dumbbells of an openwork design—two crowns separated by a central shaft. Westborough picked one of them up between his thumb and forefinger; he found it surprisingly heavy. He was about to return it to the altar when he realized with a horrified start that he was no longer alone in the Tibetan Room. Chang was standing in the doorway, regarding the intruder from a vantage point between the Red and Yellow kings. Westborough hurriedly regained the cane which he had leaned against the altar.

Chang walked across the room with deliberate slowness. He was smiling, but what his smile conveyed, Westborough could not tell. It might have been indifferent or threatening or merely amused; only one thing was certain. It was not the usual friendly smile of welcome.

"Your ankle, you will hurt it again," Chang cautioned. Westborough leaned heavily upon his cane.

"Dear me, yes. It was very stupid of me to venture to hobble down here. But I was wakeful, I could not sleep, and I believed I would disturb no one if I came hers."

He added shyly, "I am extremely interested in the gods of your people."

"Not my people," Chang said. He lifted the brass bowl of marigolds before the image of the central Buddha. "I go bring fresh."

"Do you remain a Buddhist, Mr. Chang?" Westborough asked. The question was a presumptuous one; he did not expect Chang to answer. But Chang did.

"I believe in pure teachings of the Enlightened One." His black eyes swept contemptuously from one to another of the remaining eleven images. "Not in these."

"Dear me," Westborough murmured. There was nothing else that he could say. Chang's presence had, somehow, the effect of making him feel gauche and ill at ease. He shifted his eyes uncomfortably toward the floor, "Why, whatever is that?" he cried suddenly.

Chang also looked downward, then gravely shook his head. "Does not belong here."

"Doesn't belong here! Why, what can it be?"

Chang set down the brass bowl of flowers upon the altar. "Have not seen it before."

Westborough (not forgetting to lean heavily upon his cane) stooped to the floor. The object he picked up was a small cylinder covered with red silk, a cylinder of the same size and shape as a big firecracker. Of its purpose Westborough did not have the slightest grasp, but he saw that the silk covering could be peeled away. He removed it, revealing a small roll of paper, coarse, yellowed paper that might have been of Tibetan origin. There was a drawing upon one side in faded vermilion. A simple drawing, one of the simplest possible. A representation of the fly-foot cross, the swastika.

It differed, Westborough noted, from the *hakenkreuz* of Nazi Germany, from the swastika of the orthodox Buddhism, in that the direction of rotation was counterclockwise. The so-called male form of the emblem.

"*Yun--drun!*" Chang exclaimed in a voice grown suddenly tense. "The *yun-drun* of Bon!"

II

"The emblem of Bon!" Adam Merriweather exclaimed. His voice held an uneasy note. "Do you know much about Bon?"

"Does anyone outside of Tibet know much about Bon?" Westborough countered.

He and Merriweather were seated on his small balcony, watching the sunlight sparkle over the gentle ripples of Lake Michigan. The sun had a moderately large-sized arc yet to travel before it crossed its meridian.

"I know the obvious facts, of course," Westborough continued. "Bon, the aboriginal religion of Tibet, had degenerated into an extravagant shamanism by the seventh and eighth centuries when it was superseded by Buddhism. Although the primitive cult of demon worship was unable to compete with the metaphysics of Tantrik Buddhism many Bon rites have unquestionably survived. I might mention the use of skull cups (which, I believe, were originally designed for the drinking of human blood sacrifices), skull drums and thighbone trumpets. The rather widespread employment of human bones and skulls throughout Tibet is, decidedly, not of pure Buddhist origin. Moreover, many of the aboriginal Bon deities have also survived; they have been transformed into respected members of the Lamaist pantheon."

"Yes, I know all that. It's not the important thing Bon itself still survives."

"Yes, to some extent. I understand that it has become so modified by Buddhist influence that it is now scarcely distinguishable from the state religion."

"That's the White Bon. It's harmless. What I'm talking about is the other kind—the Black Bon—the genuine, aboriginal demon worship of Tibet. It still continues under cover, though Lhasa officials have tried for years to stamp it out. Its hold is so strong, I've heard, that many Buddhist temples of supposedly good repute have secret rooms where Bon adherents may gather for their ceremonies.

"Weird ceremonies, they must be! Bon priests are sorcerers and wizards, like those of the Chinese Taoists; they are feared like the very devil the length and breadth of Tibet. That swastika is their emblem! In fact the very word 'Bonpo,' Rockhill states, is derived from 'Punya,' one of the names for the swastika worshipers."

"The device, however, is an extremely widespread emblem," Westborough informed his host. "The Greeks employed it in their art as did the Egyptians before them; even among the ruins of ancient Troy Schliemann discovered it. The meaning is not sinister; quite the contrary. The swastika—the name, by the way, comes from the two Sanskrit characters st' and asti—is almost universally regarded as a symbol of good fortune."

Merriweather shook his head dubiously. "I don't like it. I never saw that roll before in my life. Chang never saw it. Jed didn't bring it with him. How did it get in my house? It appeared so—so suddenly. Like a warning dropped from the sky."

"Warning?" Westborough repeated. "Why should you expect to receive a warning, Mr. Merriweather?"

"Look it over," Merriweather invited, unrolling the drawing. "The paper is Tibetan paper; Jed is sure of that and so is Chang. The cross is drawn in vermilion, an ink used in Tibet, with a pen. Not with a brush but with a pen—a wooden stylus such as Tibetans use. Have you seen the iron pen case which Tsongpun Bonbo brought with him from Tibet? Did you know that he was alone in that room practically all of yesterday afternoon?"

"You believe that it was he who left the drawing there?"

"I know it," Merriweather declared with conviction. "He won't admit it, naturally. But I know he left it, and I think I know why. It's some crazy kind of Tibetan warning."

"Warning? Dear me, Mr. Merriweather, this is the second time within a few minutes that you have used the word. Perhaps I may be allowed to guess the cause of your discomfort? You did not wish the Lama Tsong-pun Bonbo to know that Chang is translating the Padma Sambhava manuscript for you. Yet in some manner he has learned."

"That fool Chang blurted it out before him last night!" There was a moment's uneasy silence. "Chang's finished the translation," Merriweather added in a low voice.

"So soon?"

"Oh, the job wasn't so heavy on a wordage basis. You know what the pages of Tibetan books are like ? There are only a few lines of writing on each page."

"I should like very much to read the manuscript's translation, if I may be permitted to do so."

"It's downstairs in my filing cabinet—that is the original copy. Chang has his own file in which he keeps carbons of everything he translates."

But Merriweather did not add that either copy would be placed at Westborough's disposal. The historian was quick to notice the omission.

"May I ask the subject of the manuscript?"

Merriweather did not answer for some time. "Have you read the English translation of the Bardo Todol?"

"The one which Mr. Evans-Wentz has edited under the title, *The Tibetan Book of the Dead*? Yes, I have perused it with great interest."

"Then you'll have a good idea of what this is—instructions for the deceased on the after-death plane, tantras to stop the cycle of rebirths and assure immediate Nirvana. But that's not the---" He brought the sentence to an abrupt termination.

"There is something else?" Westborough prodded. "Other tantras, perhaps?" But Merriweather's manner was not encouraging. It was the sheepish manner of one who realizes that he may have said too much.

"Yes, other tantras. Call them magic, if you wish. It won't be accurate, but that's the only word we have in English. The entire collection has a one-word Tibetan title which Chang tells me he has rather loosely rendered as 'Spells of the Thunderbolt.'"

"Certainly an alluring name. But may I ask what the Lama Tsong-pun Bonbo said when he learned that Chang had translated the magic of his country for your benefit?"

"He didn't like it, but what of it?" There was fear beneath the bluster of Merriweather's manner, Westborough sensed. "He can't stop me from doing what I want with my own property."

"Perhaps," Westborough suggested gently, "he considers that it is still his property."

"Well, it isn't," Merriweather answered shortly. "Not in this country, anyhow."

Westborough did not dare to reveal that he knew otherwise. Yet he felt that he must say something to plead the lama's cause. "Now that you have Chang's translation the original is not so necessary," he ventured.

"Not necessary? When it's by far the most valuable thing I have in my collection?"

"But the poor lama has traveled halfway around the world to recover it!" Westborough exclaimed in dismay. "To him it means far more than it can possibly mean to you."

"Allow me to say that I consider myself to be the best judge of that matter," Merriweather said stiffly.

"Dear me, I am sorry!" Westborough exclaimed. He was Merriweather's guest, the apology was necessary, but he did not like apologizing to Adam Merriweather. "I fear that I have offended you."

"No, you have not offended me," Merriweather answered. But he rose to his feet as sign that their discussion was ended.

"Perhaps I may be able to do a favor for you," Westborough hazarded.

"A favor for me?"

"I am happy to say that the Lama Tsongpun Bonbo and I have apparently become good friends. If you wish to lend me the drawing of the swastika I shall be glad to ask him about it. Perhaps he will speak more frankly to me than he did to you. I have little doubt but that your presence awes him."

"Yes, something in that," Merriweather ruminated. He reached into his pocket for the silk-covered roll. "Very well, please talk to him." Someone knocked upon the door as Westborough was transferring the roll to his own pocket. "That brother of mine!" Merriweather grumbled. "Since he came Vincent refuses to make even a pretense of working. He won't even go down to the office. I've had to stop his allowance." He called loudly, "Yes, come in."

Their visitor, however, was the Lama Tsongpun Bonbo.

"Kusho Wes-bo-ro!" the lama exclaimed. "My joying your leabing your bed. Kusho Mer-ri-weat-her, please, your not going? My wishing talking wit' you. Here."

"Why here?" Merriweather demanded.

His voice was so truculent that Westborough wondered if the millionaire were not really frightened.

"My wishing Kusho Wes-bo-ro to hear. He priend to us bot'. Kusho Mer-ri-weat-her, my being patient. Your promising tell me when brot-her come; he come, still your not saying. Chang trans-late sacred words ob Guru Padma in tongue of pyi-ling, my saying not-hing."

"Not much you could say," Merriweather interjected ungraciously. This time Westborough was sure that his belligerence was mere defense mechanism.

"Kusho Mer-ri-weat-her, must know, please, what your doing. Please, your saying, Kusho Mer-ri-weat-her?"

In the lama's voice there lay a note of frantic, of desperate pleading. Merriweather detected it, for his own fear faded at once. The man had, apparently, the sadistic instincts of a bully.

"Suppose I've decided to keep it."

"Your not doing t'at!" the lama cried in horror. "No, Kusho Mer-ri-weat-her. No, please."

"Why not?" Merriweather sprawled back against the cushions of his chair, a pleased smile on his face. "Why shouldn't I be entitled to keep it? I paid for it."

The last statement was hardly truthful, Westborough reflected. The Padma Sambhava manuscript had cost Adam Merriweather nothing but the trouble of writing a check which had never been cashed. The lama, apparently convinced of the folly of begging from Merriweather, abruptly changed his tactics.

"It not sape, Kusho Mer-ri-weat-her; words ob Guru Padma dan-ger-ous. To you, to e-bil Reppner. Your being *na mee tet*." A shiver traversed Merriweather's pudgy body at the last three words. "*Na mee tet*," the lama repeated in a deep ceremonial voice.

Whatever the meaning of the strange Tibetan words there could be no doubt of their effect upon Adam Merriweather. The collector rose to his feet, his face a pasty gray. "Very well, I'll go get it for you."

"How my "tanking you?" the lama exclaimed gratefully. "It bringing you much merit, Kusho Mer-ri-weather."

Some of the color had now returned to Merriweather's face. "You once offered me twenty thousand dollars for it. Does that offer still stand?"

The lama bowed his head. "Your wishing more?"

"No, it's a fair offer."

It certainly was, Westborough said to himself as Merriweather walked from the room. Twenty thousand dollars for something which had cost the collector nothing and which he had no right to sell! Westborough, usually the mildest of men, was conscious of intense indignation. He must say something to the lama; he could not allow the naive Tibetan priest to be so despoiled. But on second thought he reconsidered.

The hearings on such a suit as this might be drawn out for months while the lama sickened with uncertainty. There was, moreover, the risk that justice might not eventually triumph. No, it was best that the lama pay his twenty thousand dollars to Adam Merriweather, even though the latter had no right to it.

Besides, to Tsongpun Bonbo money meant nothing. The lama had seated himself tailorwise on the stone flooring of the balcony, his face beaming like that of a child whose dearest wish is about to come true.

"Tso Map-hang," he murmured, gazing over the sun-speckled waters of the lake. "My seeing Tso Map-hang."

"I am happy for you, Tsongpun Lama," Westborough said gently. He wondered if the lama would be willing to indulge his curiosity. "May I ask the meaning of the Tibetan phrase you applied to Mr. Merriweather? Undoubtedly it was a phrase well known to him."

The lama turned his head. "My trying explain. Your haloing here power which light lights. What your calling him ?"

"Electricity," Westborough answered.

"My knowing him little. Is way in which he can be stored ?"

"Yes, there is a device known to us as a battery."

"Bat-tair-ee," the lama repeated. "Words of Guru Padma, all sacred objects same to us like your bat-tair-ee."

"I do not understand. Why are your sacred objects like one of our batteries?"

"T'ey storing power, Kusho, power like your ee-lec-tri-ci-tee, but power ob mind. Your understanding?"

"A mental power? A force of the mind?" He saw that the lama had nodded. "You mean that one's thoughts can be concentrated in focus upon a single object? That such thoughts are not dissipated but preserved as electricity is stored in a battery?"

The lama nodded vehemently. "Your understanding. Eberyt'ing in world mind; not-hing can be which is not mind. One man t'ink long time on object like words ob Guru Padma. He die, his t'ought not—what was word you use?—dee-see-pate. T'ought on object remain, surround it like cloud, cloud you cannot see. Now ot-her man t'ink; his thought making cloud grow bigger. Ebery man who t'ink making cloud grow bigger. It habing power. It being dan-ger-ous to one who not know, one who is *na mee tet*."

"A battery for thoughts!" Westborough ejaculated. He found the conception to be most startling. "But your cloud is purely a mental force? You do not mean that it can become a physical one?"

"What one, what ot-her?" the lama shrugged. "Bot' same. Mind cause all."

Westborough deliberated upon the Buddhist concept that physical and mental forces are interchangeable. He asked thoughtfully, "May this cloud of thought surrounding an object have the power to kill?"

"Sometime it may kill," the lama answered.

"Did such a force kill Mr. Reffner?"

"Kusho Wes-bo-ro, e-bil karma bring e-bil end—always. My not knowing more."

"Thank you, Tsongpun Lama. There is another question I should like to ask. Is one of your ka-tas missing?"

"My not knowing, Kusho."

"The question was, perhaps, poorly worded. How many of these scarves did you have with you when you came to Chicago ?"

"One, two, t'ree, pour." The lame spread wide the fingers of both hands. "My not knowing, Kusho Wes-bo-ro."

Only a Tibetan priest could be so sublimely indifferent to worldly details, Westborough reflected as he brought out the silk-covered paper roll.

"You have seen this drawing before, have you not, Tsongpun Lama?"

"Yes, Kusho Mer-ri-weat-her showing me yun-drun."

"Is the yun-drun a common symbol of Shod?"

"Yes, Kusho, ber-ry common."

"What is its meaning?"

"Sometime good luck. Sometime long liking, it turning same way as Wheel ob Birt' and Deat' which cannot stop till *kalpa* end."

"You are referring to what Waddell has termed the Wheel of Life? Truly a sublime conception! I am familiar with it through one of your religious paintings which I have had the good fortune to examine. But this swastika—yun-drun, I should say—does not turn in the same direction as that great Wheel. Is it not the yun-drun of Bon?"

The lama shrugged. "Yes, Kusho, yun-drun ob Bon, but man who draw may know no better, ig-no-rant people ob Bhod t'inking bot' yun-drun are same. My hearing Kusho Mer-ri-weat-her."

The lama's ears, Westborough acknowledged, were a great deal better than his own. It was not until some seconds later that he heard the ponderous tread of a man fifty pounds overweight.

The footsteps in the corridor drew nearer; the door of the room burst violently open.

"The manuscript!" Adam Merriweather gasped breathlessly. "Not where Chang put it last night. Not in the pigeonholes. No one's seen it. It may be stolen!"

III

Lake Michigan's waves swished against the shore with the velvety softness of a caress. From Westborough's balcony the sun was no longer visible. Only a tiny strip of golden-yellow sand remained on Adam Merriweather's private beach to testify that it was still in the heavens.

Westborough entertained another visitor.

"Speak softly, John," he pleaded. "I cannot guarantee that our conversation will not be overheard. Remember that you have called merely to express your sympathy as a friend for my injured ankle."

"It's the damnedest thing ever!" Mack exclaimed. But he lowered his voice as requested. "Let's have all the facts."

"They are very scanty. Chang finished the translation at about eleven o'clock last night. He insists that he then returned the original manuscript to its proper pigeonhole. No other person in this house will admit to having seen it since."

"Was it kept in that big room with all the idols?"

"Yes, in the Tibetan Room."

"Doors locked?"

"The west door is always locked; not merely locked but bolted from the inside. The north door, the one through which we entered the other day, is very seldom locked, Mr. Merriweather told me."

"So anybody in the house had the chance to steal the thing!"

"Yes."

"Was any search made for this Tibetan hocus-pocus?"

"A very thorough one. Mr. Merriweather, as was only natural, was anxious to do everything in his power to convince the lama of his good faith."

"They went through every room in the house?"

"So far as I know, yes."

"Your room too?"

"My room, I believe, was among the first to be searched."

Mack vented a shrill whistle. "You want to be careful they don't get on to you. That walk of yours this morning was a fool thing to do."

"Yes, extremely stupid."

"I mean, to let Chang catch you. All right to look around, of course—that's why you're here—but be careful or we'll both be in the soup."

"I am more sorry than I can say for my unfortunate indiscretion."

"Well, forget it," Mack said gruffly. "You're doing a good job here. Has Merriweather called in anyone from headquarters?"

"No. He is taking the attitude that the manuscript has merely been mislaid and will be found sooner or later."

"He's a damn fool," Mack opined. "However, it doesn't come under my department—yet. What's your slant on this thing?"

"I do not know that I have one. The problem is a complex one
because of the multiplicity of motives for the theft. The manuscript did
not have merely one value but three."

"What do you mean by three values?"

"First of all there is its value as a sacred object. We may term this the
religious value. That is its value to the lama. Possibly, although I think
not, its value to Chang also."

"Go on."

"The second value is due to the interest attached to it as a historic
object. I shall call this the scientific value. That is its value to Adam
Merriweather and to his brother. Like the religious value, the scientific
value cannot be measured in terms of dollars and cents, but it is an
attraction of no mean magnitude."

"And the third?"

"That is, of course, the monetary value, which we may place at twenty
thousand dollars, since that is the amount of the lama's offer to Mr.
Merriweather. Keeping in mind these three types of values, do you not
see how complicated the problem becomes? Shall I point out some of
the various possibilities?"

"Sure, let's have 'em."

"Let us first dispose of the religious value. The lama, despairing of
obtaining Mr. Merriweather's consent to his offer, may have stolen it."

Mack nodded. "Yeh, and then, when he'd got it safely tucked away,
come in and begged Merriweather to let him have it. Good way of covering up."

"That course, however, imparts to Tsongpun Bonbo a more Ma-
chiavellian quality than he appears to possess. I have so far found his
character to be simple and open. Moreover, stealing is ranked as an
offense second only to the taking of life in the five primary command-
ments which the Buddha gave to his order. Although one must keep in
mind that the lama considers—justly so—that the manuscript is his own
property and not Merriweather's. So much for the religious value. The
only other person who might have taken the manuscript for this motive
is Chang. But I do not think that likely."

"Why don't you?"

"Chang admitted to me this morning that he is an orthodox Buddhist. Padma Sambhava—no matter what else he may have been—was
certainly not that. On the contrary, he founded a sect which violated a
great many, if not all, of the tenets of orthodox Buddhism. A work of
Padma Sambhava's would hold no more religious sentiment for Chang

than a work of Calvin or Knox or Luther would hold for a devout Catholic. Probably even less."

"Maybe Chang was lying to you about his religion," Mack suggested.

"I do not believe that likely. Lying is the third offense to be proscribed by the Buddha."

"What were the other two?" Mack wanted to know.
know.

"Adultery and the drinking of alcoholic liquors."

The detective grinned. "Smart fellow, the Buddha!"

"The ethical principles of his teachings are as high—or higher—than those of any religion the world has known. However, we are now ready to consider the manuscript's second value—the scientific one. From this angle we have two suspects. Doctor Merriweather may have stolen it from his brother."

"To sell to the lama?"

"No. Remember that we are discussing the scientific value, not the monetary one. It is difficult to explain to one who has not delved exhaustively into a subject of this nature the immense thrill of owning an original manuscript of historic interest. I myself have been tempted many times into the breaking of the tenth commandment. Fortunately I have so far refrained from breaking the eighth one, but I can easily understand such a reason for breaking it."

"So you think it was Jed Merriweather who took it?"

"Dear me, no. I am making no accusations but merely exploring possibilities. Another such possibility is Adam Merriweather."

"Steal his own manuscript? There's no sense to that."

"It is not his but the lama's. He could not hope to retain possession if the lama instituted legal action for recovery."

"Does the lama know that?"

Westborough shook his head. "I think not. No one has as yet informed him that in our courts a foreigner, unless his country is at war with ours, has the same standing as an American citizen. But Mr. Merriweather may have feared that, if he kept the manuscript openly, the lama would take other action than legal."

"What could that squirt do to anyone?"

Westborough hesitated; the answer was extremely difficult to put into words. "Merriweather may fear—I think does fear—that the lama has access to powers which our Western civilization does not possess. Many oriental scholars have insisted that such powers are to be found in Tibet."

"What sort of powers?" Mack demanded.

"It is difficult to explain; the concepts are so utterly foreign to our

Western minds. For want of a better term we may group them under
the all-inclusive heading of magic."

"Nuts!" Afack growled disgustedly. "Anyone who believes stuff like
that is screwy."

"Knowing as little as I do of the matter, it would be folly for me to
venture an opinion. And yet"—Westborough hesitated once more—
"Mr. Reffner was killed under strange circumstances."

"You telling me?" Mack said. Rising from his chair, he shoved both
of his hands into his pockets. "Talk about your magic! This fellow who
called himself Hamilcar Barca must've had it. I've been in this game a
long time, and I never knew it was so easy to get away with murder."

"Surely you have some clues?"

"What clues? There weren't any fingerprints on the toothpaste tube
or on the shaving things. Must-a handled 'em with rubber gloves, if you
can believe it. No fingerprints on the doorknob. Fingerprints on the
key tag—sure, the bellhop's and the manager's both. Fingerprints in
Reffner's room—his own and the chambermaid's. Oh, he was a slick
devil, this Barca!"

"What about the powder which you had analyzed?" Westborough
questioned.

"Bath powder," Mack growled. "Bath powder---ever hear of anything
crazier? We didn't find the box in his room. Make what you can out of
it. I can't make anything but a headache."

"You tried, of course, to trace the movements of Hamilcar Barca
after he had left the hotel?"

Mack confessed dourly, "We tried. Taxis—how many of 'em do you
think there are in this town and how many fares do you think each of
'em carries during a day? At that we had some luck. We found the driver
who'd taken him to the Pilgrim Deluxe. Not much there. Driver had
picked him up somewhere on Randolph Street, but that was all we could
get out of him. All he remembered was taking a guy to the Pilgrim
Deluxe; couldn't even say for sure that his fare had a beard. We couldn't
find the cab driver who took him away from the Pilgrim Deluxe —if
there was one. And we couldn't get a lead at the railroad or bus stations
or at the airport. Sure there were guys with gray beards buying tickets.
We ran one of 'em down, and he turned out to be a minister taking the
bus to visit his married daughter in Newark. But there were a lot of
fellows without beards buying tickets also, and if you ask me Barca was
one of 'em. All he had to do was to step into a public johnny, rip off his
phony, clean up his face a little, and there you are! Last guy in the world
we'd be looking for. Probably didn't even leave town; just came back to
wherever he belonged and went on as usual. Find him? It's like hunting

for a galloping ghost!"

"It does seem to be an exceedingly difficult problem," Westborough agreed. "I am sorry that I have not been able to be of more help to you."

"Well, we're not licked yet. Stick it out here as long as you can. I want you to find out all you can about this manuscript thing. What about your third value the twenty-thousand-dollar one? Who knew that the lama had offered to pay that?"

"The offer, I have learned, was made immediately prior to our arrival on Tuesday in the presence of Doctor Walters and Miss Shelton. Miss Shelton, who told me of it, said also that she had informed her fiance, Vincent, of the news. Whether Vincent kept the matter from his uncle or not I do not know, but it does not seem probable that he would withhold such startling news. And Chang may have been informed by any of these I have named, by his employer or by the lama himself."

"Looks like everyone in the house knew it!" Mack exclaimed.

"I think that we are safe in making that assumption."

"Well then, who needed money badly enough to steal it?"

"Another difficult question to answer. The same amount of money does not always mean the same to different people or even to the same person at different times. Adam Merriweather may be excluded; if he stole the manuscript it was not for its monetary value. Doctor Merriweather, however, may be placed in the category of those needing money; I understand that he is experiencing severe difficulties in financing his projected expedition to Turkestan. Miss Shelton is entirely dependent on Mr. Merriweather's charity—not a happy situation for a girl of her caliber. Vincent Merriweather's allowance has been recently discontinued; I do not know how much it is nor how badly it is needed. Chang? I know nothing of Chang. His financial position is as much of an enigma as his past history."

"Listen!" Mack commanded brusquely. "Someone's coming down the hall." He tiptoed to the door and opened it a narrow crack through which to peer cautiously outward. Closing the door as noiselessly as he had opened it, he returned to the balcony.

"It's Jed Merriweather," he said. "I never met him, but he looks just like you described him. If he comes in here it ought to be our chance to get the dope on that guy Chang."

IV

Lieutenant Mack and Dr. Merriweather were alike in many ways, Westborough reflected as he completed the introduction. Both had the same air of confidence, the same assurance. It was the assurance of one who has battled successfully against such obstacles as the average man, securely oscillating between his steam-heated home and padded office chair, cannot even dream.

Jed Merriweather's adversaries had been the mountain ranges of Central Asia, John Mack's the machine guns of Chicago gangsters, but, for all the diversity of their backgrounds, they were none the less spiritual kindred.

And each seemed to recognize the similar quality of the other; the recognition was apparent in the way they were shaking hands.

"Lieutenant Mack, I am glad to know you. And glad to see you here. It's high time Adam called in someone to run this stolen manuscript down."

"Lieutenant Mack is here unofficially," Westborough made haste to say. "He was good enough to come to express his sympathy for my injured ankle. Moreover, the missing manuscript does not come under his department."

"Not yet," Mack added sententiously.

"You've told him about it, though?"

"One can scarcely refrain from discussing an affair of such interest. However, I imparted the news in strict confidence, as I believed it to be your brother's privilege to determine the course of action."

"Not altogether," Dr. Merriweather differed. "Now that Adam has definitely decided to return the manuscript he owes it to the Lama Tsongpun Bonbo to make every possible effort to find the thing. The lama is the real sufferer by this theft—if it is a theft."

"It is my sincere wish that his suffering may be of short duration. Perhaps Lieutenant Mack, from his broad experience, may be able to offer helpful counsel. Unofficially, of course."

"Not such a bad idea if Lieutenant Mack is willing to advise us. I'll go find Adam."

"Perhaps," Westborough began hesitantly, "it would not be well to trouble your brother at the present instant. He is now resting; the excitement, the anxiety have been a great strain upon him, he informed me."

For all the dignity of Jed Merriweather's black beard and his scholarly spectacles, his grin was the grin of a mischievous boy. "Yes, Adam is rather like that. Even when we were little fellows together it was the same way. Poor devil, he can't help it! Well, what's your recommendation, Lieutenant Mack?"

"If I was handling this I'd make dead sure of one thing first of all. Was the manuscript really put back in its place last night?"

"There can be no doubt of that. Chang's word cannot be doubted."

"Chang? Oh yes, your brother's Tibetan secretary." (Westborough, with great relief, observed that Lieutenant Mack had at last refrained from calling Chang a Chinese.) "Well, what makes you so sure of him?"

"I have known Chang for a number of years. He is as honest as a man can be—thoroughly trustworthy. If Chang said he replaced the manuscript in its pigeonhole, then he did replace it."

"Well, I'd have to know more about him before I made up my mind on that," Mack answered glumly.

"My dear Lieutenant, I am beginning to lose confidence in your discernment. Please don't tell me that you are numbered among that unfortunate class of beings who consider that a man is less of a man because his skin is of a slightly different color and his eyes slant."

Westborough hastened to pour a generous dosage of oil upon the stormy waters. "Dear me, that it is not in the least what Lieutenant Mack meant to imply. He is far too broad-minded for racial prejudices. But Chang's background is completely unknown to him, and it is a police axiom that the background of every person having the opportunity to commit the particular crime should be thoroughly investigated."

"Chang's background? Well, he's been working for Adam for the last three years. And with me for two years before that."

"And before he came to you?"

Jed Merriweather grinned his disarming grin. "Ah!" he exclaimed, expelling the breath between his teeth. "If I tell you, you'll think I'm romancing, you won't believe. Few people can believe who have never been in Central Asia."

"Chang was a member of the priesthood, was he not?" Westborough inquired.

"Did he tell you that?"

"No. I drew the conclusion from some of his statements."

"And drew it correctly. He was a *ge-long*—a fully ordained priest who keeps the two hundred and fifty-three rules. Let me tell you about the gompa where he studied. The description will have to be second-hand, since I never had a chance to see it. However, I have seen others."

Relaxing against the red leather cushions of his metal chair, Jed Merriweather began his story. A spider, Westborough fancied, a great black-bearded spider spinning a web with words for threads—a web of shimmering, diaphanous beauty.

Slowly a picture came into being. An oil painting brushed with bright splotches of color on the canvas of the mind. A valley. Bleak, inhospitable, almost barren. Lichen-clad boulders. Small patches of grass and large patches of never-melting snow. Junipers cringing from the bullying wind—dwarf trees like those of a Japanese garden. Incredible Himalayan shrubs flowering like pink-leaved water lilies. Towering from behind, from in front, from either side, rank upon rank of ermine-robed giants, row after row of domes and spurs and cones and spires. Mountains compared to which the Alps or the Rockies are as pebbles. Mountains as desolate, as inaccessible as the moon.

Gradually the works of man began to intrude into Jed Merriweather's painting. A zigzag road toiled slowly upwards from the plains, stairways were hewn at inconceivable labor from solid stone. Above the sliding scree of the hillside buildings began to rise tier upon tier. Whitewashed squares and oblongs, some many stories high, which were connected by bridges and outdoor staircases, ornamented with towers and battlements and with the gleaming gold of their upturned roofs. A city where two to three thousand male inhabitants lived celibate lives of monastic rigor. An inconceivable city of Cloud Cuckoo Land!

"Inside all was routine," Jed Merriweather continued. "Iron discipline. Enforced meditation. Endless reading of the sacred texts. Thinking not encouraged. Discouraged, in fact, as tending to obscure the higher perceptions and the intuitive wisdom of a saint, which are attainable only after years of not thinking. Does that sound like something from Alice in Wonderland? It isn't crazy to them. A thing is so because it has always been believed so; such is the unanswerable argument of the Orient. Chang took little stock in it.

"Chang, unfortunately for him, was born with a Western mind, a scientific mind. He believed in a creed of logical proof; the teachings of the holy scriptures passed through his mind as through a sieve. The doctrine of the Buddha he retained—no reasonable man could reject it—but other teachings, the outgrowths which nearly obliterated that pure core of truth, he found arrant nonsense. These thoughts he could not confine to himself any more than the Buddha had been able to refrain from telling of his discoveries under the Bo tree. But Chang's heresies were not received as well as the Buddha's had been.

"Let's give the Devil his due. Buddhism—even the Tibetan brand of it—is probably as tolerant as any religion on earth. Still there are breaches of discipline which no orthodox kanpo—committed by tradition to a ritualism of demon masks, devil dancing, blowing upon human thighbone trumpets, and rattling human skull drums—is allowed to overlook. When Chang first gave his fellow monks the opportunity of seeing the pure light of truth he was warned. Later he was flogged, and a flogging for even a small offense, mind you, amounts to fifty strokes of a cane. The whipping was as useless as the warning had been. The brethren, taking counsel among themselves, came to the conclusion that the Buddhist equivalent of a devil had taken possession of their unfortunate fellow.

"Devils may be exorcised in many ways, and Chang's fellow lamas knew every one of them. But no matter how much they blew their trumpets, jangled their bells, rattled their skull drums or bellowed their incantations, Chang's devil refused to be tempted into leaving his victim. He was a devil of sterner fiber than any the brethren had previously encountered. They came to the conclusion—very regretfully, no doubt— that Chang, for the sake of his future births, must be made to pass through the terrible ordeal that is known as 'Good or Bad Luck.'

"It's called that, they say, because it depends solely on a man's luck whether or not he is able to survive it. Most of them don't. Chang was taken to the temple court, his feet fastened by ropes, while two of the huskiest brothers in the order lashed him with whips. Something around a thousand lashes. Mercifully his face escaped, but his body! . . . Yes, I have seen the scars. When it was all over he was dragged outside of the gompa boundaries by a rope and left to his own devices.

"Chang—his name wasn't Chang then, by the way—is reticent with regard to how he lasted the next few months. But Tibetans are a hardy breed; they have to be to survive their climate. Chang's physical being, even though wounds heal slowly at that altitude, gradually recovered. His physical being, not his mental.

"The freethinking Western ideas, which had visited him like biological sports for no reason at all, still remained to trouble him. Moreover, his social position was very bad. In leaving the monastic brotherhood he had lost his profession—like a lawyer disbarred or a doctor banned from the practice of medicine, but with even more stigma attached to the disgrace. The lay population of Chang's community were outspoken in their contempt of him. All in all he was very miserable, so miserable, in fact, that he had the thought which doesn't come to more than one Tibetan among half a million: the thought of leaving his country.

"Somewhere beyond Bhod was the land of the pyi-ling. Terrible people, Chang knew, something like a cross between the gods and the lower animals, but his own people had cast him out. Moreover, a certain adventurous demon (probably the very devil that had survived the ordeal of 'Good or Bad Luck' with him) whispered that it might be well to find out for himself if the pyi-ling were as bad as painted. But his ideas of geography were of the haziest.

"Chang had learned that the world was shaped like the shoulder bone of a sheep, and this was one of the teachings of the sacred books which it had never occurred to him could be contradicted. He knew that the Himalayas were south of him, and at their foot dwelt the nearest of the pyi-ling. These pyi-ling, however, if not actually under the control of the all-powerful Dalai Lama, were at least under the protection of his army. (The foundation for that curious misconception may have arisen from the fact that the Dalai Lama, as a gesture of friendship during the World War, offered a thousand Tibetan soldiers to fight on the British side.) India, therefore, as a near-vassal state of the Dalai Lama, was out of the question. Chang decided that the only route possible for him was the one northward—across the valley of the Tsang-po River, across that tremendous range christened by Sven Hedin the Trans-Himalaya, and across the Chang Tang.

"The words 'Chang Tang' mean 'north plain,' a pitifully poor description for that terrible mixture of bleak plains and barren ranges tangled up together at the heartbreaking elevations of sixteen thousand feet and over. Add to the plains and ranges such ingredients as a little grass, a few nomad herdsmen, a good many bandits, a multitude of brackish salt lakes, and winds fierce enough to blow away a man's face, and you'll begin to have a glimmer of the Chang Tang. And the farther north you go, the worse it gets. Tibetans themselves think nothing is able to live in the northernmost portion.

"Yes, the Chang Tang has been crossed, but by explorers with large caravans. Chang started out to duplicate their feats with two miserable little ponies. Certain suicide, but he didn't know it. He had no idea of what awaited him. And his luck was bad from the first.

"A gang of bandits—one of the many such gangs which terrorize the outlying regions of Tibet—robbed him of his money and of one of his horses. But they left him the other pony and all of his food because they found out he was traveling due north, and that convinced them he was out of his mind. To leave a madman destitute on the Chang Tang was a deed beyond even the elastic consciences of those brigands.

"After that encounter Chang went most of his way on foot. He knew that he would have to spare his one pony as much as possible. Doubts began to assail him, he confessed to me afterwards. The Chang Tang was bigger and tougher than anything he had been able to imagine. Finally he came to another mountain range—you will find it on relief maps of Tibet, looking like the shadow of a long, protruding finger— and the new ascent proved too much for the overtaxed lungs of his pony. Chang flung stones to drive away the ravens who in no time at all were swooping down to gouge out the unlucky beast's eyes, carved off as many strips of horse meat as he could carry, and continued on foot. The pony's flesh lasted him a long time. Eventually, however, it was gone and with it the last of his tea and tsamba. Squatting cross-legged upon a snow-covered boulder, Chant murmured to himself a Buddhist saying which may be translated, 'One who is born is doomed to die.'

"You or I, Lieutenant, would have fought the idea of death with every ounce of strength we possessed. Chang was more sensible. He simply closed his eyes and waited for death with the sublime calm which only a fatalistic philosophy is able to give. He was still waiting for it when my party found him.

"We took to each other immediately. He was grateful to me for saving his life; I admired his pluck and his brain. I taught him English, and in return he taught me many things, including how to write a first-class Tibetan script. I've said before that Chang wasn't his real name. That, he told me, could never be mentioned again in view of the disgrace which had befallen it. Since he had to be called something, however, I christened him Chang Tang in remembrance of the place where we found him. The Tang part has managed to get dropped, and just Chang he's been ever since."

"What if he has to sign a check?" Mack grinned.

"For such uses he borrows my initials and writes 'J.M. Chang.' He is an indefatigable worker and has been, altogether, the most helpful assistant I have ever had."

"May I ask you how you were able to relinquish such valuable services even to your brother?" Westborough inquired.

"Adam, through his several agents along the Indian and Chinese frontiers, had begun to acquire a very fair collection of Tibetan sacred books and needed someone to translate them for him. When he asked me for Chang I couldn't very well refuse. Adam has been the principal backer of my last two expeditions. But I did hate like the very devil to see Chang go."

"I can well sympathize. May I ask how your brother happened to acquire such an odd hobby as the study of the sacred books of Tibet?"

"Someone told him a story." The bearded Dr. Merriweather, distinguished lecturer on three continents and author of books printed in half-a-dozen languages, was grinning again like a mischievous small boy. "The yarn about the great Masters of Mysticism living in Tibet who are supposed to have all the knowledge of the world at their fingertips. That tale circulated for a long time in certain circles and may still be running its course for all I know. Nothing in it, naturally. Although I have seen some odd things. . . . Well, all of this doesn't seem to be helping to find the missing manuscript."

"An authentic manuscript?" Westborough inquired.

The archaeologist nodded. "At least, as I told Adam, the paper and the type of script give one no grounds for saying that it could not date back to the eighth century. Whether it does or not is another matter, and it's highly improbable, of course, that the actual writing was done by that semi-mythological personage, Padma Sambhava. Such things just don't happen."

"Well, no matter whether the document is genuine or apocryphal, it is one of amazing interest. Did you plan to translate it, Doctor Merriweather?"

"Of course. Adam gave Chang the first chance at that, though."

"Have you had the opportunity to read the translation he finished last night?"

"I don't intend to read it—not unless it turns out that the manuscript is really gone for good, which I can't believe. Chang and I might differ in our interpretations, and I don't want to be influenced by his translation, even though it will unquestionably be far superior to any piece of work I am able to do."

"To a humble gleaner in the fields of knowledge that point of view is a very understandable one. The subject of this manuscript is one which appeals to the mystical side of your brother's nature, is it not?"

Westborough had expected that the question would bring another of Dr. Merriweather's boyish grins, but instead the archaeologist's manner became very grave.

"Yes, Adam's wildly excited." He repeated the last two words. "Wildly excited, and I don't like it. It isn't good for him. He thinks that he's at last found the way to the Secret Doctrine."

"I must confess my complete ignorance," Westborough declared. "Whatever can the Secret Doctrine be?"

"No one quite knows," Dr. Merriweather replied. He pronounced a single Tibetan word and added in a hushed voice, "It's the most carefully guarded mystery of Asia. And the most dangerous."

PART EIGHT: A Door Is Locked
(Thursday Evening, July 22)

THEY STOOD beside the shadowy form of the Yellow King. "I am grateful for your offer to continue the Cook's tour of Tibet," Dr. Walters whispered. He did not know why he was whispering; perhaps an unconscious response to the eerie atmosphere engendered by this room after dark.

Janice Shelton had found the light switch. She pressed it, and the room became illuminated. Dimly illuminated, like the interior of a cathedral. Under light no more brilliant than that provided by the smoky butter lamps of a lama temple, Buddhas and Buddha-gods leaped into shadowy visibility.

"Creepy!" Walters exclaimed. He was sorry the minute he had spoken. His voice was not suited to the place, not fitted to this odd little nook in space-time where the world-lines of himself and Janice Shelton had coincided. She held up her hand, mutely warning him to be silent.

"Wait!" Crossing to the altar, she pressed a second switch. Buddhas and Buddha-gods leaped into multicolored prominence. Dr. Walters caught his breath. The effect was as startling as magic. The images were bathed in blues, in reds, in greens, in amber and in dazzling white. It was like a painting. A painting with lights.

He knew how it was done of course. Floodlights with colored screens concealed beneath the altar. But to explain the mechanics of a trick does not always take away the magic of it, and the magic of this remained. Oddly enough one of his first thoughts was of the quaint, friendly little Tibetan priest whom he had met in this very room only two days before.

"Has he seen this? The lama?"

"Yes." He felt that she was reluctant to discuss the matter. "I don't think he liked it."

"Well, it is like turning his gods and goddesses into a circus."

"Yes," she owned, "in a way it is. Shall we begin with the large figure under the pure white light? That's the founder, the great Buddha, and

133

he's seated in the Witness Attitude, which is one of the most common ways of repre---"

"Just a minute," Walters interrupted, fumbling for the switch concealed beneath the altar. "There!"

"Why did you do that?"

"Turn off the floodlights?"

"Yes."

"I can't talk to you with that rainbow on." There was a roughness to his voice which he did not in the least intend should be there. "It's like—like being in the center of a World's Fair."

Even the dim temple glow that remained in the room was sufficient for him to note her glance. But he read little hope there. It was the glance of a lady who is half offended, half amused by a buffoon's impudence.

"What, Doctor Walters, do you have to say to me of such importance?"

"Plenty!" The word burst from his mouth in a violent explosion. "Everything."

She said in a quiet voice, "I think it would be better to turn on the lights."

"I know I'm a fool!" The words clung to his mouth like the taste of bitter fruit. "Worse than that. I know it's hopeless, but I love you so. Janice!"

She suffered him to take her hand, but there was no comfort in its cool, lifeless touch. She loved that fellow Vincent of course. Dr. Walters relinquished the hand he had been pressing so tightly.

"Sorry." Dr. Walters had become a pearl diver, a pearl diver battling upward through a hundred feet of black water to the ocean's surface. "I shouldn't have said it. I know you're engaged to young Merriweather." The black water once more engulfed him. "Why do you do this to me? Since we were here together the other day I haven't been able to think of anything else. Janice! Janice darling !"

She remained cool and aloof. Savagely he told himself that he could kiss her. Yes, he could hold her lithe body within his arms and press his lips against hers. But the result would be no more than if he kissed one of those jeering images. Kissed the smiling, gilded lips of the Buddha himself.

"You used the right word just now, Gay. The word 'hopeless.'"

"I know," he answered tonelessly. "You're in love with Merriweather. It's all right. Hundreds of people have to go through this sort of thing every day. Don't waste time feeling sorry for me."

"Sorry for you? No, Gay, I'm sorry for myself."

"Janice!" he cried. "Oh, my darling!"

Why had he ever thought that Janice Shelton was cool and aloof? She was like a flame—a flame soaring upward to meet the flame that was in him. Suddenly she wrenched her body away.

"It's the beginning, but it's the end too. They're mixed up together like the snake that swallows its own tail."

He said thickly, "Don't talk nonsense. You're mine; I know it now. When two people love as---"

"Don't!" she interrupted fiercely. "I know what you're going to say, but it isn't true."

"It is true."

"No. Life isn't so easy. Not for me. There's Uncle Adam. He's set his heart on my marrying Vin."

"So that's why I'm to give you up!"

"Yes. I'd break my word to Vin—even though I am fond of him— but I can't to Uncle Adam. You know what a sudden shock might do to him."

"I'd forgotten it," Dr. Walters owned in a shamed voice.

"My father was one of those who lost everything a few years ago and jumped from the top floor of a skyscraper. Because he and Father had been old friends Uncle Adam offered me a home." She rushed through the words in the manner of a child hastening the recitation of a lesson learned by rote. "Charity! I shouldn't have accepted, but I did accept. He's counting on me to marry Vin. When you have debts you pay them, don't you? This is the only way I can pay."

"I can't argue with you." Dr. Walters pressed his moist hand tensely against the glass top of one of the museum cases. "Because I'm a doctor I'll have to be honest. Frankly I don't know what a sudden shock would do to Adam Merriweather. It might not be fatal or even dangerous, but—"

She shivered. "We can't accept the risk, Gay. If anything happened we'd be criminals, murderers."

"Yes, if anything happened."

She held out her hand. "Gay, my dear! Thank you so for being honest."

She pressed his hand with sudden, desperate strength and ran from the room. He waited there in silence. How lightly she ran! He could scarcely hear her fugitive footsteps. He listened intently. She was on the stairs, now she was in the upper hall. He could hear her no longer. His last link with Janice Shelton had been broken.

He must get out of here, must leave this house immediately. As he strode toward the door he recognized the heavy tread of Adam Merriweather just outside. They met in the corridor.

"Good evening, Mr. Merriweather."

"Evening," the other answered shortly. What had come over him? Something that Walters, for all his science, didn't understand. Merriweather's face was flushed in feverish excitement; he was elated and yet, at the same time, furtive.

"I don't like the way you're looking," Walters said with genuine concern. "Please step over to your study, and we'll have another examination."

"No!" Merriweather's voice raised to a fretful, impatient snarl. "Not tonight; I haven't the time. There's going to be a thunderstorm."

"Early tomorrow then?"

"Yes, come tomorrow."

Stepping inside the Tibetan Room, Merriweather closed the door in his doctor's face. Walters, as he turned to walk down the corridor, heard the click of its lock sound behind him. Not until he had reached the front porch did it occur to the doctor that his patient had said an odd thing. Yes, an odd thing, but he could not think of it.

But as he stepped into the street he remembered that it had been something about a thunderstorm. The storm was beginning now; its threatening rumbles reminded him of artillery fire. Of the Japanese guns roaring before Peiping in a world gone suddenly mad.

II

In comparison with the overwhelming personality of Jed Merriweather his brother Adam appeared pallid, Vincent anemic, Mrs. Gestler artificial, and Westborough (the historian had permitted himself the risk of hobbling downstairs to join the others at dinner) insignificant. The great man's voice rumbled across his brother's living room like the deep notes of a twenty-foot Tibetan trumpet as he related his incredible traveler's tale.

Far out on the Takla Makan Desert a tiny caravan had plodded its snail's pace across the soft sands of tamarisk-studded dunes, across gravel and stone-hard clay, over dwindling yellow rivers and by shrinking salt lakes. Its goal had been the ancient course of a vanished stream where centuries ago, if Turki tradition were to be believed, an oasis had flourished.

"I was gambling on a buried city," Dr. Merriweather informed his enthralled listeners. "A city of the almost legendary times when the teachings of the Buddha blossomed in the deserts of Sinkiang. They have been obliterated for nearly a thousand years, those teachings, while the voices of muezzins call the faithful to prayer, yet their memory persists faintly in the race consciousness, since, of all the things in this mutable world, tradition dies the hardest.

"Do you see what I mean? Far out on the desert may be a spot of sand, no different from the surrounding terrain and yet considered holy ground. Why? The Turkis do not know, but it is because a famous shrine once stood there, a shrine which a thousand years ago countless pilgrims trooped across the desert to revere. Although the shrine has been buried for centuries, its very memory forgotten, the descendants of those pilgrims still cross the desert to pay homage to the same site. It was a tale of this nature which led my caravan across the Takla Makan just five years ago.

"We did not find what we sought. We did not uncover any of those ancient Buddhist chapels whose painted frescoes preserve the last direct influence of the dying art of Hellas. But we found something even better. We excavated a Tibetan fort.

"Of all the races which have swept through Turkestan—Huns, Mongols, Chinese, Uighurs, Turks, Nestorian Christians, it would take an hour just to name them—the Tibetan domination has interested me the most. Perhaps it was the incredible cheek of them: establishing their outposts months away from their own cities over the barren desolation of the Chang Tang and the terrible passes of the Kuen-Lun and Altyn-Tagh ranges; holding their lonely garrisons in defiance of the not inconsiderable Chinese power of the T'ang dynasty. Tibetans may look back with pride to their years of glory in the eighth century when their nation was one of the greatest in the whole of Asia."

He described the excavations in detail. The offensive ammonia smell, lingering after a millennium to attest to the homely purposes to which the Tibetan soldiers had once put their former living quarters. The ancient rubbish heap which had yielded such rich treasures.

"The trash they'd once thrown away was a gold mine to me. Digging into it, I found fragments of paper—that tough-fibered paper made from the pulped bark of the daphne laurel which grows hundreds of miles away on the Himalayan watershed. There were leaves from sacred manuscript books and—far more important—scraps of secular writing. I translated parts of the latter; you can hardly realize how similar to today was the life they were then leading. Some of my fragments were stamped with vermilion seals; these papers were official military correspondence and included orders to dispatch troops or to send provisions, inventories of the bows and arrows, shields and swords contained within the garrison, and one letter from a minor officer at a distant outpost giving himself an unimpeachable alibi for disastrously losing a frontier skirmish with the Chinese forces. Other bits of writing—not so numerous as the military correspondence---related to civil matters: account books, records of court proceedings, even letters of a purely personal nature. All in all it was the greatest find I had ever made, and it kept me happily busy for weeks. I had twelve cases of these manuscripts packed for transport when the Turki merchant with whom I had contracted for supplies arrived from the nearby oasis of Chargatik to bring me some startling news.

"A Turki revolt at Hami had plunged all of Sinkiang into a bloody civil war. The Turkis had appealed to their coreligionists, the Tungans—Chinese Mohammedans whose strongholds are the strip of oases in the southern fringe of the Takla Makan, right in the very district where I was now excavating. The Tungans, a race of brawling ruffians who would rather fight any day than eat, were besieging Urumchi, the capital city of the province. And the Urumchi administration had retaliated by dispatching an army, a partisan band of White Russians, to raid the Tungan villages and ravish them with fire and sword.

"The leader of these Russians (White only by courtesy, since they had long since lost their last vestige of political beliefs of any nature) was a noted terrorist whom the Urumchi government feared almost as much as it feared the Tungans, and the assignment was a shrewd bit of strategy in the traditional Chinese policy of letting one foe swallow another. This dreaded guerilla band had already struck at oases east of Chargatik and would come there, it was expected, almost momentarily. My Turki, with the fine fidelity that is characteristic of his race, had risked a meeting with them in order to bring me the warning.

"I had to act quickly. We were between the Russians and Chargatik and were short of supplies, since my Turki had not taken the time to bring the usual stores with him. Our only hope was to beat the Russians to Chargatik, but there was a better than even chance that we wouldn't be able to save our lives.

"Trusting that my Tibetan fort would remain unmolested until I could return to it, I ordered the ruins to be hastily covered and our ponies and camels loaded. We started off to Chargatik. It was a ghastly race. If the Russians won it we would be forced to choose between a quick death by rifle or a slow death by thirst while we hid from them in the desert. Or perhaps we wouldn't be permitted to choose anything.

"However, we reached Chargatik first, and I risked a day there in order to replenish our depleted stores. We had no trouble in obtaining everything we needed. The inhabitants—those of them who had had the courage to remain in their homes—looked upon us as a godsend. We offered them silver, which could be securely buried in the desert, in place of food and water, which were certain to be confiscated or destroyed when the Russians arrived. Or *if* the Russians arrived, I should say, since I heard many conflicting reports. There was even a rumor that the Tungan hero, Ma Chung-yin, had met and completely annihilated the Russian forces. That, however, I could not believe, since Ma Chung-yin, according to the best information available, was still with the besiegers of Urumchi, two hundred and fifty miles to the north of us.

"We left Chargatik early in the morning. If we could move quickly enough to stay ahead of the Russians I was hopeful that we might succeed in reaching Yarkand, and from there we could travel over the five highest caravan passes in the world to Leh in British territory. But the Russians fooled me. They were approaching Chargatik not from the east but from the west, and we were directly in their path.

"Fortunately we had started before sunrise. And fortunately also, we were not making as much noise as they were. We heard their shouts from a distance, and I gave the order instantly to dismount. At such moments one thinks quickly or he does not live to think at all. We led our ponies and camels behind a sand dune and waited while they passed us, riding hell-for-leather. Had a horse neighed or a camel vented its bubbling roar they would have known of our presence, but the animals displayed a rare intelligence. Or perhaps the gods of all the archaeologists were fighting in our favor.

"I counted the dark shapes as the horses passed. There were not many of them. This could not be the main force, I saw, but was merely a small detachment sent to harry Chargatik. Then, since they rode from the west, the main body could not be east, as I had been informed, but must be camped in some oasis directly ahead of us, barring our westward escape. It was a dismaying outlook.

"The present, however, was even worse than our future prospects. If there had been time to convey a warning to Chargatik . . . but there was none. A quarter of a mile away we heard the rattle of machine guns, the shrieks of the terrified inhabitants, and then all noises were swallowed by unholy silence. The sun was just beginning to show on the horizon when the Russian butchers rode past us again; they were glutted with blood triumph and whooping like Comanche Indians. When they were out of sight we returned to Chargatik to render what service we could for its wounded. But there were no wounded, only corpses."

The silence which followed the cessation of Jed Merriweather's voice held in itself something of a startling quality. "I don't know why I'm going over all this. It's familiar ground to all of you, even to Mr. Westborough, since he confesses he's read my book."

"Pray do not leave us at such a point," the historian pleaded.

"Very well. You asked for the story, so you'll get all of it. Now that the road to the western oases was barred our own position had become an impossible one. On the east lay a desert almost totally void of water; on the north was Urumchi, where the struggle between the Soviet-supported provincial government and the Tungan warriors was raging in full force; on the south was, in many respects, the very worst road of them all. To go south meant climbing up to the Tibetan plateau over one of the world's greatest ranges, the Kuen-Lun mountains; it meant making our way westward to Ladakh across the desolate expanse of the Chang Tang. However, there was no feasible alternative.

"I took my camels—those shaggy, two-humped Bactrians of Central Asia—over the Kuen-Lun mountains as the Bonvalot expedition had done nearly fifty years before. It wasn't an easy journey. Bactrian camels can stand almost any hardship, including variations of temperature from a hundred and forty degrees Fahrenheit to Arctic cold, and yet two of them died on the way up and one more along the Chang Tang. In addition I lost several ponies, so that I was forced to jettison all but one, and that the smallest, of my precious cases of manuscripts. I knew that once we had reached Leh the Indian government would never grant me permission to re-enter Tibet. Unless I could save them now, I had lost them forever. I made a desperate decision and altered our course to the south.

"In that direction is Tibet—the inhabited regions of it—and Tibet remains forbidden country. But no matter how hostile the attitude of the Tibetan officials we encountered, it was not likely that they would refuse to sell us the horses with which to leave their land. Thus equipped, we could retrace our steps on the Chang Tang, recover my cases of manuscripts and continue to Leh according to original plans. Or so I thought then.

"Some good did come out of that journey southward. We found Chang. One more mouth to feed—when we had so little---but I don't believe a man in the party ever regretted it. Well, we were arrested and dragged before the dzong-pon as I had expected. What I had not expected was that the dzong-pon would turn out to be one of the most flinty-hearted scoundrels I had ever encountered. After a conference lasting for several hours and entailing endless discussion, he allowed us to buy, at quadruple the market prices, four ponies. Four miserable ponies!

"It was diabolically calculated. Assuming that all of our transport animals survived, we were assured of reaching Leh, but unless we starved ourselves beyond endurance we could not hope to reclaim my cases of manuscripts. Not even a single one.

"The dzong-pon was as inflexible as death to all of my entreaties. He hinted that four ponies was perhaps too large a number to allow us, and if he were forced to listen to further protests . . . We started at once on our way across the Chang Tang.

"It was a heart-rending trip. One after one I passed the cairns marking the burial sites of the eleven precious cases I had been forced to sacrifice, and I could do nothing but leave them there. Worse yet! Another of my camels died, and I was forced to surrender the twelfth and last case of all. The net result of the greatest archaeological find since Sir Aurel Stein's Turkestan expeditions was exactly nothing, but it was either that or face certain starvation. Only the Chang Tang could offer such a terrible alternative.

"Mile after mile we made our way—across stone-strewn plains, over valleys green with treacherous ice, up cliff walls painted with the colors of a Grand Canyon sunrise. We toiled to the top of the 17,600-foot Chang La pass and climbed down 6000 feet in the next fifty miles. We reached Leh. Ordinarily I am very fond of Leh. It is one of those towns to which the overworked adjectives 'quaint' and 'picturesque' belong by inherent right: white houses clinging to the hillside and the flaming spires of cho-tens. But that day it was hateful. As we rode under the row of poplars overlooking the shuttered shops of the bazaar I had just one consolation. All of the men who had started with me from our camp near Chargatik were still alive.

"I pulled every wire I could command in the attempt to organize a return expedition, but, as I had feared, it was hopeless. At Leh I could do nothing, at Srinagar I found hands and feet bound fast by official red tape, at Delhi I failed, utterly and ignominiously. The Indian government refused, under any circumstances, to permit me to re-enter Tibet, even the desolate Chang Tang. They were not unsympathetic, those brisk, pleasant officials to whom I told my story; they would have liked to help me, I believe, but they were compelled to live up to the letter and the spirit of their government's treaty obligations. The twelve cases of manuscript I had brought with me from Chargatik were gone forever—an appalling loss to the world. It was almost ruin.

"A slender fragment of hope, however, remained to me. Other fragments, fragments I had not had the time to unearth, lay still buried by the desert sands of Sinkiang, and if ever I could get permission to return there . . . Well, it took me five years of waiting for comparative peace to descend upon Sinkiang, of wirepulling in Nanking. But the net result is that at last I have a passport."

"Not worth the paper it's written on," Adam Merriweather snapped.

He did not attempt to conceal the malice in his voice. "Your luck's as bad as it was five years ago, Jed. What do you think this Sino-Japanese war will do to your passport? It's sure to be revoked."

"It's a good enough passport to get me over the Karakorum range from Kashmir," Jed Merriweather returned. His voice had become tired, the voice of a man who knows he is hopelessly beaten. "The Tungans were forced back from Urumchi by the Soviet-backed troops of the *tupan*---the new military governor—but they haven't yet been driven out of the southern oases. They still pay nominal allegiance to Nanking and will recognize its passport. And the Tungan leaders are my good friends."

"By this time the tupan has probably blasted your Tungan friends out of existence," Adam Merriweather sneered. "You may be fool enough to commit suicide, Jed, but I don't see why I should allow you to do it on my money. And the fifty or sixty thousand dollars you require is by no means the small change you seem to think. All of your life you have been notoriously lax in money matters."

"Is that your last word, Adam?"

"By no means. If you are able to convince me that your project is reasonable I shall aid you as generously as I have always aided your past expeditions. Shall we, however, defer the matter for later discussion?"

Vincent sprang to his feet, trembling with pent-up emotion. "Let's get out of here, Uncle Jed. Let's take my canoe out on the lake."

"In a thunderstorm?" Mrs. Gestler asked.

"Thunder!" Adam Merriweather exclaimed. "Are you sure, Alma? The paper doesn't say that "

"Adam, my dear, I don't care in the least what the paper does or does not say. I can trust to my own ears, which, as you know, are very good ones. And I have just heard a thunderclap."

"Well, a wetting may do us good," Jed Merriweather laughed, his hand resting affectionately on his nephew's shoulder. "Come on, Vin. I'll take you up on that canoe ride."

They left the room together. When they had gone Adam Merriweather slowly raised his pudgy body from his high-backed Renaissance chair.

"Thunder! Are you sure, Alma, that it was thunder you heard?"

"Yes, certainly. What ails you tonight, Adam?"

"You take nothing seriously, Alma, so I shall waste few words." Merriweather's voice deepened, altered in tone as if some unknown agency were speaking through his mouth. "I am upon the verge of a tremendous discovery. Perhaps the greatest discovery ever known to modern times."

PART NINE: A Door Is Opened
(Thursday Evening, July 22)

WESTBOROUGH excused himself to Mrs. Gestler. There were some important questions which he wished to ask immediately of the Lama Tsongpun Bonbo. He made an elaborate pretense of hobbling down the corridor, but it was wasted effort as he encountered no one.

As he passed the door of the Tibetan Room he noticed a tiny thread of light showing from underneath. Could Adam Merriweather be in there now? Adam Merriweather, who had behaved so strangely? Cautiously Westborough attempted to open the door. It had been locked from the inside. If it were Merriweather within it was clear that he did not wish to be disturbed.

Westborough hobbled up the back stairs. In the upper hall he passed the door of Miss Shelton's bedroom. "Dear, dear!" he clucked and hurried away self-consciously. He could have sworn that he had heard the sound of sobbing from within. Heartbreaking, unrestrained sobbing.

Truly it was an odd household. Of all its members Mrs. Gestler alone seemed to be entirely normal. Westborough reached the bedroom where, he knew, Tsongpun Bonbo had retired for religious exercises. Under ordinary circumstances the historian would not have dreamed of interrupting the Tibetan, but these circumstances were not ordinary ones. Tsongpun Bonbo, and Tsongpun Bonbo alone, could answer his questions.

The door of the bedroom stood ajar, permitting Westborough to peer inside. He caught a glimpse of the lama, who was seated cross-legged upon the bare floor, telling a rosary of yellow beads. From his lips issued Tibetan prayers which had, to Westborough, a sound suggesting the purring of a huge cat.

Westborough, liking less than ever to interrupt the lama's religious devotions, knocked shyly on the door. For a few moments his knock received no answer; the lama did not look around. Then his deep, full voice said slowly in English:

"Your please coming in, Kusho Wes-bo-ro?"

The Tibetan had not turned his head. How was it possible for him to know the identity of the person standing on his threshold? Westborough felt suddenly awed. Hitherto he had regarded the lama mainly as a naive child; now he had the odd sensation that he was standing in the presence of a deeper, more penetrating wisdom than any the West could offer.

"Dear me!" he cried in confusion. "Pray forgive me for disturbing you. I would not have interrupted for the world if I had not believed it to be important."

The lama turned toward his visitor, and the illusion of a mysterious wisdom suddenly vanished. His face held only the simple, friendly smile which Westborough had always known.

"Your coming in, Kusho? Your taking chair?"

Although his guest accepted the chair indicated the lama remained seated upon the floor. He was a true follower of the Buddha who had forbidden the use of high seats to his *bhikshus*. He continued to finger his beads—deep yellow wooden spheres the size of large peas—while he waited for his guest to begin the conversation, but there was no trace of nervousness or of impatience in his manner. Tsongpun Bonbo had the gift, one so rare in the Occident, of remaining silent without ungraciousness.

"Because of your great wisdom, Tsongpun Lama, I come to you in search of the answer to a problem of great difficulty," Westborough began. This florid style of speech was the best substitute he could manage for the elaborate honorific language of Tibet in which, he knew, the priest was accustomed to being addressed. "It is a problem which has troubled me very much."

The lama's smile deepened; his hands moved in an expressive gesture. Westborough took courage to continue.

"As one who seeks enlightenment from the great dark of ignorance, I beg of you to explain to me the nature of the Secret Doctrine."

He used the Tibetan word he had learned from Jed Merriweather, wishing to make certain that the lama would understand. And Tsongpun Bonbo did understand. Although his manner, his voice remained as courteous as always there was more than a slight reserve in his answer.

"My not knowing Secret Pat', Kusho."

"But," Westborough persisted, "surely you are acquainted with those who have known it? Or at least you can tell me something of its goal."

"Who knowing its goal, Kusho, who habe not study? Perhaps reaching t'e Siddhi."

"The Siddhi!" Westborough gasped breathlessly. He recognized the

Sanskrit word as one common in the language of Yoga, into which art he had once experimentally delved. "The eight magical powers of the Siddhi? The ability to make one's body lighter, heavier, smaller, to reach any place? . . . I do not remember the others."

"Your knowing ?" It was amazing how quickly the lama's friendly smile had disappeared. "Please, your not taking Secret Way, Kusho? It not *your* pat'."

Westborough was again conscious that he stood on the threshold of an ancient, unexplored wisdom. But a wisdom perilous to explore. The lama's earnestness, even more than his words, revealed the danger.

"It is not I who plan to tread the Secret Path, but---"

A clap of thunder interrupted him from the heavens, an extremely loud one. Westborough's nerves were shaken unexpectedly, and he jumped in alarm. A second and even louder clap followed instantly.... Mrs. Gestler's prediction of a thunderstorm was certainly going to be fulfilled. He thought regretfully of Jed and Vincent Merriweather adrift on the lake in a tiny canoe. This promised to be one of those sudden summer electrical storms in which the rain pours down with the temporary volume of a Niagara. Both of them would certainly be soaked to their skins; he did hope that they would be able to make port without swamping. His thoughts were interrupted by a new sound, a sound which caused him to jump higher than he had leaped for either clap of thunder. A single word pronounced in a harsh, a guttural voice:

"Heegh!"

It had been a sound and not a word. In no language with which he was familiar could he recognize it as a word. Perhaps his ears were playing him tricks, and he had heard merely the pounding of the rain against the house tiles. (The thundershower was now confirming his worst fears of what its violence would be.)

"Heegh!"

This time there could be no mistake. A human voice had muttered the guttural sound. Was it a Tibetan word? He turned to the lama for enlightenment, but the lama's face expressed a puzzlement equal to his own. One thing only was certain, Westborough decided. It had not been a cry for help. In the deep, resolute intonation of the sound he could detect no terror.

"Heegh!"

It was coming from a distance . . . from below . . . obviously from the Tibetan Room. Westborough recalled the exultation that he had seen shining in Adam Merriweather's face only a few minutes before. He remembered the locked door to the Tibetan Room he had found

on his way upstairs. Was Merriweather in there now? If one strolled to
the balustrade one could look downward through the interstices between the painted beams. . . .

No, he decided suddenly, he was not going to do it.

His role of spy, all it entailed, had become repugnant to him. If
Adam Merriweather had chosen to dip into the murky waters of the
occult that was his own concern. Westborough told himself that he would
not, under any circumstances, rise from his chair nor take a single step
toward the railing. Nevertheless, he listened for a repetition of the
strange sound.

He expected it momentarily (it had occurred at very regular inter-
vals), but it did not come again. Odd! He wondered why his heart was
pounding so agitatedly. In sympathy with the drenching rain which beat
against the glass windows ? Or was it some other quality present in the
atmosphere? An esoteric quality of he knew not what nature.

Westborough rose shakily to his feet. In spite of his firm resolutions
something, like the pull of a giant magnet, was drawing him toward the
balustrade. The lama, as though impelled by the same unseen force,
sprang to his feet with easy agility and followed. . . . Another sound
came to them from below.

This time, however, it was plainly a sound not made by human voice.
A metallic clatter and after that the noise of a heavy object striking the
floor. Sick with horror, Westborough bolted for the railing.

He saw what he had hoped he would not see. By the west end of the
yellow altar a man's body was lying face downward.

II

The doors to the Tibetan Room were locked, both doors. Frantic
pounding brought no response. The quick-thinking brain of Jed Merriweather took instant command of the situation. He and Vincent had
just come in from the lake, their clothes dripping wet.

They were heavy doors, the archaeologist explained in quick, terse
phrases. It would take time to batter one open. Wasted time in which a
human life might be saved. There was another alternative.

They raced up the stairs, Westborough, forgetful of the miraculous
recovery his ankle was displaying, with them. A straggling group of panting, frightened people: Vincent, Jed, Alma, Janice, Chang, the lama,
Wilkins, the other servants. Everyone in the house, in fact, except its
master.

Vincent had brought a rope from the boathouse; Jed was knotting
it about the balustrade with the swift, deft touch of one accustomed to

the intricacies of packsaddles. "It may be, probably is, only a faint," he flung out hopefully. "Janice, go to the phone and call Doctor Walters. If Walters gets here soon enough we may be able to save him."

Westborough noticed the sudden tenseness of her body, the equally sudden relaxation of its taut muscles, and then she was gone with the swiftness of a paper borne by a gusty wind. The historian's gaze traveled downward to the beams above the Tibetan Room. They were spaced fairly close together; one could walk across them without difficulty and drop (about a six-foot drop, he estimated) to the floor. But there were no signs that anyone had done this. Quite the contrary. The layer of dust on the top surfaces of the beams had been at no place disturbed.

Jed Merriweather finished his knots and flung the free end of the rope over the railing. He started to climb after it when Vincent pushed him back, snatching the rope from his uncle's hands.

"I don't weigh much. It might not hold you." Before Jed could reply the boy had slid downward at a dizzy rate, doing, Westborough noted, a deal of damage to the dust on the beams. With one accord they rushed downstairs. Vincent had the door open by the time the first one had reached the corridor. The boy's face was like a sheet of white paper.

"He---he---doesn't answer!"

They dashed pell-mell into the room. Westborough, as he passed the altar, caught a glimpse of typewritten papers resting there, an incongruous note among the Tibetan oddities, but he gave them little heed. Later he was to regret many times that he had not taken instant possession of them.

Adam Merriweather was lying face downward directly before— Westborough realized with a quick start---directly before the black image of Yama, the terrifying Lord of Death. The fingers of the millionaire's right hand were clenched about a dorje, one of those mystic thunderbolts of Lama ceremonies. Westborough somehow found himself the first to raise the collector's head. He saw that the pupils of Merriweather's pale blue eyes were widely dilated, mirroring a frozen horror.

The historian had had much ghastly experience of recent years— too much not to recognize the truth. He said quietly: "Mr. Merriweather is dead."

Someone shrieked. It was Mrs. Gestler. "Please," Westborough requested, "do not touch the body—he must not be moved until the poli— until Doctor Walters comes here."

In what form had it been, the death which had overtaken Adam Merriweather behind the locked doors of this room? A natural death as the result of his weakened artery? Or death by means of which Westborough was not unfamiliar—the horrible agencies of bullet or dagger?

Merriweather's pallid face was unmarred, his white summer clothing unstained, apparently, by telltale spot of red. But it would be impossible to determine that for certain without turning over the body, a step for which Westborough did not wish to take the responsibility. There was, however, no reason why he could not examine the carpeting in the dead man's vicinity. As he stooped to do so his fingers came in sudden contact with moisture.

Westborough stifled his horrified outcry. It was water he had found and not blood. There was a large pool near Merriweather's body. He saw also that a *melong*, one of the round ceremonial mirrors, was lying on the floor— doubtless it had been its fall which had caused the metallic clatter. The surface of the mirror was wet too; where did all this water come from? Rising again to his feet, he was able to answer the question immediately.

One of the silk-wrapped vases on the altar had been tipped over and was drenching the altar cloth in the vicinity of the Thunderbolt God, Chana Dorje. Gleaming in the midst of the wet yellow brocade was a circular spot of silver—the head of a thumbtack. Westborough pried it loose from the altar; certainly an ordinary enough looking thumbtack, although one with rather a long shank.

He pushed it back where he had found it, and glanced around at his companions. Apparently none of them had seen his hasty inspection of the altar.

Chang and the lama were talking to each other in excited Tibetan; Jed and Alma were regarding their brother's motionless body in a stunned silence. Vincent had moved apart from the others and was leaning against the glass case containing the demon masks---enormous painted faces with saucer-shaped eyes and fierce scowls. Vincent's face was a mask also, a mask of tortured grief. Shocked at having intruded on the boy's privacy, Westborough turned away. . . . He recalled the typewritten sheets he had seen on the altar and felt that he would like to know the nature of their contents.

The typewritten sheets, however, were no longer upon the altar. Surprised, Westborough voiced his queries to his companions. Nobody in the Tibetan Room would admit having seen them.

III

Taking advantage of the confusion, Westborough was able to slip unnoticed from the Tibetan Room and walk across the hall to Adam Merriweather's study. There was a telephone in there, he remembered, a cradle telephone ornate with mother of pearl, which must have been especially made to harmonize with the intarsia of Merriweather's eighteenth-century bureau-desk. Picking up the handset of this aristocratic instrument, Westborough dialed a number.

While he waited for the connection to be completed he could not help but ponder upon Adam Merriweather's interest in the "Secret Doctrine." Both Dr. Merriweather and the lama had condemned that enigmatic ritual as one highly dangerous to practice. Could mystic exercises of this nature have been responsible for Merriweather's sudden death?

Westborough sighed. He was headed directly into the dark, winding alleys of the occult—alleys whose twists were just enough familiar to cause him to dislike intensely the thought of traversing them. Yet he feared very much that it might be necessary. . . . Mack's gruff tones sounded on the other end of the wire. Mack's not very emotional voice conveyed a shocked surprise.

"Stand by, I'm coming right up there. How was it done? Strangled like the other guy or what? Who's in the house now? Any ideas as to who did it? Or can you talk over the phone?"

Westborough staggered under the machine-gun fusillade of questions. "It does not look as though he had been murdered," he finally managed to say and explained the circumstances as briefly as possible.

"Nope, that doesn't look like murder," Mack agreed. "How could it be murder? Just the same I'm coming over to have a look at him. Don't let 'em move the body. And stop the servants from washing up the dinner dishes. There's a thousand-to-one shot that it might be poison."

Westborough hung up the phone and glanced toward the steel filing cabinet in which Adam Merriweather had admitted he kept his esoteric papers. The historian was surprised to see a ring of keys protruding from the cabinet's lock.

"Dear, dear, dear!" he exclaimed. The temptation was a most alluring one, but even though he were sufficiently unscrupulous to yield to it (and he sadly feared that he was) there was no time now for meandering from Mack's clear-cut instructions. Later perhaps? But someone might remove the keys. And he did not wish to keep them on his own person.

A means occurred by which he could obviate the difficulty. He locked the cabinet, removed the keys and dropped them out of sight in a nook between the cabinet and the wall. In all probability no one would find them before he was able to return. Leaving the study, he went in search of Wilkins, whom he found in the butler's pantry, putting away the last of the silverware.

Yes, the dinner dishes had been washed long ago, the butler informed him and accompanied the information with an extremely puzzled stare. Westborough did not attempt to explain; any explanation, he felt, would merely deepen Wilkins' suspicions. He turned and walked into the dining room, hoping that he would be able to rejoin the other members of the household before his absence became noticeable. But fate held no such good fortune in store.

Chang was in the dining room, waiting impassively between the sixteenth-century refectory table and an enormous credenza. The Tibetan bowed politely, but with the air of keeping a book in which all of Westborough's black marks were efficiently noted. The others, he explained pointedly, were waiting in the living room for the arrival of Dr. Walters.

Westborough desired to ask several questions of Chang, but the present moment did not seem exactly the proper time for them. He turned and hobbled ignominiously from the field. (He must never again forget that he could not walk without hobbling.)

Miss Shelton and Mrs. Gestler were the only ones in the living room. Where, Westborough wondered, were Dr. and Vincent Merriweather? They came into the room before he could nerve himself to speak to the two stunned women.

"We carried him upstairs," Dr. Merriweather explained tersely. "Afraid, though, it's too late. Poor Adam!"

They had moved the body! Westborough suppressed a horrified exclamation. Dear, dear! He did not know what Lieutenant Mack would say to this action when he arrived. But neither did he know what the Merriweathers would say when Lieutenant Mack arrived. . .. The historian was acutely conscious of being in a despicable position.

A loud, importunate ring from the front doorbell announced the arrival of Dr. Walters, who had covered the intervening distance with surprising celerity. Jed and Vincent accompanied the doctor upstairs. Westborough, although uninvited, hobbled after them, reaching the door of Merriweather's bedroom in time to see the doctor flinging back a sheet.

All of Westborough's instincts urged him to look the other way, but he felt that he owed it to John Mack to see whatever was possible. Very little was possible. The deceased was now resting on his back instead of face downward as they had found him. His clothing had not yet been removed, and Westborough noticed that the front of the white linen coat and the knees of the white linen trousers were damp. The historian remembered the upset holy-water vase, but before he could proffer this explanation to his companions Dr. Walters had closed the door, barring the three men from the bedroom. When he reopened it, after a considerable interval, the white sheet again covered the body of Adam Merriweather.

Dr. Walters stretched his hands to uncle and nephew. "You know what I have to say, I guess. If it's any consolation it must have been over in an instant—no suffering. Poor Merriweather! He was in bad condition, apt to go at any time, but I hadn't expected, somehow, that it would happen so soon."

Westborough, greatly as he disliked the necessity, felt constrained to ask a question.

You are satisfied, Doctor Walters, that his death was a natural one?"

"Of course it was," the doctor snapped. He was laboring under an unusual strain, no doubt; it was not his nature to snap at his interlocutors. "I examined him thoroughly."

A slang word the historian had learned from Lieutenant Mack seemed an appropriate one to apply to himself at the present time. It was the word "heel." Whatever this kind of "heel" might be, Westborough was sure that he was now behaving like one. Yet he had no alternative.

"Are you satisfied to sign the death certificate?"

"Certainly I'll sign it."

"Without a postmortem examination?"

"The cause of death is so clear that none is needed."

"Dear me, I am sorry to be so insistent," Westborough murmured unhappily, "but without a postmortem examination one cannot detect the presence of poison."

"Poison!" the three men shouted in one voice.

"It is a possibility which must not be overlooked. I have ventured to take the liberty of notifying Lieutenant Mack, who is now on his way to visit us."

Regarding the shocked, haggard faces of the two Merriweathers, Westborough felt himself to be more of a "heel" than ever.

PART TEN: The Secret Doctrine
(Friday Morning, July 23)

CAREFUL TO MAKE no sound, Westborough dressed as best he could in the dark. The hour of 3 A.M. was an admirable one for his purpose. By now the most restless of sleepers must be dozing in oblivion, and there remained for him a full two and a half hours until sunrise. If the opportunity to search the study were not embraced now it must be forever lost.

Unless he exhibited a degree of gall which he did not possess Westborough could not remain in the house another day. He was no longer a welcome guest. There had been an extremely stormy scene last night before Lieutenant Mack had been permitted to have his way with regard to the autopsy. As the one directly responsible for the unwelcome intrusion, Westborough knew that he had dropped to an icy zero in the esteem of the household.

Not that Lieutenant Mack had made himself in any way offensive. Indeed, the detective had been extraordinarily tactful, almost apologetic, in his dealings with the bereaved family. He had asked comparatively few questions, and his examination of the premises had been, for him, a perfunctory one. Even when he was told that Merriweather's body had been carried upstairs Mack had bulldozed no one, and that was very nearly an all-time record in restraint. But the detective himself had seemed to share the general opinion that he was stirring up an unnecessary red herring.

Westborough inserted his feet into bedroom slippers; they would not be so noisy, and the bandage around his ankle precluded the wearing of street shoes. He allowed the bandage to remain, but he did not think it necessary to take his cane. The sprained-ankle pretense "gag" was the expressive word favored by Lieutenant Mack—had now worn thin.

The upper hall was as dark as the pitch mentioned by John Bunyan. A flashlight would be helpful, but Westborough did not possess one. Nor did he dare to turn on the hall lights. Fortunately he was reasonably well acquainted with the geography of the house by this time and was able to grope his way to the back stairs without mishap.

At the staircase landing he paused to gaze out the window. The violent thunderstorm had ceased hours before, and he could see also a few stars shining. There should also be a full moon. . . . No, the moon must have long since crossed its meridian and would be visible, if at all, only from the western side of the house.

However, he must not complain of the darkness. (If only he were able to keep from stumbling on these stairs!) Darkness and black magic were singularly suited to each other, and it was black magic which he was now going to investigate. Or was it?

He closed and locked the study door before he ventured to turn on the light. The thought of invading the dead man's privacy had become distasteful. Why do it? In a few more hours he would be out of the Merriweather house, back into his own familiar world. Why not give up the investigation now? "No," he murmured softly to himself. "In the words of Talleyrand, 'The wine is drawn, it must be drunk.'" Crossing to the eighteenth-century desk, he withdrew a handful of papers.

They were letters (most of the papers in the desk seemed to be letters), and personal correspondence held little interest for him. One missive, however, seemed worthy of examination, an airmail letter with a San Francisco postmark. After noting that the postmark had been stamped on last Saturday afternoon at 1 P.M., Westborough removed the epistle from its envelope and read it without compunction.

DEAR ADAM:

Don't write that the plan is impossible in views of threatening war clouds over the Orient. It is not. I am coming to Chicago to explain what we can do to meet that contingency.

Don't say no until you talk to me. But I am confident that you will see this through as you have seen the others.

If I can make it I'll leave tomorrow night, which will bring me into Chicago Wednesday morning. Will wire to let you know definitely. Till later, then, and best regards to the best of brothers.

JED.

Adam Merriweather had died, Westborough recalled as he returned the letter to its envelope, before his brother had been able to secure the backing he sought. Merely another instance of Jed Merriweather's continued ill luck! The historian deserted the desk for the filing cabinet, which, he was now positive, held the papers he wanted to find. The keys were still in the nook by the wall where he had dropped them. He

recovered the ring, selected the proper key and was in the act of inserting it into the cabinet lock when he stopped dead still.

Westborough's hearing was moderately good, and he believed that
he had heard the tread of feet upon the staircase. He hurriedly switched
off the study light.

Leaning against the door, he listened intently, but the sound was
not repeated. He waited a short interval before he unlocked the door.
He unlocked it very slowly, so that it might not click, and turned the
doorknob in an equally cautious manner.

How black it was in the corridor outside! But Westborough forced
himself to grope around a complete circuit of it before he returned to
the study. He had seen or heard nothing. Surely his nerves had been
playing him tricks!

He turned on the study lights and opened the cabinet. Its two bottom drawers held books: there was his own copy of Kustner's *Tibetan
Mysticism* and several other works of a similar nature. He noted in one
of these books that certain sentences had been underlined. They were
references pertaining to the Secret Doctrine.

The references were all extremely general in their nature, as was to
be expected. The information which Adam Merriweather sought had
never been published outside of Tibet; Westborough was doubtful if it
had even been committed to Tibetan block print.

He replaced the books and opened the upper two drawers of the
cabinet. They were crammed with papers. Westborough scanned the
title of folder after folder. He found only translations from the Kan-gyur,
the Tibetan scriptures, or from the Ten-gyur, the official commentary.
Naturally there were many gaps. A set of the Kan-gyur is in one hundred and eight volumes; of the Ten-gyur in two hundred and twenty
volumes. Even the efficient agents of Adam Merriweather had not been
able to procure the complete sets; why, an entire caravan would be
needed to carry that many books away!

Of this enormous mass of Tibetan sacred literature only a very small
portion had hitherto been translated into European languages, Westborough knew. Chang was engaged in a great work of scholarship, one
for which posterity would be grateful, but Westborough was now searching for something else. Well toward the back of the second drawer he
found it, a bulging folder with the label "A. Merriweather---Private." He
withdrew it from the drawer and carried it to the desk for a more careful examination.

The papers it contained—unlike those in the Kan-gyur and Ten-gyur
folders—were dog-eared with much handling, confirming what Westborough had for some little time suspected. The translations of the

scriptures and their commentary were but a blind, a monumental bulwark of scholarship behind which Adam Merriweather had concealed his real reason for Chang's employment. It had not been the gospels of the Buddha which had interested the millionaire collector but Buddhism's peculiar esoteric outgrowths.

Even before he had searched through the folder Westborough had an excellent idea of what he would find there. Tantras, Yoga treatises, mantras . . . much of the material appeared to Westborough to be mere childishness unworthy of the followers of the Buddha who had forbidden his bhikshus the practice of magic. But perhaps he was mistaken in that hasty judgment and, whether he was or not, it did not matter. References to the Secret Doctrine had been underlined by Adam Merriweather, but such references, like those in the printed books on mysticism, were couched in the vaguest of vague terms, exactly as though the unknown writers had been chary of mentioning the subject.

Westborough looked for Chang's translation of the "Spells of the Thunderbolt." Surely if anyone had ever been qualified to discuss the Secret Doctrine it would have been the lotus-born Padma Sambhava and, if Jed Merriweather were right in his surmise, there was good ground for believing that he had discussed it. But the great sorcerer's secret spells were not with the other papers in the folder. Obviously they should have been in this folder if they were anywhere in the cabinet, but Westborough could not find them.

By four o'clock he had read all he cared to read of Merriweather's private folder and had learned nothing that seemed in any way germane to the collector's death. He restored the folder to its proper place in the drawer and locked the cabinet. Its keys he left where he had first found them, trusting that their temporary absence had not yet been discovered.

Turning off the study lights, he opened the hall door. Once more he stopped in sudden surprise. Were his ears up to their former tricks? Or had he actually heard something? Not footsteps this time, but the clink of metal against metal. He heard the sound again, unmistakably. It came from across the hall, from behind the closed door of the Tibetan Room.

Westborough cautiously tried the handle of the door. It was not locked. It should have been locked last night, but it was not locked now. He opened it gradually, a half inch or so at a time.

The darkness within the Tibetan Room was very nearly a fit match for that of the corridor. Westborough stepped across the threshold. It did not occur to him that he was behaving in a foolhardy manner; that the darkness could hold danger. He started to circle the Yellow King, now a mere formless hulk, in search of the light switch which, he remembered, was located there.

From behind the Yellow King moved something . . . something he could not see. He felt the touch of silk flicked about his throat, touching his skin as delicately as a lover's kiss, tightening instantly into a cruel band. He tried to shout, to scream, to yell, but though he could open his mouth no sound would issue from it. He tried to tear the silken band away; as well attempt to fight the writhing tentacle of an octopus. His legs weakened, his brain sickened, his heart gave an upward leap to meet his lungs, and he knew nothing else.

II

"Kusho Wes-bo-ro!"

From the depths of the great void where the naked soul wanders alone Westborough received the impression of someone calling. Miraculously a door opened for him, and he became conscious of other senses than sound. His hand felt the rough touch of carpeting, he realized that he was lying on a floor. The floor of the Tibetan Room of course! But why was the Yellow King calling? And why was the Yellow King bending over him? He perceived that it was not the Yellow King but the Lama Tsongpun Bonbo.

"Your not being dead, Kusho!" the lama exclaimed delightedly.

"No," Westborough tried to answer. The word issued in a hoarse, almost unrecognizable whisper. It was painful to speak, his throat was so acutely sore. The lama assisted him to rise to his feet. His forehead throbbed abominably. Little wonder, Westborough realized as he felt the large lump which had formed there.

Doubtless he had bruised his head against one of the cases when he fell. Perhaps it was that which had caused him to remain unconscious for so long a period. He had been unconscious at least an hour and a half, for he had entered this room at four and the gray light of dawn was now streaming through the skylight above his head. Sunrise, as he had taken particular note to look up yesterday, at this time of year occurred close to five-thirty by Chicago's daylight saving time.

He could not see well at all. Objects at the other end of the room were an unrecognizable blur. Where were his glasses ? The lama helped him to look for them. They were on the floor, near where he had been lying, and one lens had been shivered into fragments. He could not wear them now. Regretfully he inserted them into the case he carried in his vest pocket.

"My being glad your not being dead," the lama observed shyly.

Westborough smiled an answer. Speaking was yet too painful. But he must not complain. He had escaped death—although by a hair's breadth. If the pressure had been applied to his throat for only a few seconds longer! Westborough shuddered. Yes, he had been very fortunate.

Or was it good fortune? Had the strangler failed because he did not know his craft? Westborough did not believe so. He believed that his assailant knew it only too well. In that event his life had not been intended. Had the strangling been no more than a warning? A grim warning not to meddle in matters not his concern?

"But I will meddle," Westborough said to himself.

An hour and a half ago he had been willing to consider his part in the investigation ended. Now he wished to remain in the house if it were at all possible to think of an excuse which would keep him there. The contest had taken on the personal issue of a vendetta. He did not like to have silk cloths twisted about his neck in darkened rooms.

His first move was to visit the glass case at the eastern end of the room. He saw at once that it now contained only one Tibetan ka-ta. So? One scarf where there had once been two. Where was the other? Tied about a convenient rock and sunk in the depths of Lake Michigan perhaps? He became conscious that the lama was saying something.

"My not liking house ob Kusho Mer-ri-weat-her."

"Nor I," Westborough concurred with a wry smile.

"Kusho Mer-ri-weat-her not understanding, he liberating e-bil powers. Dan-ger-ous."

"Powers that can kill?" Westborough asked. The lama nodded gravely.

"Yes, Kusho. Soon your leaving? Staying dan-gerous."

"Dangerous indeed," Westborough agreed. "But for the present, at least, I must remain. Once more I have a question to ask you, Tsongpun Lama. Why have you visited this place before the others are awake?"

"My dreaming dream," the lama answered softly.

"A dream? Of what nature?"

"My dreaming words ob Precious Teacher hide here."

"Dear me!" Speaking had become easier now. "Did the dream show you where they were hidden?"

"Yes, Kusho, it being True Light showing all." He pointed across the room to the image of Padma Sambhava. "T'ere!"

"Under the altar?" Westborough questioned excitedly. "Dear me, are they there now?"

"My not yet looking. My seeing you, Kusho."

Westborough extended his hand. He was sorry that he did not know the Tibetan equivalent for the gesture. "You have been a true friend to me, Tsongpun Lama. We will search together for your sacred book."

But the lost manuscript was not under the altar before the statue of Padma Sambhava. There was nothing under the altar at any point but the floodlights which illuminated Adam Merriweather's twelve images and their colored screens. The lama turned disappointedly away from the search.

"Not True Light, Kusho, my dream! In house ob e-bil my not knowing True Light."

Vincent Merriweather rushed suddenly into the room. He was dressed, Westborough noticed with some surprise, in no more clothing than a pair of bathing trunks and a towel. And he was very angry.

Yes, Vincent was going to be difficult, although Westborough, remembering that the young man's father had died in this very room only last night, could not find it in his heart to blame him. The historian, moreover, was unable to furnish a convincing reason for his early morning prowl. The best explanation he was able to give sounded decidedly lame, even to his own ears. However, Vincent heard him out.

"So you heard a noise from the Tibetan Room? What sort of noise?"

"One reminding me of two pieces of metal striking together." (This much, at least, was true.) "I walked inside but could not see anything."

"Why not?"

"It was too dark."

"Dark! The sun's been up for at least an hour."

"At four o'clock it was dark," Westborough insisted.

"You mean to say you've been in here for over two hours ?"

Westborough smiled in a rueful manner. "Unfortunately I had no choice in the matter. Most of the time I was not conscious."

"What!" The towel, slipping from Vincent's shoulders, dropped unheeded to the door. "Are you telling me someone knocked you out?"

"No, I was not hit but strangled." He saw that Vincent was looking as if he didn't believe a word of it. "With a silk scarf, probably one taken from that very case. If you will be kind enough to look you may see two cards bearing the label, 'Ka-ta, or Tibetan Ceremonial Scarf.' But there is only one such scarf."

Vincent inspected the case, his face as severe as a youthful inquisitor's. "How do I know you haven't taken it out yourself? There's something queer about the way you've been acting. Where's that cane you usually carry? You don't seem to be limping this morning. And you weren't limping last night either—until you remembered about it again. If you ask me, that ankle of yours is about as much sprained as mine is. And you've been snooping around this room before; Chang told me about it. I don't know what your game is, Mr. Westborough, but I don't want any more of it. I'll give you fifteen minutes to pack your things, and then I'm going to call a taxi for you to get out of here."

Westborough wilted helplessly under the tirade. His part in the drama now seemed definitely over unless he could say something which would satisfy the new master of the house. But he could think of nothing, nothing to say in his own defense. He knew only too well that most of Vincent's rebuke was justified. The lama intervened unexpectedly.

"Can Kusho Wes-bo-ro make mark on own t'roat?"

"What?"

The lama repeated the question.

"Say, there *is* one on your throat—a red line."

"And a large bump on my forehead," Westborough added ruefully. Vincent sheepishly extended his hand.

"I'm sorry I said what I did."

"I do not in the least blame you."

"Are you badly hurt?"

"Except for a sore throat and a somewhat painful forehead I remain undamaged." While Westborough was speaking an excellent excuse for continuing as a house guest occurred to him. "My glasses, however, did not escape so well." He exhibited the interior of his spectacle case as proof. "Unfortunately I can scarcely see more than ten feet without them. I do not wish to inconvenience you at such a time, but may I be permitted to remain here until I am able to secure a duplicate pair from my opticians, who have, of course, the formula in their files?"

Vincent nodded. "Stay the weekend with us, if you want to. I'm sorry this happened. I don't understand it. Perhaps a burglar got in. Someone trying to steal something from Dad's collection."

"It is possible."

"Not Dad's any longer," Vincent amended, glancing about the room. "I can't get used to the fact that he's—that he's gone."

"You cared a great deal for your father, did you not?" Westborough asked gently.

"No," Vincent answered promptly, "I can't be a hypocrite about it. We weren't good friends. My fault, I guess. I didn't want to go into the steel business. I still don't, but I wish now---" He became suddenly conscious of his bathing trunks. "Good Lord, you must think I am a cold-blooded fish! To be going out swimming this morning!"

The historian shook his head. "Not in the least. I know that you would not have risen at such an early hour if your father's sudden death had not been a great shock to you."

"Yes, it was a shock," Vincent admitted. "I can't seem to get used to it. When I woke up, an hour or so ago, I tried lying in bed to think things over. But it wasn't any good. I felt I had to get out somewhere. So I thought maybe if I took my canoe out on the lake—"

"The lake!" Westborough interrupted. "Dear me!" The word had started a new trend of thought in his mind. "I wonder, Mr. Merriweather, if someone has not already used your canoe this morning?"

"Someone else? Who?"

"I do not know. Perhaps no one. But if you do not mind I should like to walk as far as the beach with you."

Vincent's canoe was lying overturned on the beach in front of the house. "Looks like you're wrong," the young man contended. "That's just where we left it last night."

Westborough did not answer. He had walked to the water's edge and was peering nearsightedly. Without his glasses the act of seeing was a difficult one. Suddenly he gave an exclamation of surprise. He could not be mistaken, even without his glasses. There was a shallow depression extending from the moist beach to the comparatively dry sand in which the canoe was lying. Vincent also had seen the mark.

"That's where we dragged it out of the water last night," he said.

"I beg your pardon," Westborough demurred, "but I do not see how it can be. After you came in it rained extremely hard, hard enough to obliterate, or very nearly so, the track you made then. But this gouge, as you may see, is fairly well defined. I do not believe that it was made over two hours ago."

IV

Chang's office was a surprise to Westborough, who had certainly not expected to see anything so Western and of such businesslike efficiency as its furnishings. The room was amply lighted, with windows on two sides, and commanded an excellent view of the lake. Westborough considered it distinctly preferable to Merriweather's study, and he wondered why the millionaire had not taken it for his own use. Perhaps, the historian mused, Adam Merriweather had not cared for too much light upon his occult studies.

Westborough hesitated at the entrance. He was sure that Chang's voice had answered his discreet knock, and yet the Tibetan, who was seated on a modern swivel chair before a distinctly modern flat-topped typewriter desk, did not seem to be aware of his presence. Absorbed in his work of translation, perhaps. . . . Westborough corrected himself. The paper which Chang was studying so intently was one covered with Tibetan characters, it was true, but it was not one of those long, narrow oblongs which form the pages of Tibetan books. Indeed, it looked like a sheet of ordinary American typewriter paper. Chang's red-leaded pencil was marking notations (also in Tibetan characters) here and there along the margin, just as though he were correcting an exercise. Thinking regretfully of his own teaching days, Westborough sighed. At that minute Chang looked up from the paper.

"Excuse, please, my rudeness. Will you not be seated?"

Westborough accepted a walnut office chair. "Pray do not allow me to interrupt your work."

"It does not matter. I am honored by visit from Mr. Westborough."

Whatever had come over Chang? Last night, when they had met in the dining room, he had been almost uncivil; today he was the very pinnacle of courtesy. Well, one must not too closely examine the teeth of the proverbial gift horse. . . . Westborough saw that Chang was about to put away in a drawer the paper on which he had been working.

"I beg your pardon, but am I correct in my surmise that you have been correcting an exercise?"

"You are correct," Chang replied, smiling blandly. "My privilege to teach our language to Mr. Vincent. He is very good student."

"Mr. Vincent studying Tibetan!" Westborough exclaimed. Somehow it had not occurred to him that so young a man (Vincent could not be more than twenty-one) would choose to work on such a difficult subject. Although, the historian recalled thoughtfully, Vincent had at times shown a grasp of difficult subjects remarkable for one of his years.

"He learn to write very well," Chang declared, pointing with evident pride to the characters on the paper.

"Dear me! What is his purpose in undertaking such a strange study?"

Chang shrugged his shoulders but did not reply; his manner had become suddenly guarded. Westborough smiled shyly.

"That, however, is none of my concern. I have come to ask a favor."

"Most happy," Chang murmured.

"The late Mr. Merriweather gave me to understand that you preserved copies of your translations in your own file."

"Yes, I have such a file."

"If you do not mind I should like to borrow your translation of the Padma Sambhava manuscript. 'Spells of the Thunderbolt' was your title, was it not?"

Chang's bland smile was nowise disturbed. "My poor attempt at title. Happy to find it." He walked to a filing cabinet which might have been a duplicate of the one in Merriweather's study and pulled open a drawer.

"I see that you do not keep your work under lock and key," Westborough commented.

Chang murmured deprecatorily, "It is hardly worth the trouble of theft." He withdrew a file folder from the drawer and handed it to Westborough. "Translation is poor thing but my own. Hope you will not find carbon too illegible."

" 'Spells of the Thunderbolt,' " Westborough read aloud from the folder's label. "I am deeply grateful. I assure you that I will not keep it long. Why, dear me! The folder is empty!"

Chang examined it as if he could not believe the evidence of his own eyes. "I do not understand. I put carbon here on Wednesday night after I finish translation."

"Perhaps you have mistaken the folder."

"No, it is not possible. This is folder I make out for it, as you see. If it is not here I not know where to look."

"Well, it does not matter in the least," Westborough lied in as cheerful tones as he could muster. "My reason for wishing to examine it was a very superficial one."

"Perhaps Mr. Vincent will allow you to see copy in Mr. Merriweather's file," Chang suggested.

"Thank you, I shall ask him. May I examine another specimen of your translations?"

Chang bowed and moved aside from the filing cabinet. "Take what you wish." Selecting a folder at random, Westborough withdrew its typewritten contents and studied them with the most knowing air he could assume.

"You are translating the Kan-gyur!"

"That and the Ten-gyur. Mr. Merriweather own many volumes of both."

"But this is a marvelous accomplishment! I understand that only small portions of the Kan-gyur and Ten-gyur have hitherto been rendered into English."

Chang bowed. "My understanding also."

Westborough opened another drawer and gazed upon its crowded contents. "You have performed a stupendous amount of work. Have you considered editing it for publication?"

Westborough fancied that he had caught a glint of genuine emotion in the Tibetan's obliquely slanted eyes. It was gone almost immediately.

"Thought, yes. Further, no."

"Perhaps if I speak to my own publisher?" Westborough hazarded. This time he was sure that he had not misread the gleam on Chang's face. But the Tibetan slowly shook his head.

"Thank you, that is very kind offer. Unfortunately translations not my property, since I work for Mr. Merriweather, who pay me for him."

"Dear, dear, that is unfortunate! And now that Mr. Merriweather is dead the title will, of course, revert to his heirs. Who, by the way, are his heirs ?"

He did not believe that Chang would answer that question, but Chang did.

"Mr. Vincent inherit everything. Allowance for Mrs. Gestler. Provision for me. Provision for Wilkins. Nothing for Doctor Merriweather."

"Nothing for his own brother!" Westborough exclaimed. Chang shook his head.

"Mr. Merriweather not like Doctor Merriweather, though he pretend to him he do."

"Did Doctor Merriweather know that he was not to share in his brother's estate?" Westborough questioned.

"Yes, he know. Mr. Merriweather tell him when he make last will."

"May I ask how you are so familiar with the terms of the last will, Mr. Chang?"

"He dictate letter to send to attorneys concerning same. No secret now that he is dead. Everybody know soon."

It may have been no secret, Westborough reflected, but it was the last bit of information in the world that he had expected Chang to reveal. Bret Harte's atrocious doggerel leaped to mind: ". . . for ways that are dark and for tricks that are vain, the heathen Chinee is peculiar." Chang, however, was a Tibetan (as he had so often insisted to Lieutenant Mack), and apparently a very enlightened one.

Westborough returned to the subject of the translations. He was positive that he was on promising ground there. Chang, if he had not misread, was as eager to have his labors recognized as an American scholar would have been.

"You will not object if I speak to Mr. Vincent? I am sure that he will not allow his equity to stand in the way of the publication of your translations."

"You are kind, Mr. Westborough. No, I not object."

"Then I shall speak to him today."

Chang said a little hesitantly, "Once I speak to Mr. Merriweather about publication."

"And he did not grant his consent?"

"No, he answer, my English not yet good enough. Publishers, he say, laugh at my clumsy expressions."

Westborough, however, did not laugh. "Perhaps I might be allowed to go over the manuscript with you?"

Chang bowed, and this time appeared to mean it. "Greatly in your debt. You could aid me great deal."

"I shall be most happy. By the way, since the copy of the Padma Sambhava translation seems to be gone, may I ask you a few questions concerning it?"

"Happy to answer." But Chang had stopped bowing.

"Was it a collection of tantras?"

Chang nodded.

"Many tantras?"

"Not many."

"Tantras for what purpose?"

Chang's smile displayed virtually every upper and lower tooth in his mouth. "Sorry, I not remember. I translate so many."

"Did one comprise instructions for the dead? Something on the order of the *Bardo Todol*?"

"Sorry, I not remember."

"Was one of them the Secret Doctrine?"

Chang's smile abruptly faded. "I not know what is the Secret Doctrine."

Westborough pronounced the Tibetan word he had learned from Jed Merriweather. "Do you know the meaning of that term, Mr. Chang?"

"I know it," Chang answered in a low, deep voice. The muscles of his lips were taut. His eyes surveyed the wall, the floor, the ceiling.

"Was that subject discussed in the manuscript?"

If ever face revealed a tortured soul Chang's did at that instant. "Sorry." He clipped the word to an abrupt termination. "I not remember."

Westborough left the office immediately. He knew that he would not be able to get any further information from Chang. He was doubtful if the information he sought could be secured from anyone.

V

Tsongpun Bonbo was sunning himself. The lama, wearing his rosary of yellow wooden beads, had seated himself cross-legged on the broad terrace of red flagstones overlooking the lake. In his eyes there was a rapt expression.

"It reminding me ob Tso Map-hang, Kusho, but it not being real."

"It seems very real to me," Westborough differed.

"No, Kusho, it not real. Tso Map-hang not real. Not-hing real. Not-hing we see or hear or taste or smell or touch. Our dreaming dream ob ig-no-rance, Kusho."

"Very much so, I fear," Westborough smiled, "but there is a matter upon which my ignorance desires enlightenment. Has Tsongpun Lama read the manuscript which he has traversed half the world to recover?"

"Many time, Kusho." The lama's deep voice droned like a colossal bee. "Many time he seeking com-port in cool water ob Guru Padma's teaching."

"Will Tsongpun Lama deign to explain to one so unversed as I the nature of those teachings?"

The lama remained silent for so long a period that Westborough feared the question had offended him. Finally, however, he answered.

"T'ey words ob power, Kusho. One who hear when he see True Light leabe Wheel ob Birt' and Deat'."

"To enter Nirvana immediately?"

"Yes, Kusho."

"And when does one see the True Light, Tsongpun Lama?"

"One whose karma not e-bil seeing at deaf', Kusho. Only ber-ry little while. Words must be read soon, or it be too late."

"Then the manuscript is a ritual for reading to the dead?" Westborough questioned. "Like the *Bardo Todol*?"

"Yes, Kusho."

"Does it not comprise other subjects than this? Does it not also discuss the Secret Doctrine?" Westborough once again employed the Tibetan term.

"Not Secret Pat'!" the lama exclaimed vehemently. "Guru Padma not writing Secret Way. He knowing one must receibe *angkur*—be instruct by word ob mout'."

"Dear me! If such is the case, then Mr. Merriweather's quest was foredoomed to failure."

"He seeking Secret Pat'? *He?*"

"Did you not know, Tsongpun Lama?"

"No, Kusho, my not knowing."

The lama sank into the motionless silence of an Egyptian mummy while Westborough became absorbed in a contemplation of his own. What had been the significance of the word which had been pronounced last evening? Could that strange, guttural sound "Heegh" be a mantra —one of those words of occult power whose mere vocalization Lamaists deem sufficient to obtain command over one of their weird deities? He inquired of Tsongpun Bonbo.

"Yes, Kusho, 'Heegh' is a mantra, a word ob power por he who know how it use. No wort' por he who not know."

"How does one learn its use, Tsongpun Lama?"

"He must be gibe angkur—be taught by one who know."

"By word of mouth, Tsongpun Lama?"

"By word of mout' only, Kusho Wes-bo-ro."

"I see." The historian reflected that the gate to Tibetan mysticism was not an easy portal to enter and that it was doubtful if even Adam Merriweather had succeeded in advancing very far. "I have one more question to ask of you, Tsongpun Lama. Does the mantra 'Heegh' pertain to the Secret Doctrine?"

The lama exclaimed in horror: "Kusho, learn not-hing ob Secret Way! Trail by creb-ice not being proper pat' por blind to trabel."

PART ELEVEN: "If It Was Murder, How Was It Done?" (Saturday Afternoon, July 24)

A S THEY STEPPED onto the small balcony Mack handed Westborough a somewhat blurry carbon on legal-size onionskin paper. "Here's the stenographic report of the inquest you wanted. I borrowed it from the coroner's office, and it's got to go back there when you finish with it."

Westborough thanked him and took the proffered document. He moved his new glasses a fraction of an inch backward on his nose before beginning to read. They did not fit as well as the old pair of gold-rimmed bifocals had done. Doubtless it would be necessary to visit his opticians in person in order to have them adjusted.

"What do you want it for?" Mack demanded, occupying a chair. "You were there. They called you as a witness, and you heard the whole thing."

"Dear me, yes, but one's memory is often faulty. Although the written word may err, it is at least consistent."

The inquest, held that morning in the auditorium of the undertaking establishment to which the mortal remains of Adam Merriweather had been consigned, had attracted little attention from the press. "Death due to natural causes," the verdict rendered by the coroner's jury, was not one to lend itself to screaming headlines unless it were a verdict flagrantly not justified by the evidence presented. But it had not been such a verdict; indeed, Westborough pondered, it was difficult to see how a coroner's jury could have decided in any other way.

Mack lighted a cigar, threw the match on the stone floor and leaned back in luxurious contemplation of the lake. "Nice view! Wouldn't be hard to take this sort of thing every summer."

Engrossed in his reading, Westborough did not answer. He had at last found the section for which he had been searching among the onionskin sheets.

DEPUTY CORONER: Your name, please, and occupation.
DR. WATERS: Gaylord Walters, physician.

167

Q: Was the deceased, Adam Merriweather, one of your patients ?

A: Yes and no.

Q: Will the witness please give the Court a definite answer to the question?

A: He was not one of my regular patients. I attended him in the absence of Doctor Theodore Pressinger, who is now taking a vacation in Europe.

Q: Are you familiar with the physical condition of the deceased ?

A: Yes.

Q: Through your own examinations of him?

A: Through my own examinations and the case history which had been left with me by Doctor Pressinger.

Q: Did the deceased enjoy a state of good health?

A: No, he did not.

Q: You may explain to the Court the nature of his ailment.

A: He had an aneurysm of the aorta—the great trunk artery leading from the heart.

Q: Was this injury of such a nature that it was likely to result in the death of the deceased?

A: Yes.

Q: Even without contributing cause?

A: Ye-es.

Q: Were you surprised that the deceased had died suddenly?

A: No, the aorta was liable to rupture at any time. However, the case history of the deceased shows that he had made a determined effort to take care of himself.

Q: Will the witness please explain what he means by the phrase, "take care of himself."

A: He rested frequently and avoided physical exertion.

Q: Exertion of what nature?

A: Any exercise more strenuous than an occasional brief walk.

Q: Was emotional excitement also dangerous to him?

A: Yes, decidedly.

Q: Might a violent quarrel with some other person have had fatal consequences?

A: Perhaps.

Q: To your knowledge had the deceased undergone any recent emotional excitement?

A: I know of none prior to the night of his death.

Q: You may tell the jury of the events of that night.

A: I encountered the deceased in his house at the door of the large room which contains his collection of Tibetan objects. He seemed to me to be strangely agitated. I told him that I did not like his appearance and asked him to permit me to make a medical examination.

Q: Did you make such an examination?

A: No. He refused to allow me, saying that he was too busy.

Q: Did you inquire the cause of his agitation?

A: No. His manner was such I knew he would not tell me.

Q: Did the deceased say anything else to you at that time?

A: Yes, he remarked that there was going to be a thunderstorm.

Q: What did the deceased do as you left him?

A: He walked into the room and closed the door.

Q: Which room?

A: The room containing the Tibetan collection.

Q: Did he lock the door to that room ?

A: I thought I heard the lock click as I walked down the hall.

Q: Did you try the door to see if it were locked?

A: No.

Q: Was anyone in the room with the deceased, to your knowledge ?

A: No.

Q: Would it have been possible for a person to have been in that room without your knowledge ?

A: No.

Q: On what grounds do you make that statement?

A: I had just come from that room myself.

Q: How long a period had you remained there?

A: About twenty minutes.

Q: Were you in the room alone?

A: No.

Q: What other person was with you?

A: Miss Shelton was showing me the Tibetan collection.

Q: Was Miss Shelton with you when you met the deceased r

A: No. She had gone upstairs a few seconds prior to that time.

Q: Leaving you in the room alone?

A: Yes.

Q: Doctor Walters, in your opinion what would have been the consequences of the deceased receiving a blow directly over his heart?

A: Such a blow might easily have had fatal consequences.

Westborough, noting again that Adam Merriweather's interest in the occult had not been introduced into the prosaic atmosphere of the inquest, skimmed rapidly over other testimony until he came to the sections he wanted.

DEPUTY CORONER: Your name, please, and occupation.

DR. HILDRETH: Basil Hildreth, medical examiner for Cook County.

Q: Did you perform a surgical autopsy on the body of the deceased Adam Merriweather?

A: Yes.

Q: What was the cause of his death?

A: There was an aneurysm of the aorta which had ruptured. I found the pericardium filled with blood.

Q: How could such a rupture have occurred?

A: Either through natural causes or through accident.

Q: What do you consider to be "natural causes"?

A: I would divide them into two categories: physical exertion and mental stress. In the former category I would place any form of excessive muscular exertion, in the latter such emotions as violent anger, sexual passion or sudden terror.

Q: Are you able to say whether it was physical exertion or mental stress which caused the rupture you found?

A: No.

Q: You include terror among the mental causes. Would it have been possible to have frightened the deceased to his death?

A: In my opinion a sudden fright might have had that result.

Q: What other causes for the rupture can you suggest other than those you have listed?

A: All of those resulting from accident. To cite only a few: a fall to the ground, a collision with a person running, a blow over the heart.

Q: Let us discuss the last possibility you mention. Did you find evidence that the deceased had received such a blow ?

A: No.

Q: Is it possible for such a blow to be struck and leave no after- effects?

A: There is only a slight possibility. A blow of this nature will almost always create an ecchymosis or discoloration of the skin tissues, an injury which was not present on the deceased.

Q: You mention among the accidental causes a fall to the ground. Suppose that the deceased had been seized by a sudden fainting spell causing him to fall to the floor, where he was found lying. Could such a fall have resulted in his death?

A: Yes.

Q: Is there also a possibility that the rupture may have occurred without discernible cause?

A: Any increase in blood pressure may have caused the aneurysm to rupture.

Q: Did you find any injury upon the deceased other than the ruptured aorta?

A: No.

Q: No evidence, even of slight nature, which would indicate that he had met his death as the result of physical violence ?

A: None whatsoever.

Q: Did you examine the organs for traces of poison?

A: I am not a toxicologist.

Q: Did you ask a toxicologist to examine them?

A: Yes, Doctor Jalvers.

DEPUTY CORONER: Doctor Jalvers, will you come to the stand, please?

DEPUTY CORONER: Your name, please, and occupation.

DR. JALVERS: Doctor Edward Jalvers, pathologist and toxicologist.

Q: Were you requested to make an examination of the organs of the deceased Adam Merriweather?

A: Yes.

Q: Did you make such an examination?

A: Yes.

Q: What was the nature of your examination?

A: I examined the tissues microscopically, and I made chemical tests of the stomach, intestines, liver, kidneys, spleen, lungs, heart and brain.

Q: Could you detect the presence of a toxic agent in any of these organs?

A: No, I could not.

Q: Is there a toxic agent which cannot be detected through chemical or microscopical examination?

A: A toxic agent impervious to detection is a paradox. A poison cannot cause death unless it damages some organ of the body, and any such damage is readily discovered. The matter of identification is, of course, a different question. Naturally some toxins are more difficult to identify than others.

    Q: Did you hear the testimony which has just been given by Doctor Hildreth?

    A: Yes.

    Q: Are you able to suggest any other cause for the ruptured aorta of the deceased other than those enumerated by Doctor Hildreth?

    A: No.

Westborough ceased his reading and folded up the onionskin sheets. "May I keep them for a few days, John?"

    "I guess so," Mack answered, puffing meditatively on his cigar. "Now that it's all over what do you think of it?"

    "The inquest?"

    "The verdict."

    "May I ask what you yourself think of it?" Westborough countered.

    Mack spat a small fragment of moist tobacco leaf over the edge of the balcony. "Damned if I know! If it was murder, how was it done?"

    "Shall we attempt an analysis?" Westborough smiled.

    "Ouch!" Mack groaned. "Led right into your strong suit! Well, go ahead. Guess I can stand it."

    "From the standpoint of the traditional triad of motive, method and opportunity?"

    "Take motive first. Vincent Merriweather takes everything but the inheritance tax, and that gives him the only good motive there is. Unless you want to count in the U.S. government."

    "There are other motives than financial ones."

    "Sure, sex. Dough and sex are the cause of ninety-five per cent of this town's murders. Once in a while you get a bit of grudge work. . . . Say, there's a motive for the lama. Got sore because he figured Merriweather was holding out his manuscript on him. And Chang? Can you figure him into this?"

    "His motive might be one of scholarship. He has done a very worthy work in translating large sections of the sacred books of Tibet. I know that he would like to see his translations published. Hitherto that has been impossible because the translations were Mr. Merriweather's property, and he had refused his consent. Moreover, I learned that Mr. Merriweather had several times spoken slightingly of Chang's work."

    "That grounds for murder?" Mack grinned.

    "Harsh and unsympathetic criticism has made many a person feel like committing such an act, I believe. Shall we pass now to Doctor Merriweather, who had also incurred his brother's disapproval?" Westborough reviewed the information he had learned concerning the proposed expedition. "Doctor Merriweather is badly in need of funds, but it is only fair to add that his brother had not refused them to him at the time of his death. Furthermore, Doctor Merriweather benefits no-wise financially from his brother's decease."

Mack exclaimed: "His son, his brother, Chang and the lama! How about adding the sister to the list?"

"I never heard her make a remark that would justify such an inclusion."

"And Miss Shelton? Merriweather treated her pretty decently, didn't he?"

"Yes, as his own daughter. I know that she was affectionately fond of him. And yet . . ." Westborough's voice trailed away. It seemed cruel to reveal the secret upon which he had involuntarily stumbled the other night. Yet in the interest of truth he felt that he must reveal it. He told Mack of the heartbreaking sobbing he had heard from behind a closed door.

"Crying, eh? Well, women sometimes cry for no reason at all. And on the other hand . . . well, sometimes they don't. Let's see what could make a good-looking girl engaged to Young Millionbucks suddenly start crying? Something he said to her? No, it couldn't have been him; he was out on the lake then. I remember now. She had just left Doc Walters."

Westborough said nothing. He did not like the particular side path into which their mental excursion was wandering. Yet he knew it was an important path which merited full investigation.

"Young Millionbucks isn't much of a man," Mack speculated. "Walters is. It could happen, couldn't it?"

"Yes," Westborough replied unhappily, "I suppose that it could."

"Walters was the last fellow to see Merriweather alive. And he's a doctor. He could--- No, it doesn't make sense. It wasn't the old man who was in his way, but the young one. To hell with motives anyway! Let's pass on to opportunity."

"At the hour of Mr. Merriweather's death Doctor Walters was out of the house."

"You can't check that. He wasn't at his home or his office when Miss Shelton first phoned. She told us Thursday night that she couldn't get him for a little time."

"True," Westborough admitted. "Doctor Walters' exact position at the time must remain an unknown quantity. Miss Shelton, however, I had just overheard in her own bedroom. Mrs. Gestler remained alone in the living room, while Chang was working in his office."."

"Neither of the last can be proved," Mack objected.

"True," Westborough said again. "The lama's alibi, however (if my own word is to be believed), is a perfect one. Vincent and Doctor Merriweather were together on a canoe ride, or at least," he corrected himself, "the story of the canoe ride is well supported by their extremely wet clothing. And the butler Wilkins—"

"You know all this doesn't mean anything," Mack broke in. "He was in that room alone. Nobody was there when he went in. Nobody came out after he died. Both doors were locked from the inside. Sure, I know that can be faked, but these doors were genuinely locked from the inside. No marks of pliers on the barrels of either key, no string scratches in the paint. There aren't any windows, so what's the only way left to get into the room?"

"To descend from the second story," Westborough answered.

"Sure, to swing down the way young Merriweather did. But that can't be done without smearing the dust on top of the beams. Was the dust smeared? You had a good look at those beams before Merriweather came down. Was it smeared?"

"No," Westborough replied. He had already answered this question several times before. "It was not."

"Well then, nobody could get into that room. Nobody. You can't talk about opportunity—there wasn't any. Nobody had a chance to kill him. Nobody."

"Under these circumstances would it be mere folly to consider the question of method?"

"Method!" Mack shouted. "Method! He wasn't shot or stabbed or clubbed or strangled. He wasn't poisoned. What other methods of murder are there?"

"I can think of only one." Westborough's eyes were peering owlishly from behind his new glasses. "Murder by magic."

PART TWELVE: "If We Knew That, We Might Know Everything" (Sunday Morning, July 25)

WESTBOROUGH dreamed of dinner plates which of their own accord were rolling back and forth upon the long altar facing Adam Merriweather's Tibetan gods. They were not of china but of metal . . . bronze disks, a foot or so in diameter. . . . Suddenly he recognized that they were not dinner plates, and as he did so he found himself broad awake.

The curtains of the canopied bed were stifling; he flung them aside. It was very early; the gray light of dawn had just begun to enter the room. Westborough groaned softly at the thought which had entered his mind. Twice before he had prowled while the household slept. His first excursion had been merely embarrassing, but the second distinctly dangerous. Dared he to risk a third? This time he might not escape . . . might not escape . . . so easily.

His mind, however, was already made up. Reason told him that it was not necessary, but there are higher voices than Reason, and one is compelled occasionally to listen to them. Metal mirrors had intruded themselves into his every trend of thought. He could not be satisfied until he knew.

He donned dressing gown and slippers and left his bedroom. He paused for an instant to look over the balustrade. The Tibetan Room below was void of human visitor. Nevertheless, as he stood in the downstairs hall he experienced a sharp distaste for entering. He remembered what had taken place before in this room, the quick death that had hovered in wait. . . .

His hand closed upon the doorknob; he opened the door. It seemed safe enough so far. The room was singularly bereft of hiding places. One could not crouch behind the transparent museum cases, and none of the images were large enough to afford effective concealment. Unless someone were hidden in the space under the altar—but on lifting the yellow altar cloth he found nothing except the trestles which supported the boards of the raised platform. He was alone in this room.

175

Alone? As he locked the door behind him Westborough was forced
to correct himself. He had forgotten the four Kings of the Quarters
who were regarding him so malignantly. And the twelve images behind
the altar were, he was sure, sharing the same aversion. Even the smile
of the gilded Buddha seemed no longer beneficent, and the scowl of
the frightful Chana Dorje conveyed a distinct menace. Westborough
stood before that painted image with a feeling of awe. He knew that he
was in the presence of something incredibly ancient.

The legend of the thunderbolt deity was already hoary with age
thirty-four centuries ago, an ancient legend when the Aryan invaders of
India had composed their Vedic hymns to Indra, the lord of the clear
sky, who shook heaven and earth with his "hundred-edged" darts. Indra,
Zeus, Jove, Thor, Vajrapani or Yahweh—call him by whatever name you
will, he remains basically the same conception. The wrathful god. The
god of terrible weapons.

However, it was not the Thunderbolt God which Westborough had
come to see, but the bronze mirror which had fallen to the floor on the
night of Adam Merriweather's death. He studied it intently: a flat, circular disk twelve to fourteen inches in diameter, covered with a net-
work of tiny engravings. They included representations of the wheel,
the conch-shell trumpet, the royal umbrella, the lotus, the fish and the
other eight auspicious emblems; inscriptions in Sanskrit and in Tibetan;
intricate geometrical designs whose significance it was impossible to
fathom.

Lifting the mirror, Westborough noted that the thumbtack he had
seen the other night had been removed from the altar and that the
upset holy-water vase had been restored to its normal position. The
holy-water vase, he remembered from his omnivorous reading, was usually employed in Lamaist ceremonies in conjunction with the mirror,
or melong.

The rite was one of purification, was it not? He recalled the
well-known line which a Buddhist sage had brushed in Chinese characters nearly thirteen hundred years ago: "The mind is like a mirror shining bright." In the religion of Tibet did the melong have the same symbolism ? Westborough did not know, and the question suddenly assumed
importance for him.

His conversations with the lama had revealed that every ritualistic
object, every pictured emblem, spoke a symbolic language, tunefully
eloquent to those able to recognize it. For instance one might take
such a simple example as the five small skulls in the wreath upon the
Yellow King's head. These skulls were not, like the Indian's scalps, the
grisly trophies of victims, but were merely a method of saying that the

Yellow King had renounced the vanities of the world to take refuge in
the Buddha's doctrine.

Westborough's eyes, following his thoughts across the room, rested
for some time upon the grotesque papier-mache mask. It was not a face
of beauty. Like Padma Sambhava and others of the figures behind the
altar, the Yellow King had three eyes. Two of these orbs, although optics
great and glaring, with huge black disks for pupils and enormous bushy
eyebrows reminding one of the scaly outlines of a dragon's back, were
in the normal position for eyes, but the third, much smaller in size, was
inset in a vertical position in the center of the forehead. This was the
so-called "Eye of Wisdom" by means of which the Yellow King was able
to discern at a glance the past, present or future. Below a broad, flat
nose yawned a cavernous mouth—an aperture in the mask at least five
inches long by an inch and a half wide. A bump like a bisected ostrich
egg grew from the top of the Yellow King's head; only a Tibetan could
have told what that signified.

The face of the Red King on the opposite side of the door seemed
identical in almost every detail save color, and yet Westborough sensed
a difference between them. Was it in their costumes? No, those silken
garments were exactly the same. True, the Red King wore an enormous
gilded crown in place of the Yellow King's skull chaplet. Could it be
that? Turning back to the Yellow King's wreath, Westborough saw that
every one of the five small skulls was surmounted by a tiny glass mirror.
Odd that he had never before noticed that detail! The mirror seemed
suddenly to have become as ubiquitous as King Charles's head; he must
find out about it at once.

Without doubt one of the books concealed in the bottom drawers
of Adam Merriweather's cabinet could supply the information he
wanted. He closed the door of the Tibetan Room behind him and went
across the hall to the study. In the study, however, he met with a disappointment. The keys to the filing cabinet were no longer in the lock
where he had left them; they were not in the study at all. And the cabinet itself was tightly locked. Dear me! The disaster, however, was not
irreparable.

Down the hall and around the corner was the library where there
were also books on Tibetan subjects, although none, Westborough acknowledged, of such esoteric nature as those within the cabinet.

The library was not Italian and it was not in the slightest degree
Tibetan but contented itself with merely being the most comfortable
room in the house. Westborough selected a work from its shelves, settled
into an enormous chair upholstered in green leather before the open
fireplace, and switched on a reading lamp.

Once before he had found Colter's *Handbook of Lamaism* helpful. It was an English work, still in its original paper jacket, and it opened stiffly. It did not appear to have been read a great deal, nor was it difficult to tell why. Colter, turning the kleig light of inquiry upon Lamaism, stripped it of its mysteries, the mysteries which hover in dark places, and substituted in their stead an encyclopedic assortment of brute facts. It was not the sort of book which Adam Merriweather would have relished.

But when one wished facts—merely facts and nothing more—Colter could be very useful. As, for instance:

CEREMONIAL MIRRORS

As the objects seen in the mirror exist but as reflections of what we (but not the Buddhist) term reality, the mirror (melong) is taken by Lamaists to symbolize the mind of man, which, it is believed, may exist only as a reflection from the One or Universal Mind.

A mirror covered by dust fails to reflect the light thrown upon it. So is the human mind clouded by false beliefs unable to reflect the True Light of the One Mind. The symbolism is sufficient to explain the common Lamaist rite of purification, i.e., water from a holy-water vase or *bumba* is poured upon the melong to cleanse it.

The melong is also used in the so-called forecasts of the future, and it has been made the emblem of various deities.

Had the melong and the holy-water vase been employed by Adam Merriweather in mystic ceremonial rites? Or was it mere accident that the vase had been upset, the mirror knocked to the floor? One could not know, but if Adam Merriweather had not been engaged in secret rites why had he pronounced three times the mantra, "Heegh"? Why had the dorje, that enigmatic thunderbolt of the Lamaist religion, been grasped in his right hand at the very instant of his death? Westborough consulted once again the pages of Cotter:

DORJE

The Lamaist thunderbolt or dorje has undoubtedly been directly borrowed from the *vajra*, the lightning bolt of the Vedic storm-god Indra. Indeed, ample evidence of such borrowing is furnished by the tradition that the original dorje flew through the air of its own volition from India into Tibet, where it now reposes in one of the great monasteries of Lhasa.

As Indra's vajra represented the destruction of the enemies of the Vedic Aryans, so may the dorje symbolize the annihilation of the enemies of Buddhism. In a higher sense, however, it is said to typify the conquest over self.

Westborough sighed. Colter, for all his encyclopedic knowledge of strange customs, was not being very helpful. Was there no way in which the dorje, the mirror, the vase, the mystic word thrice repeated could be linked together? Behind the locked doors of the Tibetan Room, Westborough felt sure, Adam Merriweather had been engaged in the performance of a weird ceremony. A ceremony of what nature?

He said aloud: "If we knew that, we might know everything."

But they did not know, and it was exceedingly probable that they would never know. Westborough turned the pages of Colter again, turned them at random, since he did not know for what he searched. A paragraph presently engaged his interest. So much so, in fact, that he read it twice.

MOLDED IMAGES

The art of molding papier-mache is one widely practiced in Tibet. The plastic composition is usually pressed in molds as high reliefs, thus forming two halves, which, after drying and hardening by stove heat, are joined together over a central wooden framework. The image, elaborately painted or gilded, may in addition be decorated by bits of gold, coral or turquoise which have been inserted into the moist pulp prior to drying. Internal organs of dough or clay are often placed in the hollow space between the two halves of the image, but if this piece of realism is omitted the hollow may be filled with votive offerings: jars of consecrated barley, paper rolls of prayers, citations from the Buddhist scripts or even whole textbooks. These offerings of the devout, both from clergy and laity alike, are sealed within the central cavity by an officiating lama, the ceremony being one comparable to the cornerstone dedication in more modern quarters of the world.

Westborough's brain was racing at top speed as he concluded his reading. A hollow image ? The Padma Sambhava manuscript? Was there a connection between them? Could it be possible that the lost manuscript was still concealed within the Tibetan Room? Dear me, it was possible; yes, it was very possible.

Standing up, he smoothed the wrinkles in his dressing gown with one of his small, fragile hands. Action was indicated—action which Demosthenes had termed the first, the second and the third of the three parts of oratory. Yet on the threshold of the Tibetan Room Westborough hesitated.

He had closed the door after he had left the room, and it was closed now. Doubtless it had been a wise precaution to have closed it, but he wished now that he had left it open, at least a small crack. One might then have been able to tell whether or not some other person had entered. Now one could not. He was conscious of an instinctive aversion toward entering, an inward shrinking from something, he did not know quite what.

"Can it be possible that I am at heart a timid man?"

The thought was not an inspiring one, but it forced him to open the door. The room seemed exactly as he had left it, except that more light was now streaming through the skylight in the distant roof. He glanced toward the Red and Yellow kings and received once more the impression that something differentiated the two giant figures besides the obvious differences of the color of faces, of crown and skull chaplet. The difference was a subtle one, he knew, and it bothered him that he was not able to detect it.

He started in quick alarm. He had not yet closed the door, and he could hear very plainly the sound of footsteps down the corridor. Someone was coming, someone who might enter at any instant . . . . Flinging dignity to the wind, Westborough ran at his top speed across the room. His dressing gown fluttered behind like a toga on a breezy day in ancient Rome, but his slippers, fortunately, made no sound upon the carpeting.

He ran half the length of the altar in search of a place to hide. There was just one available. Westborough hesitated only a few seconds before lifting the altar cloth. He scurried hurriedly under it and flopped prone beside the floodlights which illuminated the face of the merciless goddess, Pal-den Lha-mo. A votive offering to a savage deity! What a position in which to find oneself!

To think that he, a man of nearly seventy, should be playing a childish game of hide-and-seek! But perhaps the game was not so childish. No more childish, in fact, than the game the fox plays when he dashes panting into his lair while hounds bay their disappointment. For someone had entered the Tibetan Room.

Although he could hear the noise of a person walking Westborough could not be sure of the direction. He risked lifting a corner of the altar cloth but could see nothing. Abruptly the noise of movement ceased. Was his presence here known or suspected? Westborough wondered. Or had the visitor already left the room? It was annoying not to know which.

His muscles grew cramped from remaining so long motionless, and he ventured to stretch his arms upward. His fingers brushed against the boards forming the top of the platform; he felt the slight cracks between them. The altar, evidently, had been rather carelessly contructed, but the yellow cloth covered a multitude of sins. It covered him at that instant.

He had heard nothing for a long time now. Suppose that the visitor had at last left the room. In that event, Westborough decided, he should seize the opportunity of returning to his bedroom, for if he did not go there at once it might soon be too late to escape observation. But if he were not alone? Then the identity of this early morning visitor to the Tibetan Room must by all means be determined. And determined at once before it became too late.

Westborough was still deliberating upon the best method of accomplishing this feat when he became aware of a sound he had heard once before in this house. Not the noise of footsteps this time, but a sound from a human voice. Muttered invocations which suggested the purring of a giant cat.

He ventured to extend his head from his hiding place and saw Tsongpun Bonbo. The lama, seated cross-legged before the image of the historic Buddha, was telling his yellow wooden beads exactly—the thought came to Westborough in a sudden flash—as he had been doing at the moment of Merriweather's death.

The lama's catlike purring seemed suddenly uncanny. Was it a prayer he was reciting, or was it an incantation? Between the two words lay a world of difference. Westborough, watching the lama's brown fingers moving his yellow beads, remembered the curious power ascribed to Tibetan mystics which he had once discussed with Adam Merriweather. The power of creating a thought-form which may appear to walk and act as a man but has no real existence outside the mind of its creator.

Impossible? Well, give this strange power a name couched in the familiar English language. Call it "group hypnotism" or "hallucination induced by suggestion" and see how soon it begins to take on the aspects of a reality. It might exist, Westborough mused soberly. Western science has as yet cut but feeble paths through the dark jungles of the mind.

If it were possible for such apparitions to be created, then Adam Merriweather might have been slain indeed by one on the outside of his sealed room. Slain by a thing to which locked doors were no barrier, which had come to him as no human agency could have come. Killed by terror of a specter that did not exist. Murdered by a thought alone. A thought—Westborough carried the idea to its logical conclusion—in the mind of a frail Tibetan priest, who, in the very presence of a witness, had calmly moved his yellow globules while his enemy died.

The perfect alibi indeed!

But Westborough saw at once that this was a path he must not pursue. Not because it was too fantastic, too improbable---he was not sure that it was either—but because it was a path he could not understand.

An alien path utterly at variance with the scientific method which makes use of the laws of probability to investigate the apparent phenomena of telepathy. No matter how useless that method seemed now, he must proceed by it. He knew no other.

For shame's sake, however, he could continue no longer under the altar. Wriggling from under the cloth, he stretched himself to his feet. The lama, his gaze fixed upon the placid features of the Buddha, did not look around. Westborough coughed self-consciously.

"My not seeing you here, Kusho Wes-bo-ro," the lama observed without turning his head. "My not hearing your coming in."

The Tibetan's voice was hurt, gently accusing. Westborough stared shamefacedly across at the Red and Yellow kings. He and the lama had been friends—some kinship of spirit had hurtled the twin gaps of race and tradition to bind them together. Why could he not say simply, "I hid under the altar when I heard you coming?"

But he could not say it because he feared that the lama would not understand, that his confidence would be forever withdrawn if told he had been spied upon by one whom he had trusted. Westborough, despairing of finding an explanation that would not be a palpable falsehood, continued to stare upon the Red and Yellow kings. . . . Suddenly he turned and walked rapidly across the room.

Peering and squinting at the two kings from a shorter distance, he saw that his hasty impression had been quite true. He had found at last the secret of the subtle difference between them.

"Look, Tsongpun Lama!" he exclaimed to the Tibetan, who had risen from the floor to follow him. "See how the light is shining from the mouth of the Red King through an opening at the back of the mask. Only a small opening, it is true, and yet sufficient to allow a little light to shine through. But from the mouth of the Yellow King there shines no light. It is as though a black curtain had been placed to bar it. A curtain within his head!"

As he completed the last exclamation he stretched his hands upward to touch the Yellow King's mask. As he expected, the mask could be lifted upward; it was merely resting upon a pole protruding from the framework about which the costume was draped. He continued to raise the mask. . . .

Something dropped to the floor. Or would have dropped there if the lama had not hurried forward to catch it in both arms. It was an oblong parcel wrapped in black cambric. Stripping off the cambric covering, Tsongpun Bonbo hugged the oblong package to his chest as a mother might hold a dearly loved child.

"Oh, Kusho Wes-bo-ro, the words! The precious words!"

But no one else in the house must learn that the lost words of Guru Padma were lost no longer, Westborough reflected as he glanced upstairs at the deserted gallery of the second floor to make sure that they were not under observation. Their secret was dangerous!

PART THIRTEEN: The Words of Guru Padma
(Monday, July 26)

MACK GAVE a malevolent glance toward the sign with the Japanese characters and walked through a hallway hung with paper lanterns into the main room of the restaurant. He found Westborough seated at a table before a rice-paper window.

"John!" the historian exclaimed, rising eagerly to his feet. "It is a most welcome relief to see you."

"What'd you pick this joint for?" Mack demanded as they took their seats.

"Since it is quiet at this hour we can discuss rather delicate matters in comparative privacy."

Mack, glancing about the room, saw that their table was the only one occupied. "It's quiet, all right."

"Moreover," Westborough continued, "the oriental atmosphere did not seem inappropriate to the peculiar nature of the case on which we are associated."

Mack said: "Humph! Well, what do we eat?"

"I have taken the liberty of ordering, John. A Japanese luncheon which I trust you will relish."

A black-haired and smiling Japanese girl brought them each a covered bowl and returned immediately to the kitchen. Mack lifted the cover to find a thin soup, garnished with white cubes of soy bean and bits of coagulated egg white. "Try anything once," he grunted and dubiously lifted a spoonful to his lips. With the first taste his expression changed. "Not bad," he pronounced and finished the soup. "Well, what's happened at the Merriweather place lately?"

"A very great deal. However, I see that our waitress is now returning to cook the sukiyaki."

"What the devil's that?"

"The name means, unless I am mistaken, the 'dish cooked at the table.' "

The Japanese girl brought them tea and bowls of rice, which she placed on the black lacquer trays in front of them. Smiling in a friendly manner, she lighted the gas of the porcelain table stove, placed an aluminum skillet upon the stove and a square of suet within the skillet. Leaving the suet to simmer, she returned to the kitchen.

Westborough took advantage of the interlude to relate his activities of yesterday. He was not, however, allowed to talk long. The waitress returned with a large platter heaped with raw beef and with many kinds of vegetables, some familiar and some unrecognizable. She placed the beef within the skillet, covered it with a dark soybean sauce from a cruet on the table, stirred the mixture carefully with a pair of long wooden sticks and left the mixture to its own devices.

"So you found the manuscript!" Mack exclaimed.

"Yes, the words of Guru Padma have now been recovered." Westborough explained under what circumstances they had found them. "But that," he added smilingly, "is by no means the last discovery."

"Well, what else?"

Once more they were interrupted by their Japanese waitress-cook, who had come to add the vegetables: dried onions, green onions, mushrooms, slices of water chestnuts and glistening shreds of a white seaweed, which the soybean sauce dyed to translucent amber. She allowed the ingredients to cook for a few minutes before transferring the mixture deftly to their plates with her wooden sticks.

Mack stared with suspicion at the paper packet embellished with Japanese characters which was now handed to him. "What's this thing?"

"Chopsticks," the waitress explained. "You use them, please ?"

Mack grinned broadly and tore off the wrapping. "Sister, I'm game!" She showed him how to hold the wooden pegs between the fingers of his right hand, laughing with schoolgirl gaiety at his unsuccessful attempts to capture the elusive morsels. One may, Westborough reflected while wielding his own chopsticks, disapprove of Japan's Asiatic policy, but it is extremely difficult to dislike the Japanese as individuals.

"Stuff isn't bad at all," Mack observed when the waitress had again left them. He was manipulating the chopsticks with improved dexterity. "Well, go on. What else'd you find?"

Westborough lifted the handleless teacup to his lips. It contained a liquid of so pale a green that it was almost colorless, and he sipped slowly, relishing the delicate flavor. He lowered the cup.

"The Lama Tsongpun Bonbo was kind enough to translate a few pages of the manuscript for me. Although I have taken the liberty of editing his wording I have not altered its meaning. Would you care to hear our joint product?"

"Shoot!"

Westborough, taking a paper from his breast pocket, read aloud:

" 'This is the great Doctrine, the great Secret, the Secret of the Thunderbolt. By its means one, though destined for rebirth low on the Wheel, may raise himself to the lot of the heaven-born gods. I, Guru Padma, I, the Precious Teacher, I who sprang full-grown from the heart of the lotus, do hereby proclaim that he who reads may know, may learn, may receive the eightfold powers of the Siddhi. This is my Word, O ye who come after!

" 'Choose a night of a thunderstorm. Choose a night when the great Chana Dorje rides the heavens and his power is at its height. Take in your hand his sacred weapon, the thunderbolt. Kneel before his sacred image on a melong purged by the purifying waters of the *Samskara* you renounce."

"Sam scara?" Mack inquired.

"The most difficult to define of the five *skandhas*—the components of a personality. I employ the Sanskrit because there is no exact English equivalent for the term 'Samskara.' Perhaps will or volition; perhaps, in another sense, the ocean of birth and death which is the antithesis of Nirvana."

"Go on reading," Mack said.

" 'Thinking upon the power of the God, thinking upon the might of the God, pronounce three times the mantra "Heegh," the mystic Word, the great Word, the Word which calls the mighty Bodhisat from the storm-swept heavens. As you pronounce the Word for the final time you will note that the thunder ceases. Bow your head in token of your knowledge that the Bodhisat is now within the image before which you kneel and touch to his sacred lips his emblem, the dorje. Pronounce then the mantra "Oom," the great Word, the mighty Word, the Word of power to which even the Lord of the Thunderbolt must listen.

" 'Gaze fixedly upon the image of Chana Dorje. His lips will move, his teeth gnash, his eyes flash with the fire of the heavens. Be not afraid. Speak not, move not, take not your eyes from the face of Chana Dorje. Remain thus before him until you pass into the *Samadhi*, the mystic trance in which Chana Dorje will confer on you the eight powers of the Siddhi, the powers of the Bodhisat himself.

" 'This is the goal of the great Doctrine, the great Secret, the Secret of the Thunderbolt, which I, Guru Padma, the teacher born of the lotus, do hereby proclaim.' "

Mack snorted disgustedly: "Never heard so much bunk in my life! The words of Guru Padma! Nuts!"

"My dear John," Westborough said mildly, "those are not the words of Guru Padma. The four pages which the lama translated were forged."

II

The Japanese girl brought them each crisp cookies of rice flour and the peeled segments of an orange. "Forged!" Mack ejaculated, jabbing a toothpick viciously into an orange slice. "In Tibetan?"

"Yes, with careful attention to the spelling, language and style of writing of the original. A forgery extremely difficult to detect."

"How do you know it is forgery?"

"The lama has memorized the entire manuscript as Tibetan priests do so many pages of their sacred texts. He insists that the four extra folios do not belong. Furthermore, he informs me, the secret of the Secret Doctrine has never been committed to writing, either in Tibet or elsewhere. It is against an age-old tradition to so commit it."

"What does it all mean, then?"

"It supplies the last bit of evidence necessary to solve our enigma." Noting the wrinkled forehead of his companion, Westborough took a folded paper from his pocket. "The problem may be somewhat simplified by dividing it into ten basic questions."

"Ten thousand, you mean," Mack grumbled.

"Merely ten," Westborough smiled, handing the paper across the table. "Provide the correct answer to each of these, and you will see how beautifully they weld together into a logical whole."

Mack unfolded the paper. In Westborough's small cramped handwriting he read:

QUESTIONS WHICH MUST BE ANSWERED

1. Why was Jack Reffner strangled ?
2. Why was the drawing of the swastika left in the Tibetan Room?
3. Who concealed the original Padma Sambhava manuscript ?
4. For what reason?
5. Was Adam Merriweather murdered?
6. If murder, by what method ?
7. Why has Merriweather's copy of the translation disappeared ?
8. Why was Chang's carbon of the translation removed?
9. Why was the Tibetan Room invaded on Friday morning?
10. Why was the canoe afterwards taken out on the lake?

Mack shook his head. "You can't be too dumb and last long on a job like mine. But this is something too crazy to figure."

"On the contrary," Westborough demurred, "the pieces may be put together with the precision of a jigsaw puzzle. And it is an exhilarating mental adventure to arrange them—at least I found it so."

"You've solved this thing?" Mack asked incredulously.

"I take little credit. Once I had the lama's translation he answers seemed to be obvious."

Mack asked quickly, "Was Merriweather murdered or not?"

"He was murdered," the historian replied, "and murdered by a most amazing method. The plan was so skillful, so subtle, that it could have been conceived only by a brilliant genius. Its perpetrator made some mistakes, yes, but his crime would never have been detected had it not been for exceedingly poor luck. Perhaps, as the lama insists, it was his own evil karma which defeated him."

"Well, who was he?" Mack demanded.

"The masculine personal pronouns are used merely for convenience. At this stage of analysis one must not assume that the culprit is necessarily of the male sex."

"My God! You mean a woman did it?"

"I did not say that either."

Mack groaned. "You've got brains, and I'm the first to admit it, but you can be the most irritating mutt on earth. Come on, cut out the funny work. If you know who did it, tell me."

"Surely, John, you do not wish me to deprive you of the pleasure of working the problem out for yourself? Perhaps if I gave you a few hints?"

"Oh, all right," Mack yielded. "I'll play your way. What are they?"

"The spirit gum and crepe hair which we found in the room of Hamilcar Barca were, you recall, wrapped within a hotel towel before being thrown into the wastebasket."

"Well, what of it?"

"Why was a hotel towel used when there was a newspaper in the room?"

"Why not? Can't see it makes a nickel's difference."

"On the contrary, it does make some difference, which our schemer was subtle enough to recognize. But let us pass on to another matter. On this most perplexing and unusual case we have encountered two strange coincidences."

"Two ?"

"One pertains to the lama and Jack Reffner who, journeying across the world in opposite directions, arrive in Chicago on the same day. The other pertains to the Pilgrim Deluxe Hotel, which address, you will recall, was not previously unfamiliar to every member of the Merriweather household."

"Well ?"

"One of these two is not a coincidence, but an essential foundation for the murderer's plans. Surely you will recognize which one that is?"

"No, damned if I can!" Mack fumed. "There's no sense to this any way I figure."

"Dear, dear," Westborough sighed, "I see that I shall have to tell you."

Mack roared, "For God's sake do!"

Westborough told him. . . .

"Have you any proof?" Mack demanded when the historian had concluded.

"Dear me, no, but I have checked and rechecked my reasoning carefully."

"Didn't you examine the---"

"I did not dare to take that chance alone. Perhaps I am overly timid, but I had also the safety of another's life to consider."

"Too bad you didn't, but even that wouldn't have been proof. How the hell are we to trip this devil up?"

Westborough withdrew some more papers from his pocket. "I wished to check on these matters, and that is why I did not ask you to meet me before noon. There is an obvious line of inquiry indicated."

"Yeh, we can do that, all right," Mack said, scanning the papers.

"It is a trail which cannot easily be concealed, although," the historian added slowly, "one which our adversary had slight necessity to conceal."

"It's a cold trail now," Mack objected. "Nearly a week old." He placed all of the papers into his pocket. "Well, we'll get busy, and thanks. With any luck we ought to be able to turn up something in a day or two."

"You must find it before that," Westborough exclaimed anxiously. "You must find it this afternoon."

"Why this afternoon?"

"I am no longer a guest in the Merriweather residence. Officially I have taken my departure."

"Well ?"

"However, I have left a re-entry there. I did not remove my luggage, explaining to Vincent Merriweather that I would call tonight to secure it."

"What of it?"

"When I do go back tonight, John, you must be able to come with me."

"Short notice," Mack objected. "Don't know whether we'll be able to make it or not."

"I know, John, that it is short notice, but I have had experience on previous occasions with the rapidity with which you and your associates are able to work."

"Why tonight? You can pick up your grip just as well tomorrow night."

"Frankly I am afraid to wait longer."

"What's there to be afraid of? You're out of it now."

"It is not for myself I fear, but for Tsongpun Bonbo."

"Who's going to hurt him?"

"He is completely guileless, so like a confiding child. I have tried to stress to him the urgent necessity of not revealing that he has found the manuscript, but he is so happy over it that I am not sure he is able to conceal the important fact."

"Well?"

"There is a phrase—an expressive one—a 'plugged nickel.' Should our opponent learn that the lama now holds the Padma Sambhava manuscript in his possession I would not give a 'plugged nickel' for Tsongpun Bonbo's chance of life."

PART FOURTEEN: The Pieces Are Joined Together (Monday Night, July 26)

JANICE SHELTON glanced up from an armchair as Vincent entered the library. "Reading?" he asked.

"Trying to." Her wan smile was not convincing. "I can't put it out of my mind. The service this afternoon."

"Well, it's over now," Vincent said grimly. " 'For dust thou art, and unto dust.' "

"Don't!" she shuddered. "He was your father."

"Is that any reason why I should be a hypocrite?" he demanded.

Her book fell unheeded from her lap. "Do you have to be a hypocrite? Didn't he leave you everything he had?"

"Because I was his son; not because he liked me." Vincent sank into a chair and lit a cigarette with shaking fingers. "He had no more use for me than I did for him."

"Why are you so bitter, Vin?"

"Forget it."

"You were like two millstones grinding against each other," she said softly. "Did he hurt you a lot?"

He said angrily: "Do we have to dig up every old score?"

"No, of course not."

"The trouble with you, Jan, is you're too infernally wise. You know more than a girl of your age has any business knowing."

She smiled. "Do you want to know the trouble with you, Vin?"

"Well"—he shrugged—"I asked for it."

"The trouble with you is that you've been living on your nerves ever since Thursday. Why don't you go upstairs, take a hot bath and get some sleep?"

"Sleep!" he exclaimed. "I don't know what sleep is."

"Then it's high time you were finding out. Come now, Vin, stop looking so tragic."

"Do you have to talk as though I were a child?"

191

"Do you have to act like one?" she laughed. "Gay—Doctor Walters told me he might drop over for a few minutes this evening. Why don't you ask him to look at you?"

"Why should I? What can he do?"

"Well, you can't go on this way. Maybe he'll give you something so you can get a night's rest."

"No, thank you. I don't care to be indebted to your Doctor Walters. I don't like him."

"I do," she said softly.

"So I have noticed."

"Vin, let's stop lunging at each other's throats. Whatever became of that Mr. Westborough? I caught a glimpse of him at the funeral, but he didn't come back with us."

"No, he told me this morning that his tenure as a guest was over. 'Tenure' was his word. 'Deeply as I appreciate the hospitality so generously extended to me by yourself and your father, I feel that I can no longer intrude upon you at this unfortunate time.' "

She laughed. "Yes, that sounds just like him. But I'm hurt. He didn't tell me good-by."

"Probably expected to see you tonight. He said he was coming back to pick up his bag."

"Well, I'll be glad to see him again. You can't help but like him."

"Yes, I like him," Vincent said slowly, "but there's something queer about his visit. He dropped in to bring a book to Dad, and he stayed nearly a week."

"You forget that the stay was forced on him."

"Yes, I know. First his ankle, then his glasses. Did he tell you how they happened to get broken?"

"No. How did they?"

"He said that he heard a noise in the Tibetan Room and when he went in to investigate, someone strangled him."

"Strangled him? Oh no!"

"That's what he said."

"I can't believe it."

"Neither could I until I saw the mark on his throat."

"How horrible!" Her body quivered as though a cold draft had blown suddenly into the room. "Vin, why didn't you tell me about this before?"

"He asked me not to tell anyone."

"But who here would do such a thing?"

He shook his head. "I wish I knew."

"This isn't exactly a house of murderers," she continued.

"No. It's queer any way you look at it, but then he's queer. Take his ankle first."

"It was sprained. Doctor Walters said so."

"And Doctor Walters is an honorable man. But sprain or no sprain, it didn't stop Westborough from walking all over the house whenever he felt like it. I told him straight out his ankle was fishy, and then he sprung those glasses. Wouldn't I please let him stay until he could get new ones."

"He did get new ones, though."

"Yes, when? On Saturday. Did he have any excuse after that for not leaving? He did not, but he didn't go just the same. Yesterday he shut himself up all day long with the lama and didn't say a word about going."

"Poor Vin!" she exclaimed, smiling. "He does have so many people camping on his doorstep. A history professor and a Tibetan lama and his uncle Jed and a Miss Shelton. He's too polite to get rid of any of us."

"Don't be silly! Though the lama is something of a problem."

"He's a dear!"

"But a problem all the same. He traveled halfway around the world to find this manuscript which Dad promised to sell him and it disappears. (That's another queer thing that's happened since Westborough's been here.) Now I can't turn the lama out until we find his manuscript. It wouldn't be decent."

"Do you want to turn him out?"

"No, not particularly, he's no trouble. But he can't stay here forever, can he?"

"And your other two guests?"

"Which one?"

"Not your uncle. I know how much you think of him."

"Do you know how much I think of you?"

"No."

He sat down on the arm of her chair, his fingers caressing her cheek. "Then you ought to be learning."

"So you really want to marry me? You didn't ask me just because of your father?"

He bent forward suddenly and kissed her throat. "Don't talk nonsense. You're beautiful and you're wise and you're unselfish. You're a good sport and you have a sense of humor. You know how to put up with my bad moods, and you haven't bored me yet. Seven good reasons—count them if you don't believe me---why I want to marry you."

She said: "Yes, but you've forgotten the eighth."

"Then consider it added. What is it?"

"Just a little matter of whether or not you happen to love me."

"Good heavens, Jan! Do I have to tell you that?"

"Some girls might think it was important."

He sank to the floor and buried his head in her lap., "Yes, Jan honey, with all my heart."

Her fingers gently stroked his hair. "Thank you for saying that, Vin. It's beautiful."

"And true," he added. " 'Beauty is truth, and truth—' "

"I know better, dear." She continued to stroke his head. "Be honest with me, Vin. If you must, be cruel, but at all events be honest. That's what I want from you now more than anything else. Will you?"

"Yes," he answered in a choked voice, rising to his feet.

"Very well. Do you still say you love me?"

"Ye—oh, Jan!" He crossed to the fireplace, staring down at the polished desolation of its empty grate. "I don't know. I think so."

"But you don't want to marry me ?"

"Oh, marry!" he exclaimed. "You know what I've always wanted, Jan."

"And you were willing to give that up? For me?"

"Why not?" he demanded gruffly.

She flung her arms about his neck and kissed his lips with swift intensity. "That's for good-by, Vin dear."

"Good-by?" he repeated in a puzzled manner.

"Sorry," Dr. Walters said stiffly from the doorway. "The butler said I would find you in here, Miss Shelton, but he didn't say that you were busy."

"Gay!"

"I can come back later. Or if I don't, it's of no consequence."

"Gay, stop talking like an idiot." She ran hurriedly across the room. "I love you, and you know it. I was just telling Vin good-by."

"Yes, Janice was just telling me good-by," Vincent corroborated, thrusting both hands into his coat pockets. "A little demonstratively, perhaps, but then you must remember that we are friends of long standing. Walters, I congratulate you. It's always the best man who wins, isn't it?"

Janice caught his arm as he reached the door. "Don't go like that, Vin. Say you'll forgive me."

He removed the hand that was resting on his sleeve. "One finds it a little difficult to overlook the fact that one has just made a first-class fool of one's self. Not that it's of any consequence. Well, I congratulate you, Walters. Or did I say that before? Yes, I did, didn't I? Well then, good evening."

She watched his unyielding back disappear down the corridor. "I've hurt him," she lamented. "Poor Vin!"

"Never mind him," Dr. Walters commanded, placing his arm protectively about her shoulders. "He'll get over it."

"After all," she said, "it isn't as if he really did love me."

"If you don't forget him, Janice, I'm going to be frightfully jealous."

"Can you be frightfully jealous?"

"Terribly. Horribly."

"Well then, Doctor Walters, I think you and I are going to be able to get along."

"And we'll begin right now, Miss Shelton !"

She lifted her head suddenly from his coat lapel. "What's that, Gay?"

"Nothing. The doorbell."

"Oh, the doorbell. Wilkins will answer it, won't he?"

"Naturally. Don't pay any attention to it."

"Why does it go on ringing?"

"Does it matter?"

"A long and two shorts. A long and two shorts. Over and over."

"Special-delivery letter, maybe."

"Wilkins is so slow, perhaps I—"

"No, wait. He's just outside in the hall."

"Yes, I hear him. He walks so heavily—like an elephant in the house. Poor, poky Wilkins! A long and two shorts. 'Hear it not, Duncan, for it is a knell that summons thee to—' "

"Janice, stop it!" He shook her roughly by the shoulders. "Tell me right now what it is that's bothering you."

She smiled a little shyly. "I'm all right now."

"You're not all right. You're shaking all over. Why?"

"I don't know. Oh yes, I do. This house---that room! One man died there. Another man was strangled. Did you know that?"

"No."

"He didn't die, the second man---yet. That bell! It's still "

"It won't ring much longer," he promised grimly.

"A long and two shorts. Always the same. Is something else going to happen here in this house tonight, Gay? Something terrible?"

He drew her close but did not answer.

II

Wilkins showed them into the living room and left them to wait among the Venetian tapestries, the massive Renaissance furniture. Mack closed the door behind the butler's retreating form.

"'And we mean well, in going to this mask; but 'tis no wit to go,' " Westborough whispered softly. Mack sniffed.

"S'matter? Losing your nerve?"

"Dear me, I hope not."

"Brace up! You've done smart work on this case. All that's left now is to deliver the spiel the way we've planned. A few minutes more and it will be all over."

"'Or the right way or the wrong way, to its triumph or undoing,' " Westborough quoted, smiling.

"Huh?"

"I beg your pardon. A line from Robert Browning. Shall we review our plan of campaign?"

"Thought that was settled. We get all of 'em into the Tibetan Room, and I watch for a break while you give your lecture. But they've all got to be there."

"Yes, the innocent members of the household are needed as catalysts. When the denouement is reached their united horror of the culprit should create a most unnerving psychic atmosphere."

"Not the way we usually get confessions," Mack contended. "May work at that, though." He strode, silently as a prowling cat, to the closed door. "Shhh! One of 'em's coming now."

It was Vincent Merriweather who entered. The young man's face was flushed, and he was breathing heavily.

"Good evening," he said, nodding to each of them in a preoccupied manner. "Your bag is waiting in the front hall for you, Mr. Westborough."

"It was kind of you to keep it for me today, but I have still another favor to ask of you."

"Yes?" Vincent took a gold case from his pocket and touched the spring which flicked it open. "Will you have a cigarette ?"

"No, thank you. I am indebted to every member of this household for some kindness during the past few days, but I left in such a hurry this morning that I was unable to say good-by to anyone but you. Naturally I desire to rectify that breach of good manners. Will you be kind enough to ask all of them to meet me in the Tibetan Room?"

Vincent produced a gold lighter that was a perfect mate to the case. He applied its flame to his cigarette.

"Whom do you mean by 'all'?"

"The Lama Tsongpun Bonbo. Chang. Your uncle. Mrs. Gestler. Miss Shelton. Doctor Walters if he happens to be in the house."

"He is," Vincent answered shortly. "All of them are."

"Then will you be kind enough to ask them to come to the Tibetan Room?"

Vincent took a quick puff on his cigarette. "Why the Tibetan Room?"

"Dear me, I must not be so insistent!" Westborough exclaimed. "I merely had the fancy to make my adieux to my Tibetan friends in an appropriate setting."

"All right," Vincent yielded. "Do you want to wait here?"

"There, if you please."

"All right," Vincent said again. They walked down the hall.

The Tibetan gods were menacing shadows in the darkness, but as Vincent pressed the light switch they took on a judicial aspect. A jury deliberating behind their altar while the four Kings of the Quarters kept grotesque ward. A committee of judges presided over by the smiling Sakyamuni, whose right hand pointed downward to call the earth for a witness.

Never, Westborough mused, could he become accustomed to this room. Always must he be an alien intruder among its painted beams and pigeonhole bookcases for silk-wrapped Tibetan tomes; among its ghost-daggers, its demon masks, its skull cups and skull drums; among its gods and its guardians resentful of their sanctuary's invasion . . . but he saw that Vincent had gone.

Mack and Westborough walked together to the altar as though some voiceless signal had passed between them. Standing before the threatening figure of Chana Dorje, they flung back the yellow brocade and stooped to their knees. Their eyes focused upon a narrow crack between two boards on the underside of the altar. They saw that small wedge-shaped bits of wood, to the right and to the left of the crack, had been whittled away.

"Whee-ew!" Mack ejaculated. He smoothed down the yellow cloth they had lifted. "Good sign! Shall we have a look at the—"

"No," Westborough demurred. He was raising a metal mirror in order to place an object beneath it—a small object which glittered like silver. "If we are watched from the second floor, as we may well be, even this slight examination may have unpleasant consequences. Our expose, in order to attain its maxim psychological effect, must come as a complete surprise."

"Someone's coming," Mack cautioned in a low voice. Westborough hurriedly replaced the bronze mirror and moved away from the altar.

"Good evening, Mr. Chang."

"Good evening," Chang bowed. His Mongolian features were tonight expressionless.

"I should like to ask if your memory of a certain passage has improved since our last conversation?"

But Chang this time was not to be caught off guard. "My memory is very poor one."

"An unfortunate ailment," the historian murmured. The arrival of Tsongpun Bonbo prevented his saying more.

The lama's beaming countenance was an open secret (to anyone possessing the key) that he had carried out to the letter Westborough's instructions of that day. Others straggled into the room: Janice Shelton and Dr. Walters, Vincent Merriweather, Mrs. Gestler and the black-bearded Dr. Merriweather. Mack closed the door and unobtrusively took a post before it.

Westborough remained before the altar. "Good evening to you all," he began. "As I have already said to Mr. Merriweather, I should like to thank you for the courtesies extended to me during my stay. But that is not my only purpose in asking you to meet me here." There was a brief whisper of surprise. "I feel that I must acquaint you with a discovery which Lieutenant Mack has made. Despite the verdict rendered by the coroner's jury Adam Merriweather did not die a natural death."

He waited for the storm to subside.

"Mr. Merriweather was murdered—murdered by a method unique in the annals of crime, a method so strange, so difficult to detect that it might almost be termed 'murder by magic.' "

Pausing, he glanced about the room. On the faces before him he could read nothing but a universal astonishment. Plainly the task was going to prove a more difficult one than he had anticipated.

"Lieutenant Mack," he continued, "was first drawn to this house while investigating the murder of Jack Reffner. Since that crime was one vitally linked with the death of Mr. Merriweather's father it may be well to summarize its salient features now.

"On last Monday evening, between the hours of nine and eleven, the unfortunate Mr. Reffner was killed. He was strangled with a silk scarf, which, with his dying strength, he attempted to wrest from his throat. He did not succeed in that attempt, but he tore loose a small silken fragment—an unfortunate mischance for his murderer. The characters embroidered upon that small shred of silk enabled Lieutenant Mack to identify the scarf as a Tibetan one.

"Suspicion for the crime became directed to the occupant of a room across the hall from the unfortunate Reffner. That individual had registered as Hamilcar Barca, of Carthage, Mo., a name and address which Lieutenant Mack recognized as obviously false, and had departed from the hotel without his baggage at a time which might have been very shortly after Reffner's death. As might be expected in a hotel so poorly illuminated as the Pilgrim Deluxe, the description which the police were able to secure was a meager one: Hamilcar Barca was of medium height, wore dark green glasses and had a gray beard.

"In the room which Mr. Barca had occupied Lieutenant Mack found, wrapped within a hotel towel and thrown into the wastebasket, a braid of gray crepe hair and a bottle of spirit gum such as are used in stage makeup. Moreover, he discovered that Mr. Barca had left behind him a number of toilet articles, including a shaving brush, a half-full tube of shaving cream and a razor. The shaving brush, when found, was damp, showing that it must have been used no later than the preceding evening. All of this was strong evidence that Mr. Barca's gray beard was a false one—a disguise behind which (and the green glasses) he concealed his real features. They suggested a carefully premeditated murder.

"Upon the floor Lieutenant Mack found smudges of a white powder, which a laboratory analysis revealed as a woman's bath powder. These are virtually his only clues to the identity of Hamilcar Barca, who came out of the unknown and vanished into the unknown after committing a murder with, apparently, no other motive than the pilfering of Mr. Reffner's pockets. But robbery cannot explain the reason for that brutal crime.

"The true motive"—Westborough snatched another quick glance about the room—"was one inextricably mingled with the death of Adam Merriweather, the machinery for which had even then been set in motion. Reffner, alive, might be able to furnish damaging testimony; therefore he must be destroyed before Merriweather's murder could be allowed to proceed. What was this dangerous knowledge which the unfortunate Reffner harbored? A slight fact, but enough to seal his death warrant. A fact pertaining to the Tibetan manuscript which he had stolen from the Lama Tsongpun Bonbo.

"Did Reffner know what that manuscript contained? No, for although he spoke the oral tongue well, he could not read the Tibetan language. Nor had he had the manuscript translated, or, at least, no more than brief portions of it. Reffner's ignorance was the foundation upon which the murderer was able to base his plot. But it is now time to consider the fate of the manuscript after its arrival in this residence.

"Mr. Chang"—he bowed toward the Tibetan—"a scholar of rare ability, translated it into English for the benefit of his employer. He made two copies of his translation. Shortly after he had completed his work the original manuscript was stolen. The original copy of the translation vanished soon after Mr. Merriweather's death; I have reason to believe that it was stolen from this very room during the confusion which attended the discovery of his body. The carbon copy, which Chang kept in his own file, disappeared also, as I discovered when I wished to examine it. Furthermore, the very memory of the manuscript appeared to have been expunged from the translator's mind. Truly a mysterious set of circumstances---as though some supernal agency had taken a celestial sponge to efface all traces of the manuscript's presence in Mr. Merriweather's house.

"Why was this done? Because, ladies, gentlemen, incredible as it may seem, a Tibetan manuscript of the eighth century was the agency employed to kill Adam Merriweather."

There were cries, exclamations of surprise. Not the cry he had expected. Not the exclamation he had hoped.

"Mr. Merriweather, I fear, had become engrossed in the pursuit of a phantom, a chimera, which, if it exists at all, must remain forever hidden from prying Western eyes within that unknown depths of Central Asia. In short, he sought the Secret Doctrine."

"Secret Doctrine?" Vincent repeated. "What's that?"

"Perhaps you will know it better by the Tibetan term, since I understand, Mr. Merriweather, that you are making excellent progress in the study of that difficult language." Westborough pronounced the Tibetan name and waited for the echoes of those strange syllables to die from the room. "I shall say little about this shadowy rite, the powers which it is supposed to confer upon its initiates, because there is so little known to say. The Secret Doctrine, I am informed, is extremely dangerous for the uninitiated to explore—'A trail by a crevice is not the proper path for the blind to travel' was, I believe, the expressive language used by the Lama Tsongpun Bonbo. Dangerous it proved for Mr. Merriweather, since it was the direct cause of his death."

Although he could detect astonishment and incredulity in the voices clamoring about him he could detect no fear. What an amazing actor was their iron-nerved antagonist!

"I do not mean that Adam Merriweather's esoteric researches liberated occult forces which caused his death," Westborough hastened to qualify. "He was murdered by methods not of the East but of the West. The Secret Doctrine was merely the bait employed to lure him to his death. A recondite bait couched in the supposed words of the semi-mythical Padma Sambhava, the founder of Tibetan Buddhism and wisest of all the Buddhist sages. Padma Sambhava: demon-destroyer, sorcerer, warlock, necromancer par excellence—please bear these qualifications in mind. It is necessary to remember that Padma Sambhava may well be considered the supreme authority on matters of the occult by one who has delved even superficially into the subject. And it is now time for us to examine the manuscript he is reputed to have written."

"The manuscript!" someone shouted. "Good God, you haven't---"

"Yes," Westborough affirmed. (The lengthy lecture was at last beginning to yield results.) "The manuscript has been found and has been again restored to the place where it was hidden. Tsongpun Lama, will you be so kind as to bring it to me?"

The lama, who had been careful to remain near the Yellow King, stood on his tiptoes to raise the scowling mask. He removed the packet (again wrapped within black cambric) and brought it to Westborough.

"T'ere, Kusho! My placing in your hands words ob Precious Teacher."

"Thank you, Tsongpun Lama," Westborough said gravely. He set the packet upon the altar and stripped off the black cambric, the three layers of yellow silk. He unstrapped the heavy boards protecting the loose pages. "We must handle it with care," he said. "It is a much venerated document."

One by one he turned the individual folios face downward into a pile. Presently he placed aside four pages, casting them out as one might playing cards which have strayed into the wrong deck. He restrapped the boards, replaced one by one the three yellow silk wrappings, and returned the packet to the lama.

"I do not believe, Tsongpun Lama, that anyone will now question the fact that this is your property." The lama hugged the packet to his bosom as though he would never relinquish it. In a voice scarcely above a whisper he said:

"How may I t'ank you, Kusho Wes-bo-ro, who do t'is por me?"

"It is I who am indebted to you, Tsongpun Lama. Without the valuable help you have given this strange case would be yet unsolved."

He picked up the four sheets he had taken from the manuscript, held them loosely in the fingers of one hand. "These purport to pertain to that chimera-like rite of which I spoke a few minutes ago. I use advisedly the word 'purport.' It is an age-old tradition that the nature of the Secret Doctrine is transmitted only by oral instruction from guru to *chela* throughout generation after generation. The fact that these folios profess to expound that great enigma should alone brand them as a forgery."

He smiled quietly. "Yes, a forgery," the historian emphasized. "An excellent forgery capable of deceiving even experts. The paper closely resembles the tough-fibered, yellowed paper of the other folios—it is probably an actual Tibetan paper; the ink is a close match in shade to that of the other pages; the air of antiquity hovering about the four sheets is convincingly authentic. How was such spurious antiquity achieved? By delicate dyeing with staining fluid? By careful application of smoke? By patient brushing with fine sand? There are many methods, but we do not need to concern ourselves with them. It is the content that matters, and that, thanks to the courtesy of the Lama Tsong-pun Bonbo, I am enabled to read to you."

The paper served as a curtain behind which Westborough could observe the faces of his listeners. Eager listeners. And one fearful, timorous with apprehension which could be concealed no longer.

" 'This Is the great Doctrine, the great Secret, the Secret of the Thunderbolt. . . .' "

Westborough, as he concluded his reading, noted that the one who feared had regained a momentary lapse in poise. If the words meant anything to any person present in the room it was not now apparent.

"That is the translation of the Tibetan lines upon these four folios," the historian explained. "It seems rather long to be contained there, but Tibetan, as many of you know, is a highly compressed language. This document, coming, as it appeared to come, directly from Padma Sambhava, revealing, as it purported to reveal, the method of obtaining the mysterious powers of the Secret Doctrine, was bound to exercise a remarkable effect upon Adam Merriweather. In fact it was almost a certainty that he would obey its instructions to the letter. Keeping that in mind, several elementary deductions may be made.

"Mr. Merriweather, although heard to pronounce the word 'Heegh,' the three times directed, was not heard to pronounce the word 'Room.' The act which caused his death was therefore included in that section of the ritual between the two mantras. That act---"

He broke off abruptly, realizing that it was yet too soon. Their adversary must be shown the silken threads of logic which they had woven into their cocoon. All of those threads. This killer of two men must be made to realize that from that fine-spun cocoon there was no escape possible.

"That act I shall reserve for later consideration. Let us now return to Hamilcar Barca, who in his room at the Pilgrim Deluxe Hotel is waiting for Mr. Reffner's return. In the newspaper he has bought to while away the time he finds some startling news. The rightful owner of the manuscript, through an almost incredible coincidence, is in Chicago; his quest is almost certain to lead him to Adam Merriweather; the ingenious murder plan must be halted at once.

"Yes, but he has already been driven to desperation, as his conceiving of a dual murder shows. If he halts now he loses everything. And the lama's presence, moreover, may help as well as hinder; certainly it will provide the final touch necessary to convince Adam Merriweather that the authenticity of the manuscript cannot be questioned. Barca has several hours to weigh the pros and the cons of the matter, and he decides to accept all risks, even the close proximity of one of the few men in the world who might be able to expose his forgery.

"While the hours drag by he waits, waits until he hears a key being inserted in the lock of the door across the hall. He tiptoes to his own door, which he has left ajar, and looks into the corridor. Reffner has returned. The prologue has been finished; the curtain can now arise upon the first act of the heinous drama. He knocks upon the door of Reffner's room.

"The disguise of Hamilcar Barca has been removed; Reffner sees the natural person of his visitor. Although surprised, perhaps, he is not distrustful. Why should he be distrustful? Barca, for no other reason, it would appear, than a natural generosity of heart, has already given him valuable assistance. Reffner reveals that he has succeeded in selling the Tibetan manuscript to Adam Merriweather, and Barca strangles him with his silken scarf. All is over within a very few minutes. There is no disturbance, no outcry.

"Barca restores the scarf to his pocket. If he notices that it has been torn he fails to realize that embroidered Sanskrit characters are on the fragment remaining in Reffner's hand. He puts on again the gloves which he has worn while he waited in his room across the hall. Not until the gloves are on his hands does he venture to turn out the light, leave the room and close the door. When he entered he could not, of course, be wearing gloves, but it was his host, Reffner, who then opened the door for him and closed it afterwards. Barca knows that he has left no fingerprints in Reffner's room. And in the room across the hall he has touched nothing without gloves; not even the key to his own door, which was carried upstairs and inserted in the lock by a bellman.

"The murderer resumes once more the guise of Hamilcar Barca. He may not take his baggage with him when he departs, but the articles which he leaves behind have been brought for that very purpose. The few things which must be removed he can carry away in his pockets. He walks down the three flights of stairs to the lobby. The night clerk catches a glimpse of him as he goes out but pays little attention. The murderer disappears within the maelstrom of Chicago. Exit Hamilcar Barca!

"He has succeeded in what he came to do. He has left no clues to his identity. Yet careful as he has been, the evidence in his room is sufficient him. Now that we know Reffner's murderer is also Merriweather's, we may detect him by applying the principles of logical inference.

"Consider, first of all, the hotel itself. Old, poorly illuminated, a stupid manager, a nearsighted night clerk, a meager staff of employees—it is, in every respect, the ideal setting for such a crime as Reffner's murder. But Barca must have knowledge of this hotel before he can induce Reffner to stop there. Not firsthand knowledge that would be too dangerous—but knowledge imparted by someone who has previously stayed there. Is there such a someone among the persons in this group? There is indeed, and from this one matter alone we might be able to surmise the identity of Hamilcar Barca, but there are other clues even more reliable.

"Why, for example, have the spirit gum and the crepe hair been wrapped in a hotel towel when a newspaper was available? A crumpled-up newspaper may be thrown away unopened, but surely no self-respecting hotel employee will allow a good towel to be so treated if he or she is able to prevent it. That fact is one on which Hamilcar Barca counted. He did not want to conceal the crepe hair, the spirit gum; he wanted to make sure that they would be discovered. He wanted to flaunt them before the very eyes of the police investigators so that they might draw from them the natural inferences.

"Ladies, gentlemen, those natural inferences were the wrong ones. Hamilcar Barca did not have a false beard, but a very real one. White added to black makes gray. A few dashes of white bath powder were sufficient to make a gray beard from the black one of Doctor Jedediah Merriweather."

"Don't move!" Mack barked. "I've got you covered." There was the flash of light on steel as he took something from his pocket. "Jed Merriweather, I arrest you for two murders. It had to be you who killed Reffner. You're one of the few fellows in this country liable to own a Tibetan scarf. Do you want to make a statement now?"

Dr. Merriweather surveyed his manacled wrists and said coldly: "At the hour you say Reffner's death occurred I was on the train en route from San Francisco."

"Were you?" Mack snapped. "Let's see about it. You mailed (we'll suppose it was you who mailed it) an airmail letter to your brother on Saturday which was stamped by the San Francisco post office at 1 P.M. What else can you prove? You came in here Wednesday morning on the Overland Limited from San Francisco, and you sent a telegram at three-sixteen Tuesday afternoon from Kearney, Nebraska—right time and right place for that train. So far, so good, but now we're up to bat. Here's what really did happen:

"You dropped the airmail letter into a post-office box just before you left San Francisco, which was at eleven o'clock Saturday morning on that new streamlined train, the Forty Niner. Reservation under a phony name, sure, but that beard of yours isn't easy to cover up. You hadn't counted on us checking, though. Only about one chance out of a hundred thousand that anyone would ever suspect you of having anything to do with Jack Reffner."

"What makes you assume that I had?"

"That part's easy. Reffner had gotten in from the Orient about two weeks before, and he was broke when he landed. Most boats from the Orient dock at San Francisco, and if he was broke he'd naturally try to sell his manuscript. Everyone who knows a nickel's worth about such things knows you are one of the big guns on Tibetan stuff. You'd be the first fellow he'd hunt up. He leaves the manuscript with you a few days so you can consider buying it. While you're translating it, Westborough thinks, you get the idea of how to murder your brother and get away with it. You have access to Tibetan paper, you can write Tibetan, and you know all the tricks of making the thing look genuine. I don't think there are five other people in the U.S. who could do that job—and that's one of the biggest points against you, Merriweather. When Reffner comes back to see if you're going to buy his manuscript the forged pages are inside it. Reffner can't read Tibetan; he'll never be able to expose you, and you don't learn until way later that the lama's in this country.

"You give Reffner a song and dance. You can't buy the manuscript yourself, you can't pay him what it's worth, but you have a millionaire brother in Chicago who collects such things. If Reffner shows it to him he'll get a good price, but—there's a great big 'but' to be considered. Reffner mustn't tell your brother who sent him because you and your brother aren't on good terms. Reffner mustn't even mention your name if he wants the deal to go through. He swallows that, as anyone would, and it leaves you sitting pretty. Nothing in the world to connect Jed Merriweather in San Francisco with Jack Reffner in Chicago.

"Reffner's broke, so you play the Good Samaritan and buy his ticket to Chicago. You also give him a little money to eat on, but not much. You'll send him some more later, you tell him, but you've got to know his address. He doesn't know Chicago, but you do. There's a nice low-priced hotel in a convenient neighborhood. The Pilgrim Deluxe on Eron Street. If he'll stay there for a few days you'll send him enough money to last until the deal goes through with your brother. Reffner asked for mail when he came back to the hotel last Monday; he expected to hear from you.

"The Forty Niner brings you into Chicago Monday afternoon at three o'clock daylight savings time. You check your grip—the one with the stuff you really need—and go into the station washroom. You can hide in one of the johnnies while you powder your beard. It's a pretty fair disguise, that—if people don't get too close to spot the specks of powder. But it's plenty safe for the lobby of the Pilgrim Deluxe, which is about as dark as Carlsbad Caverns with the lights off. You know all about that hotel. Chang stayed there once, and he described it to you.

"You walked away from the station, carrying your dummy grip that you're going to leave behind, but when you reach the Loop you think it's safe to take a taxi. We found the driver afterwards; maybe he'll be able to identify you.

"You sign the register as Hamilcar Barca and pay for your room in advance so there'll be no questions about you. While you're registering it's no trick to find Reffner's room number and get the manager to give you a room across the hall from him. The manager hands you a key, but you're too smart to handle it. You let the bellhop carry it upstairs and open the door to the room. He even puts the key in the inside of the lock for you.

"When you're alone you wash the powder off your beard so Reffner will see you the way you were in San Francisco. You hope he comes in early. If he stays out too late it'll put a bad crimp in things, because you've got a train to catch. But a fellow doesn't go in for night life without money, and Reffner can't have much left out of the little you gave him. He can't borrow any—he's a stranger in town---and if your brother buys the manuscript you know he'll pay for it with a check that Reffner can't cash on such short notice. Three reasons why you expect Reffner to come in early, and it works out the way you figured.

"You go knock on his door. He doesn't suspect anything when he sees you. Hell, the guy thinks you're one of his best friends! You ask about the manuscript. You're sure your brother'd buy it on sight, but if he didn't buy it now's the time for you to learn about it. But Reffner tells you he's got your brother's check in his pocket, and from that time on his goose is cooked brown.

"Reffner doesn't suspect anything, I said. All the while you're talking with him you're holding the scarf in your hand, ready for your chance at a split second's notice, and he still doesn't suspect anything. That's the neatest touch of all. It's a *Tibetan* scarf, see! A curio which you can say you've brought along on purpose to show him.

"After you've settled his hash you go back to your own room and re-powder your beard so you can walk out of the hotel looking the same as when you came in. There's plenty of time for you to walk all the way to the station, and it's a good thing for you there is. A cab on this trip would be risky business. You go into the good old station washroom again and wash the powder out of your beard. You collect the grip you've left at the checkstand, go over to the ticket window and buy a one-way ticket to Kearney. Lots of time for you to catch train Number

27, out of here at ten-twenty---eleven-twenty, d.s.t.—which brings you into Kearney at two thirty-five Tuesday afternoon. You send the wire to your brother and catch the train back to Chicago, the train that you're supposed to have been riding on ever since Sunday night. Smart plan! But once we begin to check up we find more holes than in a hunk of Swiss cheese.

"The train crew on the Forty Niner remembers you. Black beard! Easy to trace when we know what to look for. So does the ticket seller in Chicago remember you. And the one in Kearney. And the telegraph clerk there who took your wire. Black beard again. But you didn't dare shave it. It would have looked too funny to your Chicago relatives if you came here without the well-known beaver. Well, that's the case we've got against you for Reffner's murder, and it'll hold water when we take it to the state's attorney. The motive's obvious."

"Indeed?"

"You bet it is. Reffner knew, and might tell if he was asked, that you had the manuscript long enough to add the forged sheets. You had to kill him to cover up for the murder of your brother."

Dr. Merriweather laughed in a full-throated manner. "Are you seriously saying that I killed my brother with four leaves from a Tibetan manuscript?"

"Yes," Westborough answered gently, "that is exactly what you did do, and your motive was almost as strange as your method—you killed him for a Tibetan fort buried in the desert sands of Sinkiang. What were the lives of two men—one a thief, the other a hopeless valetudinarian—in comparison with its archaeological riches? Very little to one like you who has witnessed the slaughter of the inhabitants of an entire village for no other reason than the unleashing of a savage lust to kill. You needed money for your expedition, and it could never be obtained from your brother while he lived."

"You were present, I believe, at our last interview. May I remind you that he did not give me a definite refusal?"

"Quite true. Your brother was jealous of your reputation, your accomplishments, your very personality. Your groveling to him for money afforded a comforting feeling of superiority which he would not willingly relinquish, but you understood his psychology perfectly. You knew that your brother, although he might appear to hesitate, was certain eventually to withdraw with your other backers. The only sure way to secure the funds you needed was to procure them from his estate."

"His estate! Do you know that he left me nothing? Do you think he didn't tell me of the will he'd drawn?"

"Both facts are irrelevant. Your brother left virtually everything to his only son, and your nephew, Doctor Merriweather, is extremely devoted to you."

"Uncle Jed!" Vincent cried in a tense, shocked voice. "Uncle Jed!"

"They're talking nonsense." Jed Merriweather's black beard bobbed grotesquely beneath his face. "You were with me at the very minute of your father's death. Do you remember that, Vin? You've got to remember."

"He's right!" Vincent was nearly sobbing in his relief. "We were together in my canoe. Out on the lake, blocks away from the house. How could he kill my father, who was here—locked inside this very room?"

"That," Westborough said, "is a matter which must now be considered. And may I add that I am sincerely sorry for both of you?"

IV

"One may well wonder why Doctor Merriweather did not destroy the forged folios when he had the opportunity to do so," Westborough continued. "That, I believe, may be simply explained. It was not safe to remove them because their existence was known to the translator, who, in the event the manuscript was unearthed from its hiding place, might call attention to the absence of these pages. Somewhat ironical, Doctor Merriweather, that you should be worried over what Chang might reveal. He knew even more than you dreamed, and he did not betray you.

"I think, without doubt, that Chang saw you pick up a sheaf of typewritten sheets from this altar on Thursday night. He said nothing. Perhaps he did not know then that those sheets were Mr. Merriweather's copy of the translation, but after his own copy of it had been removed from his own file he must have been able to put two and two together. What answer he received from his arithmetic I do not know, but only this theory is able to account for his amazing lapse of memory. Chang has been very loyal to you, Doctor Merriweather. I hope that you will not now make him suffer for that loyalty by refusing to confess the truth.

"Naturally you would have been safe if you had destroyed the original manuscript with the two copies of its translation, but that feat was one impossible to one of your training. Although you could kill two men with little compunction you could not obliterate an object of such great historical value. What disposition did you eventually intend to make of that manuscript, Doctor Merriweather? To recover it for yourself after the lama had returned with a broken heart to Tibet? Or were you going to restore it to him after the excitement aroused by your brother's death had quieted down and it became reasonably safe to do so? I shall incline to the latter view. You are not at heart a cruel man, I know.

"I am indebted to you for sparing my life when I surprised you on Friday morning. Or did you intend to spare it? And it would be more accurate, I believe, to say that you surprised me. Hearing my footsteps in the hall, you rushed to the glass case, whipped out one of the Tibetan scarves and unlocked the door (you would not have been working in that room behind an unlocked door, I believe)—all before I was able to reach it. Never in my life have I encountered another such example of lightning-quick thinking. I congratulate you, Doctor Merriweather.

"The evidence of your crime you, of course, removed from this room on that morning and took far out on the lake in your nephew's canoe. The objects you buried beneath Lake Michigan's waters may, however, be recovered even yet; there exist such things as dredges and divers. I mention these details to show you how intimately we are acquainted with the structure of your plot, how impossible it will be for you to escape the consequences of your crimes. It is now time for us to reconstruct your highly successful murder machine."

Westborough stepped behind the altar and laid his hand upon the skull-dotted hair of the potbellied Chana Dorje. "Of the twelve images in this room this one alone is made of papier-mache. Tibetan papier-mache images, as I read the other day in Colter's *Handbook of Lamaism*, are molded in two halves. When joined together a hollow space is formed in which are inserted votive offerings. Now let us see if the Thunderbolt God is constructed according to tradition."

He had several anxious minutes as he fumbled at the back of the image in search of the catch which opened it. He did not doubt it was there—it had to be there—but it might be well hidden. Too well hidden, perhaps. Dear, dear, whatever should he do if he could not find it?

He spied a small knob, pressed it, and with relief watched the entire back of the Thunderbolt God swing open. He reached his hand into the hollow—they were there just as he had expected they would be. Heaven be thanked!

He brought out a double handful of red silk-covered cylinders—the size, the shape of giant firecrackers. "Tibetan prayers," he explained. "Paper rolls of written prayers inserted by devout worshipers when this image was consecrated. The drawing of the swastika which was found here on Thursday morning was a prayer, too, I believe. The prayer of an ignorant layman, unable to write but able to draw the emblem he believed would bring him good fortune. A layman so ignorant that, as the Lama Tsongpun Bonbo explained to me, he did not know that he had drawn the wrong kind of swastika—the left-handed symbol of the Bon demon worshipers. Although the presence of the Bon swastika in this room caused Adam Merriweather a great amount of anxiety he did not connect it with this image. Possibly, Doctor Merriweather, you had never acquainted him with your discovery that the back of the image opened. It was Wednesday night when you opened the image—the night of the very day of your arrival. You wasted no time; the very next night might be a night of a thunderstorm, as indeed it was. But the demon of bad luck, which had followed you from Sinkiang into Tibet five years ago, had caused the recent withdrawal of your expedition's backers and had been with you even in the Pilgrim Deluxe Hotel when Reffner grasped the fragment of your scarf, was here also in this room. When you had finished your work and restored the rolls of prayers to the image, you failed to notice that one of these rolls had fallen from the altar and was lying on the floor. Perhaps all the gods of Tibet were in accord that you should penetrate no further into the ancient secrets of their homeland."

The hole was there, Westborough saw. The small hole at the bottom of the image. Even Jed Merriweather, despite his surpassing brilliance, had had to leave that trace of his handiwork.

"Perhaps, Doctor Merriweather, it may be well to refresh your memory of the instructions you had written in Tibetan and included with an authentic eighth-century manuscript to reach your brother as a command direct from the high priest of his mystic heaven. Shall I read the translation again?

" 'Choose a night of a thunderstorm. Choose a night when the great Chana Dorje rides the heavens, and his power is at its height.'

"Shall we analyze the significance of this piece of Tibetan rhetoric? The thunderstorm enables you to know in advance when the event will occur. It provides you a measure of control over your murder machine.

" 'Take in your hand his sacred weapon, the thunderbolt. Kneel before his sacred image on a melong purged by the purifying waters of the Samskara you renounce.'

"Purged by the purifying waters for an excellent practical reason, Doctor Merriweather. A wet skin and wet clothing become fairly efficient conductors of electricity. Now let us see what is underneath the mirror which your brother found so conveniently waiting before the god to which he was to kneel."

Westborough moved aside the bronze mirror to point to a spot of shining metal. He inserted his thumbnail to pry the small disk from the altar.

"Do not look so alarmed, Doctor Merriweather. This thumbtack is not the one which you removed on Friday morning, although very similar to it. Quite commonplace, is it not? Had your brother, through some unlucky chance, chosen to lift the mirror and pry loose *your* thumbtack, Doctor Merriweather, he would have found as ordinary a thumbtack as this one. A loop of wire twisted about its shank cannot be pulled through the narrow crack between the boards and through the altar cloth; the friction will cause the wire to slide off the tack and fall, unnoticed, to the floor below the altar. That is why your brother, had he pulled out your thumbtack as I did after his death, would have found no evidence of your machinations. But, unfortunately for you, in order to affix such a loop to the tack you were forced to cut away wood from the under side of the boards. Anyone who cares to look beneath the altar may see the results of your whittling.

"There are electric outlets, provided, no doubt, for your brother's floodlights, under the altar, Doctor Merriweather. Very close to the Thunderbolt God is an outlet with T-shaped slots, a polarized outlet— the last link in a wiring system in which ground wire is joined only to ground wire and live wire only to live wire in every branch and circuit throughout the house. A plug designed especially for the T-shaped slots of that receptacle is affixed to the portable cord you use. That cord, Doctor Merriweather, is divided into two insulated wires of different colors. The white wire—the one which connects to the harmless trolled side of the house circuit—is the one which you twist about the thumbtack you have inserted under the metal mirror on the altar. The other wire---the live, the dangerous black wire—is brought into the interior of the hollow image through a hole you have bored in the bottom. You solder its end to the very teeth of the Bodhisat, to his glittering golden teeth. Be ready, gods, with all your thunderbolts!'

"Your brother kneels upon the metal mirror—the wet mirror on which he has just poured the purifying waters. Fortunately he will upset the holy-water vase in his fall, rendering of minor significance the fact that the knees of his trousers are to be damp at the time of his death. Although his weight presses the mirror tightly against the head of the thumbtack he feels nothing. The contact has been completed on one side of the circuit only. The harmless neutral or ground side.

" *Thinking upon the power of the God, thinking upon the might of the God, pronounce three times the mantra "Heegh.". . .'* These instructions are merely to add the proper note of mystical verisimilitude. '. . . *touch to his sacred lips his emblem, the dorje.'*

"The *metal* dorje, Doctor Merriweather. The metal that closes the circuit and sends the 110 volts of the house current coursing through your brother's body.

"The low-voltage house current leaves no sign of its entry, no traces, externally or internally, of its passage or exit. Even under the favorable conditions you have insured, it would probably do little harm to a man in normal health, but for your brother it has the power to kill. The unexpected shock is far too much for his weakened heart.

"'Pronounce then the mantra "Oom," the great Word, the mighty Word, the Word of power to which even the Lord of the Thunderbolt must listen.'

"But your brother, Doctor Merriweather, is not able to pronounce that mantra. He is dead—dashed to pieces by the Thunderbolt God's own thunderbolt . . . but in this instance a thunderbolt of human creation. . . yours, Doctor."

The End

BIBLIOGRAPHY

THE WRITER wishes to acknowledge his indebtedness to the following authorities whose works he has consulted in the preparation of THE MAN FROM TIBET:

BELL, SIR CHARLES
    People of Tibet, The—1928
    Religion of Tibet, The—1931
    Tibet Past and Present—1924
BONVALOT, GABRIEL
    Across Tibet—1892
CARES, PAUL
    Gospel of Buddha According to Old Records, The—1894
COMBE, G.A.
    Tibetan on Tibet, A—1926
DAS, SARAT CHANDRA
    Journey to Lhasa and to Central Tibet—1902
DAVID-NEEL, ALEXANDRA
    Magic and Mystery in Tibet—1932
    My Journey to Lhasa—1927
    Superhuman Life of Gesar of Ling, The—1934
ENCYCLOPAEDIA BRITANNICA
ENDERS, GORDON B.
    Nowhere Else in the World—1935
EVANS-WENTZ, W. Y.
    Tibetan Book of the Dead, The—1927
    Tibetan Yoga and Secret Doctrine—1936
FLEMING, PETER
    News from Tartary—1936
FORMAN, HARRISON
    Through Forbidden Tibet—1935
FRANCKE. A. H.
      Notes on Sir Aurel Stein's Collection of Tibetan Documents from Chinese Turkestan (The Journal of the Royal Asiatic Society

of Great Britain and Ireland for 1914)

GOMPERTZ, M. L. A.

Road to Lamaland, The—1926

HANNAH, HERBERT BRUCE

Grammar of the Tibetan Language, A—1912

HATFIELD, JAMES TAFT

Elements of Sanskrit Grammar, The—1884

HEDIN, SVEN

Conquest of Tibet, A----1934

Flight of Big Horse, The—1936

Trans-Himalaya (2 vols.)—19O9

HOLDICH, COLONEL SIR THOMAS H.

Tibet, the Mysterious—1906

HOWARD-BURY, LIEUTENANT-COLONEL C. K.

Mount Everest, the Reconnaissance, 1921-1922

KAWAGUCHI, EKAI

Three Years in Tibet—1909

LANDON, PERCEVAL

Opening of Tibet, The—1906

LANDOR, A. HENRY SAVAGE

Explorer's Adventures in Tibet, An—1910

LATTIMORE, ELEANOR HOLGATE

Turkestan Reunion—1934

LATTIMORE, OWEN

High Tartary—1930

LAUFER, BERTHOLD

Oriental Theatricals—1923

Origin of Tibetan Writing—1918 (Journal of the American
  Oriental Society, Vol. XXXVIII)

Use of Human Skulls and Bones in Tibet—1923

MCGOVERN, WILLIAM MONTGOMERY

Manual of Buddhist Philosophy, A—1923

To Lhasa in Disguise—1924

MERRICK, **HENRIETTA SANDA**

In the World's Attic—1931

Spoken in Tibet—1933

MULLER, MAX

Science of Religion—1872

NOEL, CAPTAIN JOHN

Story of Everest, The—1927

O'CONNOR, LIEUTENANT-COLONEL SIR FREDERICK

On the Frontier and Beyond—1931

RIJNHART, SUSIE CARSON
    With the Tibetans in Tent and Temple—1901
ROCKHILL, WILLIAM WOODVILLE
    Land of the Lamas, The—1891
    Life of the Buddha and the Early History of His Order, The—
    1916
ROERICH, NICHOLAS
    Shambhala—1930
RUTTLEDGE, HUGH
    Attack on Everest—1935
SANDBERG, GRAHAM
    Tibet and the Tibetans—1906
SHAKE, SOYEN
    Sermons of a Buddhist Abbot—1906
SHEARING, CHARLES A.
    Western Tibet and the British Borderland—1906
STEIN, SIR M. AUREL
    Ruins of Desert Cathay (2 vols.)—1912
    Sand Buried Ruins of Khotan—1904
THOMAS, EDWARD J.
    Life of Buddha as Legend and History, The—1927
WADDELL, L. AUSTINE
    Buddhism of Tibet or Lamaism, The—1895
    Lhasa and Its Mysteries—1906
WARD, F. KINGDON
    Land of the Blue Poppy, The—1913
YOUNGHUSBAND, SIR FRANCIS
    India and Tibet—1910

Afterword
About Clyde B. Clason

C LYDE B. CLASON'S career as a mystery writer took up only five of his 84 years, but in the short span between 1936 and 1941 he produced ten long and very complicated detective novels, all published by the prestigious Doubleday, Doran Crime Club, featuring the elderly historian Professor Theocritus Lucius Westborough.

Born in Denver in 1903, Clason spent many years in Chicago, the setting for several of his novels, including *The Man from Tibet*, before moving to York, Pennsylvania, where he died in 1987. During his early years in Chicago Clason worked as an advertising copywriter and a trade magazine editor, producing books on architecture, period furniture and one book on writing, *How To Write Stories that Sell*. For some reason, Clason stopped selling mysteries on the eve of World War II, although he published several other books, including *Ark of Venus* (1955), a science fiction novel, and *I am Lucifer* (1960), the confessions of the devil as told to Clason. He also produced several non-fiction works dealing with astronomy as well as *The Delights of the Slide Rule* (1964), his last published book-length work.

Why Clason left the crime fiction genre, never to return, remains a mystery today. Long after they went out of print his books remained popular with readers and have always fetched premium prices in the antiquarian book trade. And modern critics, though taking the occasional potshot at his sometimes florid prose, still commend him on his research and ability to construct convincing locked room cases.

Indeed, seven of Clason's ten Westborough mysteries feature locked rooms or impossible situations. Along with John Dickson Carr and Clayton Rawson, Clason was a leading exponent of this very popular subgenre, with locked room mystery connoisseur Robert C.S. Adey referring to the Westborough canon as being among "the more memorable" entries in this narrow field. Adey had special praise for *The Man from Tibet*, calling it a "well-written. . . above average golden-age novel" that was "genuinely interesting, and well researched," and citing its "highly original and practical locked-room murder method."

Other contemporary critics also looked upon this short-lived series with approval. Howard Haycraft, the genre's first major historian, predicted that Clason was on the brink of becoming a mainstay of readers, while two-time Edgar-winning critic James Sandoe listed *The Man from Tibet* in his *Readers' Guide to Crime*, a 1946 compilation of required titles for libraries, noting that this, as well as other Westborough titles, appeared frequently on the lists submitted to him by other critics for inclusion in his guide. Modern critics like Bill Pronzini and Jon L. Breen have also offered kind retrospective reviews of Clason's work, although they disagreed on the merits of at least one of his books, with Pronzini praising *Blind Drifts* (1937) for its "particularly neat and satisfying variation on (the locked-room) theme," while Breen said "the plot is far-fetched and over-elaborate, and the killer stands out rather obviously." Both critics, however, were impressed with Clason's research in this book in describing the operation of a Colorado gold mine.

Research was obviously a passion with Clason, who certainly felt the need to provide his readers with an accurate portrait of Tibet, a country whose borders were closed to foreigners and whose religion, a form of Buddhism, was then little-known in this country. Purists might have objected to the amount of space Clason devoted to educating his readers but they can't fault the skill with which he works the fruits of his research into the narrative. Such scholarship is evident in other titles as well, including *Murder Gone Minoan* (1939), in which Clason recreates an ancient civilization on an island off the California coast, or *Green Shiver* (1941), his last mystery, in which the reader learns a great deal about Chinese jade.

Clason's narrative skills were not inconsiderable, although modern readers might wish that his characters could deliver their lines with "he said" or "she asked" rather such Tom Swifty's as "he choked" or "he opined." On the other hand, it's somewhat refreshing to read a mystery in which ejaculations refer only to exclamations of speech.

Like other mystery writers of the day, Clason threw in a perfunctory romance in *The Man from Tibet* between a couple of the secondary characters, which fortunately was as brief as it was insipid. Yet in the crime novels of the day—Georgette Heyer's mysteries spring immediately to mind—such romantic entanglements were actually useful in helping the reader sort out potential murder suspects. If you could figure out which two young people would eventually find their star-crossed way to each other, you could automatically eliminate two suspects from your list. On the other hand, Westborough, like many other central characters of the period, seems if not asexual, at least beyond or above such temptations.

Unlike many other mystery novels of the time, Clason's books are remarkably free of racial prejudice, at least on the part of the ever-rational Westborough, who on more than one occasion gently rebukes his companions for expressing racist sentiments. In *The Man from Tibet* he even manages to find a kind word or two (their foreign policy not-withstanding) to say about the Japanese, who were at the time plundering most of their neighbors in a dress rehearsal for World War II. Clason recognized that anti-Japanese sentiment was rampant among most Americans of the late 1930s. Westborough's best friend, Lt. Mack, has little use for "Japs" and when the two visit a Chicago Japanese restaurant for lunch, Clason subtly mentions that the place is nearly empty. Westborough unfailingly treats the Tibetan characters with understanding and respect, going out of his way to explain to all the linguistic differences that account for their difficulties with the English language.

Too often modern critics excuse writers of the 1930s, like Agatha Christie or Dorothy L. Sayers, for fostering racial prejudice or anti-Semitic views, by jokingly dismissing complaints about such lapses as runaway political correctness. What these apologists forget is that while it may be acceptable and even necessary for an author to show that such views were commonplace at the time (as Clason does), the authorial expression of such views is never acceptable. Take for example, Bruce Hamilton's 1930 English mystery, *To Be Hanged* (much praised by those two great snobs of crime fiction, Jacques Barzun and Wendell Hertig Taylor) in which a very minor—and very disagreeable—character is offhandedly described in the narrative as a "little Jew." It is to Clason's great credit that he was able, in the words of Ruth Rendell, to fulfill "the duty of the artist in rising above the petty prejudices of the day."

Like other fair-play mysteries of the day, Clason's books tend to end very abruptly once the murderer is revealed. Yet, even some of his biggest fans, like Pronzini, suggest that his books could have been improved by some judicious editing to cut their length from 80,000 words to 65,000. On the other hand, 80,000 or more words was the rule rather than the exception in the mysteries of Clason's era. It was not until World War II, when paper restrictions prompted publishers to use lighter paper and to cram more words on a page, that the length of a typical mystery was reduced to 60,000 words. This will fill 192 pages, the number needed to make up six 32-page signatures, a very economical size book to produce. This has remained the standard until quite recently, and it wasn't so long ago that Dodd, Mead cut—without explanation or editing to make sense—a major character from a Wendy Hornsby mystery just to ensure that the book did not exceed 192 pages.

Today, however, publishers are once again looking for bigger books, especially with "breakout" or bestselling authors, and a number of books in the crime fiction field have suffered from this verbal bloating. P.D. James, for example, started out writing tightly crafted gems, but all of her books after *An Unsuitable Job for a Woman* (1972) bog down in endless details about the contents of suitcases or in long pieces of melacholy introspection by her leading characters.

Clyde B. Clason, at least, stayed away from such pretentious drivel. Indeed, it's his asides into Tibetan culture, or Chinese jade, or the working of a gold mine, as well as his unobtrusive social commentary, that make his books as appealing to today's readers as they were to those of the pre-World War II era, even if his plots and characters are decidedly old-fashioned. Why he did not make the transition into the modern era will probably never be known, but we can't help but wonder if he was unable or unwilling to produce the shorter, more streamlined mysteries the Crime Club insisted upon after the country went to war. Whatever the reason, it's our loss, but he still left behind a remarkable body of work considering the brief portion of his life he devoted to the writing of mystery fiction.

Tom & Enid Schantz
Boulder, Colorado
January, 1998

A Catalog of
Rue Morgue Press
Titles

Murder, Chop Chop

By James Norman

A classic late Golden Age novel of detection and adventure set in China in 1938 during the Sino-Japanese War

Fans of Golden Age mysteries set in exotic lands with eccentric characters will love this long out-of-print masterpiece that many critics said should have been included in the Haycraft-Queen list of cornerstone mysteries, written by a man who fought in the Spanish Civil War and was a victim of the Hollywood Blacklist.

In these pages you will meet Gimiendo Hernandez Quinto, a gigantic Mexican who once rode with Pancho Villa and who now trains *guerrilleros* for the Chinese government when he isn't solving murders. At his side is a beautiful Eurasian known as Mountain of Virtue, a woman as dangerous to men as she is irresistible, and a superb card player as well—so long as she's dealing. Then there's Mildred Woodford, a hard-drinking British journalist; John Tate, a portly American calligrapher who wasn't made for adventure; Lt. Chi, a young Hunanese patriot weighted down with the woes of China and the Brooklyn Dodgers; Nevada, a cowboy who is as deadly with a six-gun as he inept at love; and a host of others, any one of whom may have killed Abe Harrow, an ambulance driver who appears to have died at three different times.

There's also a cipher or two to crack, a train with a mind of its own, and Chiang Kai-shek's false teeth, which have gone mysteriously missing.

ISBN 0-915230-16-X   **$13.00**

The Mirror

by Marlys Millhiser

The classic novel of two women lost in time.

How could you not be intrigued, as one reviewer pointed out, by a novel in which "you find the main character marrying her own grandfather and giving birth to her own mother?" Such is the situation in Marlys Millhiser's classic novel (a Mystery Guild selection originally published by Putnam in 1978) of two women who end up living each other's lives after they look into an antique Chinese mirror.

Twenty-year-old Shay Garrett is not aware that she's pregnant and is having second thoughts about marrying Marek Weir when she's suddenly transported back 78 years in time into the body of Brandy McCabe, her own grandmother, who is unwillingly about to be married off to miner Corbin Strock. Shay's in shock but she still recognizes that the picture of her grandfather that hangs in the family home doesn't resemble her husband-to-be. But marry Corbin she does and off she goes to the high mining town of Nederland, where this thoroughly modern young woman has to learn to cope with such things as wood cooking stoves and—to her—old-fashioned attitudes about sex. Shay's ability to see into the future has her mother-in-law thinking she's a witch and others calling her a psychic but Shay was an indifferent student at best and not all of her predictions hit the mark: remember that "day of infamy" when the Japanese attacked Pearl Harbor—Dec. *11*, *1941*?

In the meantime, Brandy McCabe is finding it even harder to cope with life in the Boulder, Colorado of 1978. After all, her wedding is about to be postponed due to her own death—at least the death of her former body—at the age of 98. And, in spite of the fact she's a virgin, she's about to give birth. And *this* young woman does have some very old-fashioned ideas about sex, which leaves her husband-to-be—and father of her child—very puzzled. *The Mirror* is even more of a treat for today's readers, given that it is now a double trip back in time. Not only can readers look back on life at the turn of the century, they can also revisit the days of disco and the sexual revolution of the 1970's.

So how does one categorize *The Mirror?* Is it science fiction? Fantasy? Supernatural? Mystery? Romance? Historical fiction? You'll find elements of each but in the end it's a book driven by that most magical of all literary devices: imagine if...

ISBN 0-915230-15-1 $14.95

The Rue Morgue Press
reprinting the kind of books that
made people start reading
mysteries in the first place

The Rue Morgue Press was founded in 1997 by Tom & Enid Schantz with the intent of bringing back in print some of the books they have enjoyed calling to the attention of their customers during the nearly 30 years they have operated their mystery bookstore, The Rue Morgue (which opened in 1970 as The Aspen Bookhouse).

The books chosen for publication by the press (with the exception of *The Mirror*—see previous page) aren't necessarily immortal classics but rather are books that mystery bookstore owners might have pushed into the hands of their customers back in the 1930s or 1940s, had such stores existed then, explaining: "This just came in. I think you'll get a kick out of it."

For example, 1942 saw the publication of Raymond Chandler's third novel, *The High Window*. In that same year James Norman's *Murder, Chop Chop* was released and although it was very popular with readers of the day and earned praise from mystery critics, then and now, it has been unavailable for almost as long as *The High Window* has been in print. In 1938, John Dickson Carr published one of the most famous and often reprinted locked room mysteries of all time, *The Crooked Hinge*. In that same year, readers also eagerly grabbed copies of Clyde B. Clason's locked room mystery, *The Man from Tibet*, which was to go out of print and be unavailable for many years to come.

For information on future titles write:

The Rue Morgue Press
P.O. Box 4119
Boulder, CO 80306